Crimson Lace

Linda Francis Lee

JOVE BOOKS, NEW YORK

CRIMSON LACE

A Jove Book / published by arrangement with
the author

PRINTING HISTORY
Jove edition / December 1997

All rights reserved.
Copyright © 1997 by Linda Francis Lee.
This book may not be reproduced in whole
or in part, by mimeograph or any other means,
without permission. For information address:
The Berkley Publishing Group, a member of Penguin Putnam Inc.,
200 Madison Avenue, New York, New York 10016.

The Putnam Berkley World Wide Web site address is
http://www.berkley.com

ISBN: 0-515-12187-8

A JOVE BOOK®
Jove Books are published by The Berkley Publishing Group,
a member of Penguin Putnam Inc.,
200 Madison Avenue, New York, New York 10016.
JOVE and the "J" design are trademarks belonging to
Jove Publications, Inc.

PRINTED IN THE UNITED STATES OF AMERICA

10 9 8 7 6 5 4 3 2 1

ACKNOWLEDGMENTS

I would like to express my appreciation to Kathy Peiffer, Judy Bougades, Nancy DiGanci, and Elizabeth Lindner for their friendship and support.

Linda Francis Lee
P.O. Box 4961
Chapel Hill, NC 27515
E-mail: LFranLee @ aol.com

For Sophie

Crimson Lace

Prologue

TARRYTOWN, NEW YORK
1896

> *March 1886*
>
> *My dearest Lily,*
>   *I hate to see the life drained out of you by a society that doesn't appreciate the type of woman you are. So I am leaving you my wealth so you can remain free . . . and I am leaving a gift, to ensure that you do.*
>
> *Hawthorne*

Lily Blakemore refolded the aged and yellowed stationery, though she hadn't needed to unfold the note to know what it said. She knew each word and space, period and comma by heart.

She set the note aside with careful movements, not because she was afraid of tearing it, in fact many times she wished she could, but because she was afraid that with any sudden, startling movement *she* might be torn into tiny little pieces—and wouldn't be able to be put back together again.

Lily tried to scoff at her foolishness—torn pieces and putting herself back together again, indeed—but could only close her eyes, and draw a deep, calming breath.

Raine Hawthorne.

As it had happened all those years ago, he *had* left her his vast fortune, along with a copy of an invitation that had been sent out upon his death to New York City's elite for a grand gala to be held at her home—a memorial gathering at Blakemore House in Manhattan. Lily had promised Raine on his deathbed that she would host the gala event upon his passing, unaware that he intended to reveal a posthumous gift.

The gift.

Which had changed her life forever. Leaving her alone to pick up the pieces of a shattered life. Sending her into exile here in Tarrytown, hours away from her home in Manhattan.

Lily could have told anyone the exact day her life had changed forever. The exact moment. Ten years ago on March 16, 1886. At eight-fifteen in the evening. She remembered all too well the sound of the grandfather clock that had tolled the quarter hour from the foyer in Blakemore House. She could have described who had been there, what they had worn.

In her dreams, both waking and in sleep, she could still see the ornate pattern of the imported wallpaper, the heavy velvet draperies pulled back from the mullioned windows, the clear night sky strewn with silver stars. It had been a beautiful night—a night, she had whispered to herself as she had gotten ready, that she would never forget. Strange how some things could come true, but turn out so differently from what had been expected. It *had* been a night she never forgot, but time after time she wished she could.

Lily could have described the crystal chandelier that had dripped golden light, and how the expressions on each and every face in that crowded parlor had changed from anticipation for the gift to be revealed to a glimmer of awe after it had been—but only a glimmer before outrage came crashing down as understanding dawned like a cruel winter day.

The gift had been scandalous.

Oh, Raine, she thought with a sad laugh and shake of her head, *you always knew how to get attention. If only you hadn't tangled me up in your scheme. Having me reveal your gift. Causing them to believe I condoned what you did. Making me an accomplice in my own destruction.*

That night so long ago, New York's elite had stood in their elegant finest, quivering with shock, speechless, before the whispers had begun. Everyone, it seemed, had known that no good could come of Lily Blakemore. *A wild child,* it was whispered behind rapidly moving fans. *Always had been. Thank the Lord her parents were no longer living to witness such a disgrace.*

Lily hadn't laughed that night. She had stood in shock like everyone else. Shock and hurt. Wounded beyond words. But what could she have said? How to defend herself? She hadn't been wild. Not really. She had simply wanted to live. Life. Wind in her hair. Laughter in her ears. But no one had understood, never had. In truth she had been branded years before she met Raine. But only after such an outrage when the gift was revealed did her family's friends feel they could say what they had felt all along. And they had said it with a perverse glee.

In reality, Lily had been ruined long before that night. Raine Hawthorne had only sealed her fate.

The scene was seared in Lily's mind like a daguerreotype, the edges frayed from endless viewings. As the years had gone by, Lily had reimagined that night a hundred different times, a hundred different ways, with a hundred different endings. As if it had only been a play, she had rewritten the scene countless times. But the daguerreotype in her mind failed to change, history refused to be rewritten.

Ten years had passed since that fateful night. Lily was no longer a very young nineteen. She was twenty-nine, and as comfortable in her life as she imagined was possible given the circumstances. She had sworn she would never go back to that house, to those people. And she had kept her vow.

But things had changed, she thought. Tomorrow she was going back to Manhattan, back to Blakemore House.

Lily packed a great many things in her traveling case without a single thought to practicality. A deep blue feather boa, several clinking bracelets, plenty of shoes—she loved her shoes—and a delicate china teacup and saucer that were her most cherished possessions. Her mother had given them to her, just as her mother's mother had given them to her a generation before. A tradition. A cup and saucer that had been handed down from mother to daughter for years. These she packed carefully to take with her. The rest of her belongings would follow later.

A coach would arrive in the morning. John Crandall had seen to the arrangements, hiring the coach and driver to take her south to Manhattan despite the fact that he had told her she shouldn't come. But how could she not?

Lily took a deep bracing breath and squared her shoulders. While Lily looked forward to seeing the man who had befriended her after the scandal broke, she was uncertain how she felt about seeing anyone else. Her days in Tarrytown might be lonely, but she had come to terms with her life. She found joy in long walks through the landscape. And while she had no one in this northern town whom she could actually call friend, people said hello to her when they saw her in the streets.

The thought of returning to the place of her fall from grace left Lily's heart pounding against her ribs and her stomach churning with concern. She hadn't been in society in years—ten years to be exact. Her many travels to the farthest reaches of the world couldn't be counted. Sharing earthen mugs of thick black coffee in the scorching deserts of Arabia with a tribe of Bedouins, or sitting down to exotic meals in the jungles of Africa had little in common with attending tea in the gilded drawing rooms of Manhattan. It had been so long since she had to think about how to sit and what to say in polite company. Would she remember how? she wondered a little frantically.

Regardless, she would return to the parlor in Blakemore House, return to the house where she had been born and raised. Her brother's will had been specific. Upon his death from what the doctors said was a failing heart some four months before, Claude Blakemore had named Lily to care for his motherless children, and she was to return to Manhattan to do so.

Claude had not spoken to Lily in the ten years since she had left Manhattan. Why, she wondered, why was Claude forcing her to return now?

But she knew. The children. Her nieces and nephew.

She only knew young Robert. A soft smile pulled at her lips. The little boy had loved her before she was sent away, wrapping his chubby little arms around her neck. Would he remember her? Lily scoffed at the thought. Of course he wouldn't, he had been two years old.

And her nieces. What were their names? Who did they look like? Claude? Perhaps a little like her?

Her brother had been so handsome. Dashing. They had gone everywhere together as children. They had laughed and played.

If she was truthful with herself, she knew she was half-excited about this trip as well as half-terrified.

Was it possible that things would be different? Was it possible that people had forgotten? After all, ten years was a long time.

A flicker of hope flared to life in her heart, silly hope, she chided herself, but a hope that she couldn't quite extinguish. The fact remained that she was going home. After ten long years of exile, even if it was after his death, her brother had asked her to come home.

One

It never would have happened had he not grown restless that night. He never would have seen.

On Wednesday morning Morgan Elliott had learned that Blakemore House was in need of a caretaker and repairman. On Thursday he had been hired. Gaining access to Blakemore House under the guise of a repairman wasn't his first preference, but his options were running out.

No matter how many years he had lived in New York, at his core he was still a man of Virginia, the manners of the South bred into his bones. Deceit of any kind didn't sit well with him. But he saw no other way to get the information he needed. To once and for all destroy John Crandall.

A fierce determination swept through Morgan's chiseled body, tensing the hard muscles that lined his frame as his dark eyes narrowed. John Crandall was a successful businessman. Confidant of governors and presidents. But Morgan was certain the man's strongest connections were to crime. It was through crime that he got the money to pay for the mansion he built next to the Vanderbilts. It was through crime that he got the money to pay for the extravagant parties he hosted, no doubt to impress all the well-connected people with whom he socialized. Morgan felt it in his bones.

And now it was rumored that John Crandall was going to run for governor. Morgan planned to see that he didn't, that he couldn't. But to accomplish that, Morgan needed proof of the man's crimes. Proof, however, had been hard to acquire. Morgan had been unable to find the evidence he needed, unable to get any sort of look into Crandall's tightly knit organization. Until now.

A woman named Lily Blakemore was reported to be the man's mistress. And Lily Blakemore needed a repairman.

Three long, hot summer days had gone by since Morgan had been hired on Thursday—three long, hot, frustrating days without catching sight of the woman he had come here to see. Not a glimpse from a distance, not a hint of her voice drifting along on a breeze. Not even a mention that would confirm that indeed she had returned to the city as he had heard, to this house where by all accounts she had been born and raised.

But this night, as he walked up the flagstone path from the cottage he was given at the back of the estate, long after the sun had spent itself on the horizon, he found her.

It had to be her, he reasoned, his dark brow furrowing against unexpected emotion. Who else could it be? Who else would be standing on the back porch, sheer white draperies billowing out around her through the windows and doors carelessly thrown open.

He stood in the shadows for a moment, only a moment. Just looking. He expected music, dancing, loud laughter— had been led to believe he would find all that and more. But there was no music, he saw no dancing, and if she was laughing he couldn't tell.

Her back was to him, her hair loose. When he looked closer he was startled to find that she wore nightclothes. Prim and soft. Buttoned to the neck. A downy sheath beneath a dressing gown of lace. White lace. *A princess in white lace.*

The thought startled him, making his jaw clench. Though he had never met her, he knew her type. She might look as innocent as a schoolgirl, but she wasn't. The demure folds of her gown couldn't hide the slim curves of a woman—a body, it was said, that men around the world, poets and privateers alike, had fought and died for.

When Morgan realized that he was just standing, staring no doubt like a thousand other men had done before him, he stepped forward with a muffled curse, anger knotting in his gut. He didn't care that propriety demanded he turn back and return to his cottage.

"Hello," he said, his deep voice rumbling through the moonlit night.

She turned with a start, whirling around to face him, the white dressing gown dancing around her ankles, revealing tiny, delicate feet without slippers.

Despite his anger, awareness slid across his skin as if she had reached out and touched him. Unexpected heat shimmered down his spine, pooling low. Hard, unbridled. He wanted her.

The thought was so sudden and so intense that Morgan swore in reaction. But then he looked into her eyes, fathomless eyes, and his desire shifted into something he couldn't define.

His shoulders stiffened, his face a mask that hid his suddenly churning thoughts. Perhaps he had been wrong. Must have been wrong. This couldn't be her. This couldn't be the woman who all of New York called Crimson Lily.

His inscrutable eyes narrowed against emotion he didn't understand, emotion he had no interest in feeling. Who was this woman? he wondered, taking a deep, sharp breath to steady his mind.

She stood so still, her dark brown hair almost black, her skin nearly as white as the billowing drapery or her prim nightdress. Her lips were full and red, sensuous. But they trembled. And her eyes. Blue. Widened. Awash with tears.

Looking into those eyes Morgan was unprepared to see a silence at her center, as if something had been taken, as if she were no longer whole.

Instincts he thought long suppressed surfaced. Without warning, he wanted to reach out, to pull this woman into his arms, to protect her. "What's wrong?" Morgan asked quietly into the still night.

She looked down then, and for the first time he saw her palms extended, covered in blood.

His heart lurched in his chest. "Good God, what happened?" he demanded. He started forward, his long, determined stride closing the distance that separated them, everything else forgotten.

She didn't answer immediately, only stared at her hands as if somehow an answer would come. "They hate me," she whispered brokenly.

Her words were barely heard, slipping into the warm night, swirling through his mind like a rustle of winter-dried leaves along the flagstone path.

"What?" he demanded, his heart pounding.

But when he reached the bottom step he could see behind her, on the white wall of the porch, in paint. Red paint—not blood.

Crimson Lily.

Two words. Painted boldly. So simple, but saying so much.

His heart stilled. He hadn't been wrong. It was her. And yes, they hated her. He knew that. It was half the reason he was there.

His mind seemed to freeze—trying in some way to reconcile all he had learned about Lily Blakemore with the vision of this desperate, innocent waif who stood before him. But comprehension seemed impossible, and before thoughts and sense could collide, she whirled away from him, fell to her knees, and started wiping frantically at her name that had been painted on the wall.

Morgan stood still, stunned. Couldn't move. She wiped and scrubbed, the fresh red paint smearing, red everywhere, tears overflowing, her words incoherent.

Later the scene would play itself over and over again in his head. The wounded woman/child. Her prim nightdress of white lace splattered with red. For now, however, he could only act. Without thinking about what he was doing, without thinking about why he was there in the first place, he leaped up onto the porch and carefully pulled her away. "Don't," he commanded in a gentle whisper. "You're going to hurt yourself. I'll do it."

A moment passed before she fell back, her legs folding beneath her, her blue eyes drawing him in. Out of himself. She was so beautiful. Words had failed to do her justice. Suddenly he had a better appreciation of why men around the world had been taken with her. Drawn to her.

Reaching out, he carefully pushed a stray lock of her loosely curled dark hair away from her forehead. "Wait here." He started to stand, but she reached out, clutching his wrist, marking him with red paint. Her gaze locked with his, her eyes wild.

"I'm just going to get some water and some paint," he explained in soothing tones.

She looked deep into his eyes as if somehow if she looked long enough or deep enough she could learn some truth. He didn't have to be told that this woman didn't trust anyone, probably didn't know how. Clearly she had been betrayed. But by whom?

His eyes flickered and his brow furrowed as he shifted his weight uncomfortably before he looked away. "I'll be right back."

Within minutes he returned from the work shed near his cottage with a pail of water, a stiff-bristle brush, a rag, and white paint. He saw her flash of relief when he reappeared. A wholly unexpected reassuring smile pulled at his lips. "See," he said with a gentleness that anyone who knew him would have not believed possible, as he raised the buckets and supplies to show her.

She didn't return his smile, only pushed herself up, then took the pail of water and the rag before returning to the angry red letters. After a moment's hesitation, he took the steps and knelt beside her.

Side by side, they worked on the wall as the moon drifted through the sky. There were no words. Only the sound of bristles and cloth against the wooden wall to mar the night. When they had scrubbed as much of the red paint away as they could, the old white paint underneath rubbed away with it, they fell back to sit on the wooden slats of the porch floor. For reasons he wasn't interested in studying, he felt a strange sense of accomplishment.

He nearly smiled, expected her to smile, too. But Lily only looked at the wall, her blue eyes still troubled, as he looked at her. What did she see? he wanted to ask. And yet again he wondered about this woman, trying to assimilate what he knew. Or what he thought he knew, he amended suddenly.

"We need to paint," she stated with conviction, still staring at the wall.

Her voice was steady but quiet. Soft like her flowing gown. Now that the crimson had been washed free, he knew exhaustion had set in. He could see it in the curve of her shoulders, the fullness of her eyelids. She needed to sleep. To forget, he thought unexpectedly.

"No, it's too wet to paint," he said.

"But we have to. If we don't," she said, her voice rising, "the children will see it."

Despite the late hour, a dog barked in the distance. Once, twice, then quiet. No sound. Amazing in a city as large as New York. People everywhere. Carriages of all kinds. Horsecars pulled along iron tracks, while drays charged through the crowded streets.

After he left Virginia, he had spent years searching for a place of quiet in this world of thunder, never finding it.

He was always moving, always working. He knew others said he was driven. Obsessed. He had never thought of it that way. The people he loved were gone. His parents. Jenny. He had given up on the quiet long ago.

"Go on inside and get some sleep," he said. "I'll wait until the wall dries. Then I'll paint it."

She turned to look at him, really look at him for the first time. He saw in her eyes that she saw him, the man, not simply someone who had crossed her path like an inconsequential street vendor who she would never see again in this vast city.

"Yes," he assured her, "I'll paint the wall before anyone wakes up."

The creases in her forehead eased slightly. "Really?

He couldn't help his smile any more than he could help his fingers from reaching out to caress her cheek. "Yes, princess, really. Now up with you. Go inside and get to bed."

She stared at him, her large blue eyes luminous, until a soft smile broke out on her lips. Before he realized what she was doing, she reached out and laced her delicate fingers with his. Almost reverently, she pressed the back of his hand to her cheek. "Thank you," she whispered.

Then she was gone, leaving him alone, surrounded by an unexpected silence in a world of thunder.

Two

"I want out."

Morgan planted his palms on the scarred desktop of his boss, not bothering to hide the paint that stained his hands.

Morgan didn't want to tell the man what he had seen last night at the Blakemore House. He was certain that as long as he lived he would never forget the blaze of red letters on the wall. Nor would he forget the look on Lily Blakemore's face, or the way it had made him feel. He didn't want his boss to know about the incident, or anyone else for that matter. Proof of which was in the white paint that stained his hands.

Oddly, Morgan felt protective. Foolishly, of course. She was Crimson Lily. But the haunted look in her eyes had touched him in a way that even hours later still left him unsettled. "I mean it, Walter, I'm not going back."

Walter O'Malley leaned back in the hardwood swivel chair and studied the younger man who stood before him. Walter was nearing sixty, his thin face lined with years of hard, dedicated work, his once flaming red hair like a stiff gray brush.

At length, Walter turned to a blue-suited patrolman who Morgan hadn't noticed. "I think we're about done here, Sergeant Collins. Keep me posted."

The sergeant moved toward the door, nodded to Morgan, then quit the office.

Without a word to Morgan, Walter pulled a fat cigar out of the humidor that sat on his desk. He didn't bother to clip the end, he simply looked at it without striking a match. "The missus hates these things," he mused, more to himself than anyone else.

"Walter," Morgan said, his voice low, commanding.

Walter hung his head and sighed. "All right, all right. Are you at least going to tell me why you won't go back? You have the perfect cover."

The sounds of drawers opening and shutting surrounded them as the night shift packed up to go home and the day shift started filtering in. Soon the noise from the cavernous office outside Walter's door would be an echoing din, but not yet. It was still early. There was only a hint of the sun outside Walter's tiny third-floor office window.

As long as Morgan had lived in New York he had never gotten used to the crowds of people or the buildings that lined the streets as far as the eye could see. He hadn't allowed himself to think of Virginia or wide open spaces. But after last night it hit him. Hard. A deep yearning. To go home. But that was impossible. He had a job to do— a quest, Walter had once remarked. Morgan scoffed at the notion. He wasn't on a quest. He was simply taking care of business, bringing men to justice.

But suddenly, Morgan was tired of this life. Tired of waking up in the morning having constantly to remember where he was, what identity he had assumed. He wanted to return to Virginia. And he would, he thought suddenly, just as soon as he put Crandall behind bars. But he wouldn't use Lily Blakemore to get it done.

"I just don't think it's wise to go back."

"Not wise. Well," Walter responded, nodding his head

slowly as if considering. "Let's look at this. You've gotten inside. Finally. With the perfect cover, and you don't think it's wise. Hmmmm," he murmured, still nodding his head.

"Damn it, Walter." Morgan pushed away from the desk, running his hands through his thick, dark hair. "You've got to trust me about this. I'll find another way." But of course as soon as Morgan said the words he knew they weren't true. He had been trying to get information from inside Crandall's circle for the last two years without success. The return of Lily Blakemore, her reported connection to his prey, and her subsequent need of a repairman had been a godsend.

Reluctantly, Walter set the cigar aside, then smiled. "Listen, I don't know what happened over there," he said, shrugging his wiry shoulders, "and far be if from me to demand an answer. In fact, I don't even want to know. You can do what you want, you know that as well as I do. You don't need this job, and quite frankly, I can't imagine why you do it. But you've worked hard on this case, Morgan, just think about what you're giving up."

"Hell," Morgan muttered.

"Hell is right, son. I know you. And I know that if there is a man alive who can get Crandall, it's you."

Walter was quiet for a second before he picked up his cigar again, rolled it along on his fingers, and considered Morgan speculatively. "I hear she's beautiful."

Beautiful? Dear God, if only it were that simple, Morgan thought, remembering how he felt when he had looked at her pale, perfect face, her deep blue eyes, and her lips that were made to love.

"Yes," Walter continued with a surprisingly dreamy smile for someone normally so gruff, "if I were a tad younger I might be inclined to play caretaker for the beautiful woman myself."

Morgan shot Walter a heated glare, his voice terse. "This has nothing to do with beauty."

Extending his hands in surrender, Walter sighed. "No,

I don't suppose it does. As long as I've known you, you've never been a man to be swayed by a pretty head. All business with you." He shook his head and chuckled. "Lucky cuss. You've got women falling all over you, but not one of them has managed to get you to settle down. Had I only managed to meet you earlier in my life I might have learned a thing or two."

"You're head over heels in love with Maisy, Walter, and everyone knows it."

"Well, yeah," Walter said with a lopsided grin that looked out of place on his craggy face. "Maisy's a fine woman. But we're not talking about me, we're talking about you. And damn it, Morgan, these last few years you've become like a son to me, and you aren't getting any younger, you know."

"At thirty-five I don't consider myself at death's door."

"True enough, but at thirty-five the missus and I already had five young ones. You need to find yourself a wife. Get married to someone who can make you smile. When was the last time you smiled, Morgan?" Walter held up his hand as if to ward off an answer. "No, don't answer that, and don't get all hot and bothered on me. I just think marriage would do you a world of good." Walter leaned forward and pointed at Morgan with his cigar. "But first, go back to the Blakemore place. Give it one more shot. Get this whole thing out of your blood, for the good of you and New York. That's all I ask. You're so close to getting a real look at the inside world of John Crandall."

Morgan stiffened at the name, the image of the man leaping to life in his head. Morgan tried to put the woman he had seen last night together with Crandall. Even after a night spent trying, it was impossible. From experience, Morgan knew that Crandall was the lowest form of life. But last night . . . Lily . . . Associated with Crandall? How could that be? Crandall was a man beyond contempt. Which reminded Morgan just how much he wanted to bring the bastard low.

• • •

Outside, Morgan didn't bother with the arched-roofed horsecars that most people took for a nickel. He didn't need the ridiculously low salary that this job paid. He hailed a two-wheeled hansom cab to take him uptown to the Blakemore's brownstone on Fifty-ninth Street, welcoming the rattle and jolting sway of the small carriage as they made their way through the rapidly thickening congestion of downtown Manhattan.

He didn't want to think about Crandall—or Lily Blakemore and what she had made him feel. But the rattle and sway wasn't enough to distract him from the fact that last night, for a time, the memories that had plagued him for so many years had been washed clean from his mind. Lily had made him forget. At least for a while. Memories washed free. No Trey. No Jenny. No hand reaching out to him. No insurmountable distance to be crossed to save her.

As long as Morgan lived he was afraid he would be plagued by the look on sweet Jenny's face as she fell, her face turned to him. Their eyes had locked, and as they did, her fear receded. Gone, replaced. But with what? he had wondered so many times. Resignation? Acceptance that she was going to die? Or disappointment? In him? Of course in him, he conceded with a sigh.

Years before Morgan had promised Jenny that he would keep her safe. And he hadn't. Dear God, he hadn't.

Morgan pressed his back into the carriage seat, trying to concentrate on the feel of the cracked and worn leather against his spine. He hadn't allowed himself to think about his promise to Jenny since her death—hadn't thought about it until arriving at Blakemore House? Why now? he wondered.

Morgan's jaw set with implacable determination as he turned his head to the tiny, grime-streaked window, away from his thoughts, and concentrated on the task at hand. His determination gave way to a curse. Blakemore House.

He remembered the morning three days ago when he

had applied for the position, walking into the house with the butler who had been in charge of the hiring. Even though the massive town house was only blocks away from the opulent mansions built of marble and granite, the Blakemore home was in a state of total disrepair. The discreet advertisement that had announced a repairman was needed was an understatement. What the Blakemores truly needed was someone to raze the property, then an architect and a builder to start from scratch. No one in his right mind would take on the task of simply making repairs.

But even as he stood in the echoing foyer that day, the house in ruin around him, Morgan's ultimate goal had never wavered. He wanted Crandall. Badly. And if he had to rebuild the pile of stone and mortar himself in order to gain access to Crandall, so be it. Morgan had been hired on the spot.

The traffic thinned out once the hired hack fought its way through the dangerous intersection where Broadway crossed Fifth Avenue. After that the clip-clop of the horse's hooves over stone became steady and rhythmic. When Morgan caught sight of the glass-framed sign that marked Fifty-fourth Street he banged the back wall of the carriage. Morgan jumped down onto the narrow, cobbled length of Fifth Avenue in front of St. Luke's Hospital. Though Blakemore House was on Fifty-ninth Street between Sixth and Seventh Avenues, Morgan needed the walk. He tossed the driver a coin and set out.

Only a few minutes later someone called out.

"Mr. Elliott!"

Morgan slowed his paced and realized that he had come around to the back of the house. "Good morning, Cassie," he said with a nod.

Cassie Blakemore was the youngest child of Claude Blakemore, the deceased brother of Lily. In fact Morgan knew it was the premature death of Claude Blakemore four months ago that had brought Lily back to Manhattan in the first place. Morgan remembered well the day he had

learned that not only had the thirty-three-year-old Blakemore passed on, but that he had left his children in his
sister's care. All of New York had been aghast, then
amazed when Lily had actually shown up. Morgan wasn't
aghast or amazed. Just thankful—thankful that she had
needed a repairman. Or at least he had been until last night.

"Mr. Elliott!"

Morgan cleared his thoughts and focused on the young
girl. Cassie was six years old and had long ringlets that
framed her heart-shaped faced.

"We've been waiting for you," she told Morgan,
smoothing her ruffled dress, seemingly proud of the lopsided bow around her waist, which looked as if she had
tied it herself.

When Morgan glanced toward the kitchen door, he
found Cassie's older sister and brother waiting on the back
steps of the house as well. In the short time Morgan had
been there, he had learned that Cassie was the sweetest.
Her older sister, Penelope, on the other hand, was eight
years old and not the happiest child he had ever met. Robert was the oldest at twelve, a self-righteous young boy
who spent most of his time peering through his round spectacles as he read one book after another.

"I was just getting ready to go look for you out back,"
Cassie added with a huge smile.

Morgan didn't smile in return. He didn't want to let this
sweet little girl think he was friendly. The last thing he
needed was to have the children wanting to spend time
around him.

"No reason for that," he said as he allowed himself to
be pulled inside the house by the child. "I'm here and I'm
starved."

As luck would have it, he was allowed to eat his meals
in the kitchen with the staff—all two of them, a butler and
a cook—rather than being left to his own devices back at
his cottage. It was luck not because he wanted to eat in
the kitchen, the only room he had determined wasn't fall-

ing apart, but because it gave him greater access to the house and its occupants.

During the time he had been there, Morgan had learned that the children took their meals in the kitchen as well. He assumed it was because the dining room was cold and drafty and needed a good deal of repair. But that task was a long way down on his list of things to do. Faulty gas valves, leaky plumbing, and loose floorboards came first. A grimace pulled at his lips. With all the work that needed to be done, with only three days under his belt in his new job, he had become quite a regular fixture in the household.

Cassie climbed up onto her chair, Penelope followed. Robert sat down, but immediately immersed himself in his latest tome. Morgan started to tell the boy to put the book away, but stopped. Robert was none of his business. His only real job was to find proof that Crandall was a criminal, not to do house repairs, much less teach the Blakemore children manners.

Morgan closed the door, intent on joining the children who sat around the table—the empty table.

"Where's breakfast?" Morgan asked, looking around for the cook when he suddenly became aware that the kitchen was cold and empty.

The children noticed the lack of activity, too. But before anyone could speak, the swinging door from the hallway pushed open, bringing Miss Lily Blakemore in on its wake.

Lily.

God, Morgan murmured silently, she was beautiful. Breathtaking. Radiant. Blue eyes shining like sapphires.

Morgan had the unexpected urge to pull her close, press her body against his. Ask her if she was all right.

After last night and at the sight of her this morning, he was suddenly forced to admit that somehow his world had changed. As if for reasons he didn't understand, she now belonged to him in some essential way.

As if he had found what he had been searching for all his life.

Despite everything he had told himself that morning, at the sight of Lily, John Crandall didn't matter. There was only Lily.

"Good morning, good morning," she practically sang as she came into the room. "I'm desperate, simply desperate for a cup of coffee."

The difference in her manner was startling, but that difference barely registered in Morgan's mind. Without thinking, he stepped away from the door. She saw him then, he knew it. He watched, mesmerized, as her breath caught and her smile grew luminous.

"Good morning," he said. He was unaware that his face grew formidable, darkened with the intensity of emotions he was unaccustomed to feeling. His heated gaze took in the length of her body, making sure that she was all right.

And in that second everything changed. The spell was broken and she drew a sharp breath. Her smile disappeared. Her eyes grew troubled, the sparkle replaced with the same vulnerability he had seen last night. For one startling second he would have sworn that she was sad and aching . . . and embarrassed. But why?

He started to reach out to her. But then she raised her chin a notch, the look in her eyes growing calm and curiously remote, making him believe he had imagined her embarrassment.

"And who might you be?" she asked as if he was nothing more than an inconsequential stranger come to call.

Morgan had expected many things, a thank-you, a shy smile. But not this. Not this uncaring indifference. He dropped his hand away.

For the first time he noticed that her prim nightclothes of last night had been replaced with an elegantly flowing peignoir of the deepest blue that left no doubt that her body was stunning. Slim curves that begged a man to touch, to feel. Her hair was up, pulled loosely back, looking as if just a mere slip of one pin and the whole glorious mass would tumble free. Wisps of feathered plumage encircled her neck. She was clad in the height of fashion—for a boudoir. He had been in many, too many, most of which belonged to the most beautiful and wealthiest women of the world. London, Paris, New York.

Morgan's dark eyes hardened to slits of obsidian. He knew this kind of woman, knew her well. The woman who had stilled his heart last night was dressed as if she waited for a lover, looking at him as if she had never seen him in her life.

Morgan felt his mind shift and change, slip back to the man he had been for years. God, he had been a fool. "I'm the new repairman," he stated with icy reserve.

"I never hired a repairman," she said, her tone dismissive.

He shrugged his broad shoulders coolly. "Perhaps not directly, but your butler did."

"Butler?"

"Yes, Lily," Robert stated as he glanced over the rim of his gold spectacles, his voice laced with disdain, "the butler whom you fired two days ago and have failed to replace."

The cool indifference in Lily's eyes wavered. But then she squared her shoulders and walked over to the stove.

She moved with a grace that most women could only dream of possessing, a grace that no doubt any male from puberty to senility could not resist—had not *needed* to resist if all the stories Morgan had heard were true. His teeth set.

"Oh, Lily," Cassie breathed, her eyes wide and adoring. "You look ever so lovely this morning. Let me get you some coffee."

Lily glanced at Cassie, her lips caught between a smile of pleasure and that startling uncertainty. "Thank you, love," she said softly. "But there's no need to help. I can get it myself."

Penelope snorted.

At this, all of Lily's uncertainty fled and she laughed.

Morgan would have sworn she was relieved.

"Good morning to you, too, Penny dear," she chimed.

"My name is Penelope." The words were spoken sharply, through gritted teeth.

"Ah yes, so you've said. Penelope it is. And no doubt if I forget again you'll remind me." Lily glanced over at the stove, which was cold. "Where is the coffee?"

Penelope crossed her arms with a huff and a glare, muttering what sounded like several less-than-complimentary epithets undoubtedly aimed at her aunt. Robert shook his head with what Morgan would have sworn was disgust, then returned to his book with grim determination. From the looks of things, Morgan surmised, only Cassie felt any sort of affection for their aunt Lily.

"No coffee *or* breakfast?" Lily trumpeted, glancing around for the missing fare.

"You fired the cook, too, a day after you fired the butler, remember?" Robert reminded her with an indignant scoff.

Her head tilted in thought. "Oh, yes." She laughed, recalling. "They were dreadful." Her look suddenly grew serious. "I think they were spies."

"Spies!?" Penelope shrieked in exasperation. "Harold and Nan had been with us for years. What could possibly make you think they were spies?"

"I found them outside talking to one of those reporters who've been poking around."

"Reporters?" Morgan asked, his eyes narrowing. The last thing he needed was some reporter he had met along the way catching sight of him, announcing that he was here. Crandall was a dangerous man. And Morgan hadn't survived as long as he had by taking danger lightly. "What reporters?"

"Oh, you know," Lily replied with a negligent wave of her hand. "Reporters from *The World* and *The Times*." She glanced around the kitchen then. After a moment she looked at Morgan, seeming to weigh something mentally. "I wonder, Mr. . . ."

"Elliott. Morgan Elliott."

"Well, fine, Mr. Elliott. Do you by chance cook?" Lily asked with exaggerated politeness. "Surely you can make coffee at the very least."

She had the audacity to smile at him, a practiced smile, and Morgan felt a stiff coil beginning to tighten in his chest. How could this be the same woman that he had met last night? In fact, he would have sworn that it *wasn't* the same woman but for the hint of telltale paint staining her hands. "No, Miss Blakemore," he bit out. "I don't cook or make coffee. I'm here to make repairs."

"Perhaps you know of a cook, then?"

"And a butler," Robert added with a snort.

"No," he stated coldly, "can't say that I do."

"Hmmm." Lily's mouth twisted comically as she considered. "Well, I suppose that settles it then," she stated finally, pulling the long flowing sleeves of her peignoir up over her elbows. "I'll have to make breakfast myself. And after that I'll find a cook and butler." Then she winked at Robert, who muttered as he quickly dropped his gaze back to the book.

Without hesitating, Lily got to work. Morgan, Penelope, and Cassie stood back and watched. Even Robert eventually pulled his nose out of the pages as Lily sashayed over to the large walk-in pantry, her slim-heeled slippers clicking against the tile floor, before she pulled open the door and peered inside. She stood there for quite some time without ever venturing inside. Morgan was on the verge of asking what she was looking for when she turned away and walked to the cool box. "Hmmm," they heard her murmur as she made a cursory inspection.

After a moment she shrugged her delicate shoulders, then whirled back—with caviar in one hand and a bottle of Champagne in the other. "Voilà! Breakfast! I knew there had to be something we could eat!"

Cassie squealed in delight, Penelope gasped and rolled

her eyes. Robert snorted. "Figures," he muttered, slumping in his chair.

Morgan stood dumbstruck. He couldn't move much less speak, until finally he planted his hands on his hips and cursed. "Caviar and Champagne, Miss Blakemore?" he said, his voice tight. "For children?"

Her full red lips curved into a mischievous smile, and with that smile Morgan had the sudden, astounding thought that she was doing this on purpose, as if she were intentionally being outrageous, her antics an act. But that was absurd. She was Crimson Lily. If nothing else, she had proved that fact to him this very morning.

"Do you have a better idea, Mr. Elliott?" she asked, her voice sultry.

"Ham and eggs, for starters," he ground out.

"I may not know much about cooking," she said with a laugh, unfazed by his harsh words, "but I do know that there is not a single egg or slice of ham to be had, at least not in this kitchen. But we have plenty of—"

"When was the last time you were around children?" he demanded, his anger shimmering through the room.

Lily's triumphant smile evaporated like a tiny spill of water on a blistering hot day. Without warning, her blue eyes grew troubled, and yet again Morgan forgot everything, only wondered about this woman, about what could have happened to put that look in her eyes. Morgan hated the surge of emotion that tried to stir to life in his chest, hated that yet again he wanted to close the distance between them and take her in his arms. And he realized as he stood there, that with that look he would paint the damn wall all over again.

"Oh, Lily," Cassie said with great feeling, clearly trying to make her aunt feel better, "I think caviar and Champagne sounds absolutely delicious, even if we *are* just kids."

Lily turned very carefully to Cassie, the smile on her lips not reaching her eyes. "Thank you, pet," she said very quietly. "But Mr. Elliott is right. I wasn't thinking. You need eggs and ham and porridge. Not Champagne and caviar."

Morgan hated the way he felt, as if somehow he were at fault. With a shake of his head, he sighed. "Come on, kids. I'll take you to a place I know. We'll eat there."

For a second no one moved. But then Robert pushed up from the table with a grumble. Penelope followed next. Reluctantly Cassie climbed down from her chair. "Will you come with us, Lily?"

Lily glanced at Morgan. Their eyes locked and held, turbulent emotions drifting across her features like dark clouds in a stormy sky. Yet again, Morgan saw what he would have sworn was a flash of embarrassment, an aching inadequacy.

But then the look was gone, and when she spoke her words were tinged with defiant laughter. "Out for ham and eggs?" she asked with a shudder, placing a bejeweled hand on Cassie's head. "I think not."

Three

Lily paced the length of the thick Aubusson carpet, an odd-looking papier-mâché bird sticking out from her hat. "I tell you, I just can't do this! Good heavens, what was my brother thinking? I don't know the first thing about children."

She whirled to a stop in the middle of the room, the bird nearly flying from its perch, a clutter of bracelets jangling to a halt on her wrist. "John! You're not listening to me."

John Crandall grimaced, returned his silver filigree pen to its holder, then leaned back against the supple leather chair of his richly appointed study. "I'm listening, Lily."

"You haven't heard one word I've said!"

"I've been listening for the last half hour."

Lily gave him a doubtful look, at which he merely smiled, then began to recite nearly word for word her long tirade against her deceased brother. He started with her being forced to return to Manhattan, wound his way through all the changes in the city that she had not found to her liking, and had just begun to recount the litany of problems that plagued her childhood home when she waved her hands in surrender.

"All right, all right," she grumbled, tossing her head. "You've proven your point." She ignored his triumphant smile.

Lily had no idea why she was acting so childishly. It was unlike her. But truly she couldn't imagine why her brother had left his children in her care. Dear Cassie, Robert, and Penny—no, Penelope, she corrected herself.

Lily felt the unexpected burn of tears in her eyes. After only a few days at Blakemore House, she reluctantly concluded that she was hopelessly inept at this mothering business. Not that she should be surprised. And not that Robert and Penelope seemed to care. They had made it perfectly clear that she hadn't been able to do anything right since her arrival.

Lily reminded herself that they had lost their father, adding that it didn't matter that four months had passed. She knew from experience that time couldn't fill the void. They could only learn to adjust to a new life. But Lily despaired that no matter how much time passed Robert and Penelope would never adjust to her. Good Lord, no doubt they would sing to high heaven if not dance in the streets if she packed her bags and took the first coach back to Tarrytown.

But Cassie would care. Precious Cassie. A deep abiding joy filled Lily's heart. And as always at the thought of her youngest niece, Lily knew that she would try again. She would return to the house, get them to talk, ask them about their lives, and see if she couldn't find some crack in the armor they had erected so solidly around their hearts.

"Now, Lily," John said, standing. He wasn't particularly tall for a man, but there was no doubt that he was commanding, handsome in his own way. His hair was thick and blond, his eyes brown.

With a few short strides, he came around the wide expanse of mahogany desk to stand before her. They stood nearly eye to eye. Very gently he touched her chin. "You belong in Tarrytown, Lily. I told you it was a mistake to come here.''

Lily turned away.

''You know I'm right, Lily,'' he added, all but preening. ''Let me arrange for a carriage. You can be back in Tarrytown this evening.''

''No, John, I can't,'' she responded, holding on to her determined resolve with a tenuous grip. ''My brother wanted me to do this and I will.''

Lily glanced back suddenly and was startled by the flash of sizzling anger that crossed John's face. But then his countenance settled and the look was gone as if it had never been there.

''Then fine,'' he said, the smile she was so familiar with back in place. ''Stay. It just never occurred to me that you would want to.''

''What's that supposed to mean?''

''Just that, nothing more. If you want to care for your brother's kids you can.'' He looked her in the eye, his head tilting in question. ''I just never realized that you wanted children.''

She turned away sharply. ''I don't,'' she stated with force, hating the sudden tightening in her chest. Children and a home. A real home. Not a cavernous mausoleum in Tarrytown. But that was impossible. ''And it's not like I asked for them. But I've got them. And somehow I've got to take care of them. Raising horses is a very different task from taking care of children, let me tell you. Horses don't talk back.'' At this she groaned. ''Which reminds me . . .'' She frowned, her porcelain skin creasing. ''I need to find a butler and a cook. And quickly. With the exception of little Cassie, precious child that she is, no one appreciated my breakfast this morning.''

John looked at her, surprise sparking to life in his eyes. ''I didn't realize you knew where the kitchen *was* much less knew what to do in it.''

''Funny, John.'' She sniffed. ''Kitchens simply have

never interested me. If I wanted to cook I could. But I don't want to cook, thank you very much. That's why I need someone to do it for me."

Suddenly she shook her head and turned back to him. "I haven't the foggiest notion where to start looking for a cook or a butler. Would you help me, John? You are my dearest friend."

"I'm your only friend, Lily."

She cringed. "Thank you for reminding me." She started to push away, but he took her shoulders and pulled her back.

"I'm sorry. Don't get angry," he said, his voice smooth.

"Oh, John, I'm not."

He looked at her, his gaze doubtful.

"Really, I'm not," she added with more conviction.

"You know I'll help you in any way I can," John said, "haven't I helped you whenever you have needed me these last years?"

"Yes." She sighed.

"Good, and I will continue to do just that for years to come. To begin with, I believe you said you needed a butler."

"And a cook."

John smiled. "Yes, and a cook. What did you do to the ones that were there?"

Lily scowled in memory. "I fired them. I saw them talking to the reporters who've been lurking outside the house." She glanced toward the windows, pain much like she had felt the night before flickering to life in her eyes. "I don't think I could stand to see my name in the newspapers again." She took a deep, fortifying breath. "I need a butler and a cook, yes, but I need people I can trust."

Trust. She wondered if it was possible anymore. She reminded herself that she trusted John. But it had taken years.

With John's help, she had established a life for herself, and truly was as content as she could be. Until this. But

if she was truthful with herself, her childishness and uncertainty had less to do with her nieces and nephew than
with the new repairman. Morgan Elliott.

A shiver of awareness raced through her body. Lily
shook her head as if she could shake off the unsettling
feeling. Dear friend or not, Lily didn't dare discuss any of
this with John, or anyone else for that matter. She didn't
want to tell anyone about last night when she had turned
to find Morgan Elliott on the pathway. Nor did she want
to tell anyone how she felt this morning when she had
found him again. Like a schoolgirl, giddy and elated.

Morgan Elliott had saved her. A knight appearing before
her to banish the darkness. He hadn't asked about the letters on the wall, hadn't asked why some mean-spirited
child or self-righteous adult had put them there. He had
simply knelt beside her, their shoulders brushing in the
silence as they worked magic on the wall. For one precious
night she had felt safe.

But then this morning he had seen her, really seen her.
Good morning, he had said simply as she stood there and
watched the hardness fill his eyes and his heated gaze slid
over her. She was certain what she saw was disgust. She
had seen it countless times before.

After all these years she should have been used to it,
usually was. But not with the memory of last night still
fresh in her heart.

John straightened. "I would come over myself to help
but I am leaving for Europe in the morning."

"John! You're leaving?"

"It can't be helped. But I'll be back as soon as I can.
In the meantime, I know two fellows who can help you
out. Marcus and Joe. I'll have them at your house this
afternoon."

"You will?"

"Absolutely. So wipe that sad look off your face."

"Oh, John," she said quietly, tugging at his lapels,
"you are so good to me."

• • • •

Lily sat back in a maroon-enameled, five-glassed landau as the carriage made its way north on Broadway. She was just on the verge of directing the driver to take Fifth Avenue when she noticed that they had come to the stretch of Broadway between Fourteenth and Twenty-third streets known as the Ladies' Mile. They passed shops of every kind, the finest in the world. It was said this was the most expensive length of real estate in the city—not because of the actual property values, but because a man had to spend a good bit of time in the financial district to make enough money to pay for what his wife purchased along the nine blocks of shop-lined street.

Lily remembered the cherished days when she and her mother had made a day of shopping, starting at Madison Square, the tree-lined park at Twenty-third Street and Broadway, where all the ladies gathered in their fine carriages before starting out down Broadway to shop. Madison Square was still there and by the looks of the crowd of carriages circling its border, the long days of extravagant shopping still occurred. But those days were over for Lily. Her mother was gone, and Lily couldn't quite bring herself to go shopping alone.

Nearly forty-five minutes later, Lily returned to the town house on Fifty-ninth Street. Once inside she made her way through the first floor, as stunned now as she had been that first day at the shambles the house had become. It wasn't a case of broken windows and walls with holes. It was more a case of neglect. The paneling covering the walls was dull and scratched, the fine silk wallpaper stained and ripped, the imported carpets thin and threadbare. The portraits that graced the stairwell were dusty and dull from lack of care. City soot covered the multipaned windows. Many of the gas fixtures no longer worked. Lily could only surmise that not a single repair had been made since she left years before. What had happened? she wondered. Why hadn't Claude taken care of the house?

But the battered rooms held no answers, and Claude had left no communication other than the simple will that designated Lily as sole guardian of his children.

The house was quiet, the children nowhere to be seen, and Lily breathed a guilty sigh of relief. Tossing the oversized hat onto the entryway table, she took the stairs up to the second floor to change her clothes. She longed for a bracing ride through the countryside. But since most of her belongings, including Midnight, her favorite horse, had yet to arrive she would have to wait.

Lily had just turned down the hallway toward her bedroom when her heart suddenly skittered and her breath caught. Her steps faltered. Morgan Elliott kneeled on the floor as he measured something along the base of the wall.

For the first time in years she felt shy. "Hello," she said, when he seemed unaware of her presence.

He turned around slowly, his gaze hard. After a moment, he nodded coolly, then turned back to the work at hand.

Lily felt an unaccustomed blush of embarrassment singe her cheeks at his blatant dismissal, the same embarrassment she had felt that morning. Though she knew it was absurd, she had felt one surge of inadequacy after the next when they had stood in the kitchen earlier, the children looking on. She had tamped the feelings down with effort, hiding her embarrassment with defiance. This afternoon, however, she was determined to be polite. "Thank you for taking the children to breakfast."

Without a word to her, he jotted something down on a scrap of paper with a blunt-leaded pencil, then took another measurement.

Her embarrassment drained away, but her cheeks were still stained with red. "I said *thank you,* Mr. Elliott," she said more pointedly.

He glanced back at her, his dark hair falling forward on his forehead before he raked it back with one strong hand. "You're welcome, Miss Blakemore."

That was it, nothing more before he returned to his

work. Lily was astonished. Half-angry. Half-mortified. What exactly she expected she didn't know. Common sense demanded that she proceed on to her room. But somehow she found she couldn't let it go.

"Please leave me the bill for breakfast. I'll take care of it," she said, her voice growing taut.

"Forget about it," he said still facing the wall.

"The children are my responsibility, Mr. Elliott, not yours," she said in a voice more clipped than she would have wished.

He turned back to her, one brow cocked. "Glad to hear you realize that," he responded, his voice low and harsh.

His comment struck her with the precision of a bowman's arrow, fast and deep. A moment as brittle as fine, crystalline glass passed before Lily spoke. "What is that supposed to mean?"

His cool gaze ran the length of her like an angry caress. She felt heat surge through her body, along with embarrassment, anger, and something else something she couldn't name.

"Forget it," he said, turning away.

He took one last measurement, wrote it down, then pushed up from the floor. Lily hadn't realized how tall he was, well over six feet, she guessed, a good head taller than she. As she looked up at him, her heart unexpectedly pounded. His shirt was damp, as if he had been working outdoors, only to come inside for a second to take the measurement. The thin material clung to his shoulders, broad and muscled, tapering down into narrow waist and hips. Strong thighs. And his hands. Long but carved, fingers strong.

Lily had always believed you could tell a great deal about a man by studying his hands, how they moved. With confidence? Without?

Morgan Elliott's hand were beautifully rugged, capable. Hands that had never faltered, she thought suddenly. Her heart clenched in her chest. With effort, she concentrated on his clothes.

A man's clothes were telling, too. Did he care too much? Would he go out of his way to avoid a puddle, keeping his boots unscathed? Though he was well kempt, Morgan Elliott clearly was not a man who spent a great deal of time in front of a mirror, and he had undoubtedly walked right through a good many mud puddles in his day. He possessed an innate masculinity. Lily hated that she noticed these things about him, hated even more that she was pleased.

"Do I pass?"

His tone was sensual. Insolent.

Startled, her head shot up.

Dear God, she had been blatantly staring at him. A heartbeat passed before she purposefully crushed what was left of her shyness, and she met his bold gaze. She had learned long ago that it was easier this way, and she didn't know why she had forgotten, especially when the lessons had cost her so much.

She looked deep into the dark pools of his eyes, not even a trace of embarrassment this time as she considered him. After a moment she took a deliberate step to the side. "Of course you may pass," she responded, waving her hand in front of her with a flourish, purposely misunderstanding the meaning of his question.

Morgan raised a brow. Then with a look and a tone that sent a raw shiver down her spine, he said, "Well, well, well."

He took the few steps that separated them, a predator's gait, until he stood scant inches away from her in the suddenly cramped hallway. His voice was low and deep, arrogant. "So you're not just another pretty face after all."

Her jaw set like mortar. "Meaning?"

Slowly his lips curved, though no one could have mistaken the expression for a smile. He raised his arm and braced his hand against the scarred wall above her head, leaning close, too close.

"Meaning," he responded, his voice low and sensual, "that I'm impressed."

She realized suddenly that he was enjoying himself. She could see it in his eyes. His words might drip with blatant sexuality, but he was toying with her. He the cat, she the mouse.

Her hand clenched, and she felt the furious beat of her heart. She forced her voice to work over the knot of emotion that was lodged in her throat. "Were you just born mean, or did you learn the skill?"

Morgan looked at her for one long-drawn-out second as if he must have misheard. "Mean?" His booming laughter suddenly filled the hallway. "I can't remember the last time anyone called me mean." His laughter died away and he simply looked at her, his gaze as dark and suddenly grim as a thunderstorm. "To my face, at any rate."

The frantic beat of her heart shifted, changed as she became all too aware of his nearness. His dark hair was silky, brushed back from his forehead. His tall form, strong and hard with muscle, was close to hers, so close that she had to tilt her head back to maintain eye contact. If he moved ever so slightly he would touch her. She sensed his power, barely contained, his masculinity used as a weapon.

Lily told herself to duck beneath his arm and run as far away and as fast as she could. But whether it was the unexpected scent of him, sawdust and sunshine, that wrapped around her, or her refusal to let him intimidate her, she remained still, facing him, looking at him. Denying him success in this battle of wills.

But then he moved even closer and touched her arm. Not in passing, not simply to help her. Intimately.

The touch was electric, and her breath caught. She could feel the rough callused skin of his hand warm through her thin cotton sleeve, and she could do little more than watch as his glance dropped to her lips.

"No," he said so quietly that she almost couldn't hear, "it's been a long, long time since anyone called me mean."

He ran his hand down her arm, slowly, seemingly innocent if it weren't for the darkness in his eyes. She recognized it. Had seen the look a thousand times before. But this time, for reasons she didn't understand, with this man, it was different. Despite his harsh gaze and insolent manners, she would have sworn that he looked at her in a way that called out to her. With his simple touch she felt a burning, an aching poignancy, exciting feelings she had never known before.

"Someone should have said it long ago," she stated, her voice shaky as she tried to drop her gaze. "Clearly you have gotten your way for far too long."

His eyes grew heated. He brought his hand slowly up her arm, burning a path to her jaw. With his thumb he gently tilted her chin upward, refusing to let her avoid him. "Will I get my way now?" he asked boldly, his voice deep.

He lowered his head until she could feel his warm breath against her cheek. Then he leaned closer, pressing against her. Her breath caught when she became acutely aware of the unmistakable ridge of his desire, thick and hard.

"Will I enjoy it?" he asked. "Will you?"

Lily's breath hissed through her teeth. Her mind reeled and she jerked away, out from beneath his arm, her chest rising and falling painfully. She realized then with sudden heartbreaking clarity why he hadn't asked about the letters on the wall—because he already knew what they meant. He had known all along that she was called Crimson Lily, just like all the other men had who had looked into her eyes with desire. And she hated that he knew.

She looked at him, just looked, and couldn't seem to move. Foolishly she was disappointed, and angry at herself for the aching poignancy she had felt. She had accepted long ago that she would never fall in love, never marry . . .

never have children. Raine Hawthorne had seen to that years ago.

But understanding didn't stop the tears from burning in her eyes or her heart from beating in hollow despair.

Lily took a deep breath. She told herself to fire Morgan Elliott right then and there. He was insolent, disrespectful, and well beyond the pale. But somehow the words stuck in her throat and she knew she wouldn't. Despite everything he had said and done, for one brief moment as they had knelt side by side in the night, she hadn't felt so alone.

Regardless of his insolence, Lily wanted to know how it had happened. She wanted to know why. Why him? Why could this man do what no other had ever been able to do before him?

On a black night of despair, Morgan Elliott had banished the darkness.

So she didn't utter the words that anyone else in their right mind would have. Not yet, at least. Instead she raised her chin in defiance, falling back on the stance and tone that she had used to hide her true feeling for years. She had learned the hard way that it did no good to let people see that they had the power to hurt her. "You are no gentleman, Mr. Elliott. Now if you'll excuse me," she said with effort, forgetting about changing her clothes. "I must see to lunch."

Morgan stood quietly, his hand still braced against the wall, his eyes boring into her. Moments passed before he turned his head away sharply, those dark emotions seeming to overtake him. But then his face settled, his ironclad control once again in place.

"I hope you can do better with lunch than you did with breakfast," he said finally, just when Lily had started toward the stairs.

In a flash, Lily whirled back around, too many conflicting emotions raging within her. "I'll have you know that I am a great deal more capable than you seem to think, Mr. Elliott."

"Really?"

Lily watched as he pushed away from the wall. He stood in the hallway, his massive form blocking out much of the light. Chiseled and solid. Strong.

"Yes, really," she breathed.

She turned away, had to for fear that she might close the distance that separated them. She hastened down the stairs, desperate to escape. But Morgan followed, coming up to her side. She quickened her step, trying to get away. But just as she took another step, her shoe snagged in the hem of her skirt. For one startling moment, her balance deserted her. But in the next, Morgan caught her, pulling her back to safety.

"Careful, princess."

Princess.

She emitted a strangled gasp as her throat tightened. He had called her princess last night when he banished the darkness. Why was this happening to her? she wondered desperately. Why was her world being turned upside down by children who loathed her, and a man who called her princess in one minute, then hated her in the next?

With effort she forced herself to speak. "Regardless of what you have heard, Mr. Elliott, I am truly a great deal more capable than you think."

His cool smile was doubtful.

"I'll have you know, sir," she began, forcing strength back into her voice, welcoming the anger that stirred to life in her breast, "that in a few short hours I have found a butler and a cook."

Morgan cocked his head.

"Don't look so surprised. I've managed on my own for the last ten years." She pried her arm free of his grip. "And quite well, I might add."

He opened his mouth to speak, but a shout cut him short. "Lily!"

Lily and Morgan halted midway down the stairway overlooking the dull marble foyer.

"Lily, where are you?" came the impatient shout again.

"I'm here, Penelope."

Penelope waited at the front door, which stood partially opened. "There are two men here," the child stated, her eyes narrowed in accusation. "They say they're the new butler and cook."

Lily clasped her hands together. "Splendid! Let them in!"

With obvious reluctance, Penelope opened the door the rest of the way and stepped aside. Two men entered. One was tall and barrel chested, with a long slashing scar down the side of his face. The other was short, wiry, and menacing, looking as if he might just lop off Penelope's head at any moment.

"What are you looking at?" Penelope snapped at the shorter man, clearly unimpressed by his forbidding appearance.

"You Miz' Blakemore?"

The larger man asked this of Lily, or grunted actually, she was forced to concede, her excitement beginning to wane. She hoped against hope that these were not the men John had sent. "Yes, and you might be?"

Morgan leaned close. "Scarface and Shorty," he answered for them, laughing softly into her ear.

Lily shot him a venomous glare.

"Like the kid said, we'se the new butler and cook, Marcus and Joe. But everyone calls us Marky and Jojo."

"Marky and Jojo?" Morgan remarked quietly. "Astounding what one can find in 'a few short hours.' "

Though Morgan's face was as serious as a prophet's, Lily knew better.

"Where did you find these exemplary servants?" he continued. "In a nice dark alleyway somewhere on the Lower East Side? Perhaps they were just washing their hands after tossing some poor unsuspecting bloke into the East River and you thought, 'Aha! The perfect cook and butler for me.' "

Lily ignored Morgan, and she was going to kill John just as soon as she could. But first . . .

"So, Mr. . . . Jojo," she began, addressing the taller of the two men, as she took the steps to the foyer.

The shorter man came forward. "No, I'm Jojo, just Jojo, no mister," he barked.

"Yes, well," she began, flustered, "how nice for you. But there seems to be some mistake."

The man named Marky crossed his arms. "Mistake? What are you talkin' about? Are you Miz' Blakemore?"

"Yes, but—"

"Is this Blakemore House?"

"Well, yes, but—"

"Then there ain't no mistake. Now, where do you want us?"

Marky, Jojo, and even Penelope waited expectantly. Morgan looked on with amused interest. Lily closed her eyes and prayed for guidance. Truly she was going to kill John. For now, however, the fact remained that she needed a cook and she needed a butler, and if John had sent them they couldn't be all that bad, could they?

Taking a deep, fortifying breath, Lily turned smoothly to her niece and smiled. "Penelope, would you be good enough to show . . . Mr. Marky and Mr. ah, Jojo to the servant quarters."

Penelope harrumphed and started to protest, but as soon as she started to speak, Lily saw Penelope's glance suddenly shift, as if looking at Morgan. Instantly the tirade ceased. Lily turned sharply to look at Morgan, but he merely gave an innocent shrug of shoulders.

"Come on," Penelope stated curtly. "I'll show you where to go." A hint of a smile wafted across her lips before she turned to Jojo with a renewed scowl. "And you better know how to cook."

"You ain't never seen cookin', little missy, until you've seen mine."

"Hopefully," Penelope grumbled, "we can do more than look at it."

A tiny smile cracked on the short man's lips. "A feisty one, are ya?"

Penelope's glower and Jojo's laughter slowly disappeared as the new staff members were led away.

Lily and Morgan stood alone. Lily had to will herself not to look at Morgan who was no doubt smirking, or doing something equally infuriating. Suddenly she felt every one of her twenty-nine years. Actually she felt more like she had lived *one hundred* and twenty-nine years, but who was counting, she thought with a grim shake of her head.

"I believe, *Miz'* Blakemore," Morgan began in utterly polite tones, "you were just telling me how capable you are."

Her patience spent, and any sense of propriety long exhausted, Lily shot Morgan a withering glare. "Go stuff yourself, Elliott."

With that she squared her delicate shoulders, turned on her fashionable heel, and headed back upstairs, the amazingly satisfying image of Morgan Elliott's surprised countenance blazing in her mind.

Four

It was easy enough to gain access to *The New York Times* archives, and late the next afternoon Morgan sat at a large wooden table with newspapers spread out before him. The copies were old and yellowed, brittle enough that he had to turn the pages with care.

It had never bothered him before that no one seemed to know what had caused Lily Blakemore's fall from grace. People simply seemed to know that she had. But somehow, for him, that was no longer enough.

Morgan had come to the basement of the newspaper building in downtown Manhattan determined to find out the cause of Lily's fall, reasoning that surely something had been reported all those years ago.

He told himself he needed to know more about Lily Blakemore in order to better understand John Crandall, and he left it at that. He was unwilling to think about why it had become so important to understand this strange woman who should mean nothing to him.

Lily.

A woman, it was said, with whom men around the world were enamored.

Morgan narrowed his eyes in derision, and started to snort his disdain when a flash of memory came to mind. Lily in the hallway. His body so hard it had hurt.

Morgan's gut clenched. What had happened to him? He had responded to her as if he were no better than a besotted schoolboy. He shook his head in frustration. But something about the way she had stood up to him, held her ground despite the fact that she was a good foot shorter than he had kicked his senses into high gear. The feel of her skin, the smell of her hair, the sound of her suddenly rapid breathing. God, he had wanted her right then and there. On the floor. Privacy be damned.

And that made him as angry now as it had the day before. He had no business wanting Lily Blakemore. Crimson Lily.

A fallen woman.

Morgan cursed into the poorly lit room, the sound echoing off the barren walls of the newspaper's research room. He was as bad as the rest of those besotted fools. Lusting after sensuous lips, tantalizing curves. Innocent blue eyes.

And that, he had to admit, was part of the problem.

Morgan had met many a fallen woman in his day, and he was quickly having to admit that not one of them had anything in common with Lily Blakemore. He was forced to concede over and over again that while she had acted outrageously in the kitchen and with less propriety than someone of her station in life should display, she no more seemed like a criminal's moll than young Cassie. No heavy face paint or loud voice. No profanity or smoldering cigarettes.

Moreover, the fact of the matter remained that in all the days Morgan had been at Blakemore House he had not seen so much as a glimpse of the man he sought. But his sources had been specific—his best sources. And they all agreed, Lily Blakemore was John Crandall's mistress. And

Morgan planned to use that information to find a way to bring the man down.

Before arriving at Blakemore House, Morgan had learned that Lily's father had been Orville Blakemore, of the prominent Jackson Blakemore line. Orville had built Blakemore House for his wife, Delia. Delia had been a Vanderwelt, one of the few true Knickerbockers who had founded New York. Orville and Delia had two children, Claude and Lily. By all accounts the family had lived a happy, loving life amid Manhattan's finest families until fifteen years ago when Orville and Delia had died in a boating accident. Claude, then eighteen, had taken over the Blakemore estate as well as the responsibility for his four-teen-year-old sister. Two years later Claude had married a woman named Abigail Holmes, a year later she had given birth to Robert. Morgan had also learned that the year Cassie was born, Abigail had died. He suspected, given the date, she had died in childbirth.

With that knowledge, Morgan started in on the aged newspapers.

Time passed quickly as he read issue after issue, starting ten and a half years earlier in November of 1885. He learned that not until nearly five years after Orville and Delia Blakemore had perished did Lily and Claude once again become part of the social whirl. Morgan found references to sightings of the pair at many a function that winter season. Charity balls. The opera. Always Claude and Lily, he noted, and he wondered where Abigail had been. Only once was there a mention of another man, one Beauford Tisdale, rumored to be a suitor pursuing Lily's hand. Beyond that, time and again, Morgan found references to some antic that Lily had been involved in. An impromptu swim in the Central Park pond despite the frigid cold. A horse race up on Fifth Avenue which, Morgan noted with a grumble, she had won. Attending a gala dressed as a man and demanding a duel with some poor, unsuspecting fop.

Slowly a picture began to emerge. A wild child. And oddly it wasn't hard to imagine Lily Blakemore dancing in the streets or brandishing a gun, all in the face of New York's wealthiest families. He started to smile.

Morgan knew that if she had been born into Regency England with the money and beauty she possessed, she would have been called an original. But then his smile faltered. Lily hadn't been born during that time. She had been born into and raised within a strict and proper society. A society that wouldn't take kindly to anyone, even one of their own, defying its prescriptions for behavior. Morgan knew. Though he had been born hundreds of miles away, he had been born into the same class of people. Which he knew could only mean one thing. To be outrageous in the latter part of the century, no matter how beautiful or wealthy, was not an asset.

Morgan knew that New York society was strict and rigid—a place where propriety and modesty were all-important. A place where matrons covered up not only every inch of their own bodies, but every inch of their furniture as well. God forbid someone catch sight of an undressed, and hence, indecent table leg. While mores were brought over from England, Americans, as they are wont to do, made certain they did everything bigger, better, to greater extremes. No, Morgan conceded, being an original in New York was no recommendation at all.

But even this did little to answer his plaguing question. Based on the things he had read so far, he could have understood them calling her Outrageous Lily or even Reckless Lily, but Crimson Lily? No, that he couldn't understand. What had sealed her fate?

It was as he started on the newspapers from a few months later, in March of 1886, that Morgan's eyes narrowed in concentration and he began to read more carefully.

March 2, 1886.

A short article about the death of a man named Raine

Hawthorne. Wealthy. Socially prominent. The mention would not have been significant had it not been for the fact that it was reported that Lily had been at the man's bedside upon his passing.

March 3, 1886.

An announcement for a grand gala to be held on March the sixteenth at the behest of the deceased Raine Hawthorne. How odd, Morgan thought, a gala event to celebrate his own death? And Lily was to be the hostess. But Morgan was further amazed to learn that at this event, to which only the elite were invited, the man's will was to be read, after which a gift was to be presented.

As Morgan continued day by day through the fragile, yellowed newsprint, there was at least some mention, however insignificant, about the rapidly approaching gala. The women out shopping. The shopkeepers letting slip that their customers were having a difficult time finding suitable attire. What did one wear to a gala for a dead man? Beads? Black? Neither seemed appropriate.

Morgan's eyes narrowed in confusion as he sat in the confining, airless room. But he was determined and he continued on, reading every word until he reached the designated day.

March 16, 1886.

Blakemore House. A reporter had gone to the gala, but had been barred from the home. Standing outside, the reporter had watched and noted the dignitaries and social elite as they arrived. The Astors. The Widmars. The upstart Vanderbilts. Morgan noticed that Lily's supposed beau, Beauford Tisdale, had attended as well. The reporter waxed eloquently about the gowns and the jewels. The extravagant carriages. Who arrived with whom. And he promised a follow-up the next day.

But nothing followed.

No article. Not a single line or snippet. No mention of Raine Hawthorne, Lily Blakemore, or the grand gala, nothing until weeks later when Morgan found a brief item noting that Lily Blakemore had moved away.

Leaning back in the hardwood chair, Morgan wondered what could have happened in that house that night? How was it possible that a follow-up report had not been printed about an event that had been talked about for weeks beforehand?

Morgan thought back to the fact that he could find no one who knew what had caused Lily's fall. It was as if New York's elite had thrown her out, closed ranks, then made some pact never to speak of it again.

What had happened that night? Morgan wondered again. What could have happened that would make them turn one of their own away?

The newspaper clearly wasn't going to provide the answer. But who could tell him? Then Morgan recalled the two references he had seen to Beauford Tisdale. He would track the man down.

Morgan glanced at his pocket watch. For now, however, any further search would have to wait. He needed to get back to Blakemore House before someone noticed his absence.

Morgan slipped out onto the streets of downtown Manhattan. Traffic was tangled and snarled, and he couldn't find a single available hansom cab. Resigned, he jumped up the wooden steps of a Fifth Avenue horsecar. Despite the arched roof, Morgan had to duck as he walked up the center aisle to drop his nickel into the tin box at the front of the car. Then a whip snapped in the air and the team of gaunt horses trudged on, the wooden bus jerking forward as they made their way north.

Morgan jumped down from the horsecar at Fifty-ninth, mixing in with the hack line that queued up along the southernmost edge of Central Park. He walked the distance to Blakemore House, his mind filled with thoughts of Lily. He was just about to step through a crowd of people when he caught sight of a man he knew to be a reporter lurking across the street from Blakemore House. Lily had been right. She was being watched.

Morgan cursed. After a moment, he turned back and retraced his steps, then made his way to Fifty-eighth Street so he could come up through the back of the property.

Minutes later Morgan was walking up the flagstone path when he met the children who were coming around the house from the front yard.

"Mr. Elliott!" Cassie called.

"Hello, children," he said, using an aloof voice so as not to encourage them.

But the children didn't seem to notice. They walked the last few steps to the back door together, Cassie regaling Morgan with their adventures in the park.

"Are you allowed to go alone?" he asked, despite his intent to remain uninvolved.

"I guess," Cassie answered. "We don't have a governess anymore to take us."

"Thank God," Robert muttered.

Morgan scowled. "Did your aunt Lily run her off too?"

"Oh, no," Cassie said with great seriousness. "Wilhelmina quit."

"Yeah," Penelope added with a sniff of indignation, "after she got one look at Lily. No respectable governess in her right mind would dare work in our house now."

Morgan would have pursued the issue had they not come to the back door and he noticed something strange. The small windows of the basement kitchen were covered. What in the world was going on now? he wondered with a silent curse.

Telling the children to wait, Morgan went up the steps quietly, then turned the doorknob, pushing inside. It took a second for his eyes to adjust to the darkness. But when they did, all he found was Lily, the two shady servants, Marky and Jojo, and an unknown fourth party intently huddled around the kitchen table.

Morgan stepped deeper into the room. "What the blazes—"

"Shhhh!" all four hissed in unison.

"Shut the durn door," Jojo demanded.

The children pushed in behind Morgan, and Cassie squealed in delight.

"Madame Paulie!"

"Madame Paulie?" Morgan muttered.

The children raced forward to squeeze in around the table.

"Shut the door," Marky demanded.

Morgan was too astounded to speak, much less do as he was asked.

With an impatient huff, Penelope raced back around Morgan and slammed the door. The glow of several beeswax candles burned on the table, washing the room in a dim golden light.

"What is going on here?" Morgan finally demanded.

"Shhhh!" was his only answer.

The room filled with silence, an eerie quiet that Morgan didn't like. Then he heard a strange noise—a noise, he realized in disbelief, that was coming from the unknown fourth party, an outlandishly dressed woman sitting next to Lily. Good God, the woman was humming!

Just when Morgan decided to pull the thick woolen blankets away from the windows, the woman said, "I am starting to see."

"What?" Lily asked excitedly, leaning forward, her bracelets and necklaces clanging against the wooden table. "What do you see, Madame Paulie?"

"You. I see you."

"Hell," Morgan muttered. When would Lily Blakemore cease to amaze him? A gypsy. Right there in the kitchen. And based on her nieces' and nephew's reactions, this was not the first time the woman had been there.

"Yes," the gypsy continued, her voice laced with an eerie excitement. "I see you clearly now."

"What else? What else do you see?"

"Ah . . . your parents?"

Lily's gasp was audible.

Madame Paulie glanced up quickly. "Yes," she added more definitely, returning her attention to the bowl of water that sat before her. "Oh, yes, I can see them perfectly."

"My parents?" Lily breathed.

Morgan nearly groaned, but the sound died away at the look in Lily's eyes. Sad. Desperate. And very lonely.

"Yes, your parents. They are grateful to the revered Madame Paulie for contacting them."

Clearing his throat, Morgan spoke. "What is Miss Blakemore's mother's name?" he asked boldly into the quiet room, wanting to show this woman for the fraud she was. He didn't want to admit that he wanted to erase the sadness from Lily's eyes.

"Oh, my word!" Lily gasped. "Can you tell those kinds of things?"

Madame Paulie shot Morgan a censorious glare. Morgan merely shrugged his broad shoulders and quirked his brow.

"Of course," she said, with an insulted sniff. "Let me see. Her name begins with the letter . . . *V*."

"The letter *V*?" Lily asked, her tone skeptical.

"No, no," the gypsy said quickly. "The letter is more rounded."

"Yes!" Lily laughed delightedly.

The gypsy looked encouraged. "A *U*. I am starting to see a *U*."

"*U*?" Morgan demanded. "What kind of a name starts with a *U*?"

"*U*genia," Madame Paulie shot back proudly.

Morgan prayed for patience. "In the future you might find it helpful to know that Eugenia starts with an *E*."

Madame returned her attention to the dish of water with a scowl, then said, "I see a *B*."

"Well, that's closer," Lily responded, biting her lower lip.

Madame Paulie's jaw set. "*D*."

"Yes!" Lily squeaked excitedly. "It's a *D*!"

"Oh, good God," Morgan burst out. How could anyone with half a brain be so naive? "She's running out of letters in the alphabet, for chrissakes."

Everyone at the table swiveled around to stare at Morgan, but he would not back down. "Ask her to be more specific. Ask her what your mother's name is, hell, I mean was!"

Lily's brow furrowed. "Perhaps you're right."

She turned back to Madame Paulie with an apologetic though questioning gaze.

But Madame Paulie was as shrewd as she looked, Morgan noted. She flung herself up from the table. "I cannot commune with the dead if such doubt is flowing around the room like thick black smoke of angry hatred and mockery!" she cried indignantly. "It blocks my ability to see! It's all your fault!"

Morgan might have applauded her performance had he been a mere observer of her farce. But then he cursed. He *was* a mere observer, he reminded himself harshly.

"Morgan!" everyone around the table chided in indignation, then turned back to the seeress.

"Please, Madame Paulie," Cassie cried, "try again. Mr. Elliott won't say another word."

He held up his hands in mock surrender. "Not another word from me."

"No," the gypsy cried dramatically. "It is too late. I must leave."

There was no convincing her, and once she had her money, she banged out the back door.

"Look what you did!" Lily accused.

"Me?" Morgan asked innocently. "What did I do?"

"You insulted Madame Paulie."

"Madame Paulie?" he demanded with an impatient scowl. "The woman who left because of 'thick black smoke of angry hatred and mockery'? That woman?" He said the words with a flourish, gaining a few giggles from Cassie and Penelope for his efforts.

Lily was clearly not amused. "She was going to talk to my parents."

"She was lying."

"Madame Paulie is not a liar! She is a gifted seeress."

"And I'm the king of England. She's a charlatan, and I've seen a few in my days."

"She is not!"

"All right, have it your way. Pay her all your money. See if I care. In fact, if you hurry, I'm sure you can catch her before she gets too far. Or better yet, pay me. I'll commune with your dead parents, or anyone else you have an interest in chatting with."

"Can you really, Mr. Elliott?" Cassie asked with genuine awe.

Morgan grimaced and hung his head. "No, Cassie. I can't. And neither can Madame Paulie."

Robert wore a look of I-told-you-so, while Cassie and Penelope scowled their disappointment. Even Marky and Jojo seemed disgruntled.

After that, the children lost interest and went upstairs. Marky and Jojo disappeared.

Lily pushed up from her seat at the table, intent on stomping indignantly from the room right behind her young charges. Instead, she found herself trapped between the wall and Morgan who leaned all too casually against the counter.

Since he didn't seem inclined to move, the only way out was to ask him to step aside, or squeeze by between his chiseled body and the table. She eyed the meager space, and suddenly her heart beat erratically.

"Is something wrong?" he asked.

His full lips pulled into an infuriatingly knowing smile. She wanted to slap the smirk right off his handsome face and scream, *Yes, something is wrong!* Everything is wrong. Him in this house. Her heart beating like an Indian drum run amok. Not to mention the infuriating fact that she didn't seem to have an ounce of control whenever the man was near.

But, of course, she wouldn't say that. And if he thought he could get the better of her, he could think again. Morgan Elliot was child's play compared to some of the men she had dealt with, or so she told herself.

With that she raised her chin and curved her lips in what she hoped resembled a smile. "No, Mr. Elliott, nothing is wrong."

Squaring her shoulders and gathering her long skirt, she started forward. Surely he would move, she told herself.

One step, two. But she was the only one who appeared to be going anywhere.

Her chin rose a notch and their eyes locked, hers determined, his amused.

But the infuriating man still didn't move. He simply waited and watched, his tall form a wall of heat and hard muscle.

Lily could barely swallow, much less speak. And when she came to stand just before him, she was forced to stop or brush up against him if she continued on. "Excuse me," she said tightly.

One corner of his full lips quirked up, and his gaze raked over her. But his heavy-lidded eyes shielded their expression.

She remembered all too well his touch in the upstairs hallway. The heat. The yearning.

The disdain.

Lily forced herself to be calm, not give in to her quavering nerves. But then he reached out and very slowly touched her cheek, his thumb running over her jaw. The touch startled her. So commanding yet gentle. No trace of the insolence he had shown so clearly before.

Without warning she was aware of the feel of his skin on hers. She was not thinking that he was in her way, or was more trouble than he was worth. She was thinking that he was a man, a powerful man who drew her like a magnet, despite the fact that he shouldn't.

For as long as she could remember, in Manhattan among her acquaintances, with her parents and even with Claude, Lily had never felt she belonged. Like a traveler in a foreign land.

But when she looked into Morgan Elliott's eyes she felt a certain recognition. A language they both understood.

Of course, when she thought about this she knew it was irrational. The man had made it clear that he thought little of her. Not to mention the inescapable fact that he was in her employ. Language indeed, she chided herself. She should jerk free and demand that he keep his hands to himself.

"Leave me alone," she barely managed.

His gaze met hers, and without warning his teasing smile disappeared. He looked at her closely, his brow furrowing. For a moment, Lily was certain that he was going to ask her something.

"What?" she breathed. "What is it?"

Her question clearly startled him. His countenance grew troubled, but he never answered, nor did he move away.

Yet again, he smelled of sawdust and sunshine. Things she wasn't used to. She was used to men's pomades and powders, heavy colognes and tonics. She couldn't remember standing so close to a workingman. His dark hair shone, falling forward onto his brow, the back overlong, brushing the collar of his cambric shirt. Her fingers ached to feel the silky strands.

His smile returned then, as if he could read her errant thoughts, and his gaze lowered to her lips. His fingers brushed along her cheek once, then again, before he leaned closer.

She felt a shiver of fear run up her spine, fear not of what he might do, but of what she might do. Throw herself in his arms and beg that he kiss her.

She yearned to feel his lips on hers, to feel his hand

lowering until he wrapped her in a lover's embrace. The thought shocked and unsettled her.

"Are you going to kiss me?" she asked before she could stop herself.

A moment of stunned silence passed while she realized what she had said. She regretted the words as soon as she spoke them, then regretted them even more at the look that came into his eyes. Hard and cold. Condemning.

"No," he said, pulling his hand away. "I was just wiping the candle soot from your cheek." With that he stepped away.

Embarrassment racked her body, leaving her flushed. Good Lord, what had she said? But years of being forced to defend herself in any way she could manage turned her embarrassment to anger.

"You really are a very mean man, Mr. Elliott," she said with effort.

Morgan laughed, his dark eyes glittering over her. "So you told me, yesterday, I believe." His laughter trailed off. "And you'd do well not to forget that fact, Miss Blakemore."

Her breath caught, and the shiver of fear she had felt earlier returned, only this time it was caused by the sound of his voice. "Why, Mr. Elliott? Why is it that you want me to be afraid of you?"

Her mind swirled as she witnessed a myriad of emotions rush across his features—emotions she recognized. She knew in that instant that this man wasn't at peace.

Lily knew there were those who spent their whole lives searching for something. For some people it was an indefinable search. For others their search was for something specific, something frequently beyond their reach. Morgan Elliott was searching. She recognized the look in his eyes. It was the same look she saw in the mirror.

But what struck her as odd was that other than the look, that fleeting shadow in his eyes, nothing about this assured and confident man ever would have told her he was a man on a quest.

Whatever it was, Lily wondered if he would ever feel the shock of recognition that people experienced when at last their world slipped into place. Would he? Would she? Or were they both destined to travel through life mere observers of an indifferent world. Travelers, as she had thought earlier, in a foreign land.

Was that why she couldn't utter the words that would send him away when she knew she should? Was that why the darkness had fled when he knelt beside her? Were they truly two like souls who traveled the same path?

Had their lives intertwined for a reason?

"Do you believe in magic?" she asked quietly.

Confusion creased his brow. "Magic? What are you talking about?"

A blush stained her cheeks. "Madame Paulie," she equivocated.

Morgan scoffed. "As I told you, Madame Paulie is a swindler."

"Regardless, surely you believe in destiny and fate." She couldn't seem to help herself. For reasons she didn't understand, it was important.

"Miss Blakemore, I don't believe that our lives are pre-determined any more than I believe in Madame Paulie. We make our lives what they are, we are responsible for what happens to us, good or bad." His features were hard and unyielding. "Now if you'll excuse me, I have a house falling apart that needs to be repaired. And *magic* isn't going to get it done."

Five

If Morgan thought that by reading articles or spending time near Lily Blakemore he would come to better understand her, he was badly mistaken.

Two days after Madame Paulie's indignant departure, the front door fell back on its hinges and Lily flew into the house like a whirlwind. She wore a simple cotton day dress, the delicate folds swirling about her ankles as she breezed inside.

Morgan looked on from the parlor where he worked on a gas sconce. Robert watched from where he sat on the first landing in a shaft of summer sunlight, a book lying forgotten in his lap. Penelope perched three steps below, her face glumly in her hands. Cassie leaned her head against the banister.

Lily didn't appear to notice any of them as she hurried down the three steps from the front door landing to the sunken foyer. Pulling her hat off, Lily tossed it aside with little regard for where it landed. For one precarious second the wildly feathered concoction caught an edge of the mahogany entry table, only to fall free and slide to a halt on the marble floor. Her beaded reticule didn't fare much better, but her crocheted gloves snagged on a battered Empire chair and held on, though barely. Lily scowled, but she didn't bother to retrace her steps to gather her scattered belongings.

Morgan's eyes narrowed. Lily Blakemore frustrated him like nothing before her ever had. With her talk of magic and the memory of the feel of her skin beneath his fingers, Morgan was spending far too much time thinking about the woman.

And her question. *Are you going to kiss me?*

He swore silently. He had thought of little else. Before or since. He had been on the verge of doing just that. It had been her breathless question that had steered him away from the dangerous path.

He knew he should have moved aside the second she stood up from the table, just as he should have moved aside in the hallway the day before. But again and again, reason deserted him whenever she was near.

Without warning, Lily stopped and whirled around. "Where are you?"

Morgan along with Robert, Penelope, and Cassie opened their mouths to answer, only to snap them shut when a strange young boy staggered in behind Lily, a mangy dog at his feet. "I'm hurryin', I'm hurryin'!" the boy called, gasping from beneath a wooden crate overloaded with an assortment of goods.

"This way, Albert," Lily stated, her voice lilting, before she marched on toward the kitchen.

Albert tottered off behind her, the dog scurrying at his heels.

Morgan exchanged quizzical glances with the children. "What's she up to now?" he asked drily.

Cassie smiled and leaped up from her place on the stairway to follow. "Who knows. But if Lily's doing it, it must be fun."

With a dramatic sigh, Penelope stood. "I don't have anything better to do," she announced.

After a moment, Robert pushed up and followed after his sisters. Morgan scowled, turned back to the wall, and shoved in a bolt with more force than was necessary, determinedly ignoring the clatter and bangs coming from the kitchen. He didn't want to know what madness the woman was up to now.

Lily stood in the kitchen. Albert, the young boy she had found on the street corner and had asked to help her, waited expectantly by the counter with his dog. But Lily hardly noticed.

Her stomach churned. She felt foolish. Making a grand lunch. Ha! What had she been thinking? But early that morning she had been certain of her success. In the early morning light it had all seemed so easy. If she could make the children lunch, a wonderful lunch just as her mother had made on special occasions for her and Claude, surely she could finally win Robert and Penelope over. Now uncertainty snaked down her spine.

But then she took a deep breath, quelling any doubt. She *would* win them over, she told herself firmly with a decisive nod of her head. How hard could it be to make lunch?

"Lily!"

At the sight of Cassie, Lily smiled and pulled bright yellow lemons from the crate. "Hello!" she said, her voice singing like chimes.

"What are you doing?" Cassie asked, Penelope and Robert behind her.

Lily tossed the child a lemon with a laugh. "I'm going to make lunch!"

"Lunch! You?" they asked in unison.

"Yes, me. Toasted cheese and lemonade. I haven't had lemonade since I was about your age, Cassie. Would you like to help?"

"Oh, yes!" Cassie hurried forward, dragging a tall stool over to the worktable that stood in the center of the kitchen.

Climbing to the top, Cassie knelt on the stool and started rummaging through the crate.

Albert had regained his breath and stared openly at Penelope. "Ain't you a purty one," he said with a wink that was no doubt intended to be lewd, but looked, instead, like some sort of eye spasm.

Penelope, a good head taller than Albert, looked him over calmly. "Pretty? Me? Do you think?"

Had Albert spent more than a few meager seconds in this household he would have known that the look in Penelope's eyes was not one of mutual interest. But he hadn't. Encouraged, he took a step closer. "Yes, oh yes, my lovely!"

Lost in the throes of a young boy's infatuation, his usual streetwise defenses were down. When he saw her hand curl into a tight fist, he was incapable of associating violence with this blond goddess who stood before him with a smile so sweet he thought he had died and gone to heaven. And heaven was just where he was convinced he was going when Penelope let loose with a blow to his midsection that would have done a champion boxer proud.

"Ugh."

Then silence.

Lily, Cassie, and Robert turned with a start to see what had happened. Penelope stood looking as innocent as an angel in front of Albert who was buckled over in front of her, the dog cowering at his feet.

"I think," Penelope began, her eyes wide with concern, "he might have had too many sweets. He must have a stomachache. Perhaps, Lily, you should pay him and let him get home."

"Oh, my Lord, if he's ill we can't just send him away," Lily said, hurrying forward.

Penelope scowled, then gave Albert a meaningful look,

at which the boy straightened as best he could, then said, "I'm fine. Really. I'll just be going."

"Are you sure?"

"Yeah. Real sure."

Lily looked around. "Where's my reticule?"

"In the foyer," Robert supplied, "on the floor with the rest of your things."

"Of course. Could you be a dear, Robert, and get my purse and pay Albert?"

Albert hurried out of the kitchen as quickly as his doubled-over form would allow. Robert followed him, then returned just as Lily announced, "First for the lemonade."

Lily glanced around. "Surely there are some aprons around here," she stated as she looked through drawer after drawer.

With cool movements, Penelope pulled out an apron from a deep drawer.

"Perfect," Lily said, pulling out three more. "One for each of us."

"I'm not wearing one of those frilly things," Robert announced disdainfully.

With a shrug of shoulders, Lily tossed the extra apron back to the drawer. After tying on her own apron, then helping Cassie, Lily pulled a large knife from a holder with a flourish.

"Stand back, everyone," Robert said in a wry voice that failed to hide the trace of seriousness. "She doesn't have very good aim."

Lily only laughed as she rummaged around the kitchen for the rest of the implements she would need. "There," she announced, an assortment of items gathered in front of her. "We're ready."

Very carefully she cut the lemon in half, then squeezed the juice into the pitcher. Soon the children were helping.

"How many do we need?" Cassie asked.

"Well, I'm not exactly sure. But plenty," Lily responded with a nod.

Before long they had the pitcher filled about a third of the way with lemon juice, squeezed and discarded lemons lying all over the place.

"Now for water and sugar," Lily stated.

She took a pitcher of water, then poured. In the crate Penelope found a bag of sugar. With great care, Lily poured some in, stirred, then tasted. Her face twisted and her lips puckered. Robert, Penelope and Cassie screamed their laughter, bringing Morgan into the kitchen at a dead run.

"What happened?" he demanded, just as Lily upended the sugar bag into the pitcher.

Everyone gasped, then watched with mouths agape as Lily took the long wooden spoon and stirred vigorously. With hands wet and sticky, and sugar still swirling, Lily pulled out several glasses and began to pour.

"That's sugar water," Morgan exploded.

"Do you have to complain about everything?" Lily asked with a needling glance as she handed the glasses around.

Morgan's jaw tightened. "I don't complain."

Lily's unladylike snort filled the room. "Of course not. You never complain and you are the most pleasant man I have ever known."

She snorted again, causing Cassie to giggle. Penelope even smiled. But Morgan wasn't amused. He glowered at Lily, but she ignored him as well as she possibly could.

"Now," she said, "who's in the mood for toasted cheese with their lemonade?"

"I am!" Cassie declared.

Penelope looked bored. "Fine."

"We can only hope it will taste better than your lemonade," Robert stated, setting his glass aside.

Lily ignored him too.

After much clanging and carrying on, Lily pulled a skillet out of a cabinet.

"Where's Jojo?" Penelope asked when several pans

clattered to the floor after Lily pulled one out.

Lily shoved the other pans back into the cabinet, then slammed the door shut before they could fall out again. "Jojo and Marky have the day off."

"They had yesterday off," Morgan interjected.

Lily cocked her head. "Yes, I suppose they did. Hmmm. I'll have to talk to them about that. Robert, there is some butter in the bottom of that crate of groceries."

"It's all melted!"

Lily came over and peered inside. "No, it's not. It's just soft. Just the way we want it. You can't make toasted cheese with butter that hasn't softened."

"I find it hard to imagine that you can make toasted cheese at all," Morgan grumbled.

"That's because you have shown you are sadly lacking when it comes to imagination." She turned away, but at the last minute glanced back. "Now are you going to grouse about that too?"

Morgan's eyes widened, then narrowed in turn. After a long moment in which Lily guessed he was attempting to master his emotions, Morgan turned to Robert. "I'll be in the dining room. Call me if she starts to burn the place down."

Lily's heart only started to beat again once the door swung shut. Shoring up her crumbling resolve, Lily pulled a tin of matches from the crate then stared at the stove. After a bit, she handed them to Robert. "Would you do the honors, please?"

Robert huffed, but snatched the matches.

Lily took a deep breath. It was going to be fine, she reassured herself.

The children eyed the ragged pieces of bread Lily was cutting. Penelope sighed, then pulled up another stool. Without a word, she took the knife from Lily, then began to cut smooth slices of bread. As Penelope sliced, Lily took two dull butter knives and handed one to Cassie.

Cassie worked diligently, and just when she had one

slice buttered, she pushed back to show everyone. Her stool wobbled, but Robert caught her just in time.

Lily glanced up and saw the protective smile that curved Robert's normally hardened mouth. "Careful, Cas."

Lily felt a pang in her heart. There had been a time when Claude had smiled at her like that. A time when they were young, before life had changed so drastically.

"Now, a little butter in the pan," Lily said, forcing memories from her mind, popping up from her stool. "And Robert, would you be so good as to slice the cheese?"

She dropped a goodly dollop of melting butter into the heating skillet. Next came the slices of bread filled with a layer of cheese.

Lily stared at the sandwiches. Robert, Penelope, and Cassie crowded around the stove as Lily peered into the pan, trying to determine if things looked as though they were going all right. So far so good.

After a moment had passed and all still seemed well, Lily stepped back. For a second, Lily closed her eyes. The smell of toasting cheese sandwiches filled the room. Her heart ached with a sweet poignancy.

Her mind filled with memories of her mother making toasted cheese. Lily and Claude had always helped. Just the three of them in the kitchen, laughing. Invariably, her mother would start singing some song, cajoling Lily and Claude to sing along. "The Merry Wives of Windsor." "Sweet Sally Sagehill." And always ending with "Onward Christian Soldiers," with Lily and Claude marching around the kitchen. Then as if on cue, just in time for the last chorus, her father would come down from his study, his deep baritone filling the warm kitchen. It had been rare that the four of them were together, but on those days, the kitchen warm all around them, Lily's life had seemed perfect.

It was easy to forget that so many years had passed as Lily stood in the middle of the very same kitchen, with the very same smells all around her. It was easy to forget that outside the swinging door the house was a shambles. It was easy to forget that her parents were dead, that Claude was dead. And Lily was alone. She opened her eyes. No she wasn't alone. She had Robert, Penelope, and Cassie.

She cringed. What was she going to do with these children? she wondered as she had been wondering since receiving word that Claude had left them in her care. With that her chin came up. She was going to make them lunch and win them over, she reminded herself with a determined nod of her head. She had to, and she would.

"Lily!"

It took a moment for Lily's mind to settle back into the present, but when it did she was assailed with a pungent scent—of something burning.

"Lily!" Cassie cried again.

Lily whirled around. "The toasted cheese!"

But by the time Lily made it to the stove the sandwiches matched the bottom of the skillet. Black. Everything was black.

"They're burned," Lily cried, waving the smoke away.

Just as she grabbed a thick dishrag and pulled the skillet away from the flame, the house shook with a heavy pounding that grew nearer by the second. Abruptly the swinging door slammed open.

Morgan stood in the doorway, a warrior ready to do battle. The children froze at the sight. Lily froze, too, the pan held precariously in her hand. All was silent except for the sizzle of burned butter in the pan.

He was stunning. Fierce and capable. Lily's heart beat against her chest with an intensity that matched what she saw in Morgan's eyes. Why was it that this man made her heart pound and her hands tremble? Why this man of all men?

He made her wish for things that couldn't be.

Given the nature of her life over the last ten years, the

apparent differences in their stations in life meant very little to her. Perhaps in some way the hard life that a workingman ultimately led might have made it easier for him to understand. But workingman or not, Morgan Elliott didn't understand. She had seen the look in his eyes. And that would always stand between them more firmly than class differences ever could.

With that her heart turned back to stone. She couldn't afford to care. "What in the world is wrong with you?" she snapped, coolly ignoring the burnt pan she held in her hands.

"What's wrong with *me*?" he demanded. "I thought the house was burning down."

"Well, it's not," she replied with an indignant sniff.

Lily turned, raising her chin a notch, fighting back silly tears of embarrassment. Without another word, she walked over to the pantry, inside of which stood a heavy tin trash pail. Metal clanged against metal as she dropped her burden into the pail—skillet, sandwiches, burnt butter and all.

"What are you doing?" Morgan demanded outraged.

"Cleaning."

"Cleaning?" Morgan sputtered. "Cleaning?"

"Yes, and yes." Lily turned away sharply, her throat foolishly tight.

"You threw the pan away!"

"Yes again."

"The pan should be washed!"

Lily cocked her head, uncertain if she could make it to the door without tears of defeat and embarrassment finally spilling over. "Go ahead. I certainly won't stop you."

Holding on as best she could, she walked over to a slip of paper that lay out on the counter next to Morgan. She picked up a pencil, then quickly wrote something down.

Morgan looked down at the paper. " 'Lamp. Table. Frying pan,' " he read, then glanced at Lily. "What is this?"

But it was Robert who answered. "All the things Lily has ruined since she's been here."

"Ruined? You've ruined a lamp and a table, in addition to that frying pan?"

"Oh, I forgot that little Empire chair," she said with a grimace, walking back over to the list.

"A chair? How did you ruin a chair?" Morgan choked out.

"She used it to prop open the storm door to the cellar," Robert supplied.

"Propped open the cellar door?" Morgan shook his head as if to shake it clear of cobwebs.

"Do you have to repeat everything that is said?" Lily asked, her voice growing defensive despite her efforts to keep the emotion down. "And yes, I did use it to prop open the cellar door."

"Why?"

"There was a less than pleasant odor emanating from the nether regions of the house."

"It smelled down there," Penelope clarified.

"It was awful," Cassie supplied. "Just awful."

"Had *you* seen to it," Lily stated, with a pointed look at Morgan, "I wouldn't have had to."

"It was a grand idea," Cassie added, making Lily blush. "She brought the chair outside while Robert held the door open. Then she set the chair underneath and Robert lowered the door until it rested on the seat part." At this point Cassie cringed.

"Then what happened?" Morgan asked, his tone grim.

Robert and Penelope burst into laughter. Cassie looked apologetic, but didn't answer.

Morgan turned to Lily. "Then what happened?" he asked again.

Lily looked him in the eye, then forced the words beyond the coil of tears that tightened in her throat. "The weight of the door snapped the chair in two." She dared him to say a word. "Now, if you are through with your questions, I need to find something else to make for lunch."

The children groaned.

"That's all right, Lily," Cassie said. "We've found a man in the park who sells the most delicious sausages."

Lily drew a long, quavering breath. She had failed. Miserably. Yet again she was forced to concede that she didn't know the first thing about being a mother, couldn't even make lemonade and toasted cheese. How did she ever think she could possibly win Robert and Penelope over?

"Of course, go ahead," she said, forcing a smile. "Just get some money out of my reticule."

With that she turned and walked very carefully toward the door.

Morgan watched her go. Just staring as Lily pushed through the swinging door. He had no idea what to say. The woman did that to him frequently. Left him speechless. Burned pans and snapped chairs. Half the time he was convinced she was crazy.

The children stood as well, staring at Morgan. Robert shook his head. "She's a loon," he said with a disdainful scowl.

Though Morgan had thought very nearly the same thing only seconds before, he hated hearing the sentiment uttered out loud. And he had no idea why. Robert was undoubtedly correct. Lily must be crazy. But still . . .

"Come on," Robert announced. "I'm hungry."

The back door slammed shut. Not wanting to think, not knowing what to think, Morgan moved toward the long thin windows near the ceiling that brought light into the basement kitchen. They opened easily, though he knew it wouldn't be as easy to clear out the smoke and smell of the burnt butter and cheese.

He glanced to the side and caught sight of the edge of the metal trash pail. Just an inch or two of cast iron skillet handle stuck out of the pail. She really had thrown the pan away, he thought with a shake of his head. Not that he needed proof. The clang of metal on metal had nearly deafened him.

He ran his hand through his dark hair and sighed. Lily Blakemore very easily could be crazy or mad—a loon, as Robert had said. But a woman of fallen virtue?

Morgan was finding it harder and harder to believe.

Shaking his head, his lips curved with a reluctant smile. "She threw the pan away," he said into the quiet room.

But his smile evaporated when a crash reverberated through the house.

"What now?" he blurted out.

And then it happened again, and again.

Morgan spun around and dashed out of the kitchen, following the noise upstairs. He raced up the next flight of stairs to the first floor, around the corner, then down the hall.

And found Lily.

For a second he couldn't move much less think. Lily wielded a hammer, furiously hammering the doorjamb that led to her room at the end of the hall.

"What are you doing?" he demanded.

But Lily didn't seem to hear.

Morgan took the last steps that separated them, and just as she raised the hammer to strike again, he caught her arm.

Lily spun around, her blue eyes wild.

"What the blazes are you doing?" he demanded, hating that the sight of her set his blood singing through his veins.

"I'm fixing the *blazing* door!"

Her porcelain skin was stained with red, her full lips pursed with emotion. Anger? He didn't think so.

"Hammering on the doorjamb is supposed to fix the door?" he asked incredulously.

"Yes. And next I'm going to hammer on this stupid carpet." She pointed to the carpet, one of the few things in the house that looked in order. "I tripped. Then I hit a nail that had pulled out of the doorframe."

For the first time Morgan noticed that Lily's skirt was torn. "The carpet looks fine to me. It's those damned backless shoes you're always wearing. If you'd wear some decent footwear for a change you might be able to walk.''

''They are called mules and they are the height of fashion.''

''They're about as smart as a mule, I'll grant you that.''

She narrowed her eyes. ''Whatever you think they are hardly signifies. The fact of the matter is, that if *you* had done your job and repaired this doorframe, *I* wouldn't be standing here with a ripped gown.''

She turned away and that's when he saw that she hadn't simply ripped her dress, the nail had ripped through her stockings and had caught her calf. Through the ragged tear and ruined summer stockings he could see blood. His dark gaze grew ominous. ''You're hurt.''

For the first time, Lily turned her leg and looked down, seemingly as surprised as Morgan at the sight of blood. ''Oh,'' she gasped, ''look at that.''

In a flash, Morgan took her by the hand, and when she started to protest, he swept her up into his arms and strode to the bathroom that adjoined her bedroom. Though it was in disrepair like the rest of the house, it had hot and cold running water, thanks to the fact that Morgan had repaired the boiler the day before.

''I'm fine, Mr. Elliott. Really,'' Lily said, her voice rising as she tried to pull away.

But his grip held her captive. He lowered her to a hard bench and directed her to sit down. When she tried to scramble away, he firmly guided her down.

Lily felt like an errant schoolgirl. ''I can take care of this myself, Mr. Elliott,'' she said crisply.

''Humor me.''

''Humor you? I didn't realize you knew what humor was,'' she said before she could stop herself.

Morgan glanced at her, one slash of dark brow rising, before he turned the hot water on. Muscles rippling, he lowered himself to one knee before her, intent on getting a better look at the wound. Without a thought to propriety, he lifted the hem of her skirt.

"Mr. Elliott!"

Morgan sighed. "You don't ignore cuts from old nails."

Then before she could respond, he tossed her shoe aside, ripped her stocking all the way, took a small towel he had soaking in hot water, then wrapped it around her calf.

"Agh!"

"Sit still."

"You're burning me."

"No, I'm not."

He lifted the towel and the cut was bleeding even more.

"You're making it worse," she cried.

"I'm making it better. I'm making it bleed more to pull out any impurities."

She snorted. "You make it sound like I've been bitten by a snake. Next you'll wrap your lips around my leg and suck."

Morgan's head shot up, surprise glittering in his eyes, before a slow, devilish smile broke out across his lips and one eyebrow tilted rakishly. "Not a bad idea."

Lily's eyes widened. "I mean . . ." Then she glowered. "I mean nothing at all, you licentious old goat. Don't you look at me like that."

"Like what, Miss Blakemore?" he asked, his voice a sensual drawl. "I was simply considering what that would entail—to get the poison out, of course."

"And I'm the tooth fairy."

"Are you?"

Lily jerked her leg away, but when she did the towel fell away leaving her leg exposed from her knee down, her foot bare. Morgan's teasing countenance evaporated.

It was all he could do to keep his hands at his sides. It was one thing to tease this outrageous woman, but quite another to touch her in the way he suddenly felt a desperate need to do. Her leg was smooth and shapely. He had a sudden flash of Lily in his arms, naked, their legs entwined. He felt his loins tighten. He drew in his breath and cursed, pushing away from her.

"I have enough work around here without having to play nursemaid to you, not to mention having to fix whatever else you have managed to destroy. A Chippendale chair, for chrissakes," he snapped, shaking his head.

Lily went hot beneath his words. "An *Empire* chair," she corrected him to cover her dismay.

Morgan's eyes narrowed. "Chippendale, Empire, it hardly signifies. A chair is a chair, and shouldn't be used to prop up doors that are three times as heavy. You don't know the first thing about making repairs, Miss Blakemore. In the future leave a man's work to the men, and we'll get along just fine."

Lily's jaw set, and one delicate brow cocked in disbelief at his presumption. Dismay was forgotten, and the heat drained from her cheeks. "Just because you wear pants, Mr. Elliott, doesn't make you a man."

She pushed up from the bench, intent on getting away from him, away from the suddenly too confining space. But before she could take a step his formidable body blocked her way, his fingers locking on her arm, his dark eyes burning with a predator's heat.

"You want a man, Miss Blakemore? I'll show you a man."

He pulled her rigid body to him, and just as she started to protest, demand that he unhand her, her words were smothered by his mouth. She was stunned by the initial contact, hard and bold. Demanding. Her heart pounded. Never had she been kissed like this before, as if he were claiming her as his own. It was not a kiss of passion or desire, but a kiss of possession.

Lily pushed against him, but gained no leverage. Despite her writhing form, he held her to him with an iron grip, his tongue parting her lips with expert proficiency to plunder her softness. With one hand, he tilted her head so he could taste her more deeply as he pressed her body closer to his. His desire was unmistakable, his rigid shaft hard against her abdomen.

With effort, she forced herself to grow very still in his arms. Limp. At length he pulled away, his breath ragged, though his hard gaze was neither pleased nor apologetic. Their eyes met, burning, seething.

With slow, deliberate movements, Lily lifted her arm and wiped the back of her hand against her mouth. She forced her lips to tilt in a coldly amused smile, though tears of anger and humiliation burned in her eyes. "And that was supposed to convince me you're a man?"

Their eyes locked, and her heart pounded. An aching fire suddenly burned in his gaze. She had insulted him, as she had intended. But with that look in his eyes she felt a pang of regret—and a desperate need to flee.

Before she realized what was happening, she was back in his arms. But unlike the first time, this time his lips came down on hers in a lover's embrace. Not hard, not demanding. They touched her own with a gentle fire— sensual, intense. She felt his body shudder, and she had the fleeting thought that he was giving in to feelings that he had been holding tightly inside.

He kissed her with infinite care, the corner of her mouth, her cheekbone, desperately, hungrily. When her eyelids fluttered closed, he kissed her there, too. His mouth slanted across hers, his tongue tracing her lips, cajoling them to open, drawing her out.

When she yielded, he tasted her sweetness, their bodies so close that she felt his groan shimmer against her. His kiss made her yearn for more. She craved the feel of his hands on her. The feel of skin against skin. In that moment, she wanted to press closer to his gentleness, his caring, even if it was not real. If only he would fold her against his chest, she would willingly forget for the moment that he didn't really care.

She tasted him hesitantly. She sucked in her breath, and it was as if she had breathed him in, into herself. She loved the feel of him, and just as before, she loved the rugged scent of him.

She felt his hand reach up, his palm lining her jaw, his fingers trailing back into her hair, tilting her head so he could take more of her.

"Yes, open for me," he breathed raggedly against her.

And she did. She opened for him. Gladly, willingly.

Was it possible for something so wrong to feel so right? she wondered as his hands burned a path down her neck to her shoulders.

He nipped at her lips before he kissed the shell of her ear. She could feel his breath, hear his desire whispering in her head like a rush of air, causing the feelings to change. Her fingers curled into his shirtfront when his arms wrapped around her, folding her into his chest as she had wanted. He made her feel small and delicate. Wanted and cherished, like her treasured china cup.

It didn't matter that it was all make-believe. It didn't matter that he didn't really want her or cherish her. Or so she tried to tell herself as she experienced the amazing feeling of another person's heart beating against her own. Lily realized that she could stay in his arms forever, letting his strength surround her. And that was impossible. He might desire her now, but in reality this strong man hated her.

A tremendous sense of loss filled her.

But she shook it away forcefully. She was strong too, she reminded herself. She didn't need his strength. She hadn't needed anyone in a long time. And she would have pushed away from him right then, but, before she could, he pulled away with an oath that made her blush.

She started to say something, though what exactly she didn't know. But whatever words would have come stilled on her lips at the look in his eyes. He stared at her, the dark depths of his eyes intense. Was it yearning that she saw in his eyes? Did this strong man yearn as she yearned?

Her heart fluttered and she started to reach out, to touch

his cheek, as if somehow if she touched him she would learn the answer. But then the look in his eyes shifted and changed. His dark eyes hardened.

"As I said, Miss Blakemore, in the future, leave the repairs to me."

Then he turned on his heel and left the room, and her gaping sense of loss threatening to overwhelm her.

Six

The next morning, Lily sat at her dressing table and groaned. Morgan Elliott. Surely she hadn't really kissed the man.

But no matter how she tried to rewrite events, she was unable to erase what had transpired between them.

Lily felt heat rise in her cheeks. Whenever she was near him she lost all sense. Things she had never given a second thought to, regardless of what others had said, now gave her pause. Looking at her life through his eyes made her flush with embarrassment. And that was absurd. She owed Morgan Elliott nothing, and she certainly was not about to start living her life motivated by what he thought of her. And that was that.

Lily nodded her head as she purposefully wound her long hair into a loose twist at the crown of her head. Determined to have a better day than her dreams had portended, she went to the armoire and pulled out one of her favorite ensembles, a bright turquoise gown made with layers of stiff lace that she had bought on one of her trips to Mexico. It always reminded her of fiestas and flamingos, making her feel cheerful. For good measure, she wound her favorite feather boa around her neck, and just before she left the room she added flowers to her hair. Surely, dressed like this, she couldn't possibly have a bad day.

Lily hadn't taken more than a dozen steps down the hallway when she found Marky peering inside a built-in cupboard in the wall.

"Marky, what are you looking for?"

Marky whirled around. "Miz' Blakemore." Nothing more. He stood very still, staring.

"What's wrong, Marky? And what are you looking for in there."

"Looking for?" Then he smiled. "No, I ain't lookin' for a thing, Miz' Blakemore. Nothin' atall. I was putting clutter away. Yes, ma'am, that's what I was doing. Puttin' things away, finding a spot for all the bric-a-brac that is constantly in the way. Now if you'll excuse me, I'd best be gettin' back to me duties."

He all but slammed the cupboard shut, then whirled around and hurried away.

Strange man, Lily thought, continuing toward the stairs. If her dear John hadn't sent him, she would have been concerned.

Lily entered the kitchen from the hallway just as Morgan entered through the back door from the yard. They both stopped at the sight of each other.

Lily hated that her heart fluttered. He was so handsome. Virile. Rugged. Despite the fact that she was a fool to have kissed him, her gaze was drawn to his lips. Lips that had touched hers. Gently, reverently, his predatory strength tightly controlled.

"Good morning," Morgan said with a nod, breaking into her errant thoughts.

"Good morning."

"Lily," Cassie called, pushing in behind Morgan. "Finally! You're up!"

Lily felt heat flush her cheeks, but once again she

tamped it down. "Yes, I'm up." She walked over to the stove. Jojo stood to the side.

"Mornin' missy," he said, handing her a cup of coffee.

"Good morning, Jojo." She took a sip. "Mmmm. You make the most delicious coffee."

"O' course it's delicious. I made it," Jojo grumbled, picking up a bowl of scrambled eggs and poured them into a hot skillet. "And now I suspect you gonna want some breakfast."

"No, coffee is fine."

"No, coffee is not fine, missy. You're gonna have some eggs. You're as skinny as a rail. Now sit yerself down." Jojo glanced back. "And you too, Miss Penelope. Don't think I didn't notice that you didn't eat anything worth a hoot earlier."

Amazingly Penelope sat. "Only because I'm starving, not because you told me to," she pronounced, crossing her arms over her chest.

Lily held back her smile. "I thought that I would go and get a few things from the store today."

"Like a frying pan?" Robert muttered.

Glancing at her nephew, she said, "Yes, as a matter of fact, like a frying pan. And do you know what else I need?"

"A mirror?" Morgan asked, his voice dry as his gaze ran the length of her attire.

A stunned moment passed in perfect silence before the children and even Jojo burst out laughing.

"Funny, Mr. Elliott," Lily snapped, fighting back sudden tears of mortification. She loved her dress, thought it the most beautiful in the world. But for the first time it occurred to her that perhaps it was a tad outlandish. Though that shouldn't surprise her. When was the last time she had thought about what was the right thing to wear? When was the last time it had mattered?

Lily bit her lower lip, welcoming the anger that began to build, replacing the hollow feeling inside. "Did it ever

occur to you that *you* are in *my* employ, Mr. Elliott? I
could fire you on the spot. In fact I'm not quite sure why
I don't.'' Banishing darkness or not, the man was infuriating, not to mention too forward by half.

Cassie sucked in her breath.

But Morgan only laughed. ''Go ahead. If you think you
can keep this house from falling down around your ears,
or find someone else who is crazy enough to do it for you,
have at it.''

Lily fumed but didn't respond. Really, who would take
the job? She knew that the previous butler had had a very
difficult time filling the position. And the house really had
to be repaired.

''Well, Miss Blakemore, what will it be? Am I fired or
not?''

Eyes narrowed, Lily shot Morgan a venomous look.
''No, you are not fired.''

''Yea!'' Cassie cried out, jumping up and down.

Even Penelope looked relieved. How had Morgan Elliott
entwined himself so deeply into their lives? Lily wondered,
disgruntled.

''Well then,'' Morgan said, a smile glittering in the
depths of his dark eyes, ''if it is cookware you want, it is
cookware you shall have. I was going to take the children
with me to the store after lunch. Why don't you come with
us?''

At twelve-thirty, Morgan set out from the house, Lily and
the children at his side.

''Are you sure we shouldn't take a coach?'' Lily asked,
opening her parasol against the oppressive summer sun.

Cassie tugged on Lily's skirt, a new skirt into which
Lily had changed, Morgan noted, the feather boa and flowers miraculously gone. Even Morgan had to admit that
dressed as she was, Lily couldn't have looked more respectable.

''Morgan promised to take us on the horsecar,'' Cassie said.

''Why don't *you* take a carriage,'' Penelope added, ''we'll meet you at the store.''

Lily eyed her delicately wrought silk shoes that had never been intended for any kind of walking, then she shrugged. ''No, the horsecar will be fine.''

''This way,'' Morgan announced, having no intention of walking out through the front drive. ''It's a shortcut.''

The five of them made their way along the cobbled paths that wound through the grounds until they came out the rear gate onto Fifty-eighth Street.

''I'd forgotten all about the back way,'' Lily mused, glancing at Robert. ''Your father and I slipped out through this gate many a time.'' She laughed.

''Did you ever get caught?'' Cassie asked.

''Good heavens, no. Claude was much too cagey for that.''

''My father wasn't cagey!'' Robert stated the words with such vehemence that his spectacles fell forward on his nose.

Morgan halted next to Lily who had stopped on the walkway. Robert marched ahead.

''My father was good and smart,'' Robert shot back. ''Better than a dumb woman like you.''

Morgan caught up to Robert in a few bold strides, catching his shoulder and whirling him back. ''Apologize to your aunt.''

''No! It's true. She can't say bad things about my father.''

Morgan held Robert's shoulder. He could feel the boy was shaking, and when he looked at Lily, he knew she was as disturbed as her nephew.

''I didn't mean anything unkind, Robert,'' Lily said quietly. ''I only meant that your father was very smart—just as you said.''

Morgan watched as Lily looked at her nephew, her eyes

strained with concern. But then she simply sighed before she hurried past the boy on to Sixth Avenue. "We're going to miss that horsecar you all are so excited to take," she called back, her smile clearly forced.

The incident left Morgan with an uneasy feeling. For the first time since coming to Blakemore House the reality of the situation hit him. Sure he knew that Lily had lost a brother, and that the children had lost a father, but he had been so wrapped up in finally gaining access to John Crandall that he hadn't thought about what these people must still be going through despite the fact that nearly five months had now passed since Blakemore's death.

But orphaned or not, the boy had to learn to respect his elders. Morgan gritted his teeth and started to say something. But then he cut himself off. The undeniable fact remained. Lily Blakemore and her nieces and nephew were none of his concern.

"Come on, your aunt is right, we need to hurry," was all he said in the end, his eyes dark as he led the group on.

They picked up a horsecar traveling south. Morgan helped everyone aboard. Then he watched, bemused, as Lily simply sat down on one of the hard wooden benches that ran the length of the long car.

Just before he leaped up the wooden steps himself, an older woman bustled up to the horsecar. Morgan stepped aside and helped her alight, after which she made her way to the front and dropped her nickel in the slot. Morgan nearly smiled when Lily's eyes shot open and she scrambled in her reticule.

"I'll deal with it," Morgan said, walking up to the front of the car, dropping five nickels into the slot.

"There was no need for that, Mr. Elliott, I assure you."

"Humor me," he said easily, lowering his towering frame onto the bench across from her.

"For someone who makes a living taking orders from others, you certainly have a way of giving all the orders yourself. Are you sure you're a repairman?''

Morgan sat very still and studied Lily, his body tense. But after having been around her as much as he had, he knew that the look on her face was nothing more than her usual irritation at him. She didn't suspect. ''If you're unhappy, Miss Blakemore,'' he said, his voice a practiced nonchalant, ''you can still fire me.''

Lily rolled her eyes. ''If you want to hear me say yet again that I'm not going to fire you, forget it. Once a day is enough for me.''

Their gazes locked across the narrow aisle. Morgan could see the blue of her eyes darken. He wondered suddenly if her eyes would darken as he slid his hardness into her. Slowly. Deeply. Would she cry out with the intensity? Would she try to turn her head away?

He knew he wouldn't let her look away. He would force her to look into his eyes, force her to watch him as he made love to her body. He wanted to see her. And he realized then that he wanted her to see him. Really see him.

His thoughts froze. Good Lord, what was he thinking? Making love to this woman. With a silent curse, he looked away.

The children chattered the whole way, kneeling on the benches, peering out the grimy windows.

''Where are we going anyway?'' Lily asked.

Morgan sat on the hard bench, his legs crossed as he stared out the window. ''Macy's Dry Goods on Sixth Avenue,'' he answered without looking back.

''Macy's is still in business? It seems like everything has changed in the years I've been gone.''

''Not everything. Macy's is alive and well. I hear they might move soon, but I'm sure they'll be around for years to come.''

Morgan pulled a pocket watch from his vest, glancing at the time. When he looked up he noticed that Lily was taking in his attire. He didn't wear his usual work clothes. He had worn a suit.

"Do you always get dressed up to go to the store, Mr. Elliott?"

Morgan shifted uncomfortably on the bench. After a moment he said, "I have an appointment later today. In fact, as long as you're with us, why don't you take the kids back to the house and I'll go from the store." It suddenly occurred to him that as her employee he should have gained her consent. "You don't mind if I go, do you? To meet a banker?"

"Why, no."

She seemed startled by his question, as if it had never occurred to her that she should monitor his comings and goings. True, she hardly monitored the children much less the staff.

Yet again Morgan wondered how Lily could possibly think she could manage to raise three children on her own, and yet again he wondered what her brother had been thinking when he had left his children in her care.

Lily and Morgan grew silent. The children laughed and called out sights as they made their way down Sixth Avenue.

"You forgot your hat," Lily said suddenly.

Morgan turned back to her. "My hat?"

"Yes, a hat to wear to the bank. A fine silk hat. If you're going to a bank no doubt you want to impress them."

Morgan laughed. "I don't have a fine silk hat." At least not with him at Blakemore House.

"You should. You'd look smashing."

At the simple words, Lily blushed. It was at times like this when Morgan wondered if the name Crimson Lily hadn't been given to her because her cheeks stained with embarrassment more easily than anyone he knew. How could a woman of lesser virtue blush like a schoolgirl with amazing frequency?

"I agree," Cassie said, plopping down beside Lily to

give Morgan a thorough once-over. "You would look simply smashing in a fine silk hat, Mr. Elliott."

"I'll keep that in mind," he replied, not liking the direction of his thoughts. "But for now, we're here. Come on, children."

The horsecar pulled to a halt. The children leaped down onto the cobbled street. Morgan climbed down, then turned back to help Lily. Her waist was slim beneath his hands, and he held her for longer than was necessary.

"Excuse me, young man," the older woman called out as she tried to step down from the horsecar. "I hate to interrupt such a lovely scene, but I need to get down from here. Besides which, you'd best be hurrying yourselves as it looks like your children have disappeared into the store."

Morgan and Lily leaped apart and moved out of the way. It took a moment for Morgan's mind to settle, but then he quickly helped the woman down.

"Such a dear boy you are," she said, then looked at Lily. "And such a beautiful wife you have. I'd say you're a lucky man, sir."

Then she was gone.

Morgan and Lily stood on the walkway, neither knowing what to say. After an uncomfortable moment Lily cleared her throat and scoffed, "Husband and wife. No doubt we'd sooner kill each other than marry."

Then before Morgan could utter a word, she added, "We'd best hurry if we don't want to lose the children."

They entered R. H. Macy & Company, Morgan holding the door. No sooner did they cross the threshold than someone called out.

"Lily! Lily Blakemore! Is that you?"

A tall man about Lily's age stood next to a table of fabric with a woman just a few years younger at his side.

"It *is* you," the man said with great enthusiasm. "How long has it been?"

"Well, I'm not certain," Lily said. "Since I'm not sure

who you are, I can't say that I remember the last time I saw you."

The man threw his head back and laughed. "Ahhh, Lily Blakemore. You're always the same. It's me, Bart Mayhew."

"Oh, my goodness. Bart Mayhew." Lily extended her hand. "I can't believe I didn't recognize you."

They clasped hands warmly.

"And you remember my sister, Edith?"

"Of course. It's so nice to see you."

"Yes," the petite woman said tautly. "Hello, Miss Blakemore."

Morgan noted that the sister's enthusiasm failed to match her brother's.

"I can hardly believe my eyes," Bart said. "To find you standing here in Macy's as if not a single day has gone by."

Morgan would have shaken his head and gone on, intent on finding the things he needed, but as he started to turn, he saw the features of Lily's face soften. He was stunned when he realized that Lily was truly happy to see these people, even the sister, from the looks of things. Was it possible that Lily failed to notice the way the sister looked her over with disdain, or how the brother looked her over with lust?

Morgan felt a surging need to pummel Bart Mayhew, but quelled the urge with effort, then forced himself to move away.

"I was so sorry to hear about your brother," Bart continued.

"Bart," Edith said tightly. "We really need to hurry. Mother is waiting in the carriage."

"Yes, of course. Lily, might I call on you? I would love to catch up. In fact, Edith and Mother are having a small gathering of people over to the house. I know they would love for you to come. Isn't that right, Edith?"

Edith turned very carefully and looked into her brother's

eyes for one long charged second before she turned to Lily. "Yes, Miss Blakemore," she said, her smile tight on her lips. "We will send an invitation over." She tugged at her gloves. "Come along, Bart. We mustn't keep Mother waiting."

The bell over the door rang, announcing their departure. Lily stood very still. Morgan expected her to whirl towards him and the children and scoff, make one of her outrageous and wholly inappropriate comments about Bart Mayhew and his sister.

"A party," she breathed instead, clasping her hands together. "I'm going to a party."

Morgan and Robert exchanged glances. Robert shrugged his shoulders.

"Who was that woman?" Morgan asked.

"Edith Mayhew, a friend from childhood. Sweet Edith Mayhew."

"Sweet?"

"Yes, and she's sending me an invitation to a party."

Morgan looked at Lily. He opened his mouth to speak, but at the last minute he forced it shut. "Hurry up, kids. We don't have all day."

Morgan made sure Lily and the children were safely on a northbound horsecar before he walked the short distance to a hack line and caught a hansom cab. Thoughts of Lily circled in his mind. She had chatted endlessly about Edith Mayhew and her party as they had made their way through the store, picking out the items she had to have.

Morgan would have sworn that Edith Mayhew hadn't been sincere. Edith Mayhew felt the same way about Lily as the person or people who had painted the name on her back porch wall. And he didn't believe for a second that he could have misread the situation. All too often his life depended on his ability to read every nuance. He would bet money that an invitation to the Mayhew's party would never arrive.

Despite what Lily had been told, he wasn't on his way to a bank. As he had said, he was on his way to see a banker, a banker by the name of Beauford Tisdale, the same Beauford Tisdale that Morgan had learned had once been a suitor of Lily's.

Over the last few weeks, Morgan had learned as much as he could about Tisdale. He had learned that the man had eventually married and now worked in the family bank. But Morgan wasn't going to meet the man at his office. He was going to the Union League Club where Morgan had learned Tisdale spent every Wednesday afternoon.

Morgan knew that he should be spending more time finding proof of John Crandall's wrongdoing. But the man had yet to arrive at Blakemore House, and though Morgan could easily believe that Marky and Jojo were sent by Crandall, he had yet to find proof of that either. Though it didn't really matter, Morgan reasoned. A person could hardly be convicted for providing lousy help.

Morgan started to smile. Lily didn't seem to care if the help was lousy or not. She seemed to move through life with few cares. She seemed to think that food would find its way to the table and chores would get done. And amazingly, that is what happened.

The cab rolled to a halt at Fifth Avenue and Thirty-ninth Street in front of the Union League Club. Pushing through the double doors, Morgan entered a quiet foyer that could have been someone's home rather than a club for men to while away their hours reading newspapers, gambling, and discussing the ways of the world. Morgan knew that more than a few momentous agreements affecting the United States as a whole, and in some cases the world at large, had been struck not in the hallowed halls of Washington, but here in the monied corridors of the Union League Club.

A door opened and Morgan tensed. He wasn't a member, though fortunately he had been there before and still remembered the layout of the building. But he breathed a sigh of relief at the man who called his name. "Morgan. I was hoping you wouldn't come."

"Wouldn't?" Morgan asked with a smile.

"Yes, wouldn't."

Mario Respaccio was a heavyset man of about forty years and had worked at the club for the last ten years.

"No such luck," Morgan responded with a warm smile, shaking Mario's hand. "How's Magdalena?"

"Good. Got another young one since last we saw you. You gotta come over. Someone's gotta feed you better."

Morgan laughed, but then he grew serious. "Is he here?"

Mario grumbled. "Yeah, he's here. I can't believe I'm letting you do this. Last time I helped you out I almost got fired."

"You didn't almost get fired."

"I would have been if you'd gotten caught!"

"It wasn't even close and you know it."

"Yeah, yeah. But your luck is bound to run dry one of these days, Morgan, my friend. Someone's gonna remember that the last time they saw you, you were a cab driver, or a brothel owner. You live a dangerous life."

"I'm touched that you worry," he said with a wry smile.

"I don't worry about no one but me and my family," Mario said gruffly, though unable to hide the affection he clearly held for his friend. "I just don't want your undoing to happen here while I'm minding the store. I got too many mouths to feed at home."

"Nothing's going to go awry today, Mario, or ever. No one's going to find out who I am. Now, point out Tisdale," Morgan said, slapping Mario on the back, "so I can find out what I need to know. Then I'll get out of your hair."

Morgan strolled into the small study where Beauford Tisdale sat in front of a low table neatly lined with an assortment of newspapers. The smell of fine leather and cigar smoke at three o'clock in the afternoon bespoke men of leisure and money. Only a handful of other gentleman occupied the high-ceilinged room. As Morgan had intended.

It was early yet. By the time the club began to fill up, Morgan would be gone.

Lowering himself into a tufted leather arm chair across from Tisdale, Morgan casually picked up a copy of *The Times*. Tisdale glanced up and nodded before returning his attention to his own paper. Morgan simply returned the gesture then began to read.

After a moment, Mario entered. "Your brandy, sir," he intoned, extending a silver tray with a deference and manner that had not been apparent in the foyer.

Morgan took the crystal glass, then leaned back in the chair and sighed. "Ah," he said to no one in particular, "such a day."

Tisdale glanced up again. Morgan met his eye, then quirked his head ever so slightly as if surprised. "Tisdale?" he said. "Beauford Tisdale?"

Beauford instantly looked puzzled. "Why, yes," he said cautiously.

"Good God, old man, how long has it been?" Morgan set his glass down and stood up, extending his hand.

"I'm sorry. But I don't seem to recall your name."

Morgan laughed jovially. "Samuel Whitley," he supplied.

"Whitley?" Beauford inquired, clearly confused as they shook hands.

"Don't tell me you don't remember. Harvard. We graduated together. God, I miss those days. Remember Teddy Roosevelt? Do you see him anymore?" Morgan sat back and picked up his glass of brandy, and before Beauford could answer, Morgan called out to Mario. "A brandy for my friend, good man."

The brandy appeared all too quickly, but Beauford Tisdale didn't seem to notice. Beauford was still trying to connect Morgan's face and the name provided, with himself and his days at Harvard. Morgan knew the exercise well, had done it many times before.

"I talked to Roosevelt just last week," Morgan continued, knowing that to mention the man who was fast becoming a driving force in New York City and rumored to be eyeing higher office was certain to gain Tisdale's attention.

"Really. I haven't seen him in ages. Though of course I hear about him at every turn. Doing quite well for himself, I'd say."

"That's the God's own truth." Morgan shook his head and took a sip of the fine brandy. "How goes it with you? I've heard you're doing great things at the bank."

Beauford's head cocked, then he leaned back and took a contemplative sip from the glass he had been handed. "I've implemented a new work system. Checks and balances, you know."

Beauford Tisdale had taken the bait and run. Morgan sat back and listened with half an ear to the many facets of Beauford's new banking system. Not until Morgan sensed that Beauford had exhausted his cherished topic did he venture closer to his goal.

"Such a shame about Claude Blakemore," he said with a heavy sigh.

Beauford shook his head. "Yes, the man was young. Younger than me." Beauford took a long swallow. "Makes a man think, I tell you."

"I hear his sister has returned to town."

Beauford's hand stilled midair, the glass in his hand. "Lily? Lily's back?"

"That's what I hear. By all accounts, she has custody of Claude's children."

"Lily?" Beauford repeated.

"That's right. I forgot. You courted Lily Blakemore, didn't you?"

Beauford's gaze grew distant. "It seems like ages ago.

Actually, it doesn't seem real. I can't believe she's back. I wonder if she'll stay."

This time it was Morgan who stilled. "Of course she'll stay," he said with more force than was necessary.

Morgan didn't understand his conflicting emotions. Despite his lack of confidence in her abilities to manage a home and children, it had never occurred to him that she would give up—and leave. "She has the children now. She will stay."

A fond smile pulled at Beauford's mouth. "Lily never did what anyone expected her to do." He shook his head. "She was the most headstrong person I have ever met, then or since. Mercy, she was beautiful."

Morgan hated that it bothered him to hear Beauford talk about Lily this way, especially considering he had come here with the sole purpose of getting the man to do just that. But still, something about the tone of voice, the reverence, left him feeling uneasy.

"No doubt it was being headstrong that got her into trouble," Morgan said.

Beauford seemed to consider, then shrugged his shoulders. "Perhaps. But deep down I have always felt that it was the painting classes that led her astray. If she had never enrolled in that art school I often think she and I would be . . ."

His words trailed off, and Beauford looked down into the crystal glass as if seeing something other than the brandy that filled the bottom.

"What art school?" Morgan asked, sitting forward in his chair. "What are you talking about?"

"The Gardner School of Art. Surely you remember."

Morgan didn't remember, had never even heard of the Gardner School of Art. But it wouldn't do to say he hadn't. "Now that you mention it, I do recall."

"Mrs. Gardner shut the school down within months after the scandal, you know. Not a decent parent in town would send one of their own to her school after what happened. Melva Gardner closed her doors and I can't say that I've heard of her since." Beauford scoffed. "And they said Lily had talent."

"The school was shut down?" Morgan asked, his tone incredulous, forgetting for the moment that he shouldn't be so obvious.

But Morgan realized his mistake as soon as Beauford looked at him closely, his eyes narrowing. "Surely you heard. Everyone was talking about it."

By everyone Morgan knew that Beauford was talking about everyone in his elite group of friends. The upper crust of Manhattan. Morgan had already surmised that in regards to Lily Blakemore society had closed ranks around the scandal and had not spoken of it outside their circle since.

"Of course I heard," Morgan said smoothly, but he knew the damage had already been done.

Beauford Tisdale didn't look convinced. Morgan knew he would get no more out of the man.

"It's just that I still find it incredible." Morgan shook his head and sighed. After a moment he pulled his watch from his vest. "Look at the time. I'd best be off," he said, standing. "It was good to see you, old man. Hope to see you again."

Before Beauford could say another word or ask any questions, Morgan walked out of the room, the thick wooden door clicking shut behind him.

Seven

It was as if her encounter with Bart and Edith Mayhew at Macy's Dry Goods had been an announcement to all of New York that Lily Blakemore had returned. Three days after Lily's trek to the long-established store, visitors arrived at Blakemore House with tiring regularity. Morgan overheard Marky grumble more than once that "they should just leave the blamed door open."

Morgan was inclined to agree—about the number of callers, that is. He differed, however, on the solution to the problem. Morgan would just as soon hammer the door shut as leave it open. He had never seen so many pompous prigs in all his life, posturing and preening. All men, of course. Not a single lady had arrived at the door with a calling card in hand.

This fact, however, seemed to have escaped Lily, Morgan noted early Friday morning as he stood in the front parlor, a cup of coffee in his hand. In the nearly two months since he first saw Lily, he had never seen her so happy. As she sailed through the house, her deep laughter rushed up to greet him wherever he was.

Sooner or later, Morgan knew her excitement was going to be crushed beneath the callous heel of some priggish society fop. Sooner or later, she was going to realize that the men who arrived were not there to court her or take her home to mother. And the women weren't coming at all.

Morgan felt a gnawing anger at the worthless dandy's twist in his gut, but underneath it he felt what seemed suspiciously like relief. His jaw tightened. What was wrong with him? Relief? No, he told himself. It was lust. He had never wanted a woman so badly. Any woman. All he had to do was think about her and his body leaped to life, leaving him hard with wanting. His frustrated growl resounded through the early morning light.

More evidence, if any was needed, that society wasn't throwing open their doors for Lily Blakemore, was that the promised invitation to the Mayhew's party had failed to arrive. Morgan cursed yet again when he realized he felt the need to march over to the Mayhews' house and demand the invitation for Lily himself.

He shook his head. Hell, he was losing his mind.

The morning light filtered in through the cracked and grimy panes of window glass. It was still long before any one else would be up and about and the house was quiet. Forcefully turning his attention away from the woman of the house, Morgan surveyed a particularly difficult repair that needed to be made to a crumbling marble pillar—a repair that would take hours of his time over several days if not weeks.

Morgan's dark features creased with frustration. The repairs were taking up most of his days when he should be learning what he could about Crandall. But no sooner did he fix one problem than he found yet another to demand his attention.

He told himself to forget the house, to do what he needed to do to make it appear as if he really were working, but actually spend his time ferreting out what infor-

mation he could about Crandall. But again and again he
found that it was nearly impossible to ignore the problems.

How could he let the decrepid boiler go unattended?
Another week, a month at best, and that heaving beast in
the basement would have blown. And the pillar. The ceiling above it sagged so badly that Morgan was afraid at
any second one of the children would take a wrong step
and fall right through from the floor above. Either them or
Lily.

Morgan shook his head, anger mixing with his frustration. He should be concentrating on Crandall, not Lily and
her house. But there was the catch. He couldn't get at
Crandall without being in her house. And by being in
Blakemore House somehow he found he couldn't ignore
the blasted repairs. Or Lily.

The heavy brass knocker fell solidly against the front
door. With no one else about, Morgan went to the door.

A burly man in clean work clothes stood on the front
step, hat in hand. "I have a delivery here." He peered at
a piece of paper. "For L. Blakemore."

Morgan stepped across the threshold and looked out toward a heavily loaded delivery wagon. But it wasn't the
multitude of boxes and crates that gained his attention,
rather a second wagon where another man was unloading
a sleek black thoroughbred. The horse stood a good seventeen hands high and was stunning. Proud. Defiant.

Like Lily, Morgan thought unexpectedly.

"Who does the horse belong to?" he asked, certain he
already knew.

The delivery man glanced back at the horse. "L. Blakemore, I guess, since that's who I'm supposed to deliver it
to. Ornery cuss, though," he added, shaking his head.
"Can't imagine anyone wanting anything to do with that
horse."

Before Morgan could respond, Lily came flying out the
front door. Lily who never rose before eleven in the morn-

ing. Lily who never noticed a single domestic issue such as deliveries.

"Midnight!" she cried.

As proof of her haste, Lily wore a variety of garments, none of which matched, everything askew. She hadn't even bothered with shoes. Though for all the good those blasted mules would have done her, Morgan muttered, with the way she raced across the porch.

Gathering her skirt, Lily hurried down the steps to the yard. Morgan felt a surge of raw desire at the sight of her bare ankles, but the desire gave way to the same frustration that seemed his constant companion these days. But even that gave way when Lily flew across the front drive and surprised Morgan by throwing her arms around the horse's long neck.

The scene took Morgan aback. Tender. Loving. She ran surprisingly competent hands over the horse, down its legs, pulling each up to check the hoof. Only after this was accomplished did she smile, coming to stand before the horse to look it in the eye. If Morgan hadn't known any better, he would have sworn the horse was as glad to see Lily as Lily was glad to see the horse.

In quiet tones that Morgan couldn't hear, Lily spoke to the massive animal, which nickered in response. Then Lily leaned forward and pressed her face into the smooth flesh of the horse's neck.

In all the time Lily had been in Manhattan, Morgan had never seen the woman show such love for anything. The sight of this woman lavishing her love on her horse moved Morgan in unexpected ways.

"Isn't he beautiful?" Lily called back to him.

"Yes, he is," Morgan replied, still stunned by her caring.

"He's a direct descendent of Brendan the Great," she explained, joy at the reunion bubbling over. "I have another horse, a mare, that has a link to Brendan, but not directly. It is amazing the differences in the two."

"You have more horses?" Morgan asked.

"A lot more." She walked back toward the house. "And I would have had some others brought down if there had been more than one useable stall in the stable here." She smiled sweetly. "I'm hoping in the not-too-distant future you'll work your way around to the stable. I raise horses and I'd like to—ouch!"

Lily jerked one foot up and froze. The delivery man started toward her, but Morgan got there first.

"What have you done to yourself now?" he muttered, sweeping her up in his arms.

"I stepped on a rock, you oaf. Now put me down."

Marky, Jojo, Robert, Penelope, and Cassie piled out of the house just then, halting on the front stoop, all looking as if they had dragged themselves from a deep sleep. But Morgan hardly noticed the others. His thoughts were fixed on Lily. Lily who he didn't understand. Lily who felt so right in his arms. But he nearly dropped her in surprise when she popped him in the shoulder with an amazingly strong left hook.

"I said, put me down," she ground out, her jaw clenched.

"Why? So you can hurt your other foot? Have you ever considered wearing shoes? Real shoes?"

"Put me down," she repeated, her voice tight.

Morgan ignored her until he reached the front steps, where he set her down in front of the small group. "Let me look at your foot."

He started to reach out, but Lily slapped his hands away. "Leave my foot alone, Elliott."

Ignoring her, he made for her foot again. This time she smacked him in the chest. "Don't you have some repairs to do? Nails to hammer, screws to turn?"

Morgan considered her for long minutes before he shrugged his shoulders and glanced at the delivery wagon. "It looks like I have some crates and baggage to see to first." He looked at Marky, Jojo, and Robert. "Come on, men, let's get this thing unloaded."

The sudden sound of wheels on gravel drew everyone's attention. A black-enameled brougham pulled to a halt behind the carriage. A liveried servant climbed down and walked toward the house.

"An invitation for Miss Lily Blakemore," the man announced, obviously never dreaming that the barefooted hoyden standing before him was the lady in question.

Lily gasped and started to reach out, but Penelope quickly interceded. "I'll see that she gets it."

The servant nodded, then retraced his steps to the carriage. Penelope turned to Lily with an angry grimace as she handed the invitation over. "Next time you start to tell someone who you are, I would hope you'd at least be dressed properly. We have our reputations to consider."

Morgan expected hurt feelings or a blush of embarrassment. Lily only threw her head back and laughed wickedly up to the heavens. "Yes, Penny, love, we have our reputations to consider."

With that Lily whirled around and started toward the front door, excitement dancing along her features. "Bring my things up to my rooms."

Then she raced through the door, only a hint of a limp to be seen, disappearing up the curving stairway, the invitation held securely in her hand.

Lily sat down on the edge of the chaise longue that dominated the corner of her sitting room. She held the invitation in her hands without opening it. She hated that it meant so much to her that indeed it had arrived. She should toss the hand-engraved vellum back into the Mayhew's faces. She should not be so eager to be welcomed back into the folds of New York society. She knew it, but that didn't stop her desire to wipe away the past. She wanted to go to the party, she wanted to believe that the people she had once called friends were now ready to call her friend again.

Taking a deep breath, she held the wax-sealed missive tightly to her chest, offering up a small prayer that indeed it was what she was hoping for. With careful hands, Lily broke the seal and unfolded the thick sheet of paper. Sure enough, it was an invitation to the Mayhews' party.

"I'm going," she breathed, her eyes closed. "To a tea."

First being asked to come home, now an invitation to a party, she thought, her heart beginning to pound in her chest. She disregarded Penelope's and Robert's obvious dislike of her, a dislike that had been present before she'd had a chance to utter a word of hello. She didn't think about the house being a disaster, or about any of the other things that were not so perfect in her life.

Lily concentrated on being home, being back.

And sitting there, the sense of hope that had never totally been diminished in all the years of her exile began to grow in earnest. She would be whole once again. And happy. She wouldn't have to return to the opulent mansion in Tarrytown with its echoing corridors and empty rooms. She wouldn't have to fill her days with travels to the farthest reaches of the world.

For the first time since arriving, she truly felt as if she had come home.

Lily sprang from her seat. What was she going to wear?

As if in answer to her question, the trunks and crates of her belongings began pouring into her room. No sooner was one trunk set down than Lily tore into it, pulling out dresses and linens and whatever else she came upon.

Cassie came in and wrapped herself up in a long sheer veil. "Lily, it's beautiful. Where did you get it?"

"From a sultan in Arabia."

"You've been to Arabia?"

At the sound of Robert's voice, Lily turned to find the boy hovering in the doorway. She also noticed that Penelope leaned against the wall just inside the room.

"Yes, Robert. To Arabia and India and even China."
She thought to impress the boy, but she saw the ever-present uninterest cloud his eyes. With a shrug of her shoulders, she turned back to her things. She would not let him ruin her excitement.

"Look at this!" Cassie walked over and picked up Lily's china cup from a small table.

Lily's eyes widened, then hastily but carefully she took the cup away.

"It's beautiful," Cassie breathed reverently.

Lily smiled, a soft smile that tilted her lips. "Yes. It's my most treasured possession. In fact, it has been passed down from generation to generation. From mother to daughter for over a hundred years."

She looked up to find Morgan standing in the doorway staring at her. In fact, everyone in the household was staring at her.

"Maybe we should put the cup someplace else," Lily said, determinedly ignoring the shiver of awareness at Morgan's penetrating gaze as she studied the room.

She walked over to a series of shelves perched above a low bureau. "Perfect," she announced, setting the cup high on a shelf.

She turned back with a flourish to find Morgan still in the doorway staring at her. His enigmatic look gave no clue to his thoughts.

"Well," she said, forcing her attention to the multitude of crates, "I think it is safe to say that I don't have a thing to wear to the Mayhews' party."

Everyone looked around at the mounds of clothing strewn about. Clothing of every color and description. Day dresses and ball gowns. Frippery and fine jewels, all lying about in a jumbled mess.

Lily looked at the children, her eyes shining with excitement. "Who would like to go shopping?"

"I would, I would!" Cassie cried excitedly.

"How about you, Penelope, and you, Robert? No telling

what we might find for you along the Ladies' Mile.''

The prospect of gifts won a grudging bit of interest from her older niece and nephew. And for the first time since Lily's arrival, she looked forward to going shopping just as she had years before.

''Wonderful! Let me get dressed, then we shall be on our way. We are going to find gifts for everyone, and the perfect gown to wear for my entry back into society!''

It took little more than thirty minutes for Lily and the children to depart. But it was several hours before they returned.

Morgan was in the parlor where he had spent the better part of the day erecting a wooden brace next to the crumbling marble pillar to keep the once-beautiful tin ceiling from crashing down. He would have been pleased with his accomplishment had it not been for the fact that yet another day had been wasted on repairs instead of seeing to Crandall. How had he gotten himself into this mess?

But of course he knew.

And with that thought, the front door banged open, rattling the windows. Morgan quickly checked the sagging ceiling and his wooden brace. The children had to be more careful.

But when Morgan walked out of the parlor and into the foyer only Lily stood on the landing, packages piled high in her arms. Morgan knew she couldn't see him as she was too busy glancing around, the barely visible sight of her face showing her lips twisted in indecision. Very carefully, she turned toward the entry table, and just when Morgan started to step forward to take the packages, they teetered and tipped.

''Lily, watch out!''

Lily turned with a start, causing the packages to tumble to the floor.

''Hell!'' he muttered.

Lily's head snapped up, and her cheeks stained with

embarrassment. "You have the most limited vocabulary of anyone I know. *Hell. Damn.* Every time I turn around you are cursing at something."

"Every time you turn around I am cursing at *you*," he barked unkindly as he strode forward to stand before the upended boxes. "Where are the children?"

"Outside. They're bringing in some more packages."

"Morgan! Morgan! Look!"

Cassie burst in behind Lily. Morgan's eyes widened, and it was all he could do not to groan. Six-year-old Cassie was painted and dressed to look like a miniature Lily. Feather boas and fly-away skirts. Bracelets clanging on her arms, necklaces wrapped around her neck until he wondered how she could breathe.

"Don't tell me she bought you some of those damn— darn backless shoes, too?"

Cassie smiled proudly, pulled up her skirt without a thought for propriety, and stuck out her foot. "They're called mules!"

She nearly toppled to the floor when she lost her balance, but Robert walked in just in time to catch her. "I told them not to buy those shoes," he said.

Next, Morgan heard Penelope though he couldn't see her. If Penelope had on a feather boa and mules, he thought in disbelief, he'd join the ranks of professional repairmen full time.

When Penelope entered, however, she didn't have on an outrageous hat or shoes or clothing as Cassie did. But she looked shy and belligerent all at the same time, holding a velvet bag reverently on her arm.

"Look at Penelope's new reticule," Cassie announced.

Penelope ran her hand over the bag.

"And Robert got a spy glass."

"It's a telescope," Robert stated importantly.

"Presents for everyone, I see," Morgan said with a re-signed shake of his head at this outrageous group.

At this, Cassie's eyes widened and she gasped, before

she glanced around. For the first time she noticed the jumble of boxes on the floor. Morgan expected the child to gasp or shriek, question the mess at the very least. Instead, she merely picked her way through the pile until she found the box she wanted, the size of it making her wobble on her new high heels. With great ceremony, Cassie extended the package. "This one is for you, Mr. Elliott."

Morgan felt his chest constrict. Everyone looked at him expectantly. Even Lily seemed to hold her breath in anticipation.

Morgan suddenly wanted nothing more than to turn on his heel and quit the room. He didn't want a present, he didn't want their interest. But most of all, he didn't like the quiet look of budding excitement in Lily's eyes.

"Go on, Mr. Elliott," Cassie prompted. "Open it!"

Seeing no way out of the situation, Morgan forced a smile and took the box. He untied the string, pulled off the top, then stared inside without moving.

"It's a hat!" Cassie explained excitedly. "A fine silk topper. The finest we could find. Lily insisted it must be the very best. What do you think?"

Morgan could only stare. Indeed it was a fine silk topper. *The very best.* He knew the quality well since he already had one just like it. In truth, he had more hats than he could possibly wear in a lifetime, all packed away, stored for the day he could return home. Back to the south.

And in that second Morgan realized yet again that he was tired of this life. Though his parents had passed away many years before, Morgan felt a nearly overwhelming need to return to his family's home—a woman at his side with whom he could share his dreams. Who would have his children. And as Walter had said, who could make him laugh. Someone like Lily.

An uncomfortable heat raced down his spine, both as a result of the unexpected directions of his thoughts, and because of the gift he held in his hands. But still he couldn't speak. What could he say? Certainly a thank-you was in order, but somehow the words stuck in his throat, emotion barring the way.

He glanced up, his heart like stone in his chest, and caught Lily's gaze. He watched as Lily's tentative excitement gave way to a flash of disappointment. Guilt seared through him.

"What do you think, Mr. Elliott?" Cassie demanded again, her nose wrinkled in disapproval.

Morgan still looked at Lily. "It's a fine topper," he finally managed.

Lily turned away, her face slipping into a mask of nonchalance. "It's nothing," she said with a negligent wave of her hand.

She started toward the parlor and Robert headed for the stairs up to his room.

"I think it's the finest of hats," Cassie persisted, clearly disgruntled by the lack of enthusiasm for the hat. "My papa wore a hat just like it. I remember," she stated obstinately. But then her smooth brow creased with worry. "I think I remember. Lily, did my papa wear hats when you knew him?"

If Morgan's eyes hadn't been fixed on Lily as she walked away he wouldn't have seen the stiffening of her shoulders when she stopped.

"Did he?" Cassie persisted, needing to know. "Am I right or am I wrong?"

Robert had stopped too, one foot halting on the step above. "Of course he wore hats, Cas."

"But what about before," she demanded. "Did Papa always wear hats?"

Lily looked at Cassie, emotion racing across her features until they settled into a reassuring smile. A forced smile, Morgan was certain.

"Yes, Cassie, love, your father wore hats when I knew him. Lots of hats." Her smile eased, became genuine. "You are absolutely right about your father. You remember perfectly. Claude always loved a fine hat. In fact," she looked at Robert, "he started wearing hats when he was about your age."

Robert turned around on the stairs.

"I remember the day quite well," she continued. "Claude and I went to the haberdasher ourselves. I'd never been to a store before that sold ready-made goods. It was a very special treat."

"What kind of a hat did he buy?" Cassie asked.

Lily's smile grew playful. "Your father insisted on a wide-brimmed gambler."

"A gambler?!"

"Yes, and quite the handsome fellow he was, strutting about the streets on the way home, that hat tilted rakishly on his head." Lily smiled mischievously. "I wore that hat once."

"You?"

While it was Cassie who asked the questions, Morgan noted that Robert and Penelope were as interested as their younger sister. They wanted to know the answer—as did he.

"Yes, me. It was years later, but the hat was still quite dashing."

"Why were you wearing a man's hat?"

"Because I was dressed up as a man."

Lily glanced up as if just then she remembered that Morgan was standing there. Amid the children's spontaneous gasps, red crept up into Lily's cheeks. Hastily she turned away.

"Why were you dressed up as a man?" Robert blurted out.

Lily glanced at her nephew and her blush of embarrassment retreated entirely, mischief dancing in her eyes. "Because a certain no-good loafer called . . . someone I knew a . . . a bad name. What else could I do but demand a duel?"

What else? Morgan thought with a grim shake of his head as the children shrieked with excitement. Suddenly

he remembered the article in the newspaper describing
what must have been the incident. It had appeared to be
nothing more than one of Lily's many antics. But he saw
now that right or wrong, foolish or not, she had only
wanted to protect someone she cared about. Why did he
feel certain that the someone had been her brother and that
she hesitated to tell the children that fact because she didn't
want them to know someone had called their father a foul
name? Would Lily really do something so generous?

He remembered the way she had treated her horse, and
he knew in that second that she would. Lily Blakemore
would defend anyone she loved, even at the cost of herself.

Morgan felt a reluctant surge of pride.

"Did you win?" Morgan asked with a smile he couldn't
quite hold at bay.

At once, all eyes were on him. But it was only Lily he
saw.

"No," she replied, disgruntled, "I wasn't afforded the
opportunity to test my skill. The no-good lout whipped the
hat from my head and my hair came tumbling down." She
cringed. "Anyone who was not gasping in shock was
laughing." She pulled a deep breath, shaking off the memory. "But enough of that. I have to make room for my
new packages."

Lily hurried up the stairs while Morgan watched her go.
After a moment the children departed as well, leaving
Morgan alone in the foyer, the topper cradled in the paper
wrapping.

A hat that Lily bought for him because she thought he
didn't have one of his own. A simple kindness. For him.
When he was there under false pretenses.

He glanced out the window, into the sun, his eyes narrowing. Trusting him, she had bought him a hat. This
woman whom he was certain didn't trust easily trusted
him—when she shouldn't.

Guilt surged through him. He had never felt guilty before when he had assumed a disguise—taken the position

of a hack driver or brothel owner, or whatever else he had done over the years to get a job done. He might not have liked it, but it was what he did. Guilt had never been a part of it. But somehow this time was different.

His hand fisted at his side. This time wasn't different, he told himself firmly. He was there to do a job. And he would do it. As he always did.

Eight

It was true that Morgan was there to do a job—to find the secret to John Crandall that would bring him down. And that was just what Morgan told himself he was doing when he left the house the next morning under the pretense of needing more supplies, and went instead to an old wooden building shared by several tenants.

If anyone had asked Morgan how talking to the woman who was purported to be Lily Blakemore's former art teacher furthered his goal he couldn't have explained. He told himself he was only being responsible, learning all there was to know about Lily in hopes that some piece of information would be the key to bringing John Crandall down. Yet again, Morgan disregarded the voice in his head that said he was obsessed with learning everything he could about Lily for reasons that had nothing to do with the man alleged to be her lover.

Frustrated with the direction his thoughts were taking, he pounded on the wooden door. He had learned the address the night before at a late, secret meeting with Walter back at the office.

"Who is it?" a woman called through the door.

"My name is Samuel Whitley, ma'am," he said, using the same name he had used with Beauford Tisdale.

"I don't know you."

"True. But I'd like to talk to you about a student you once had."

"I don't talk about my students," came the muffled response. "So just get yourself on out of here before I holler for the police."

Morgan knew that in this part of town a woman could scream and carry on for days and not gain so much as a second glance. There weren't many officers who patrolled this area. But mentioning that fact would no doubt get him nowhere faster than he was getting there already. "No need to call for help, Miss Spencer. I just want to talk to you."

"I told you. I don't talk to anyone about my students."

"Even if that student is Lily Blakemore?"

Morgan could almost feel the woman suck in her breath, and he was certain that if he could have seen her she would be holding her hand to her chest.

"Lily?"

He barely heard her, but the quietly spoken question whispered through the plank of wood. "Yes, ma'am. Lily Blakemore."

"She's all right, isn't she?"

He wasn't exactly sure he knew how to answer that. He certainly didn't want to tell the woman that as Lily's employee he had seen her only minutes before and was now sleuthing around gathering information behind her back. He intended to avoid telling this woman that he knew Lily at all.

"I'm sure she's fine, and if you'll open up the door I'll tell you why I'm here."

A moment passed that Morgan was sure was filled with indecision on the woman's part. But finally he heard the many locks give way and the rusty hinges creaked.

The woman was short. He noticed that right away, but only because Morgan found himself staring at the far wall of the apartment when she opened the door a crack. He dropped his gaze a good foot and a half until he found a pair of dark eyes peering out at him with caution.

"What do you want to know about Lily?" the woman demanded suspiciously.

"Miss Spencer, I'm not going to hurt you. Please, can we sit and talk for a while. If you'd like we could sit out on the front steps, in broad daylight." He didn't really want to sit out in broad daylight. He had taken enough chances by going to Macy's and the Union League Club. But he knew that if he appeared not to care she would not be as suspicious.

She sighed as she considered. After an eternity, she pulled open the door. "If you so much as lay a hand on me I'll have you singing soprano so fast you won't know what hit you."

A smile pulled at Morgan's lips, and it was all he could do not to chuckle. The thought of this little woman doing him bodily harm seemed preposterous. "My hands will be in clear view at all times."

"Then go ahead and have a seat."

Morgan glanced about the tiny apartment. He had been in worse areas of town before, but this apartment was more depressing than most. There was only one upholstered chair with a kerosene lamp next to it. A small table with one straight-back wooden chair sat in the corner. In another corner stood an easel. But he saw no art supplies.

Miss Spencer gestured for him to take the one good chair. Morgan declined and pulled out the wooden chair from the table. He waited for her to sit down before he did.

"A gentleman," she murmured to herself.

But Morgan suddenly didn't feel much like a gentleman. Sitting in this shabby but mercilessly clean room that had virtually no conveniences, he felt like a cad for being there.

"So you've come about Lily, have you?"

It took Morgan a moment to focus. "Miss Spencer—"

"Trudy. Call me Trudy. I'm too old to be called Miss Spencer. I don't feel much like a miss, besides."

"Well then, Trudy—"

"Lily. Ah, Lily. I haven't seen her in so many years." She looked at Morgan. "I think about her all the time, though. I've often wondered how she has managed."

In the end, it didn't matter if Morgan felt like a cad or not. Trudy simply talked. And talked. It was as if she were lonely and hadn't spoken to a single soul in months, but also as if she had so many memories of Lily all bottled up inside her and now suddenly found a release.

"She was talented, that girl. The things she could do with a paintbrush and canvas. Such a waste. And pretty, too. Lordy." Trudy laughed. "All I had to do was mention that Lily Blakemore was going to be in one of my classes that day and the school would be swamped with men of every calling. Men who had never given a thought to a paintbrush in all their lives would show up with a sudden yearning to learn to paint. I had more students than I knew what to do with back then." Trudy shook her head. "If only I'd saved my money."

She sat for a moment, morning sunlight drifting in through the tiny window. Morgan didn't prod her, he just sat with her, the image of Lily sitting in front of an easel filling his mind.

Once Morgan had gotten over the surprise that Lily was a gifted painter, not just some bored society woman taking art classes to fill her days, he realized he shouldn't have been surprised. The emotion he saw in Lily's features, the feelings. It seemed only natural that she would find her release in art.

"But regardless of the money, I wish I had warned her," Trudy continued, looking out the window, suddenly very sad. "I should have warned her about Raine."

Raine. The man whose bedside Lily had been at upon

his death. The muscles along Morgan's back tightened.

"But I didn't," Trudy said. "His sister Mary warned me. But I only laughed. I never saw it coming."

Morgan leaned forward in his chair, intent. "Saw what coming?"

"Surely you know."

Morgan saw that she looked at him oddly, looked at him as if for the first time she realized she might have said too much to a man she didn't know.

"Who did you say you were?" she asked, her milky eyes peering closely at him.

For a second he had to think. What had he told her? For a man whose job had always come naturally to him, Morgan was unsettled. "Samuel Whitley," he remembered, "and—"

"Why do you want to know about Lily?"

He looked the old woman in the eye. "I'm simply trying to understand," he said with great feeling, his words truer than even he cared to admit. "I am trying to understand what happened to her."

"You love her, don't you?" the woman asked unexpectedly.

The question threw Morgan off balance. His dark eyes narrowed and he turned slightly away as if he could turn away from her words. Love her? Love Lily Blakemore? Good God, never. He had never disliked a woman so much in his life. Or so he told himself, as it was easier to understand hate and disgust for a fallen woman than to put names to emotions he couldn't fathom.

"I can see in your eyes that you do," she continued on at his silence. "You love her in spite of the fact that she was ruined." She smiled at him in sympathy. "Unfortunately I don't have all the answers for you. But perhaps Mary Hawthorne does."

Only long years of practice helped Morgan rein in his racing thoughts enough to concentrate.

"All I know," Trudy went on, "is that Lily could

have been a great artist. She had such feeling, such passion, and she poured it into her work. But I have often wondered, given society's disdain of women artists, if the scandal wasn't bound to happen.''

The woman smiled fondly. ''She had built a studio of sorts in the attic of that house of hers. I wonder if it's still there.''

Morgan suddenly thought of the day he had found Lily standing at the attic door. Just standing, staring. As if afraid to go in.

''Well, now, Mr. Elliott, I've gabbed enough for now. Would you like some tea?''

Morgan cleared his head and considered the polite offer. He really didn't have the time. He had to get back to the house by ten and he still had to pick up some supplies to make his excuse to leave the house in the first place good. But he was left with more questions than answers. If he had a few more minutes with the woman . . .

''A cup of tea,'' she added, ''and then you can tell me all about how you met dear Lily.''

She started to stand, but Morgan stood, too. ''Thank you for the invitation, but I really can't stay.'' When he saw her flash of disappointment he couldn't help adding, ''I'm sorry.''

Trudy sighed, though Morgan could tell it was due more to resignation than to disappointment. ''Perhaps you'll come back some other day and tell me more about her.''

Morgan walked out into the bright morning sunlight. He blinked at the brightness after sitting for so long in the darkened room with Trudy Spencer. He thought about Lily and what he had learned in the weeks he had been trying to fit the pieces of the puzzle together that was Lily Blakemore.

He knew her parents were dead and had left her in the care of her brother, Claude, now also deceased. She had been stunningly beautiful as a young woman but full of a spirit that Morgan knew wouldn't be considered desirable in a woman of her station. She had nearly become engaged to a man who clearly remembered her with deep sentiment and fondness, but that man had married another woman whom he didn't speak of with any apparent feeling.

Why hadn't Beauford Tisdale married Lily? No doubt because of the scandal, Morgan felt certain.

Frustration assailed him. While he had learned a great deal more about Lily Blakemore in the last few weeks, he had yet to learn the cause of the scandal.

Did it have to do with her art? Or was it this man named Raine Hawthorne?

Morgan didn't like the feeling that churned in his gut. Was it Lily's artwork itself that had outraged society? Had she become the man's lover? Or was it something else altogether? But how to find out?

Suddenly, he remembered Trudy Spencer's mention of the man's sister. Though he shouldn't, Morgan knew as he headed down the bustling street that he would find Mary Hawthorne next.

Morgan stopped at the masoners' to order a new marble column for the parlor before he made his way uptown. As had become his habit to avoid an encounter with lurking reporters, he went through the back way. He stopped at the work shed and retrieved his box of tools. Morgan had finally found the cause of the compromised ceiling and pillar. An unprotected upstairs window that wouldn't close, the hinge long broken.

Whenever it rained, water spilled in, seeped through the floor to the ceiling above the marble pillar. If he didn't repair the window, the rest of his work would be for naught.

He took the stairs to the second floor, intent on going to the window. The house was silent, everyone seemingly gone, and just when he should have made the turn to walk down the long hallway to the room with the broken window, he took a different course and continued on up the next flight of stairs instead.

The quiet grew heavier as he took yet another flight of stairs, this time steep and narrow, the worn carpet muffling the tread of his heavy boots. At the top there was a door. His spine tensed when he saw that it stood open. Knowing he should turn around and return below, Morgan nonetheless continued on up the stairs and through the doorway.

The light struck him first. Light filling an expansive room of white walls, high ceilings, and more windows that he could take in with a single glance. In a house falling apart at the seams, Morgan never would have guessed a room in this condition could exist.

But these thoughts barely registered before he noticed Lily.

Sweet Lily, he whispered like an involuntary breath.

She stood in front of a long narrow table. Reverently she ran her hand along the smooth surface. He watched, his gaze taking in her form, as she picked up something. With his mind lost to the vision of her slender curves, his body filling with the heaviness of instant desire, it took Morgan a second to realize she had picked up a paintbrush.

It was then that his mind mastered his body and he noticed the easel and a smattering of stretched canvases lined against one wall. Even from this distance he could tell the canvases were yellow with age.

It was an artist's studio. Just as Trudy Spencer had said. And given the way Lily held the brush, running her thumb over the soft bristles, he knew that everything he had learned was true. Lily was an artist. Or, based on the cobwebs and forgotten canvases, she had been.

Morgan watched as Lily looked out the window, staring off into the distance, unaware of his presence, the paintbrush forgotten in her hand. Her chin rose a notch to catch the sunlight. The expression in her blue eyes was unguarded. Pain. Anger. But most of all, Morgan saw a desolation that hammered him straight in the chest. In spite of everything, Morgan felt the crazy need to pull her into his arms, not to feel the smooth curves of her body, but to protect her.

"What are you thinking?" he asked softly before he could stop himself.

Lily turned sharply. At the sight of Morgan the unguarded look in her eyes evaporated without a trace.

"What are you doing here?"

Her voice was harsh and sharp, slicing through any concern Morgan felt. Thankfully. He nearly shook his head. What was it about this woman that made him constantly forget what she really was?

"I just wanted to see what repairs were needed up here," he said casually, stepping farther into the room and looking around. His bootheels rang on the hardwood floor, echoing in the almost empty room. He ran his hand through a cobweb. "Looks like this room doesn't need much more than a good cleaning."

Lily looked at Morgan with a calm she didn't feel. She was angry that he was there, in this room, in this place of all places. It had taken her weeks to gather up the courage to pass through the door. Weeks of getting so close, but never actually turning the knob.

But today she had. She had pushed through to the brilliant sunlight, a wealth of emotions washing over her like the tide rushing back to the sea.

"I wore the hat today," he said.

Lily watched as he reached up and casually wiped another cobweb away. His hands were gentle despite their size. Strong hands that had touched her, caressed her.

"I don't think I thanked you properly earlier," he said.

His words tangled in her mind, tripping up her thoughts of hands and caresses. "What?" she stammered.

He looked at her curiously. "I said, I don't think I thanked you properly. For the hat."

Lily pulled a long, calming breath. "Properly? You

didn't thank me at all. But if that's your way of saying thank you now, then you're welcome.''

"Yes, it is, and thank you.''

"Was that so hard?''

His dark eyes grew serious. "I haven't had much practice with thank-yous in a while. I can't remember the last time someone gave me a present.''

"Well, if you're as ornery around everyone else as you are here, then I'm not surprised that people haven't bothered.''

A long moment passed before Morgan laughed. "Ornery? Me?''

"Yes, you. But an ornery man with a beautiful hat.'' Lily looked back out the window, remembering so well her father and the assorted hats he always wore. "I love a hat on a man.'' She smiled wistfully. "A fine silk hat. Wide brimmed, short brimmed.'' She chuckled. "As long as it's not one of those silly bowlers men are wearing more and more.''

"No doubt if it were up to you, you'd have men in hats loaded with feathers and bells.''

Her delighted laughter wafted through the room, like the motes of dust that drifted in the long rays of sunlight. "Not for a man,'' she corrected him.

She walked to a massive armoire, running her hands along the smooth hardwood. Grasping the high handles, she pulled the doors wide.

Paint supplies lined the shelves and hanging space. Reaching inside, Lily took a single brush from a clutter of brushes, but when she did the entire bunch clattered to the floor. She jumped back, staring at the brushes lying in disarray on the floor. After a second, she looked back into the cabinet. "I'm astounded it's still here.''

"The paint supplies or the armoire?'' he asked.

She glanced up at him, then shrugged. "Both, I suppose. It looks no different, as if I just walked out of this room yesterday. This used to be a playroom. All of our toys were stored inside the armoire. See, the handles are high. I couldn't reach, nor could Claude for many years. Our governesses had control over what went in or what came out of this cabinet.'' She smiled. ''It was with great relish years later that I flung open the doors, tossed the toys aside, and made it my painting cabinet.''

''Controlling your destiny?''

She looked back at him, her forehead creased. ''You said before that we are responsible for what happens to us. Did you really mean that, or were you just angry about Madame Paulie?''

She wanted him to deny his earlier words, she wanted him to say that a person doesn't determine the path they eventually take, but rather a greater power makes those choices. It was hard enough to deal with her ruination. But to have to believe that she had caused it left her aching and alone.

''Yes, I think that we are responsible for what happens to us.''

If he had struck her physically she didn't think she could have hurt so badly. But what did she expect? Morgan Elliott never said anything he didn't mean. ''No doubt you're right,'' she said at length. ''Somehow we make things happen.''

She moved away, walking about the room, running her fingers along the walls and odd pieces of furniture. ''I had a doll when I was young. Miss Bellingham. I loved her terribly.''

''Did you toss her out of the cabinet, too?''

The image of Miss Bellingham flashed through her head. Then Claude, dangling the doll above her head, just beyond her reach. With effort, she looked back at Morgan. ''No toy was spared,'' she answered. ''Did you have many toys when you were a child?''

''Toys?'' he stated, his voice suddenly clipped.

Lily cringed. So lost in her thoughts, she had forgotten all about Morgan's life. ''But surely you had toys. Everyone has toys, no matter who they are or where they come from. Something, even if it's a rock imagined to be a ball.''

"Yes, a few. But I didn't spend much time playing. My father believed in hard work.''

"That doesn't surprise me. I've never seen anyone work as hard as you do. Good heavens, the progress you've made in this house in such a short time is miraculous. You're very good at what you do.'' Her look grew curious. "Though I never would have pegged you for a working-man, at least not a repairman, in all my days. You clearly are a man who has been in charge.''

Morgan remembered that she had said this before, on the horsecar the day they went to Macy's, and again he grew uncomfortable. The last thing he needed was for this woman to draw the undeniable conclusion. That he wasn't a repairman.

But suddenly he wished she would. Guess what he was about. Denounce him. Demand that he leave.

Without warning he was tired of this charade. He was tired of one minute despising her, then the next wanting to strip her naked and thrust deep inside her.

Or relish the way she could make him laugh.

She did that to him, constantly. Turn his thoughts upside down. He had always prided himself on the fact that he never mixed work with pleasure. Not that he found any-thing about Lily Blakemore pleasurable. Only maddening.

"What did you do before you came to work here?'' she asked, as if reading his thoughts.

She had offered him an opening. But for all his lament, he couldn't bring himself to set the record straight. "How did we get from you telling me about your toys to my work?'' he asked with a practiced laugh.

"Well,'' she said with exaggerated patience. "I was asking you about your toys which apparently you didn't spend much time with. What about brothers and sisters?''

"None.''

"Then friends. Surely even you must have had friends."

Morgan became very still, his dark-eyed gaze growing troubled. He was barely aware that Lily studied him curiously. "Yes, I had friends," he said quietly.

The image of Trey flashed through his mind. Trey, Jenny, and him. The three of them had been inseparable.

"What were their names?"

"Jenny," he said at length, his voice tight, unable to say the other. He closed his eyes briefly, and when he opened them again Lily was studying him intently. He forced a smile. "We didn't play in a playroom like this, but we had streams and fields."

"Jenny? *You* played with a girl?"

Despite everything, her incredulous tone made him smile. One slash of dark brow raised as he crossed his arms on his chest. "Are you surprised?"

He expected a laugh, or at the very least one of her unladylike snorts of disdain. Instead she grew distant, what little levity that had surfaced in the room with the talk of toys and childhood evaporating into the long rays of golden sunlight spilling into the room. It was always this way, he realized. No sooner did he predict she would do one thing than she did something else entirely. He had lived for years predicting the unpredictable. But with Lily he failed repeatedly regardless of the fact that he longed to understand her with an intensity that gave him pause.

"Are you surprised that I played with a girl?" he repeated, wanting to pierce the quiet.

"No, I'm not surprised." She glanced back toward the window. "I was Claude's friend. His only friend, actually. We spent hours up here, talking, laughing, sometimes working side by side without a word spoken between us. For years we understood each other's thoughts without having to speak them out loud."

"Your parents must have been pleased that their children got along so well. Though I never had a sibling of my own, I've been told that not all children get along so well.''

"Pleased?'' The word seemed to surprise her, as if she had never given the meaning behind it a thought. ''I can't say. I'm not sure they even realized how close we were. They were rarely at home. My parents traveled, going here and there. Africa, India. And when they were in town, they were always at some party or having one of their own. I've often thought that Claude spent so much time with me because once I was born he was no longer alone. He had someone. Mother and Father had each other. Then when I came along Claude had me.''

"He must have loved you very much.''

Her heart hammered against her ribs. ''Do you think?'' She saw Morgan's startled look. ''I'm not sure I know what love is anymore. An illusion perhaps.''

"Sure you do,'' he stated with conviction.

"No. I'm sure *you* do, though. You who are so certain you know everything.'' She smiled softly to ease the hard edge of her words. ''You have all the answers, don't you, Morgan Elliott? You know with great certainty what is right and what is wrong. Some would call you self-righteous, wanting to impose your views and beliefs on everyone else. Despite the fact that you drive me to distraction at every turn, I don't think that's what motivates you, or at least not entirely. The world is black-and-white for you, but the rest of us live in myriad shades of gray. I wonder who is the luckiest, who has the easiest time surviving.''

Morgan didn't know how to respond. He had lived for so long with a single purpose. He'd had such a determined path he hardly remembered that there were shades of gray.

Lily laughed suddenly. ''I'm being absurd. It's difficult for everyone, no matter what they believe.''

She turned back to the armoire and sank down to the floor, her long skirt billowing around her. With graceful fingers she started to gather the fallen paintbrushes.

Morgan crossed the room in a few easy strides. As he lowered himself to her side, intent on helping, their fingers brushed.

The touch was electric. He could see that the contact unsettled her when her head jerked up and her balance wavered. Morgan reached out to steady her.

"Let me help," he said.

An aching sadness drifted across her porcelain features, until he thought she might shatter. At length she said, "Help me, Mr. Elliott? You can't help me, no one can."

"Lily, I just wanted to—"

"No, please. Just go. Leave me alone."

"Lily—"

"No, Morgan!"

They stayed that way for long moments, their eyes locked in battle.

"Please, Mr. Elliott, just go."

She was right, he realized. He should leave. He had no business there, and while his offer to help had been directed at the fallen paintbrushes, he knew that deep down he felt a need to help in a way that far exceeded the supplies that were scattered on the floor. Why? he asked himself once again. Why did he feel the need to help her? Was it guilt because he was using her to corner his quarry? Maybe, but even he realized that was only part of the answer.

He found himself tangled up in something beyond his understanding. His feelings for her were anything but clear. She was a woman of lesser virtue, a woman who didn't care about right or wrong, while he was a man who had lived his life bringing her type to justice.

A flash of Jenny came to mind.

He was forced to concede that his search for honor had begun the day Jenny had fallen much like the paintbrushes. His throat tightened in a way that he didn't understand. Guilt, pain. And anger.

Oh, Jenny. Why?

Nine

The next few days passed uneventfully, at least when compared to the events of the previous days. Lily started riding daily, and Morgan saw little of her. He was thankful because when she was near, all he believed in seemed to waver.

For years Morgan had thrown himself into work, keeping Jenny from his mind. But somehow, here, with Lily, on this job, Jenny circled in his mind relentlessly. He worked as tirelessly as he did to forget, but all he had done since arriving at Blakemore House was remember.

Morgan told himself that it was impossible not to remember when faced with a woman who was Jenny's exact opposite. Jenny had been innocent and naive. Lily Blakemore was anything but. She brazened her way through the world. But at unexpected moments, traitorous thoughts surfaced in Morgan's mind, thoughts about how similar Lily and Jenny actually were. And that made him angry. Lily was a fallen woman of no virtue. Jenny was . . . Jenny—and she was gone.

Friday evening Morgan knelt in the garden, replacing a

broken window in a front basement window well. The children were upstairs and as usual Marky and Jojo were nowhere to be seen. Morgan grumbled.

Suddenly he heard the fast and furious pounding of horses' hooves in the distance. Seconds later the pounding was followed by shouts and exclamations, colorful speech that anyone within a quarter mile must have heard. Straightening, Morgan dusted off his hands and looked to the west where the noise was growing louder.

The instant the horses and riders rounded the corner from Seventh Avenue, Morgan's heart stilled in his chest. Three riders galloped at breakneck speed. Dangerously. Carelessly. One misstep, one wrong move, and a horse and rider would go down. But from the laughter and the expletives, no one would have guessed that anyone was in danger. The trio was racing.

And Lily Blakemore was in the lead.

"Hell!" Morgan cursed, just as the children rushed out onto the front porch.

"Oh, my stars," Cassie cried in an amazing imitation of Lily herself, "it's Lily!"

Morgan watched the rapid approach, mesmerized despite himself. The sight was breathtaking, Lily bent low, her hair flying like a rebel flag behind her shoulders. She was alive as he had never seen a woman. Radiant. Charging through life.

He had seen it before in men, though rarely. But never in a woman. Life was too precarious for most people. But not for Lily Blakemore. She disregarded the fragility of life. She had no sense of her own mortality.

The riders came to an abrupt halt in front of the house, the horses dancing nervously after the wild ride, snorting and puffing in the warm early evening air. Lily threw back her head and laughed, and when she jumped down, ignoring her companion's extended hands, Morgan could see that her blue eyes blazed with fire. A goddess set down among mere mortals.

Morgan remembered the articles he had read about Lily. Yes, she was a wild child, he conceded. She thrived on life and excitement, she walked the precipice of danger and loved it. Though he shouldn't, Morgan felt a flash of admiration for this outrageous woman.

He realized after a moment that one of the men at her side was Bart Mayhew whom they had met at Macy's. The other was a man he recognized as a younger son of a prominent family, a youth with too much time on his hands who had been known to get into trouble.

Lily led her guests up to the house. They took the steps boldly, Lily boldest of all. At the top, she smiled at Cassie before passing by unfazed that her charges stood on the porch, mouths agape at her brazen arrival.

His eyes narrowing, Morgan rewrapped the sealing putty in cheesecloth, returned it to its shallow tin, then wiped his hands. After gathering his few tools, he remembered that his toolbox was still in the parlor. He considered simply going around the house to the back, leaving the box inside. But he wasn't one to leave a job unfinished. Or so he told himself as he headed for the front porch.

The children still stood at the top of the steps.

"She should be shot," Robert grumbled.

"She's a disgrace," Penelope agreed.

"She is not!" Tears glistened in Cassie's huge eyes. "She is nice and you are just hateful!"

Cassie twirled on her tiny feet and raced inside the house, her footsteps pounding up the stairs until they heard her bedroom door slam.

Morgan looked at Penelope and Robert.

"Well, she is," Penelope stated, as if she needed to defend herself.

Morgan shrugged his shoulders. No need to argue the case to him. Hell, he thought as he stepped through the doorway his features grim, he happened to agree with Penelope.

Inside the house, the laughing and boisterous talk had

not abated. If possible, it had grown louder.

"C'mon, Lily, just a couple of hands."

Morgan's fingers curled into a fist, clenched at his side.

"I said no, Melville," Lily said.

Morgan came into the room. Bart was pouring drinks. Melville took one for himself and extended another to Lily. She started to decline, but just then she noticed Morgan.

Oh, Morgan, she thought, her heart skittering against her ribs. She had an unexpected yearning to smile at him, to ask him about his day. Ask him if he had seen how beautifully Midnight had galloped through the streets. Inconsequential conversation, anything to hear him talk, hear his deep voice wash over her.

But her smile faltered when he glanced from her guests to her, disgust transforming the chiseled planes of his face.

Her heart lodged in her chest. Hard and cold. Painful. How could she have forgotten? Even for a moment. Suddenly she was tired of trying, desperately tired of being in this house where everyone believed the worst of her. The lonely outpost of Tarrytown suddenly seemed appealing. Anything, anything to escape that damning look in his eyes.

But on the heels of that thought a sizzle of anger raced through her, burning away disappointment, bringing defiance to the surface in welcome relief. Like a kidnapped child colluding with her captors, Lily became what Morgan expected. What Morgan believed her to be.

Damn him, the thought whispered through her head, her gaze locked with his, before she took the drink and tossed back the amber liquid as if she were a sailor in a tawdry saloon.

"On second thought, Melville," she said, once her breath had returned, her eyes never leaving Morgan's, "poker sounds like a fine idea. Deal me in."

"Grand! Simply grand," Melville exclaimed.

Lily picked up a cigarette, and when Morgan didn't step forward to light it she leaned over to Bart, who obliged.

Morgan's jaw worked. His box of tools sat on the floor next to where Lily stood, a cigarette smoldering between long tapered fingers. With his tin of putty, he strode across the room to her, while her companions busily cleared a place to play their game.

"I'm glad to see that you can do *something* well," Morgan drawled sarcastically in a tone that only Lily could hear. "What does it matter if you don't know the first thing about children if you can smoke, drink, and gamble as well as any man? I'm impressed, Miss Blakemore."

For a second she seemed to sway, pain washing across her gaze. Or so he thought, before her blue eyes hardened like sapphires and she took a long, deep pull on her cigarette.

She exhaled with a hard laugh. "If you had spent the last ten years as a ruined woman, you'd be good at gambling, too."

Her eyes locked with his, and with measured movements she took one last leisurely pull on her cigarette, then put it out in Morgan's tin of putty. "Now if you'll excuse me, Mr. Elliott," she added, exhaling, "one of the *few things* I'm good at is waiting."

She turned away without another word, leaving Morgan standing stock-still, the ruined putty smoldering in his hand. His mind smoldered much as the putty did. He had been scraped raw on the inside over the last weeks—trying to understand this woman, the need to protect her, and always close at hand, the desire. No, lust, he corrected himself forcefully. He hadn't had a woman in months. It was no wonder he was lusting after Lily Blakemore, he reasoned coldly. Never had he met such a woman. Hard, wild. Reckless and outrageous.

The pieces of the puzzle were falling into place. The Lily Blakemore he had come here to find was present in all her glory. The only piece missing from the picture that he had imagined all too well was John Crandall. But he would arrive. Soon. Morgan felt it in his bones.

With barely contained anger, Morgan picked up the toolbox. Straightening, he headed for the door.

"We can't play with only three," Bart stated, tossing back a single-malt scotch as if it were lemonade.

"Sure we can," Melville scoffed.

"No, we can't," Bart insisted. "We need four people to make it any fun. You, there," he called out.

Morgan continued up the steps.

"Hey, there, Mr. Repairman!"

Morgan stilled in the doorway, then turned back slowly, his dark eyes menacing.

Bart muttered and shifted his weight, obviously regretting his choice of words, then said, "Good sir, how about joining us in a hand of poker."

"Bart, really . . ." Lily's words trailed off, red surging to life in her cheeks.

Disgust riddled Morgan's brow. And with that, he watched as Lily's face transformed. Her embarrassment, if that's what it had truly been, receded. Her eyes narrowed and she met his gaze boldly.

"Actually, Mr. Elliott, why not? Why not play a friendly round of poker?" Her gaze grew coy. "Or are your . . . delicate sensibilities offended by such a thought?"

Morgan's jaw clenched. How was it, he wondered, that since arriving at Blakemore House his belief in right and wrong had been turned upside down.

Goaded on by her tone as much as her words, Morgan walked back into the room. "If *your* delicate sensibilities aren't offended by playing a sordid, base game, why should mine be? Though I hope, Miss Blakemore, you know how to play. Where I come from we play for keeps."

"Don't worry your little head about me, Mr. Elliott, I wouldn't have it any other way."

"If I were you, Mr. Elliott," Bart said with a laugh,

"I'd be worried about myself. Unless Lily has lost her touch, she's a damn fine poker player."

The foursome gathered around a table that had seen better days. Lily produced a deck of cards. "You do have money, don't you, Mr. Elliott? If not, I'll be happy to provide you with an advance against your wages."

"That won't be necessary," he replied tightly. "I'll be right back."

Morgan went out to his cottage and retrieved a sack of coins. When he returned, Bart and Melville sat at the table laughing over something. But Lily was gone. When Morgan stepped farther into the room, he found her standing at the window, a drink held forgotten in her hand.

For a second his chest tightened, his stomach knotting low. Though he could only see her profile he had come to recognize the look on her face, the particular tilt of her chin. How was it possible for one woman to jerk his emotions around in so many directions? One minute he could cheerfully strangle her, the next he wanted to pull her into his arms and tell her everything was going to be all right.

But then she turned back, never affording him a glance, and strode to the table.

"Cut the cards," she stated coolly as Bart and Melville both stood to help with her chair.

Morgan sat down across from Lily. He studied her for some time before she glanced up. But this time she wouldn't hold his gaze. She seemed to grow self-conscious. Turning to Bart, she snapped, "Quit shuffling and deal."

The startled look on Bart's face quickly evaporated when Lily reached over and laid a penitent hand on his. "I'm sorry, Bart. Please deal."

The cards were dealt all around. The laughing and talking ceased while everyone but Lily studied their cards. After little more than a quick glance, she asked for one card, then sipped her drink.

A glass of bourbon sat at Morgan's right hand. After

asking for two cards, he took an appreciative swallow. When he lowered the glass Lily was looking at him, though she quickly looked away.

The round of poker went quickly, Lily barely beating Morgan out with a pair of kings to his matching tens. Bart and Melville had nothing between them much less anything worth looking at on their own.

"Luck," Morgan found himself grumbling.

A tiny smile flitted across Lily's lips, the tension of moments earlier starting to ease.

After a few hands, it became apparent to Morgan that luck had no more to do with Lily's abilities than did a full moon. He hadn't been wrong when he had said Lily was a proficient gambler. Clearly she had gambled before and gambled well.

It quickly became apparent that the only real contest was between Lily and Morgan. Bart and Melville were more interested in exchanging stories and throwing back whiskey than concentrating on their cards.

Morgan consumed his share of bourbon as the night wore on. Lily did the same, impressing Morgan with her control.

"Here, now," Melville muttered, his words beginning to slur, "I call."

The cards were shown and this time Lily beat Morgan's pair of kings with three queens. After that, it was Lily's royal flush to Morgan's four of a kind. Her full house to his flush, a straight to a pair.

"Hell," Morgan muttered, well into the night.

"Would you like to quit?" Lily laughed, reaching out to sweep the prize into her growing pile of coins.

"Not on your life," Morgan grumbled, straightening in his seat and rolling back his shirtsleeves. "Deal."

With graceful fingers, Lily did just that. Morgan watched, a strange sensation snaking through his body as her fingers ran over each card she dealt. He felt his loins tighten at the thought of her hands caressing him, pressing against him, guiding him to her.

Long years of self-control were forcefully put into play. Morgan suppressed the fiery feelings that churned low with ruthless acumen. He concentrated on the cards, refusing to consider the woman who sat across from him. And with that concentration came a slow, steady comeback that had Bart and Melville laughing and exclaiming. Lily looked on with an arched eyebrow and a wry smile as Morgan took yet another pot.

"I believe that makes us even," Morgan said an hour later with a cool smile as he stacked his coins in neat rows.

"For you and Lily maybe," Bart said, the words by now badly garbled. "But you've got me beat soundly, old man."

Bart made to push up from the table, but his thigh banged the underside, jostling everything that sat on top. Drinks sloshed, spilling over the rims. Morgan and Lily leaped up to stanch the flow.

"I'd say, good friend," Melville said, seemingly unaware of the spillage, staggering up from the table himself, "it's time we make our way home."

"Can you make it all right?" Lily asked, steadying Melville.

"Of course, of course."

It didn't take long before the guests were on their way out the door.

"I don't know if it's safe for those two to ride," Morgan said, watching Bart and Melville attempt to mount.

"You're right, they could get themselves killed."

"I was concerned about their mounts."

Lily looked up, startled. But at the look of mischief that played in Morgan's eyes she couldn't help the laugh that bubbled up inside her.

But she hid her mirth, then turned and went back to the parlor. "Their horses will pick their way home with great care as they have done no doubt a thousand times before."

"No doubt," he said.

When she turned back, not realizing he had followed her, she was startled to find him close, too close.

He stared at her. Only hours before he had sworn she was the lowest of women. But now he found himself wanting to defend her, to come up with reasons why she couldn't possibly be what she appeared. He hated the realization that he wanted her to be something he had learned full well she was not.

Morgan Elliott, always logical, practical and realistic, wanted Crimson Lily to be innocent.

How was it, he wondered his mind raging, that this woman could twist his thoughts around until his brain felt like a bowline knot? And she had accomplished it by doing nothing more than playing poker, cursing like a sailor, and tossing back liquor like there was no tomorrow.

"Who are you, Lily Blakemore?" he asked, his voice deep and rough. "Why do you make me feel things I don't understand?"

Lily's heart hammered in her chest. She could tell from the look in his eyes that he didn't expect an answer, not that she could have provided one. She didn't understand the strong currents that wrapped around them any more than he did. In moments of sanity she scoffed at her melodramatic thoughts of banishing the darkness, of travelers on the same path. She had never met any one person who made her so angry, and did it without even trying. All he had to do is walk into a room and look at her in that way that spoke volumes and her blood began to boil—or she cringed with embarrassment.

He was everything she didn't like in a man. Overbearing. Bossy. Brandishing his brute strength like a weapon. Angry. Burning. But then he stepped closer.

He was so tall, so powerful, the raw danger of him only banked. She had noticed his potency from the start, had been drawn to it. But tonight the thought sent a shiver of panic racing down her spine. She knew she should flee, out the door and up the stairs. Dismiss him in the morning. Instead she stood her ground, thinking not of impropriety, but of the chiseled strength of him. What would it feel like to touch him again?

She was appalled at her brazenness, and would have stepped away if just then he hadn't touch her cheek. His strong finger traced her jaw, reaching her chin, tilting it ever so slightly until their eyes met.

"I'm going to kiss you, Lily."

His voice was raw with sensuality. She knew as she knew her own name that his desire was barely controlled. He wanted her, had for some time. She saw it in his eyes, could hear it in his voice. His meaning was clear. He was giving her warning.

He hated her, but he wanted her as well. And Lily knew that he hated that wanting. She couldn't plead innocence.

Again she told herself to flee. But like a moth rushing headlong into the flame, she only wanted to feel him brush his lips against hers.

He kissed her then. The touch was like fire, the flame reaching out to lick at her lips, his fingers still holding her chin. She inhaled sharply and her eyes started to close, but Morgan pulled back.

Her eyelids fluttered open.

"Tell me you want my touch, Lily. Tell me you want to feel my lips on yours."

She leaned into him in response. He kissed her again, softly, before he pulled back. "Say it, Lily. Say the words," he demanded hoarsely against her lips.

She groaned her frustration, her hands fisting against his chest. "Yes, damn you. Yes, I want your touch."

With that, his mouth came down on hers possessively. He kissed her as if he had been waiting for years. He devoured her, his mouth slanting over hers. His strong hands pulled her closer, the heat of him searing her through her clothes. His arms were like bands of iron, holding her securely as his hands caressed her back, then lower, until he cupped her round, firm hips.

She felt the hardness of his desire pressing insistently against her belly, shocking her. Making her yearn in ways she failed to understand.

"Don't be scared, Lily. I won't hurt you," he whispered against her ear, the sensation making her tremble.

His mouth seared a path to her neck and her head fell back. Then lower, until he kissed her breast beneath the material of her thin cotton riding shirt. Wrapping her arms around his broad shoulders, Lily caressed his silky hair, letting her fingers roam. But her breath caught when she felt the material of her shirt give way and his mouth closed over her breast.

"God, you are so beautiful," he murmured against her, his hand coming up and pressing her breast high. "Full and lush."

She wanted to be closer to him. Wanted to feel more of him. Have him whisper sweet words of love in her ear. *Love.* The word seared her. Scorning her.

Love was impossible.

If nothing else, Morgan Elliott had made it clear how he felt about her. He might be drawn to her in some inexplicable way, he might want to kiss her, but he didn't love her, didn't even like her, he loathed her in some deep, elemental way. But most of all, she knew he believed the stories about her. He saw her as Crimson Lily. And after he had spent weeks in her childhood home, seeing her, watching her, he had seen nothing more.

In that moment Lily wished she hadn't tossed back the drink or played poker like one of the boys. Hadn't become what Morgan expected. She had wanted Bart and Melville to leave after the ride, had been on the verge of telling them to do just that. But every time Morgan looked at her with disgust, defiance flared to life in her breast. And that defiance damned her more thoroughly in his eyes than she had been damned before.

She understood that, always had, but had never been able to stop it—hadn't been able to quell the defiance.

With Herculean effort, Lily's hand came up. She braced herself against his chest.

Despite all she knew to be true, her mind had been filled with improper thoughts of him ever since the day he kissed her. No, before, she conceded, mortified. Ever since the day she had encountered him in the hallway. But despite every attempt she had made to force Morgan Elliott from her mind she had been unsuccessful.

In the weeks Morgan had been at Blakemore House, when Lily least expected it, she would catch sight of him fixing a pipe or hammering a nail. His hands strong and capable. Bold. Always self-assured.

Shamelessly she had wished his hands would touch her—proving everything she had ever feared about herself. She was shameless. Improper. Beyond redemption.

Proving to herself that she *was* Crimson Lily.

But she wasn't! her mind raged. She couldn't be.

Despair hit her unmercifully. With a strangled cry, she tried to wrench free of his hold.

"Lily," he breathed raggedly, "what's wrong?"

"What's wrong?" she demanded, tears spilling down her cheeks. "Everything's wrong! Everything! Let go of me."

She jerked away but failed to break free.

"Lily," he said, his voice forceful, the passion cleared from his eyes. "Tell me what's wrong."

"Let go of me, damn you!"

He held her for a second longer, his obsidian gaze boring into hers as if looking for some truth. After an eternity, he did as she asked. "By all means," he said stiffly.

Lily hated the disappointment that flared to life in her heart. But that was absurd.

"Now if you'll excuse me," she replied with a calm that she didn't feel, "it's late, and suddenly I feel quite exhausted."

Ten

Lily's eyes flew open with a start. The morning sun filtered through the mullioned window, casting rays of golden light around the room, forcing her from her dream-filled sleep.

It took a moment for her surroundings to come into focus, then another before she remembered she wasn't in Tarrytown overlooking the river. Nor was she on some grand adventure in Asia or Europe. She was at Blakemore House where children hated her and repairmen looked at her with disgust.

With a sigh and a punch to her down pillow, Lily flopped over onto her stomach. "Arrggh," she groaned.

But her groan of frustration quickly turned to a groan of mortification when she remembered not only where she was but what had happened last night.

"Good Lord, what have I done? Again!"

Lily rolled over onto her back, throwing her forearm over her eyes. "Why do I keep doing this? With Morgan Elliott of all people."

If she wanted to experiment with kissing then why not kiss Bart or even Melville? But Lily knew that it wasn't about experimenting. It wasn't about Bart or Melville. It was about Morgan. And the way he made her feel.

Embarrassment singed her cheeks despite the fact that she was all alone as memories of last night and Morgan Elliott played havoc in her mind. His touch, his lips kissing her so intimately. At the thought, her traitorous body began to tingle, and she caught a moan just before it escaped her lips.

Forcefully she jerked her head to the side. She would not think about Morgan Elliott or his kiss. But the memory was not so easily eluded.

How was she ever going to face the man again? she wondered dismally. He had thought her lower than low before she had acted so wantonly. Good heavens, she had allowed him to touch her breast.

She could bet any amount of money on what he thought of her now, and not be afraid to lose. How was she ever going to go downstairs and face the man again?

"Arrggh," she cried again, pounding the bed with her fist.

But then she stilled, pressing her eyes closed. She was not a coward. Never had been. If there was one thing she knew about herself, it was that she had always stood proud in the face of cruel comments and disgusted stares. She had faced them all, and she had faced them with courage. People could argue that she had no honor or dignity. But if she had nothing else, she had courage. Lily clung to that thought like a drowning man clinging to a lifeboat in a raging sea.

With that, Lily kicked her feet free of the tangled sheets, ready to face whatever scorn or humiliation the day brought.

But then she remembered. It was Saturday. The day of the Mayhews' party.

"Oh, my stars!" she exclaimed. She was going to tea!

Uncertainty came easily on the heels of last night's humiliation. But even her uncertainty couldn't hold up against the shimmer of excitement that bubbled up inside her. She was stepping back into the life she had left behind so long ago.

When Lily came downstairs for a cup of coffee, Morgan was nowhere to be seen. Thank God, she murmured to herself firmly, though it was hard to deny the flutter of disappointment she felt. What would he have said? she wondered, then snorted. She knew exactly what he would have said. Nothing. He would have merely gazed at her with one of his stern, formidable looks, then walked right past her without so much as a by-your-leave. And Lily had no interest in waiting around for that.

Morgan walked in the back door almost the instant Lily pushed out through the kitchen's swinging door.

"Jojo," he said with a nod.

"What do you want now?" Jojo demanded. "Oh, botheration," he whined at the sight of Morgan's mudspattered boots. "Not on my clean floor."

Morgan glanced down. "Jojo, you're starting to sound like an old woman."

The cook puffed up like a craggy-faced blowfish. "I ain't no old woman! I'm just trying to keep food in everyone's mouth and my kitchen clean to boot."

Morgan cocked a doubtful brow. "You spend more time doing anything but keeping food in everyone's mouth."

"Yeah, like cleaning up after you just about a thousand times this morning alone. I've never seen anyone go in and out of a house so many times. Dagnabit, the young'uns aren't as bad as you. So don't be telling me about work."

"You work awfully hard at becoming familiar with the back side of your eyelids, if you ask me." Mogan paused. "That or searching the house."

Jojo's hands tensed. "What are you talking about? I ain't snooping around nothin'."

When Morgan had walked the premises late last night, he was certain he had seen the cook in the attic room where Lily had once painted. Now, based on Jojo's guilty response, Morgan knew he had been right. "What are you looking for, Jojo?"

"I told you," he snapped. "I ain't lookin' for nothin'."

Morgan knew he'd get no answers, and least not this way, but he had put the man on notice. Enough for now. "Have you seen Miss Blakemore this morning?"

Jojo eyed Morgan. "Of course," he grumbled. "But she's taken herself back upstairs to primp up for that blasted party."

Morgan didn't like the sting of disappointment he felt at having missed her. He had been in and out of the house all morning, telling himself each time that he really *needed* to check the crumbling pillar or a gas sconce, when in truth he was hoping to see Lily.

He had spent a long, sleepless night with unsettling thoughts about her. Last night he had left the house stiff as a young schoolboy with wanting her. A bucket of cold water had helped his heated loins, but nothing had helped wash away the image of her from his mind.

He wanted to see her, to look into her eyes. He'd had the nagging feeling for weeks now that perhaps he was wrong about her. Though last night, when she had galloped up to the house in defiant glory, he had admitted that she obviously was the fallen woman whom all of New York City called Crimson Lily. But that was early in the night, before he had touched her intimately—and seen the look in her eyes.

Innocence.

Surprise.

As if she had never been touched before. Beyond which Morgan still *had not* seen hide nor hair of John Crandall, not even a mention that could lead him to believe she even knew the man. It was insane that he was pleased. But he was.

Today he was going to visit Raine Hawthorne's sister. Morgan hoped once and for all that he could put to rest the mystery of how Lily had been ruined. And standing there, he could no longer deny the effect she had on him. He wanted her, yes, but he realized then that more than anything he wanted her to be as innocent as she had seemed when he had held her last night.

The day progressed much the same as it started, and at three o'clock when Lily came down to set out for the Mayhews' party Morgan was nowhere to be seen. She had dressed in all the finery she had purchased for the party. She had been assured by the dressmaker and milliner her mother had used from years before that she was dressed properly for the occasion. She hadn't thought to ask the women when they had last made anyone a hat or gown.

"Oh, Lily!" Cassie breathed with enthusiasm, her tiny hands clasped to her chest. "You look ever so lovely!"

Lily twirled around, her eyes sparkling. "Do you think?"

"Oh, yes, yes."

Twirling to a halt, Lily stopped just in time to see Penelope roll her eyes. "You don't like it," Lily stated, her nose wrinkling with concern.

Penelope's eyes widened, then she shrugged indifferently. "It looks old." She hesitated. "And I don't know why you want to go to such a stupid party anyway."

"It won't be stupid," Lily breathed. "It will be wonderful. Tea and cucumber sandwiches. Lemon tarts and tiny iced cakes." And long-lost friends. Please, Lily pleaded silently, let her find friends.

Penelope eyed her for a moment, her lower lip protruding. "I don't care if you go or not." Then she hurried up the stairs.

"What's wrong with Penelope?" Lily asked.

Robert sat in a chair looking out the window and didn't answer. Cassie hesitated before saying, "Mr. Elliott said you're silly to want to go to this party."

Heat flashed through Lily's body.

"He said," Cassie continued apologetically, "that they didn't want you there."

Lily had to reach out to steady herself.

"I guess Penelope doesn't want you to get hurt," Cassie explained.

"I don't care!" came a not-too-distant shout.

Everyone turned to find Penelope at the top of the stairs looking defiant. "I don't care what you do!" Then she fled in a flounce of skirts and petticoats.

Lily took a deep breath. "Well, dear heart, Mr. Elliott is wrong." He had to be, she added silently.

Before she could lose her nerve, Lily picked up her reticule and slipped it on her wrist. Then she picked up the lace fan that had been her mother's. "Of course they want me there. They invited me."

Lily arrived at the Mayhews' home just a few minutes past three o'clock in the afternoon. The house was a massive structure with paved paths and wrought-iron fencing. Inside the foyer was a rotunda boasting a beautifully curved marble staircase.

Her heart pounded in her chest as she stepped into the magnificent foyer. A silk-stockinged servant took her invitation before another silent servant led her through a luxurious line of drawing rooms.

"Where are we going?" she asked.

"The garden room, madam."

In the distance, Lily heard voices. Women talking, laughing decorously. Just when she was led around a corner, Lily stopped, her heart lodging in her throat. Beneath an ornate archway, a group of women stood. She recognized a few of them, but not many.

The women kissed each other warmly before preceding her into the room. Lily couldn't seem to make her feet move. With the exception of Edith Mayhew, she hadn't seen any of these women in years. What if Morgan was right? she suddenly wondered. But if that were true, then why would they have invited her if she hadn't been wanted?

"Madam?"

Startled, Lily focused and found the liveried footman staring at her in confusion.

"Are you unwell?" he inquired.

Yes, she almost said. But she would not be a coward. She would not hide any longer. "No, I'm fine. Please proceed."

The buzz of voices ceased the minute her name was announced. Lily stood very still, her smile frozen on her face as she looked out at the sea of women who had turned to stare at her. Lily prayed that at any second they would smile, call out in welcome. But a moment passed, then another. The women didn't smile and they didn't call hello.

Instead, a hiss of voices shimmered across the room like a surging wave as the women of New York society began talking all at once.

"I can't believe it's her," Lily heard a woman say.

"I can't believe she would have the nerve to show her face."

"No decent woman would."

In that instant, with sinking certainty, Lily realized that Morgan had been right. She was a fool. Only a blind man wouldn't notice the angry brows, the pursed lips, the furious eyes that stared at her.

Lily nearly cried out, nearly turned on her perfectly proper heel and fled from the room. But she had been Crimson Lily for far too long.

She quelled every ounce of uncertainty and embarrassment. And just like last night in the parlor with Morgan, Lily became what they wanted. What they expected, slipping into the part she had been assigned ten years before.

"Edith!" she called out loudly to her hostess, with a deep throaty laugh. "Darling girl."

Edith Mayhew blushed painfully as the group of women

turned their startled gaze onto her as if turning on a traitor.

Lily's hand tightened on her fan, but her lips wore a radiant smile as she walked boldly forward into the room, her long stride provocatively sleek.

"Look at that dress," someone hissed.

"Leftovers from a charity offering?" another asked coyly. "She must have lost her long line of wealthy lovers."

Several women gasped and twittered nervously at the outrageous comment spoken in polite company. But appropriate or not at such a gathering, that didn't stop them.

"The woman's charms must have worn off," a woman added, satisfaction tingeing her words.

"Why is she here?"

"Surely she wasn't invited!"

Hearing the comment, Lily stopped in front of Edith Mayhew. "Dear girl, thank you so much for asking me to join you," she said loudly. "It has been so long since I have seen my dear, dear friends." Lily turned. "Like Winifred, here."

Winifred Headly sucked in her breath and looked as if she would swoon. Everyone knew that Winifred was self-righteous and demanding, quick to point fingers at anyone who stepped out of line. She was the head of the women's organization that strove to return decency and propriety to the sadly declining upper classes of New York society.

"My, my, my," a woman tsk-ed. "I never would have believed it of you, Winny."

Winifred shrieked. "I . . . I . . ." But she didn't bother to find a defense. She turned with a huff and flounced out through the arched doorway.

A handful of women followed suit. But the vast majority of New Yorkers stayed. Curiosity was piqued.

The party went from bad to worse, and the worse it got the more outrageous Lily became. She laughed and talked as if every woman there were her very best friend.

But finally, Lily couldn't take it anymore, her outrage

at her former friends beginning to subside, leaving despair in its place. Calling out an extravagant farewell, she strode from the room with the grace of a queen.

Walking with careful steps, she retraced her path through the long line of drawing rooms, then up the entryway steps and out the door. She didn't wait for a groom to hail her a cab. She walked down the drive and out to the street. A block had passed before it occurred to her that she couldn't walk the entire way. A hired hack had pulled off to the side. She scared the driver half to death when she knocked on the carriage. The man scrambled to his feet, pulled on his hat, and hastened to help her inside. Within seconds they pulled out onto Fifth Avenue.

Lily sank back into the cracked leather seat, but when they came to Fifty-ninth Street she instructed the groom to continue north. She didn't want the ride to end. She wanted to flee, return to Tarrytown. The empty house and loneliness were far easier to manage than this.

She wanted to be as far away from Manhattan as possible. The women hated her, Robert and Penelope hated her, Morgan hated her. Her throat tightened and her eyes burned.

Why did she care? she railed silently. Why after all these years had she given in to foolish hope?

They passed Central Park on the left, but Lily had no interest in turning. She wanted to continue on, up beyond the confines of Manhattan. She wanted to breathe. But most of all she hated what her life had become.

A mockery. And she had made it that way. Morgan had been right after all. A person controlled her destiny. A person caused the things that happened to her. Just as her antics at the tea only reaffirmed her position in society. She groaned in the small space. But somehow she couldn't seem to help herself.

Year after year it had been impossible to accept that she had been banished. She had hoped that New York would welcome her back. But whatever trace of hope there had

been before was now lying in ruins at her feet much as
the dreams of girlhood and innocence had lain in ruins at
her feet ten years before.

Lily wanted to scream, to rail at the injustice of the
world. For all the good it would do. She was Crimson Lily
then, she was Crimson Lily now, she would be Crimson
Lily forever.

How would she survive?

She pressed her eyes closed, trying to lose herself in the
smooth rattle and sway of the carriage, tried even harder
when the motion gave way to a great jostling as they left
the paved road. The houses were few and far between beyond the park, though the area was rapidly being devel-
oped. When she was a child, this far north had been
considered the hinterlands. But no longer was this true as
the horsecars and elevated trains began reaching these
northern limits.

But Lily didn't care about the development of the land.
She cared about very little just then. She only cared about
fleeing. To her house in upstate New York. Where she
didn't have to face the smirks and knowing looks of the
people she met.

Morgan arrived at the dilapidated tenement building where
Mary Hawthorne was said to reside. He entered the building, then took the stairs up to the second floor. As was his
way, Morgan hadn't notified the woman of his arrival. And
as he frequently did when he was ferreting out information,
he would wait to see her reaction before he determined
which of his stories he would use to explain who he was.

Mary Hawthorne answered the door within minutes of
his knock. She was a tall woman and must have been striking in her day. But what he noticed most of all was her
age. He judged her to be well into her sixties. He hadn't
given a thought to the woman's age. But for the first time
Morgan wondered how old Raine Hawthorne had been
when Lily had known him.

"Yes?" she demanded belligerently, opening the door a crack.

"Miss Hawthorne?"

"Yes?"

"I wondered if I might speak to you about your brother?"

Even through the barely opened door Morgan saw the woman's eyes flash first with surprise, then with what he would have sworn was an aching pain. "My brother is dead."

Morgan was surprised by her harshness. "Yes, ma'am, I realize that, but I was hoping I could talk to you about him . . . and a woman named Lily Blakemore."

The woman's flash of pain gave way to a sweeping bitterness. Morgan could see it. Feel it. And with the bitterness, she pulled open the door with force. "I heard she was back," she hissed, her tone accusing.

Morgan hesitated, trying to make sense of the situation. "Yes, she is."

Leaving the door open, Mary Hawthorne walked back into her tiny apartment and dropped herself into an overstuffed chair that had seen better days. She motioned Morgan to take a chair opposite her.

Closing the door behind him, Morgan followed. As soon as she started to speak he realized there would be no need to make up a story about who he was. In fact, he wondered if she would even bother to ask his name.

"So it's true. Lily Blakemore has returned." Mary shook her head with a hiss. "I can't believe she would show her face around here ever again." The woman's eyes narrowed. "You know, of course, that every penny of her money should be mine."

Only long years of experience held Morgan's surprise in check.

She nodded her head. "Yes, I took care of Raine after our mother deserted us as children. I even continued to help him after he was full-grown and struggling to make ends meet. And then he made his fortune. Money on top of money. It started small. But he invested wisely." Her bony fingers gripped the armrest. "He never would have made it though, if it hadn't been for me."

"Lily got her money from your brother?"

"Of course she did. Where else do you think she got it? From that fool spendthrift brother of hers? Have you seen that house of his? A mess, I tell you. She obviously never gave a penny of the money to Claude. Though for all it matters now. He's dead, too, just like my Raine."

Morgan tried to make sense of what he was hearing. Lily hadn't inherited her money from her family? She had gotten her money from Raine Hawthorne? His blood began to churn. What would a woman have to do to gain a man's fortune without marrying him?

The answer that came to mind made his jaw tighten. A confirmation of his greatest fear. Lily had given herself to another man.

But his anger gave way to greater confusion when Mary spoke again.

"I took care of everything for Raine while he painted. Night and day. I cooked his meals and washed his clothes. I even found him the rich people who paid him to paint their portraits."

His mind stilled. "Your brother was a painter?"

"The finest. His paintings started to sell, a rarity for a living artist, but he was good." The harshness of her features softened. "So very good." Her gaze found a single painting in the gloomy room.

Morgan was amazed he hadn't noticed the work when he first walked in. It was beautiful.

"He painted that the year before he died. For my birthday."

The painting was a landscape with a nondescript woman gazing off into the distance, or so it seemed until he looked closer and noticed that the woman was not nondescript at all. The woman was Mary Hawthorne, younger, happier. A beauty.

"Painting portraits earned Raine a decent living," she continued, "but not the kind of money he had when he died. Raine had a head for money. And he invested. I always told him he should have been a banker." She hesitated, her features growing angry again. "And the money should have been mine."

Morgan sat in his chair taking in all that she said. And as the woman spoke, all he had come to hope wasn't true was only confirmed. He hated that he cared. He hated that he had come to wish that indeed Lily wasn't ruined after all. He cursed himself for a fool.

Lily Blakemore was a woman who didn't know the first thing about morals or virtue. He had come to Blakemore House knowing that, he didn't need this woman here telling him that. But he had allowed Lily to turn his head. And foolishly he had hoped this woman would clear Lily's name.

Morgan was lost in his thoughts, barely hearing, until Mary banged her fist against a small oak table next to her chair. "Mine. It should have been mine. I shouldn't be living in a place like this. He promised me!"

Mary visibly tried to calm herself. Morgan wanted nothing more than to leave. He didn't want to hear any more. He no longer wanted to learn the specifics of what Lily had done. He knew enough.

"But no," she continued. "He fell for a girl half his age, a girl with no money but a fine old name. And you know how she got that money?"

Morgan didn't answer, couldn't speak over the terrible scream sounding in his head.

"She let him have her way with him. Like a common harlot." Her voice was low and venomous. "She mesmerized a man who had yet to have his head turned by a single other woman. Like a witch, I tell you, performing magic and casting spells. Mark my words, she spread her legs for my brother. Then she let him paint her. Naked as the day she was born.''

The air in the room seemed to disappear. The summer heat was unbearable. Anger and rage shifted through Morgan's body. *Painted her. Naked as the day she was born.* Lily was worse than he had feared.

Morgan had suspected that either Lily had lost her virginity or had painted something outrageous on her own. He had never guessed that she had allowed herself to be painted.

He thought of the infamous painting, *Madame X*. The woman had been ostracized for allowing Sargent to paint her with merely one thin strap of her gown falling down her arm. Madame X had been dressed. And based on what Mary Hawthorne said, Lily had been nude.

For all the world to see.

Shamelessly.

''Where is the painting now?'' he asked, the words sticking in his throat.

''I sold it to Lily's brother years ago.''

Morgan's head cocked in surprise.

Mary smiled crudely. ''Oh, yes. Claude Blakemore wanted that painting badly. Which was fine by me. I certainly didn't want it. And I made a pretty penny on that sale, let me tell you.'' She laughed, the sound harsh. ''But I made even more on an old packet of undoubtedly worthless sketches that I sold him as well. The fool.''

Lily didn't return to Blakemore House until nearly seven o'clock, a great deal later than even the worst of hangers-on would have stayed at an afternoon tea.

The children were waiting on the front steps when the hired hack pulled up. Marky and Jojo waited by the door.

''How was it, missy?'' Jojo called out as she came up the steps.

Lily's step faltered, and for the first time she noticed

everyone was waiting for her. She drew a deep breath. "It was fine. Just fine. Lovely, really."

They studied her curiously. "Are you sure?"

"Of course I'm sure."

Once inside, Lily dashed off a quick if shaky note, handed it to Marky, then hurried upstairs, fighting each step of the way to hold back her tears.

"What does the note say?" Jojo asked.

"None of your blamed business," Marky said with a newly practiced air of superiority, before he hurried out to the hired hack that still stood in the drive.

After a few words were exchanged, Marky sent the grumbling driver off with the note and a coin.

"What's going on?" Cassie asked Marky.

"Nothing, Miz' Blakemore, nothing at all."

Marky returned indoors, leaving the children to their own devices.

"I don't think that whatever's going on is nothing at all," Cassie said with a sigh as she lowered herself back onto the step next to Penelope. "Maybe we should go upstairs and ask Lily what's wrong."

"Go ahead," Penelope replied, plopping her chin in her upturned palms. "But she won't tell you. Grown-ups never tell you what is wrong when something is wrong."

Morgan banged out Mary Hawthorne's front door, leaped into the closest hansom cab and instructed the driver to deliver him to Blakemore House. "And fast, man."

Morgan could hardly contain his raging thoughts. Despite all he had learned, he didn't want to believe the things that Mary Hawthorne had told him. But more than anything else he wanted to see Lily, to see her face. And he knew that he had to ask her if it was true. Once and for all he had to ask Lily to explain, to tell him the truth. No more searching out information behind her back. No more speculation. He wanted the truth. From Lily Blakemore's lips.

The two-wheeled carriage skittered along Sixth Avenue at breakneck speed, but still it was hardly fast enough for Morgan. His heart raced and his palms were wet. He banged on the ceiling when they reached Fifty-eighth Street. After paying the driver, he ran down the street to the back path.

Morgan didn't stop at his cottage to change from his dress clothes. He raced up the flagstone path and up the back porch steps where he had first seen Lily, not bothering to go down through the kitchen. He didn't allow himself to think about the blazing white wall he had repainted only weeks before. He had to see Lily. He had to see her face, touch her.

Have her tell him all he had learned wasn't true.

But his racing steps came to an ominous halt when the front door swung open just as Morgan entered through the back. His thoughts reeled, his heart slamming to a halt as abruptly as his footsteps. He could hardly make sense of what he saw.

John Crandall stood in the high-ceilinged foyer of Blakemore House.

Morgan slammed himself against the wall, out of sight of the front door. His head spun, his thoughts careening out of control.

Crandall had arrived.

Morgan's head pounded, blood surging to his temples. It was all he could do to hold himself still instead of leaping forward and grabbing Crandall by his suit lapels, then pounding him into the floor.

But he didn't. He couldn't. At least not yet.

His churning thoughts were diverted when the sound of Lily's voice filtered through the chaos in his mind.

"John," she cried, hurrying down the stairs, "you came!"

"What's wrong, Lily?"

She threw herself into John's arms, and if Morgan had ever hoped that Lily had nothing to do with John Crandall, his hopes were dashed against the sheer cliff of their embrace.

Morgan's heartache and denial, chaos and rage, came together and solidified, melding into something far greater than anything he had ever felt before.

On silent feet, Morgan turned away and slipped out the back door, blinded by a cold, icy rage.

Eleven

Morgan woke late, exhausted and disoriented. He had been up most of the night. His mind circling. Raging. And still he couldn't believe it.

Lily. Posing nude for a wealthy man.

Why had she done it?

To gain the man's money? Or because she had loved him?

Morgan didn't like either answer. He didn't like to think that Lily would sell her body. But the thought of Lily having loved the man, posing to show her feelings, brought a flash of violence streaking down his spine.

And then Crandall had arrived. The very event Morgan had come to this house to witness. The man he wanted to see. Finally he could start making progress on this case. He should have felt relieved. But he only felt fury. Fury and rage for having allowed himself to hope. To hope that Lily Blakemore was an innocent—had come to believe that it was possible. She had worked her wiles on him, taking him in, making him believe that she was something other than what he had learned.

Morgan scoffed at his own stupidity.

Throwing back the sheet, Morgan pushed up from the small bed, his long hard musculature rippling as he moved. With a minimum of ceremony, he shaved and washed, then pulled on work clothes before heading up to the house. Even though he was late getting started today, he imagined Lily would still be abed. Thankfully. If there was one person he didn't want to see this morning it was Lily Blakemore. He had a great deal of work to do, none of which involved the house. The place wasn't finished by a long shot. But that wasn't his concern—not any longer. It was time to concentrate on Crandall. It was time to finish what he had come here to do.

But as soon as Morgan stepped through the kitchen doorway, the first person he saw was Lily.

He stood there, the door open, his hand on the knob. Despite everything, he was struck by her fragile beauty. His simmering rage merged with the same intensity of feeling that never failed to make his heart reel. Even now.

Oh, Lily, how could you have done such a thing? The thought sliced through his mind before he could stop it. But thoughts of her beauty and unanswerable questions gave way to a sudden certainty that something was wrong.

It took a confused second for Morgan to make sense of the situation. Lily sat at the table, Robert across from her. Penelope and Cassie were nowhere to be seen. Marky and Jojo stood behind Lily's chair. But no one said a word. There was only quiet. In a house that was so frequently full of noise, the quiet was unsettling.

Marky and Jojo looked up at Morgan, their eyes imploring him, though to what he had no idea.

Just when Morgan opened his mouth to speak, to ask what was going on, Lily looked up from the table and met his gaze.

For a second Morgan couldn't breathe. She looked at him, her eyes wide, vulnerable, much as they had looked the first night he found her.

Clearly something was very wrong.

"Good morning," she said, her voice barely a whisper. "I think I'll go upstairs," she added, standing up from her place at the table.

Morgan still hadn't moved when the door swung shut behind Lily. He was furious that after everything he had learned, he still wanted to follow her. He hated that he wanted to wrap her in his arms and wipe the anguish from her blue eyes.

Damn it, he cursed silently. She was Crimson Lily. A fallen woman. The mistress of a man he hated with every fiber of his being. How many times did he have to remind himself of that fact?

With hands clenched, he came farther into the kitchen. "What happened?" he demanded.

No one spoke, not Jojo who normally could not keep his mouth shut, not even Robert who generally loved to enlighten Morgan on Lily's latest folly. At length, it was Marky who stepped forward. He reached out and retrieved a newspaper from Lily's place at the table that Morgan had failed to notice.

"This is what happened," Marky replied, offering up the copy of *The New York Times*.

Morgan glanced from Marky to Robert before he grabbed the newspaper, holding it so tightly that the pages nearly ripped apart. He read once, then twice. Front page. Headline.

CRIMSON LILY PAINTS TOWN RED

Morgan couldn't move, couldn't find enough air in the room to force himself to breathe. A maelstrom of emotions swirled through his mind.

All at once Marky and Jojo were talking, sound all around, echoing in Morgan's head like a cacophony of confusion.

What did he feel?

Focusing, he forced himself to read the article that followed the blazing headline.

For those of you who know, or knew of, Lily Blakemore, she has returned. Brazen and bold, she is doing and saying what she pleases, wearing clothes that are a cross between blatant bad taste and a circus performer's costume. Either way, her attire makes a mockery of decorum.

Is that what attracts men to this woman, men like John Crandall? Lily Blakemore's escapades are well known and certainly well remembered. Given that, one is forced to wonder why a man like John Crandall would associate with the woman. One is forced to question the morals of a man who reportedly is about to announce his candidacy for governor of New York this week.

Will you run, Mr. Crandall? And if so, what kind of precedent do you set by consorting with a woman known to all of New York City as Crimson Lily?

The article continued on, but Morgan read no further. The room closed in around him. He looked toward the door through which Lily had fled—hurting, though she tried with every ounce of her being to hide her pain.

Morgan glanced back at the newspaper. There didn't seem to be anything there that wasn't true, in fact, it seemed to be an image of Lily that she herself appeared to nurture with a great deal of determination. Lily seemed to have gone to great lengths to let everyone know that Crimson Lily had returned.

Riding through the streets as though the devil were on her heels.

Playing poker.

Tossing back liquor like a sailor home on leave.

But no amount of reasoning could wipe the image of her pain from Morgan's mind.

''I can't believe those slimy vermin would write such

lies,'' Marky said, breaking into Morgan's thoughts.

"They're not lies," Robert hissed. "It's the truth. Lily is a disgrace."

The words were spoken bitterly. Morgan recognized the words as something he himself could have said. Then why did he hate to hear it?

"Now, you listen here, young feller." Jojo's voice hissed through the room in time with his angry, uneven footsteps as he jerked his wiry body over to Robert. "Miss Lily is not a disgrace. It's the likes of society la-di-das that are afraid of anything or anyone with a little life in them! So they cut people like your auntie to shreds, wounding them to the core. Anyone a tad different scares them silly."

After his angry outburst, Jojo whirled away, his face contorting. Robert looked suddenly more like the twelve-year-old boy he was. In that second, Morgan realized with gut-wrenching insight that the children had been set adrift in a tumultuous sea with a single guiding hand to show them the way, and that hand belonged to Lily. In truth, Robert wanted to be cared for, he didn't want to have to do the caring.

How had he missed it? Morgan wondered. Robert had wanted the rumors to be false, because Lily was all he and his sisters had left. Their only hope. They hadn't been trying to run her off. They had wanted her to prove them wrong.

Just as Morgan had wanted her to prove him wrong.

But her actions over the last several weeks had done nothing more than lend credence to the rumors. Crimson Lily had proven that she deserved the name.

Then why did he feel so badly?

Without a thought for what he was doing, Morgan crossed the room and pushed through the swinging door. He took the stairs from the basement kitchen three at a time intent on finding her. But he didn't have to go far.

Lily stood very still outside the parlor, her body tense.

When he came up behind her, though he stood no more than scant inches from her, he knew that she hadn't heard him. He opened his mouth to speak. He wanted her to talk. He wanted to hear her voice. Once and for all he wanted her to explain.

But the words froze in his throat when he heard voices coming from the parlor.

"Ooooh, Penny, dear," Morgan heard Penelope say, "I've burned the pan. Hark, what should I do? I know, I'll just throw it away."

"Stop it, Penelope! It's not nice," Cassie responded, her voice a cross between outrage and despair.

Penelope only laughed. "Stop? Good God, why?" she demanded in a dramatic voice. "I'm a frivolous creature if ever there was one," she added, sashaying into Morgan's view, walking and using hand gestures that were a remarkable imitation of Lily. But it wasn't a kind imitation. Penelope was mocking her aunt. Cruelly. Hatefully. And Lily stood frozen in the hallway, her breath caught in her chest much as Morgan's words had stuck in his throat.

But it only took a second to shake it off. He'd had enough. "Penelope!"

His voice sliced through the room and Penelope whirled around, her long hair swinging out around her head, her feather boa swirling in the air. Guilt lined her features when she turned. But when she saw Lily the guilt melted into something else. Something aching and devastated. Something very similar to the look that etched Lily's own features.

"Penelope, apologize to your aunt."

Penelope looked at Morgan, her lips beginning to tremble.

"No, no," Lily said very softly. "Penelope is right. I *am* a frivolous creature who snaps chairs in two and throws pans away instead of washing them."

Lily turned then and started for the stairs. But a solid bang on the front door halted her progress.

She stared at the entrance as if not understanding what she was supposed to do. Morgan came forward and answered the door.

"A message for Miss Blakemore."

Morgan took the envelope from the messenger and handed it to Lily. She took the thick vellum and read. Her breath came out in a sharp puff of air before she dropped the letter on the entry table and hurried up the stairs.

The message lay on the table unfolded, opened for anyone to see. Was it long years of clandestine work that made Morgan pick it up, or his obsessive desire to know everything about Lily Blakemore? Morgan wasn't about to examine his motives. He picked up the missive.

> Lily,
>   Forgive me, but I must leave town again. Just until things blow over. Try to understand.
>
>   John

The bastard.

Morgan felt a surge of anger sizzle down his spine. He tossed the note on the table, before taking the stairs to the attic.

Where he knew he would find her.

The door stood open, morning light spilling out into the darkened hallway. There was never a thought that he should turn back. He entered the high-ceilinged room she had once used to paint in, and found her staring out the window at a world that wanted little to do with her.

At the sound of his footsteps, she turned to look at him. A pain he did not understand turned like a knife in his chest. The smile that she had forced earlier was gone. Her eyes were wide, unfocused, just as they had been that night they had scrubbed the paint off the wall. Only this time there was no simple word to wipe clean. A scrub brush and white paint couldn't erase the pain and humiliation he saw in her eyes.

"He swore he loved me."

Her words rang softly in the room, echoing in the nearly empty space. He hated the sliver of jealousy that sliced through his soul.

"He swore he cared for me."

Morgan waited, his body tense.

"He said he would always be there for me."

"Who?" he asked when he could wait no longer, assuming she meant John Crandall. But Morgan wanted, needed, to hear the words from her lips.

Lily blinked, focusing on him, then after a long moment she looked away without answering. She walked to the massive armoire, running her fingers along the contours. But she didn't open it this time. She continued on, her fingers trailing along the walls and window casings.

"Lily, who swore he loved you?" Morgan hated the gnawing frustration that laced his words.

"Love me? What are you talking about?"

"You just said that someone swore he loved you."

"Oh, that," she said, her steps faltering. "It's nothing."

"Damn it, Lily. Don't do this—" He realized with a start that he nearly finished the sentence with "to me." *Don't do this to me.* He curbed his irrational feelings with an ironclad self-control. "Don't do this to yourself. Who cares what the paper says?" He realized with stunning certainty that he meant his words. He realized in that moment that she shouldn't care, no one should care what she had done.

He had come here this morning, fury dogging his every step. But standing there in the morning light, his icy rage chipped away in the face of her desolation.

He thought of the words his father had once said to him—words he had never believed. But somehow, for this woman, they seemed true. "Lily, everyone makes mistakes."

His intent was to offer comfort. But he would have sworn she flinched as if he had struck her. And when she looked at him, when she raised her chin and met his gaze, her blue eyes glistening with tears, he saw an unaccountable defeat.

All the times he had felt the need to protect her came crashing in on him. He wanted to pull her close. But just as he stepped up to the window next to her she spoke.

"What was your mistake, Morgan Elliott?"

She could have asked him many things about himself that he would have been prepared for. She could have asked him what he meant by saying everyone made mistakes? Did he really think his words were true? But not this.

"What are you talking about?" he asked.

Lily looked at Morgan, her head tilting quizzically. "I've seen it in your eyes. A look I recognize. You've made a mistake in your life, too."

Had she really seen? he wondered, blood rushing through his veins. But he knew in that instant that she *had* seen. Suddenly it all made sense. Morgan finally understood why he couldn't forget her, why he found himself repairing her walls instead of pursuing Crandall as he had come here to do.

It wasn't simply that he wanted her physically as he had told himself. It was that she understood him, had since the night they met. An affinity had formed the minute she turned to face him, red paint staining her palms. She was someone who had looked into his eyes, had seen the darkness in his soul, and hadn't turned away.

Guilt seared him. Nearly felling him. How could he have stayed in her house after that first night? How could he have used her to get at his enemy?

"It was your childhood friend Jenny, wasn't it?" she asked softly.

Morgan closed his eyes.

"Jenny was your mistake."

"Yes." One word, strangled, tightened in his throat. Tightened in his chest.

He turned to look out the window. He could see Lily's reflection as she studied him, but then he looked out into the streets and beyond. He felt Lily turn to the window, looking out as he did. Two souls staring out at forever, desolation the only view.

"We were seventeen," he began to explain as he had explained to no one else in his life. "She came to me for help."

He sighed. "She found me in my favorite spot, high above the Mississippi River."

"You're from the South?"

A slow, troubled smile broke out across Morgan's lips. "Yes, ma'am," he said, his voice thick with a southern accent that had faded away after years of living in the north. "Born and raised."

"I never would have guessed."

"What?" One slash of dark brow quirked on his forehead. "I don't remind you of the perfect southern gentleman?"

Lily studied him for a moment, a smile beginning to pull at her lips. "Actually, it's not so hard to imagine you sipping a mint julep."

"Bourbon, my dear, straight," he drawled. "A southern gentleman always drinks bourbon." His smile disappeared. "And they never fall short. They help the people they love when they're in need."

Morgan grew silent, remembering that day.

"What are you saying, Morgan? How did you fall short?"

"I don't know," he stated vehemently, then quieted. "I don't know. Jenny and I talked, for hours it seemed. About her parents, about mine. And then she started talking about Trey."

"Who's Trey?"

"A friend." Or was he? God, she had talked about Trey. Morgan felt the same burning anger now that he had then. Jenny talking about Trey. Telling him about Trey.

"Where is Jenny now?"

Sound roared in Morgan's ears, the sound of her scream. "She's dead."

Then silence.

At length Lily spoke, touching his arm. "I'm sorry, Morgan."

His pain burst then, the words flowing over. "I was angry. So angry. I started walking, pacing, trying to make sense of everything she told me." Disbelief raging through his mind. "I didn't realize she had walked to the edge of the cliff, but when I turned around she was there." Morgan ran his fingers through his hair.

"What happened?" she asked breathlessly.

"I don't know," he groaned. "I don't know what happened." His breath hissed in through his teeth. "Just suddenly Jenny was falling."

"No!"

"She reached out to me, her hand extended. God, I started running. But I had walked too far away." Morgan shook his head wearily, a groan of despair working its way to the surface. "If only I hadn't gotten angry and walked away. She asked for my help but my anger got in the way." He drew a deep breath. "Years earlier I promised to keep her safe." And it was that simple promise that haunted him as nothing else ever had.

Leaning back against the wall, he willed Jenny's face into his mind. But somehow he only saw Lily. Lily on the back porch. Lily at the kitchen table, the damning newspaper article before her.

Lily broken beyond repair.

How to reconcile all the conflicting emotions he felt for this woman?

He didn't know. Anger seared through his mind as yet again he felt a need to try.

Lily was diverting him from his path.

He might have come to this house because of Crandall,

but the reason he was still there had nothing to do with the man. He was there because of Lily.

And that was wrong.

He was in her home under false pretenses. His role was not that of her protector. And even if it were, he couldn't protect her from himself.

An honorable man would leave.

The realization brought a stark emptiness snaking through his soul.

But standing there, wanting to touch her with an intensity that left his body swollen with need, he told himself he would leave. As he should. First thing tomorrow morning.

Twelve

As he had vowed, the next morning Morgan set out for the house to announce his departure. The few belongings he had brought with him were shoved into his small case, waiting on his bed.

Though it was nearly noon when Morgan entered the kitchen, the children were huddled together as if conferring, unfried bacon and unscrambled eggs sitting on the table before them.

"What's going on here?" Morgan asked.

Cassie turned. "We're thinking about breakfast."

"It's almost noon." He glanced around the kitchen. "Where's Jojo?"

"He's sick."

"He's hungover," Robert clarified from his place at the head of the table.

"Hung over what?" Cassie asked with wide eyes.

Penelope snorted.

Morgan shook his head. "Where's Lily?"

The children hesitated for a moment.

"She's upstairs," Cassie said finally with a heavy sigh.

"Being strange," Penelope added.

Morgan forcefully tamped down the concern that flared to life in his chest. Lily was none of his business, besides which he was leaving. But still he found himself needing to know. "What do you mean she's being strange?"

Penelope shrugged her shoulders. "She's just all quiet."

"Walking around the house looking at everything," Robert scoffed.

Cassie's full lower lip quivered. "I found her standing there, just staring. At nothing. She didn't hear me. So I left and came down here. Oh, Mr. Elliott. Something is terribly wrong with Lily."

Without warning, a sudden pounding reverberated through the house.

"Oh, no," Penelope groaned. "She's got that hammer again."

Morgan pulled a handful of coins from his pocket and palmed them down in front of Robert. "Take your sisters to get some lunch." Then he flew out of the kitchen.

He found Lily upstairs kneeling in the hallway, taking a hammer to the same bit of carpet she had sworn had tripped her weeks before.

"Lily."

No response.

"Lily!"

Lily jerked back. "Good Lord, you don't have to yell."

"What are you doing?"

"I tripped again." The words were spoken softly, as if she didn't want to speak too loudly. Then she ran her hand over the carpet, before taking up the hammer again.

"Lily," he demanded, reaching down, pulling the hammer away from her. Tossing it aside, he dropped to his knees beside her. "Tell me what's wrong?"

She stared at him, her blue eyes troubled. God, how he wished they had met under different circumstances.

The thought stunned him.

He was disturbed as much by the thought as he was by

the fact that he had never been one to hope for things that couldn't be. Until Lily. Again and again.

He had scoffed at people who beat themselves against a wall of desire for something that they would never have. And he couldn't have Lily. Ever. Even if her past didn't exist, things had gone too far to ever be set right.

"This house is a mess," she said forcefully, her chin rising.

The vulnerable waif was gone, replaced by a Lily who was closed and distant. Guarded.

"This house?" Morgan asked, his thoughts still tangled in the sudden change in her. "What are you talking about?"

"Just that. This house is a shambles, and it's time I set this place to rights."

She pushed up from the floor and started down the hallway. He heard the soft tread of her heels on the carpeted stairway when he finally forced his mind to work.

With a few bold strides he caught up to her, passed her on the stairs, then turned back, halting her progress. His dark hair had fallen over his forehead, and with agitated fingers he raked the strands back. "How is it that you are just now noticing the shambles? What is really happening here, Lily? What is really bothering you?"

"That's none of your business, Mr. Elliott. Now if you'll get out of my way, I have a house to see to."

As the day wore on Morgan knew Cassie was worried about Lily. If Morgan hadn't known better, he would have sworn that Penelope began to worry as well. Only Robert stood back and retained the crossed-armed disgust that he'd had since Lily's arrival.

Regardless, Lily didn't appear to notice. She existed in some distant place in her mind. She rarely spoke, never left the house, simply walked from room to room, studying a wall here, sitting in a chair there.

Later that day Morgan found Lily in the parlor.

"This room needs work," she said, studying the ripped wallpaper on the side wall.

"Work?" he asked.

"Everything is so dark and dreary. Hmmm." Her brow furrowed uncertainly. "But maybe not." She looked at Morgan. "What do you think?"

He opened his mouth to answer, but she cut him off. "Never mind."

She turned to go, but without thinking, Morgan reached out and gently took her arm. He could tell that he startled her and her breath caught. It was foolish that he was pleased he had managed to break through the distance she had erected between them like a barrier wall to keep her safe. Her suddenly stormy eyes glanced from his hand on her arm to his questioning gaze. But she offered no answers.

"Let go of me, Mr. Elliott," she said, her voice small and trembling.

"I just want to know if . . . everything is all right." he asked again, not knowing what else to say.

He felt her tense.

"You keep asking me that. I'm fine, Mr. Elliott." She tried to pull her arm free with little success. "I'm perfectly fine."

"Then why have you spent all day inside walking from room to room?"

"As I told you. The house is a shambles. And I'm going to return it to its days of glory." She glanced down at her arm. "Now if you will let go of me," she said with haughty disdain, "I have a great deal of work to do."

Morgan didn't leave Blakemore House as planned. He told himself he would leave the following day. Then it was the next after that. But it was irresponsible to leave the house when Jojo and Marky were still lying abed and Lily was walking aimlessly through the house. He couldn't leave the children to their own devices, or so he told himself when yet another day went by and still he hadn't left.

As it turned out, Jojo and Marky weren't hungover or sick. They were gone. Packed up and departed without so much as a word of notice.

When Lily heard the news, she said nothing more than that she wasn't surprised, then continued her aimless journey about the house.

It was the same for days. The house was eerily quiet. Callers stopped calling. Even the hopelessly enamored dandies who had swarmed around Lily failed to visit after the damning article had run.

Morgan should have been pleased when the callers stopped calling. Hadn't he wished for that very situation? But somehow he hated the quiet far worse than the revolving door. He hated the way Lily drifted about the house, never venturing outside.

Lily Blakemore's strength had deserted her, leaving the vulnerable waif permanently in her place. As much as Morgan disliked the careening madcap, or so he told himself, he hated even more to see this vulnerable woman.

It was late Saturday afternoon when he walked into the quiet house. Morgan knew that Robert, Penelope, and Cassie had gone to Central Park. With a shake of his head Morgan wondered how long the children could drift along unattended. Though Robert was older than his years, every child needed guidance. A parent to show them the way.

But Morgan pushed that from his mind, just as he had pushed Crandall from his mind these last few days. For now he could only focus on Lily and his undeniable need to make things right.

Before he could take more than a handful of steps the silence was interrupted by a bang, followed immediately by a yelp of pain.

"Good God," he muttered. "What's happened now?"

He found her in the hallway, cradling her fingers. Kneeling beside her, he took her hand despite her resistance. He cradled her palm, hers so small in his, his heart pounding.

And when he looked up there were tears in her eyes.

He reached out to brush a tear away, but she jerked away. She grabbed for the hammer, but he held it away.

"Let me finish here," he said.

"No. I'll do it." She looked at him. "I told you before to leave me alone."

"Damn it, Lily. Why won't you let me help you?"

Her eyes grew desperate. "Help me?"

With those words and the look in her eyes, Morgan knew she was no longer talking about hammers or nails.

"What are you going to do?" she whispered. "Turn back time? Keep my parents from going out on that boat, point out that the weather was bad, that they'd had too much to drink?"

Her tears spilled over. The picture he had held in his mind of what her past had been was fixed. All that he had learned about Lily in the weeks he had been at Blakemore House had done nothing more than confirm his beliefs. But since the article had appeared, that picture was rapidly changing. The things Lily had said, first about her brother and how she didn't know what love was, now this about her parents, didn't mix with his vision of what this family had been.

Lily, the pampered daughter. Spoiled and frivolous. Loving parents who doted on their children. And from the articles Morgan had read, it was clear that Lily and Claude had been seen everywhere together. By Lily's own admission the two of them had been inseparable, at least for many years. Clearly Claude Blakemore had been devoted to his sister.

But if their relationship had been so close, how could Lily have wondered about her brother's love for her? How could she wonder what love was?

And her parents. Sailing in bad weather? Leaving their two children to their own devices since birth? Morgan remembered Lily's story about her brother and her going out on their own to buy Claude a hat. And what kind of parent would allow their young daughter to attend a ball dressed as a man in the first place? A parent who didn't know. A parent who left their children to their own devices.

Morgan had the sudden startling insight that if this was true, it was no wonder that Lily didn't offer the children guidance. She didn't know how.

The pieces of the puzzle he had put together, seemingly with such skill, fell apart as if someone had run their arm across the table, sweeping the pieces to the floor in an unrecognizable mess.

"Lily," he whispered, reaching out to her.

But she drew back. "Are you going to give me back ten wasted years? Are you going to make New York accept me?"

He stared at her, uncertain what to say.

"No, Morgan. You can't. I can't."

"If you wanted that, you should have fought all those years ago. Fought to make them understand you—to make them forgive you if you wanted it so badly."

Her laughter held no mirth. "Forgive me? Is that what you think I should be asking for? Did it ever occur to you that it's New York that should ask for my forgiveness?"

Of course not, and he nearly said it out loud. *She* had posed nude, not the rest of New York. But the look in her eye squelched the words. "You should have fought to stay here," he said instead. "Fought instead of running away."

"How?"

"With Claude's help. Whether you're willing to admit it or not, everyone could see that he loved you."

"*Everyone* could see?" The words were stricken. "Then everyone was wrong."

"How can you say that? He obviously tried to help you."

"How?" she demanded.

"The painting."

Lily sucked in her breath, her thoughts colliding in her mind. *The painting.* Morgan knew about the painting.

She had only seen it once, ten years earlier. There were times even when she had an eerie sensation that she had imagined it all, that the painting didn't really exist. But with Morgan's simple words, ten years faded away, and she couldn't deny her greatest shame.

"You know about the painting?" she asked, the words strangled.

"Yes, Lily. I know."

It had been bad enough that he had known she was called Crimson Lily. But to learn that he knew more than that—to learn that he knew *why* she was called the horrid name was unbearable.

If she had ever doubted that he thought her the lowest of women, she need not doubt again. He thought her the lowest kind of woman—a ruined woman.

"I also know," he continued, "that Claude bought it."

The change in her was quick and sudden. Lily reached out and grasped the doorjamb to steady herself. "Claude bought the painting?"

"If you hadn't left you would have known. You see, he did love you, Lily."

Lily turned sharply. "You're wrong. He didn't love me. He didn't love me!" she railed into the quiet room.

Morgan watched her, watched emotion play havoc on her face. She grew silent, and she closed her eyes. And just when Morgan thought she would say nothing else, she spoke.

"After the painting was revealed he screamed and cursed, told me he never wanted to see me again." She looked back at Morgan. "You're wrong about Claude," she repeated. "I didn't flee, I wasn't trying to hide. I didn't want to leave, I was desperate to stay. But my brother sent me away."

Morgan had expected her to rail about some perceived injustice done by her brother. He hadn't expected this. Why would he buy the painting if not to protect her? A nude portrait of his sister. Morgan didn't like the answer that began to form in his mind.

"He wouldn't even let me come home when Abigail, his wife, died—not even for the funeral. Not to help, not to see the children. As if I would somehow taint them."

Her tears came with renewed force, as if this admission pained her more than any other. And this time when he reached out to pull her close, she let him. She came into his arms, so tiny and delicate, her head pressed against his heart. Her tears soaked through to his skin as he stroked her hair, murmuring words that even he didn't understand.

Morgan felt again the fierce need to protect her, blocking all else out of the way. He had fought the need for so long. But how could he not? John Crandall, the article, the painting? All these things had blocked the way. But now they were gone, or at least pushed to the side as he rocked her gently in his arms.

They sat together on the floor in the hallway, sun streaming in from the bedroom. How was it possible that with this woman in his arms, he had never felt so right? Because she understood him as he had thought before?

He remembered the night he had painted the wall, the night that he had thought about a bit of silence in the world of thunder. He realized that he had achieved the silence back then when they had kneeled together in the moonlight. And he had achieved it again, here in this dim hallway with the woman who all of New York knew as Crimson Lily in his arms.

He held her close, holding her with an intense fierceness. His lips found her hair. He kissed the silken strands, trying to comfort her. He kissed her forehead, the softness of her skin searing his mind. Then her temple and cheek, slowly, gently, as her tears trailed off.

Crimson Lily was gone, only Lily was left. His Lily, he thought unexpectedly. His Lily who had seers in her house and threw out perfectly good cookware.

He kissed her, his lips touching hers, and she stiffened.

"Lily," he breathed against her. "Let me kiss you."

This time when he caressed her lips with his tongue she opened to him and he captured her sigh. His groan sounded deep in his chest. He slipped his tongue into her mouth, not deeply, not thrusting. Gently. Inviting her to taste him.

"Yes," he murmured when she hesitantly flicked his tongue, his body hardening.

Careful not to scare her, he gently sucked her tongue. He felt her body tense with feeling, but at the same time melt against him. His hands ran down her back, pressing her body to his.

Their kiss was a gentle seeking. A discovery. He nipped her lower lip, biting and tasting. He cupped her face in his hands, tilting her chin until he could taste her more fully, more boldly.

He kissed her deeply then, their tongues entwining. When his long, strong fingers found her tresses, they tumbled free from their moorings.

She pushed away from him and her hand flew to her head. "No," she whispered heatedly, red staining her cheeks.

"You have such beautiful hair," he murmured, pulling her back.

Her hand clenched on his chest. "Hair that I don't keep covered like a lady," she said, pounding with each word for emphasis.

"Shhh, don't. Don't do this to yourself."

"Why not? Everyone else does."

"Not everyone." He sighed. "Not anymore."

And it was true. Everything had changed for him. And while Crandall was not behind bars, Morgan knew that if he ever gained the information to achieve his goal—no, not *if*, rather, *when*—that information would not come from something he had learned through Lily. He had wronged her enough already by being in her house under false pretenses.

Morgan told himself yet again to leave. But as he held her in his arms, he wasn't certain that he could.

But where did that leave them? How could he continue to live a lie? He couldn't. But how could he tell her that he wasn't who he had said? That he wasn't poor. That he wasn't a repairman. That he was wealthy, probably wealthier even than she.

He didn't have the answers, not yet. He only had Lily held close to his heart.

And for now he could do nothing else.

"What are you thinking about?" she asked.

"I'm thinking about forgetting," he said, surprising himself with his candor.

She pushed back to look at him. "What are you trying to forget? To forget Jenny?"

If it were only that simple. "I don't know." He ran his fingertips down her arm, mesmerized. "I've already forgotten."

"That's the easy answer."

His smile curved on the hard planes of his face. "Yes, it is. But we are all trying to forget something." His eyes met hers. "Just like you are."

He saw that she recognized the truth of his words.

"But unlike you," she said, "everyone already knows what I don't want to remember, and takes great pleasure in reminding me."

Her words weren't bitter, just resigned.

His heart twisted another turn. And he forgot just a little more.

He kissed her again. She started to resist, but he murmured against her lips, gentling her. "Yes, love. Let me."

When he pulled back slightly, her eyes had fluttered closed. He took in her body, then without a word, he brushed his fingers along the skin at her throat before they trailed down, over her collarbone, slowly, down farther, grazing the fullness of one breast.

Lily sucked in her breath and her eyes flew open. Morgan kissed them closed, a delicate whisper against her skin. His fingers lingered at her nipple, circling slowly over the cotton of her gown, until he could feel the bud rise with desire.

"Sweet, sweet Lily," he murmured.

"I shouldn't be here," she said, her voice hoarse.

"I want you here." The backs of his fingers crossed over to her other breast. "God, I want you here," he whispered, his fingers circling.

Her head fell back and he kissed her neck.

"Morgan," she breathed, the sound like music to his ears.

He pulled her into his lap, still facing him.

"Morgan!" she said.

"Shhh, princess."

"The children!"

"They've gone to the park." Thank God, he thought. He wanted Lily. His body pulsed with desire, his loins demanding release. "They won't be back for hours."

She moaned when he lifted her skirt, pulling her closer until she straddled his thigh, her knees pressing into the soft rug. He could feel her wetness, could feel that she wanted him, too. If possible, his loins tightened even more and he groaned.

He pulled her down to him, his back braced against the wall. Wanting her. Needing her. Relishing her passion.

Kissing her, he deftly undid the tiny buttons down the front of her chemisette. With her eyes still closed, she bit her lower lip. Morgan flicked his tongue over her mouth, coaxing until she offered her touch.

She held on to his shoulders as he cupped her hips, his fingers gently caressing. He brought one hand around and touched her intimately and she tensed, her breath locking in her chest.

"It's all right, Lily," he whispered, his voice hoarse with desire, "let me love you."

But clearly it wasn't all right. Not to her.

With tremendous strength, she pulled back, bracing her hands on his chest. "No!"

"Lily," he said, his mind still circling with a passion he had never experienced, pulling her to him.

"No! Do you hear me, no! I am not Crimson Lily."

Her face was ravaged, tears streaking her face.

"Lily," he said softly, confused as he caressed her cheek. "I wasn't thinking about Crimson Lily."

"How could you not?"

She broke free, scrambling to her feet, yanking her skirts down. Morgan got up from the floor and they stood a few feet apart, staring at each other.

"Since I have met you," he said, his voice rough with emotion, "I have forgotten again and again about Crimson Lily. And just now I was thinking of Lily Blakemore, a woman who has drawn me in since I first saw her. A woman who I have learned is kind and caring despite what she wants everyone to think."

He realized in that second how true his words were. "Why, Lily? Why won't you let people know who you really are? Why do you make people think the worst of you?"

She pressed her eyes closed and sighed. After a moment, she looked at him. "You're wrong, Morgan. I am just me, always have been. It is everyone else who has taken it upon themselves to interpret my actions in ways that fit their preconceived ideas—without ever asking me how I felt."

"How *do* you feel, Lily?" he asked intently. "I'm asking. What do you feel?"

He wasn't certain what he expected. Perhaps something about existing in a world that maintained such strict guidelines in order to demarcate the classes. About rules that somehow over the last ten years she had forgotten or perhaps, given her parents, he thought suddenly, she had never mastered.

"I'm tired," she replied instead. "I'm tired of caring."

She started to turn away, but Morgan reached out and held her there. "*Do* you care, Lily?"

Her flash of anger was immediate and harsh. "Of course I do! I always have."

"Then why, why all the outrageous behavior?"

Her lips pursed and he thought she would break free and flee.

After a moment she took a deep breath, then said, "You don't know what it's like to walk into a room and have conversation stop. You don't know what it's like to have women cross the street so their skirts won't brush against your own. Yes, I care, Mr. Elliott. But showing it only gives others one more weapon to use against me."

Thirteen

Morgan jerked to a sitting position on his bed feeling raw on the inside. Out of breath. Uneasy.

He had been dreaming. Of Jenny. Reaching out. Falling.

Sitting up in the narrow bed, Morgan dragged his hand across his face. The early morning sun was only a hint on the horizon as he ran his hands through his hair, trying to wipe away the unsettling images from his mind. But he couldn't shake the utter helplessness that filled him at the memory.

Morgan dropped his head into his hands, his elbows planted on his knees, his broad naked back glistening in the growing light.

He had kept Jenny from his mind for so many years. He had left the South and traveled to New York. He had been seeking to right wrongs ever since. He had started small, learning. His targets had gotten bigger over the years and more important, until he had turned the full force of all he had learned on John Crandall. And all the while he had been able to forget Jenny's whispered declaration.

I need your help.

Guilt racked his body.

Yesterday he had tried to do everything he could to forget again. And he had for a while. With the touch of Lily's lips his memories were washed clean. The feel of her in his arms had been so right, as if it were meant to be. He had never felt so whole. So alive. For the first time since the fateful day that had altered his life, he had wanted, needed, to forget forever. He wanted to forget a girl named Jenny, a boy named Trey, and a man named John Crandall. All because of Lily.

Morgan's frustrated groan slid through the small cottage as he pushed up from the mattress, pacing the wooden floor like a caged animal. But he couldn't forget. He had promised himself he would bring Crandall down.

His life since Jenny had been his training ground. He had spent years bringing other men down, making them pay for the injustices they had wrought on others. He was considered the best. But even being the best had not helped him achieve his goal this time. He hadn't learned anything so far about John Crandall that would prove he was a criminal. But Morgan knew that he hadn't found anything on Crandall because of his obsession with Lily. So many images of Lily circling in his head that he could concentrate on little else.

Yesterday he had been willing to throw it all away because of Lily—because of a woman who turned him upside down at every turn.

Lily wounded. Lily vulnerable.

"No," he ground out, the word echoing against the thin walls.

Lily might be wounded, but she had brought her fate down on herself.

His anger grew and mounted, guilt and frustration fueling the fire. And then he remembered that his dreams had shifted and changed as they had worn on during the restless night. Turning into fire, flames licking and flaring to life. The dream had been so real that the acrid smell of char and smoke that had swirled through his mind in his sleep remained. So real. Burning his nose and eyes.

Too real.

"Sweet Jesus!"

Morgan leaped up from the bed, threw on his pants and boots and bolted out the door without bothering with a shirt. He raced through the property with his heart pounding in his chest. He hadn't been dreaming.

The house was on fire, or so he thought until he came careening through the tall hedge to a small clearing at the rear of the main house. He stopped dead in his tracks. In the middle of the yard a fire burned, lighting the early morning sky.

Lily and the children stood on the porch like spectators watching a play, mesmerized by the flash and leap of flames that licked the air. Morgan watched as well, stunned, unable to move.

But then a small explosion sounded, the flames leaping even higher. Penelope and Cassie squealed. Robert stiffened, and Lily's eyes widened with apparent surprise.

"What the hell is going on here?" Morgan demanded, marching around the fire to the porch.

"Really, Mr. Elliott, such language," Lily began before glancing down at his chest.

Her eyes widened still further and she seemed more surprised by his bare torso than the fire that burned brightly in the yard. She jerked her eyes away. "Your . . . language is most improper."

A comment on his language from Lily Blakemore? he wondered in disbelief, transfixed by the red blush staining her cheeks. Or could it be she was remembering what they had shared yesterday. Had she lain awake tortured by the remembered feel of him? Had she tossed and turned, unable to sleep, just as he had done?

The fire forgotten, he had the sudden urge to cross the distance, pull her close, press her body against his.

"Lily said we could roast marshmallows next," Penelope stated.

"What?" Morgan asked, his brow creased, unable to comprehend Penelope's simple words as he dragged his thoughts away from Lily with effort.

"We're going to—"

"I heard that. What I want to know is what is going on here?"

Cassie lost interest in the fire. She came over to Morgan and studied him as if she had never seen a man without a shirt on in her life. And no doubt she hadn't, he realized when she reached up and very carefully petted the narrow strip of dark hair that bisected his midsection as though he were some sort of exotic pet.

"Oh, Mr. Elliott," Cassie said, amazed, "you have a lot of hair."

Robert groaned and Penelope giggled. Lily's face flared red.

Morgan muttered a silent curse and stepped back, forcing a casual smile for little Cassie. "Yes, and I seem to have forgotten my shirt since I was startled out of bed thinking the house was burning down," he stated with a meaningful glare directed at Lily. "Cassie, do you think you could run out to my cottage and get me a shirt?"

"Of course!"

"You're just a baby. I'll get it," Penelope pronounced.

"No, Morgan asked me!"

In a flash, both girls took off down the steps, though Penelope skidded to a halt at the bottom, her arms swinging like windmills to keep her balance. "Don't start the marshmallows without me." Then she was gone, pursuing Cassie along the worn path, around the fire, until they disappeared through the tall hedge.

Pivoting slowly, Morgan narrowed his gaze and turned his full attention on Lily, his dark eyes slits of fiery coal. "You built a bonfire so you could roast marshmallows?" he asked incredulously, his temper barely mastered.

"It's not a bonfire, and you know it."

"Have you lost your mind?" he snapped, control forgotten.

Lily smiled wryly and shrugged. "Not so lucky."

Morgan barely managed to tamp down the urge to strangle her. The anger and frustration he'd woken up with had not dissipated, had grown stronger at this spectacle he found in the backyard. All he could think about was the fact that he was obsessed with a crazy woman.

"Do you mind telling me what's going on here?" he asked again with strained calm.

Lily glanced at him and cocked her head. "Well, there is a fire going on here." Her voice dripped with sarcasm.

"I can see that," he said tightly. "The question is why is there a fire burning here?"

Lily shoved her hands deep into the pockets of her outlandish gown, suddenly seeming young and innocent, her slippered foot circling on the wooden porch. "I was doing a little housecleaning," she said with forced nonchalance, "and I found a few things that I no longer needed. I told you this place was a mess."

Disbelieving, Morgan glanced back at the fire. For the first time he noticed odd shapes that were barely discernible in the flames. Another explosion made Lily jump.

"What the hell was that?" he demanded.

"Turpentine, I suppose," she offered, biting her lower lip.

"Turpentine?" He suddenly recognized some of the shapes in the fire. The easel he had seen in the attic. The case of supplies. The high stool. She was burning her things from the attic.

He looked back at her incredulously. "Why didn't you just ask me to get rid of this stuff?"

"I wanted it gone." And she had. She had wanted the easel and paints and supplies gone right then. Not in a week, not in a day, not even that afternoon. Burning them had seemed the only answer.

She started to return indoors. But Morgan leaped up the steps, then reached out and grabbed her arm, forcing her to face him.

Lily looked down at his hand on her arm, just looked. Morgan could feel her tremble, could see her breath still in her chest. After a moment, she glanced up, her blue eyes troubled.

"Lily," he breathed, drawing her near his fingertips brushing her skin.

He didn't think about Robert standing on the porch, or that Cassie and Penelope would be back at any time. He only thought of the feel of her beneath his fingers.

"Morgan! Here's your shirt!"

"No, *I* have his shirt! Morgan, you have to wear mine!"

Lily's eyes widened and Morgan's head jerked up just as Penelope and Cassie charged around the fire with not one shirt but two.

With supreme effort, Morgan stepped away from Lily and took both offerings. "Thank you, girls."

"Which one are you going to wear?" Penelope demanded.

They both looked at him expectantly. Finally, Morgan said, "Both."

"Both!?"

"Both," he repeated, pulling on first Penelope's shirt, then Cassie's.

"He likes mine best," Cassie announced.

"No, he doesn't, he likes mine best because he has it closer to his heart."

"Does not!"

"Does so!"

Morgan shook his head. "Girls!"

Instantly the squabbling ceased.

"Go inside," he said carefully, his patience spent.

"I don't want to go inside," Penelope protested, her eyes growing suspiciously damp.

"I said go inside. Now!"

Cassie scrambled up the stairs. Penelope followed in her

wake, shooting a hateful scowl not at Morgan but at Lily.

Without a word, Lily turned back toward the house as well.

"Lily," Morgan demanded, his tone dark and brooding. "Why are you really burning all this stuff?"

"There is so much to do. Broken furniture, moldy rugs. As I said, I am going to get this house in order if it's the last thing I do."

"It may very well be the last thing you do if this fire burns the place down."

She looked back at him. "You're the caretaker. See that it doesn't."

With that she turned away and walked into the house.

"She's a loon, I tell you," Robert said, looking at the flames. "Lily Blakemore is a loon." Then he too turned and disappeared inside the house.

Morgan watched them go. At length his gaze returned to the flames that licked and destroyed the painting supplies and who knew what else.

Get the house in order.

Morgan shook his head. He knew as surely as if she had spoken the words aloud that her goal was something very different than simply straightening the house. Why else would she be burning things rather than having them hauled away or repaired? What else would Lily burn in her attempt to erase her past? he wondered. He had said last night that she was trying to forget what she had done. Did she really think she could by destroying everything? If she burned her paints did she really think she could forget the infamous painting?

Morgan focused on the blaze and shook his head. She had started a fire in her backyard. The woman never ceased to amaze him.

In truth, the flames weren't in any immediate danger of burning anything down. The early morning air was still, and the fire burned in a clearing. The yard had long ago fallen into disrepair. There was not a blade of grass or shrubbery close enough to be in danger. But still Morgan would need to watch it to make sure.

He tucked in the shirttails. Fortunately it was early enough that it wasn't too hot yet. Though in a matter of hours the summer heat would be pounding down on the city.

The bang of the back door gained his attention. When he turned he found Lily on the steps, dragging a haphazardly folded rug. Morgan could only stare, dumbfounded.

"Are you going to just stand there," Lily asked primly, "or are you going to help me?"

Morgan clenched his jaw. "I don't think this is the way to go about . . . getting your house in order Lily."

"I take it that's a no. Then out of my way." She dragged the rug across the porch before she took the steps, the rug thumping down behind her to the dirt.

Morgan took the rug roughly from her hands. "Stop this, Lily. Stop trying to burn away the past."

Her blue eyes darkened. "My, aren't you fanciful this morning, Mr. Elliott. I'd have to say you've been reading too many dime novels these last weeks. No wonder the house is still so far away from being finished."

Morgan's jaw set, frustration washing through his veins. "You're right. What was I thinking? It's your house, your things. You can do anything you want with them!"

With a resounding grunt, Morgan hefted the unwieldy folds of woolen rug, and with one great heave, flung the carpet into the fire. "There. Are you happy?"

She eyed him dubiously. "Yes," she said after a moment. "Thank you very much."

"Next you'll want to burn the sofas and chairs."

"Now that you mentioned it. . . "

Morgan made a noise deep in his chest that sounded suspiciously like a growl, his anger burning bright, raging. His scorching gaze raked over her. "Damn it, woman, a fire in the backyard, burning priceless carpets and furniture. And you bring the children in on your exploits. Telling them they can roast marshmallows, for God's sake! What kind of woman are you?"

He saw her flinch, but his own inner conflicts burned out of control, pushing him on. "You don't know the first thing about taking care of Robert or Penelope or Cassie. If anyone got one look at the way you deal with the children they would be whisked away from you so fast your head would spin. When are you going to realize that you're here to save them from ending up in an orphanage? They need your help, not these outlandish escapades you brew up at every turn. You're supposed to keep them safe, Lily. Not get them sent away."

Lily stood as still as a statue. He saw emotions churn on her face, her eyes troubled and stormy. But then as if the storm had passed, her features calmed and she looked him straight in the eye.

"Keep them safe, Mr. Elliott?" Her tone was deadly, her eyes hard. No hint of vulnerability. "I'd have to say, then, that you and I are a great deal alike in that regard. As I recall, you didn't keep your dear Jenny safe either."

He felt his chest constrict, all air expelled in one painful breath. His blood chilled, his face growing grim. The pain was like a vise around his heart.

He hadn't kept Jenny safe. And no matter how hard he tried, no matter what he did in his life, he could never right that wrong.

At length he said, "That's right, Miss Blakemore. I didn't."

With that he turned on his heels and headed back to his cottage, failing to see the despair that darkened Lily's eyes.

Fourteen

Lily cursed her wretched tongue.

You didn't keep Jenny safe either.

How could she have said such a thing?

The faded eyes of ancient Blakemores captured in oil stared down at Lily from the walls, chiding her as she paced the confines of the parlor. Lily chided herself as well. Morgan had told her his story, had shared his pain. And churlishly she had tossed it back in his face. She pressed her eyes closed, riddled with shame.

People who callously and uncaringly hurt others with sharp words had been a part of her life for so long. She hated them. And now she had done the very same thing. She had been angry and hurt, and she had lashed out. Unfairly.

And to make matters worse there was the issue of the children. Ridiculously, it had never occurred to her that the children could be taken away. Claude's will had been specific.

But what if Morgan was right? Was it possible that they could take the children away?

Her blood ran cold at the thought. She no longer had hopes that New York would ever accept her. But she loved Cassie, and Cassie loved her. Lily suddenly couldn't imagine a life without her niece. Strangely, she couldn't imagine a life without Robert or Penelope either.

How odd that she had become so attached to the children. But she had, and she realized that if they were taken away she would miss Robert's huff of disdain and Penelope's sour faces as much as she would miss sweet Cassie's smiles. Well, almost as much, she conceded with a sigh.

And then there was Morgan.

Lily pressed her eyes closed and drew a deep breath. "Oh, Morgan," she whispered into the room, "how is it that you have come to mean so much to me?"

As the day wore on, Lily paced the house, hoping Morgan would appear. Over the past weeks, every time she had turned around he was there, his exacting eyes making some new demand. Why wasn't he there now? she wondered. Though what she would say to him if he were she didn't know. What could she say to undo her unkind words? A simple apology seemed wholly inadequate.

She finally turned her attention to straightening her room and making a list of all the many other things she wanted to do around the house now that she had decided it was time to move beyond simple repairs. But by the time her room was straightened and the list had filled the page, the sun was low on the horizon and Morgan had yet to appear.

Lily dropped down into an old chair in the parlor in a cloud of billowing skirts she had found on an adventure in India. Soft, whimsical material. A loose, draping blouse over a thin skirt that she had always loved.

At the sound of footsteps she sat up, her heart willing it to be Morgan. Robert was in his room, not likely to come out, and Cassie was asleep.

But it was Penelope who stuck her head in the doorway,

not Morgan. Just what she needed, Lily sighed silently. One of her niece's sarcastic remarks.

"What is it, dear?" she asked.

The girl stared at Lily, her young face working with emotion.

"Penelope?" Lily asked, her voice softening as she stood to walk over.

But Penelope's face abruptly deflated, and she turned on her heels and fled, the sound of her feet dashing up the stairs receding in the distance.

Lily groaned her frustration. What should she do? She was supposed to be the mother, a caretaker. Some instinct Lily would have sworn didn't exist led her up the stairs. Clearly Penelope wanted to say something. Good or bad, Lily was going to find out what it was.

Once upstairs, Lily went to her niece's bedroom. "Penelope," she called, knocking on the door.

"Go away."

Lily would have liked to do nothing more in that moment. But Morgan's words whispered through her mind, calling into question her ability to be a good mother. Resolved, she turned the knob.

Penelope sat at a dressing table brushing her long hair. Their eyes caught in the mirror.

"Penelope?"

"What?"

Sitting there on the elegantly padded bench, Penelope looked calm and self-possessed, so unlike the little girl who had stood in the parlor doorway only minutes earlier.

"Nothing," Lily said, feeling suddenly foolish. "Good night."

Lily went to her own room, the thick door clicking shut behind her. She wished she could find a way to break through the barrier that stood between her and Penelope. Even though her niece had been less than enthusiastic toward her, every now and again Lily felt cracks beginning to snake through the brick and mortar of the wall Penelope had erected from the start. Or at least sometimes Lily felt this way. Other times, such as a few minutes ago when she had gone to Penelope's room, Lily felt she must be fooling herself. No doubt Penelope was just like Robert, unwilling to accept her.

Lily walked about the room, her fingers gliding over feather boas and crocheted shawls. When she came to her precious china cup she stopped. Always such a reminder of hope and happiness in the past, but all hope and happiness now seemed gone forever.

Lost.

Everything was lost.

Which meant, she realized, her hands beginning to tingle with excitement, that she had nothing to lose.

Her spine straightened, her shoulders pulling back as her mind raced. *She had nothing to lose.* And she knew then what she was going to do.

Hurrying, Lily splashed water on her face and stared at herself in the mirror. "You can do this, Lily Blakemore."

She raced to the doorway, but at the very last second, slid to a halt and retraced her steps. Tearing through her drawers and closet, Lily found an appropriately decorous gown, silk shawl, beautifully proper gloves, shoes, and a hat. Perfectly proper attire in which she would make a perfectly proper apology.

She was going out to the cottage to face Morgan Elliott. And she would apologize. Tell him how genuinely sorry she was. She owed him that.

Hastily she pulled the apparel on and when she glanced in the mirror, even she had to admit that she looked every inch the lady.

Lily almost laughed, feeling giddy with purpose. With her heart pounding in her chest, she let herself out the back door. It was dark except for a bit of deep purple sky in the distance. The days were growing shorter as summer came to an end. Picking her way around the charred remains in the yard, high spots of embarrassment marred her cheeks.

What had she been thinking? she wondered dismally.

But she would not address that now. She had an apology to make.

Her determined steps slowed as she neared the rear of the property. She had not been to the cottage since she was a child. Memories swirled through her head. Sweet memories of a time before her life had gone awry.

But it *had* gone awry, and memories did her no good now.

It occurred to her suddenly that she had no idea what she was going to say.

"I'm terribly sorry," she whispered into the growing darkness.

"Please forgive me," she tried next.

But she tossed this out before she had taken another step. She would not beg. Would she?

"Mr. Elliott," she began again, "please accept my most sincere apology for my unforgivable behavior."

But if she said that, she reasoned, it implied she would understand if he didn't forgive her. And he had to forgive her. Had to.

She was trying yet another phrase when she came to the cottage. Her already hesitant steps slowed even further. Her heart pounded with trepidation. But then she raised her chin a notch and walked straight up the wooden steps to the small veranda and stood before the door. It was dark inside, too dark, and her heart sank.

Taking a deep fortifying breath, she brought her primly gloved hand up and knocked. Her heart all but stopped in her chest. Not a sound came from within the small dwelling.

She knocked again, her heart having jerked back into motion.

Still no answer.

What if he had already left? she wondered suddenly. For good.

Without thinking, desperate to know, Lily tried the handle. The door pushed open with ease.

The interior was dark. It took a moment for her eyes to adjust and when they did she knew she was the only one there. The room was empty and bare except for a few pieces of furniture.

Morgan was gone.

A stinging disappointment filled her heart. He was gone. She would never be able to offer her apology.

Lily walked through the room with a sigh, holding back useless tears. She told herself that it was best this way. An apology wouldn't have changed anything. Their differences went well beyond words spoken unfairly in anger. She could never apologize for being called Crimson Lily, just as she couldn't change it.

The moonlight drifted in through the open door and small windows. The cottage was sparsely furnished. A chair and wooden table. A small desk. A cabinet for clothes. And the bed. Made. Crisply. She started to smile at how typical of him this seemed. But it was then that she saw his few things—boots, the shirt he had worn countless times over the weeks he had been there, always clean, worn to a babylike softness by many washings. He might leave such things behind, but when she came closer, she found a pocket watch she had never noticed before. Beautifully wrought of silver.

Carefully picking it up, Lily felt the cool metal against her palm. She held it tightly, thinking of Morgan.

"I'm sorry," she whispered into the room with heartfelt sincerity.

The silver warmed to her touch. She felt the fine etchings swirling against her skin. Though she knew she shouldn't, she popped the lid.

For my son,
Father

A strange yearning filled her. Such a fine gift. A gift, based on what little she knew of Morgan, that his father could ill afford. But one he must have given with great love.

"Oh, why," she cried softly, "why couldn't things have turned out differently?"

But they hadn't. And just as she had said to Morgan last night, the past couldn't be changed.

She snapped the watch shut, then set it back down. The past was finished, it was only the future she could affect now. She would make her apologies to Morgan. If nothing else, the watch had made it clear he hadn't left—at least not for good. He would come back for this if nothing else.

She only had to wait.

At this, Lily decided she didn't want to be found rummaging through his belongings. She would wait for him outside.

The veranda had no chairs, so after she closed the door behind her, Lily sank down onto the top step, determined to wait as long as need be. There was still the very real possibility that he could return for his things and be gone without a word of good-bye.

The night was warm despite the late hour. The perfectly proper shoes felt tight and restricting. She longed to toss her gloves aside, along with the light shawl. But she would not, even if it killed her. Her hat, however, was a different story. She would look no less the lady for taking off her hat, she reasoned.

Slipping the pins from her hair, she pulled the hat from her head with a sigh and set it beside her on the step. It was moments like these when she conceded that there were advantages to being a fallen woman. If she wore gloves no one noticed. But if she didn't they just assumed that it was in keeping with her decadent nature. No surprises. Ever.

Until Morgan.

He noticed. He cared. So she kept the silly gloves and

shoes on and very nearly put the hat back on her head. She knew she would need all the help she could get with the apology she was determined to make.

The night drifted on. With her chin in her palms and her elbows planted on her knees, she stared down the path that led to the main house, the flagstones shining dully like black pearls in the moonlight. With her eyes, she followed the curves of the old and worn mortar that held the slabs of rock together. It was just as her gaze reached the tall hedge when he appeared.

Tall, more handsome than any one man had a right to be. Caressed by silver moonlight.

She felt a tightening in her chest. The world seemed to close in around her, her thoughts echoing in her head.

He was beautiful. So beautiful. Etched like a carving. He moved with a predator's grace, smooth, no wasted energy. His steps were long and unhurried. At ease.

She braced herself as he came closer, prepared herself for harsh words. Lily wouldn't have been surprised if he very coldly asked her to leave. But she would take what he doled out, sit quietly beneath a barrage of anger, or sit tightly if he asked her to leave. Then she would apologize.

She knew the minute he saw her. His stride faltered before he continued. It wasn't until he drew closer that she realized he wasn't at ease after all. His chiseled features were weary.

When he came to the bottom of the steps he stopped. Her courage nearly deserted her beneath the intensity of his darkened gaze. Instinct begged that she dash down the stairs and run for the house. But that was the coward's way out.

"Hello," she said, her voice weaker than she would have liked, her fingers nervously toying with the feathered hat that lay by her side.

He didn't speak or nod his head in greeting, only studied her with his cool dark eyes.

Lily drew a deep breath, forcing herself to continue before she lost what little nerve she had managed to muster. "I want you to know that what I said about Jenny was unkind and unfair. You didn't deserve that."

His dark gaze bore into her. Intense. Intimidating. But Lily would not turn away. Not this time. She held his gaze, willing him to see that she meant her words.

After a long, agonizing moment during which Morgan didn't utter a word, he simply started up the stairs, his dark eyes formidable, and Lily's heart sank. He didn't believe her, or if he did, he didn't care if she apologized or not. He would pass her by and leave her there, her apology unaccepted. But just as he drew up beside her, he leaned over and picked up her hat before continuing inside.

Lily sat very still, her heart pounding, her mind racing. His message was clear. Propriety demanded that she leap up, hurry down the path, and never look back. Instead she stood up from the steps and followed him inside.

When she entered, Lily noticed that Morgan had lit a gas jet. A soft, golden glow filled the room. Across the room he leaned against a windowsill, the multipaned window pushed wide. He looked out into the night, never looking back at her as she stood uncertainly just inside his door.

They remained that way for what seemed like an eternity. Lily couldn't bring herself to move forward or even back. And just when she would have blurted out his name, unable to take the uncertainty any longer, he spoke.

"I should be apologizing to you," he said quietly, his voice pained. "And you were right. I *didn't* keep Jenny safe."

Her heart broke, and she cursed herself yet again. "I wish so badly that I could take back those words. Truly I'm sorry."

"You shouldn't be sorry for telling the truth. I promised her years before that I would take care of her."

"You must have loved her very much."

Morgan sighed. "Yes, I loved her." He hesitated. "Our

families were close friends. Our fathers were old school-mates. Our mothers had grown up together. Jenny was an only child, as was I. We were born within a week of each other, and since birth our parents had wanted us to marry.''

''Is that what you wanted?''

''It never occurred to me not to marry her.'' He dropped his head forward, sighed, then straightened. ''When Jenny was ten her parents were killed in a carriage accident. Jenny was devastated, as were the rest of us. Within days she moved in with us permanently. At night she would sneak into my room and crawl in bed beside me. It seemed like I didn't sleep for months, just held her while she cried until I couldn't imagine she had any tears left to spill. She was so afraid of what would happen to her.''

Lily wanted to reach out and touch him, but something stopped her. ''Is that when you told her you would keep her safe?''

''Yes.'' The word seared the room.

A shiver of something, jealousy? she wondered, slid through her body. To have someone care enough to promise to keep her safe, whether or not they actually could, how cherished that would make her feel.

''I have told myself over and over again,'' he continued, ''that if I had loved her more I could have saved her.''

''You're being too hard on yourself.''

''I made a promise!''

''Morgan, what did you expect of yourself? That you could have run faster to get to her? That you should have stayed closer to her? Good Lord, how could you have known that she would fall?''

His breath hissed through his teeth. ''She didn't fall. She jumped.''

''Dear God,'' she breathed.

''She came to me for help.'' Morgan inhaled sharply. He remembered that day as if it were only hours before. ''I was surprised when she showed up at the cliffs. She had never liked the spot. She hated the heights.'' A faint smile crossed his lips before it disappeared. "She told me she loved me. More than anything or anyone. I started to pull her close, but she stopped me and told me not to say anything—yet. That's when she told me she was pregnant."

"You got her pregnant!?"

Morgan shot Lily a heated glance. "No, I didn't get her pregnant! It was Trey. My friend. Her friend."

"Jenny lay with Trey? Did she love him?"

"I don't know," he ground out. "I don't think so. She told me it only happened once. Like that would make a difference." His tone was violent. "She said it was a mistake. That it had just happened. Just happened," he raged, his fist pounding the wooden sill. "She was supposed to marry me!"

He turned away from the window and looked at Lily. "Before she came to me, she went to Trey and told him. But the bastard wouldn't marry her. She didn't know what to do, so she asked me to marry her still and give her child a name."

"And even knowing what she had done," Lily whispered, "you would have married her."

Morgan reeled. He had thought before that Lily had seen his darkness and hadn't turned away. He saw now that, yes, she saw the darkness, but she saw his truth as well. His throat tightened with emotion, grateful that someone could see. "Yes, I would have. Of course I would have. But when she told me, I was shocked, I was angry. I walked away to clear my head. That's all. I would have married her. But she jumped before I could tell her. If I just hadn't walked away I could have saved her."

What could she say to him? How could she combat his pain? "Oh, Morgan, I said before that not everything or everyone can be saved."

"But she could have been saved. Sweet Jenny. I've lived my life trying to right that wrong."

The words broke her heart, emotion burning in her

throat. Lily had known all along that nothing could come between herself and Morgan. It shouldn't matter that he loved a girl named Jenny. Not her. It was Jenny he couldn't forget. If he had any feelings for her at all it was impatience and frustration . . . and the tawdry lust that so many men had felt for her.

Her chest constricted. Yet another reminder of what her life was. She started to turn away, biting her lip in hopes of keeping everything she felt safely inside. She wanted to get as far away from this place as she could. Then, only then, would she allow herself to feel. But when she moved, Morgan reached out and caught her arm.

"I haven't been able to move beyond that day. Or at least I hadn't until I met you."

It took a moment for his words to sink in, but when they did her heart froze in her chest. She could hardly believe she had heard correctly.

"You tipped me over, Lily. I have no room for you in my life, but somehow I can no longer imagine living without you."

Her breath caught. Her mind stilled. "Morgan," she whispered.

"You are the most maddening person I have ever met. Outrageous. Fires and snapped chairs, for Christ's sake." He shook his head and groaned. "Half the time I wonder how any one person can get into so much trouble." He pressed his lips to her hair. "But truly I can't imagine a life without you."

"I'm not sure if that should make me feel better or worse," she said, unable to look away from his mouth.

"That makes two of us," he whispered as he leaned down with infinite care, his muscles rippling beneath the soft cambric shirt, and pressed his lips to hers.

The touch was like fire, searing her.

"Morgan," she said, turning her head away, wanting this path, but afraid of where it would take them.

His lips trailed back along her jaw.

She tried not to feel, tried not to want his touch. "Morgan—"

"I'm tired of talking. I'm tired of thinking," he responded on a faint breath of air as he nipped her ear.

A shiver of yearning coursed down her spine. She wanted to give in to her desire, but didn't know how. Her hands clutched him to steady herself.

"Yes," he murmured, "touch me, Lily."

He moved even closer until his hard chest brushed against the folds of her proper chemisette, the sensation like liquid fire.

She tried to step free, to force her mind to regain control of her unruly senses. But Morgan pulled her back.

"No, Lily," he whispered, "let me love you."

She wanted to feel him, touch him as he had asked. And she wondered for a moment if she had known all along where this night would lead, had come here only under the pretense of needing to apologize? Shame singed her cheeks.

"What's wrong?" he asked, his voice rough and sensual.

"I shouldn't be here."

He kissed her jaw then tilted her chin with his finger. "This has been coming for a long time now. I'm going to make love to you, Lily. Tonight. I'm not going to let you go."

And that was her undoing.

Her desire overwhelming whatever fragments of sense she had left, she ran her hands up his arms to his shoulders. She relished the feel of hard sinew beneath her fingers, she relished as well his jagged intake of breath.

"Lily," he groaned against her ear. "I want you as I have never wanted anything in my life."

She knew he did, she could feel his yearning in the pounding of his heart. Many men had wanted her. What was different was that she wanted him, too. She wanted him in ways she shouldn't, but just then neither the propriety nor the common sense that had helped her survive these many years held sway. In that moment, she wanted him without regard for what was right or wrong.

He coaxed her lips apart. He tasted of brandy and cigars, but also of the sunshine and long grasses that she loved. When she groaned her pleasure, he pulled her even closer, his hand cupping the fullness of her breast beneath her chemisette. He brushed his hand across the peaks, his tongue tasting her.

"Yes, Lily," he said, pulling her full lower lip gently between his teeth.

His fingers found the tiny buttons of her gown, working them deftly. He opened the folds until he revealed her breasts. He stared at her for an eternity, with something that she would have sworn was reverence in his eyes.

"You are so beautiful."

She tried to cover herself, unused to the scrutiny.

"No," he breathed.

And before she could respond, he swept her up in his arms and carried her to his narrow bed. He laid her down as if she were a precious china doll, fragile, breakable, then reverently removed her clothes.

"I've thought of this moment since I first saw you. I've imagined you a thousand different ways, but even my dreams didn't come close to revealing how beautiful you are," he said, his hand brushing over her breasts.

Though she lay there shamelessly, Lily had never experienced anything that had felt so right. She wanted him to love her. And when his hand came to rest on her belly, she wanted nothing more than to cover his hand with her own. To keep it there, to keep him there. With her. Forever.

With an infinite slowness, he leaned over her and brushed his lips against her skin, making her body quiver with sensation. She pulled at his clothes, and he tossed them aside until he stretched out beside her. Tears burned in her eyes with the aching poignancy that shimmered through her.

"Morgan," she whispered, unable to get anything else beyond her throat. Was it possible that he felt anything close to what she felt? Or did he simply desire her—desire her body as so many others had.

But when she opened her eyes, Morgan looked so desperate and aching that she knew that he had to feel the same as she. He must. He had to feel the same overwhelming intensity she did.

But before she could ask, he kissed her with a desperation that left her breathless. He caressed her body, making her shimmer and writhe with wanting. And then he came over her, settling between her thighs, raising her knees as he thrust his tongue deep in her mouth. He pressed against her secret opening, teasing, pulsing until he thrust inside her.

The pain was swift and heated, her maidenhead yielding to the intrusion, and she gasped. Morgan reeled back, his dark brows furrowed.

"Lily," he began, confusion etched across his face.

Lily didn't respond, couldn't. She only pulled him closer. "Love me, Morgan," she whispered, moving against him until he groaned and began to move within her, slowly but steadily. Making them forget.

He loved her then, as if trying to become one with her. Lily didn't think she could feel any more, didn't know how anything could be as intense as what he had made her feel before. But as he moved within her, the intensity of her desire commandeered her body.

And she was certain, just as sensation overtook her, that she would never be the same again.

Fifteen

Lily woke slowly. She had been dreaming again. Of Morgan. Holding her. Kissing her.

Making love to her.

The murky state between being asleep and awake shattered into a thousand tiny pieces. Her eyes flew open, but she didn't move. Didn't breathe. She hadn't been dreaming. Morgan lay at her side.

Dear God, she cried silently, *what have I done?*

Lily was afraid to move. Morgan was sound asleep, one arm beneath her holding her securely, the other flung over his head. His chiseled features were softened in sleep, his hair tousled, making him look more the schoolboy than the ruthless man she knew him to be.

After a moment more, she realized with a silent groan that beneath the thin sheet she wore no clothes. Crimson stained her cheeks when she noticed her perfectly proper gown, shoes, and gloves discarded about the room in flagrant disregard. Morgan's shirt and trousers mixed with hers. Condemning her.

Dear God, she cried silently again, *what have I done?*

The answer, unfortunately, was too clear to deny. She had made love. To this man. Who had made it more than clear that he thought little of her.

Until last night.

Her heart burgeoned in her chest as she remembered.

You tipped me over, Lily.

Last night he had wanted her in a way that went beyond desire. But then her heart slowed. He had said nothing of love.

Unable to think about what she had done, Lily knew she had to get out of the cottage and back to the house before the children woke. Preferably without Morgan knowing.

Despite what Morgan thought, she really did try to do right by the children. It was just that she rarely knew what to do for them. Beyond that, she didn't think she could face him this morning. How would he look at her? Would he feel regret? Desire? Or disgust?

Lily started to move, but she had to stifle a surprised groan. Her body was tender after their night of lovemaking. And it had been all night. As if he couldn't get enough of her, couldn't get close enough.

She inched off the bed, thankful that she had sole possession of the sheet. Morgan lay peacefully underneath a bit of blanket. Her movements froze, however, when she saw the sheet that had been beneath her. Stained with blood.

Further proof of what had transpired during the night.

She pressed her eyes closed, then very carefully inched her way off the bed until she managed to stand by the side, the sheet wrapped firmly around her, with Morgan still asleep.

Or so she thought.

"Lily?"

His deep, guttural voice slid down her spine much as his hand had only hours before.

Bracing herself for whatever she would find in his eyes,

she turned back to him. What she found took her breath away.

Love?

Suddenly she remembered the night he had come upon her as she was trying to wipe away the red letters from the wall. The emotion had been there that night, too. This man felt something very intense for her, had for some time. But she knew as well that it was wrapped up in other feelings that were not as clear.

"Come here, Lily."

His voice was rough from sleep, sensual. Her heart leaped in her chest.

"I can't," she stammered. "I've got to go."

"It's early yet."

"For me, maybe," she said wryly, chastising herself for the maddening way her body suddenly pulsed with awareness, "but not for anyone else around here."

"Come here, Lily," he repeated, the words a lover's demand.

He swung his legs over the side of the bed. She realized with a start that he had on no more than she, his lap barely covered by the blanket's edge. But even the blanket couldn't hide his insistent arousal. The sight mesmerized her as she remembered the feel of his skin beneath her fingertips, the remembered feel of his desire when he had wrapped her fingers around his hard shaft.

Before she could clear her mind, he reached out and caught the sheet. She held firmly, but he didn't let go. With measured movements, he began to pull her close.

Her fingers trembled, though the tremor had very little to do with fear. "No, Morgan."

"The choice is simple. Either let go of the sheet or come here," he told her, his voice like gravel, his eyes dark with passion.

Let go or go to him. Not a good choice as far as she was concerned. If she let go of the sheet, she would be left standing there without so much as a stitch of clothing on, though going to him meant something very different. Her heart pounded at the thought. But Morgan didn't seem to be concerned about her trepidation as he pulled her closer still.

"Morgan, I really have to get back to the house." She was so close by now that she could feel the heat of him and she had to force herself to breathe. "You yourself told me I need to think of the children."

"The children can do without you for a few more minutes." He pulled her between his legs, his erection pressing against her thigh. "But I can't."

"Yes, you can." She forced the words from her throat. "Now, close your eyes and let me gather my clothes."

"Too late for that." His voice was thick, hoarse, as if he was using every ounce of his control to speak.

The sheet remained clutched in her hands nearly to her neck. Morgan ran his knuckles over her fingers. "Let go, Lily," he added, before gently tugging the sheet free.

It fell in a puddle at her feet and she gasped. She stood before him, naked. Morgan groaned deeply in his chest, and when she tried to cover herself he moved her hands away.

"No, Lily."

He drew her still closer. She knew she should pull back, clothes or not, then gather her belongings and flee. But his hands ran down her arms to her hands, making her tremble. With incredible gentleness, he lifted them to his lips. "I have never met anyone like you," he whispered against her skin.

Her eyes burned with emotion. She could see the reverence in his eyes, the sincerity. And when his hands drifted up her belly, over her ribs to cup the fullness of her breasts, she did nothing more than sigh.

Winding her fingers through his hair, she gasped when he pulled one nipple deep into his mouth. His tongue laved the bud into a taut peak, before taking the other, sucking and laving, a slow lava beginning to churn low in her body. As if sensing the yearning, his fingers drifted lower, to tease the lips of her sex.

"Morgan," she cried out in surprise when he moved one strong thigh between her legs.

"Shhhh, love. Open for me."

"I can't do this." Her throat worked, but even as it did, her body warmed in response.

"Of course you can." He widened her stance. "Let go, Lily."

He stroked her hip until she relaxed.

"Yes, princess," he crooned, then very gently stroked her secret folds.

Her gasp rapidly gave way to a sigh that caught in her throat. Her embarrassment fled when the yearning turned rapidly into an intense desire, burning for his touch.

"Yes, Lily." With those words, he penetrated her with one strong finger.

Her body tensed, but he didn't stop. He stroked her, his finger sliding gently inside her, slowly but firmly, until she sensed her own wetness.

"God, you have such passion," he breathed against her skin, then slipped a second finger inside her, cradling her when she trembled.

He stroked her deeply, until his breath had grown ragged. With infinite tenderness he pulled out of her, then guided her down until she straddled his hard thigh. Carefully he rolled back onto the bed, bringing her with him, their bodies so intimately entwined. He cupped her hips as he kissed her, running his hands up her back. She was timid on top, not certain how to kiss him. His strong hands guided her, his tongue thrusting into her mouth as his body began to move.

"Sweet Lily," he groaned, his breath quick and sharp, "I need you. I want to be inside you."

He rolled to the side, coming over her, his elbows pressing into the mattress to support his upper body.

"I can't wait," he groaned, pulling up her knees, settling between her thighs.

Calling her name, he thrust inside her. She felt the tension in his body as he waited for her body to adjust to him. And then he began to move, slowly at first, until they were both panting and yearning. He cupped her hips, pulling her body up to meet his bold, fevered thrusts.

She clutched his shoulders, his face buried in her neck, panting, thrusting, until she felt her body convulse with her release. He cried out her name, and when he did, she could feel an explosive shudder rack the hard length of his body as he spilled his seed deep inside her.

He collapsed on top of her. She bore his weight, the heaviness comforting, until he rolled to his side, bringing her with him. She could feel the beat of his heart, strong and rapid. They lay that way wrapped together, silence all around them. She wanted to stay just that way forever.

But then he spoke, shattering the silence.

"Did you love him, Lily?"

Her mind jarred, trying to understand what he had asked, denying the meaning that crashed down on her. "What are you talking about?"

He buried his face in her hair. "Did you love Raine Hawthorne so much?"

Lily gasped, her chest on fire, her mind pitching violently, no longer able to deny. Raine whom she had thought had cared about her. But he had care about fame so much more.

She should have realized it back then. But hadn't. She had let him sketch her; she sitting for hours as she talked about her hopes and dreams, he listening—telling her to believe that she could do anything, telling her not to let society extinguish the fire inside her.

He had laughed with her, talked with her. She had trusted him. And he had betrayed her to the world.

"Love him? No," she responded, her voice tight.

Morgan pushed up onto his elbow. "Then why did you do it? Why would you pose?"

Tears burned in her eyes. She wanted to scream, to rage. She realized with Morgan's words, lying there beside him, and despite the fact that she had shared with him a gift she had given no other man, that he couldn't move beyond her past.

In that moment, she hated Raine Hawthorne more than she ever had before. And as much as she could never forgive Raine, Lily wasn't sure she could ever forgive Morgan for not holding out some hope that she had not so completely fallen.

She tried to move away, but his hand was like a band of iron, holding her captive.

"Once and for all, tell me, Lily. Why did you pose?"

Lily calmed, meeting his troubled gaze. "Perhaps because I wanted to."

She tried to roll free. But when she moved, he pulled her so close that for a second she couldn't breathe.

"Lily," he whispered, his dark eyes washed with regret.

"No, Morgan. Let me go."

"I'm sorry."

"For what? For asking the question, or because you regret my answer?"

If possible, his stormy gaze grew more turbulent. "I wish it were that simple. But I hope that one day . . . you can remember my words. I am sorry, Lily."

Their eyes locked, so many words between them left unspoken. She would have questioned him further, demanded that he explain, but just then he eased his grip. Freeing her. After a heartbeat she rolled to her feet. Snatching up her discarded clothes from the floor piece by piece, she ignored his penetrating gaze. She yanked on her gown, gritting her teeth with frustration when the maddeningly little fastenings didn't button as easily as they had unbuttoned the night before.

"Here, let me."

"No!" She jerked out of his grasp. "No," she whispered. "No, no, no," she added with each trembling movement of her fingers.

"Damn it, Lily."

He stood up from the bed and yanked on his trousers, then raked his hands through his hair. The small room suddenly seemed even smaller. He took the few steps that separated them, then pushed her clumsy fingers away.

"I can do it," she said, her voice breaking.

"No, you can't."

With angry motions, he worked her dress. When the last button was secure, she pulled away and hurried to the door. But at the last minute she stopped. She had the urge to race back to him, to try to explain how it had happened. She wanted to explain how she had been young and foolish to have believed in a man like Raine Hawthorne.

Morgan stood there like a Greek god, strong but tortured. There was a stillness about him that she had never noticed before, a stillness that came from an anger that she knew burned much as the fire had burned in the backyard that day—a fire ready to burn out of control. And like that fire, Morgan kept his own carefully contained.

In the end, she was unwilling to try to explain. She knew as she stood there that after what they had shared, if Morgan had to ask the question, answers no longer mattered. It was too late for explanations. In truth, it was too late years ago when she had posed for Raine Hawthorne.

With a start, Lily turned and fled. She couldn't afford to have second thoughts. Morgan desired her, yes. But he didn't love her—and she had lain with him intimately without the sanction of marriage.

If she hadn't deserved the name all of New York called her before, she deserved it now. She had acted shamelessly.

After years of trying to prove to herself she wasn't what society thought of her, she had only proved that they were right.

Her stifled moan wafted through the rapidly brightening sky. She had acted like the very woman she had sworn she would never be. She had come to this cottage, hadn't left when he made it clear what he wanted. Instead she had asked him to make love to her.

Dear God, she *was* Crimson Lily.

Sixteen

Lily. A virgin.

Morgan stood on the cottage porch, leaning against a post, smoking a cigar, his features darkened as he looked out into the early morning light.

Lily had been a virgin.

What did it mean? he asked himself for the hundredth time. He didn't have the answer, but he was sure of his soaring feelings. She may have posed nude for Raine Hawthorne, but she hadn't slept with him.

Nor had she slept with John Crandall.

Morgan still didn't understand Lily's relationship to Crandall, but he knew she wasn't his mistress.

Though it shouldn't mean so much to him, it did. She hadn't shared such intimacy with any other man but him. It was an unexpected gift.

But combined with the amazement was a prodding sense of unease. Why would she have posed nude for Raine Hawthorne if she hadn't been intimate with him? For the man's money? Had she thought that society wouldn't care?

Morgan shook his head. He couldn't imagine that Lily

would be greedy enough to do anything for money.

Then why?

The question circled in his head, answers teasing just beyond the reaches of his mind as days passed, each minute that ticked by a breathless suspension.

Lily ignored Morgan after the night in his cottage. Whenever Morgan sought her out she either slipped away or surrounded herself with the children. She made it clear she wanted nothing to do with him.

Morgan told himself he should have left Blakemore House long ago. But he couldn't bring himself to go.

He had told Lily the truth, that he had never wanted anyone as he wanted her. It was like a tightening in his chest that he couldn't loosen no matter what he did. At night he lay awake, wanting to go to her. But he would get no farther than the back door when he would chide himself.

In truth, nothing had changed, he reasoned. Not really. They had shared an intimacy that he would never forget, but that didn't change the fact that he had a job to do. And he had promised himself that he wouldn't use Lily any longer to get what he needed.

Leave, he told himself. *She doesn't want you here.* But as long as he lived he would never forget the night they had shared. And dear God in heaven, the morning after. As a result, the days flowed by and he didn't leave.

To compound matters, Morgan was growing concerned about Lily. If the house had been a shambles before, it was a disaster now. She had already burned almost everything that had been in the room at the top of the house—everything she could manhandle down the stairs. Only the armoire remained.

Now, as if having decided that burning was the best method to dispose of unwanted goods, Lily had methodically gone from room to room, setting fires in the clearing on what was fast becoming a regular basis.

More than once the clanging brass bell of the fire wagon

was heard making its way to Blakemore House. And more than once Lily had left Morgan to make explanations. If things didn't change very soon Morgan was certain he was going to be hauled off to the city jail for breaking city ordinances.

Though he cursed himself for a fool, Morgan couldn't bring himself to tell the fire marshall that it was Lily who had set the blazes. If anyone was going to get tossed in jail for breaking the law it would be him.

Not that she cared about his gallant intentions. Lily had not said more than a handful of words to him in days, and the words she had uttered were of the Is-that-the-fire-truck-I-hear? variety.

Morgan went up the stairs from the kitchen. He hadn't seen the children or Lily leave the house that morning, but all was quiet. Too quiet, he knew from experience.

"Hell," he muttered, "what is going on now?"

He went from room to room, but didn't find anyone. It was just as he was heading down the upstairs hallway when his steady gait faltered. He heard voices raised in anger. After a moment he realized the sound was coming from Lily's room.

"Put that back!"

"Quit being a baby. I'm just going to look at it."

"Get down from there, Penelope."

Morgan quickened his step as the voices grew more agitated. But he arrived too late. Just as he reached the door the sound of something breaking crashed through the house. The shattering noise was followed by two very young and very frightened gasps.

"Now look what you've done!"

Morgan pushed open the door of Lily's bedroom to find Penelope and Cassie standing in the middle of the floor, jagged pieces of shattered china at their feet. Morgan realized in an instant what had broken. Lily's treasured china cup, though the saucer had been spared.

Very slowly he turned his hard gaze on the girls. They

stood scared and speechless in the all-too-quiet house.

"What are you doing in here?" he demanded, his voice harsh with anger.

Morgan didn't hear Lily's footstep come up behind him, didn't know she was there until she stood beside him.

"What happened?" she whispered, staring down at the broken pieces of china at Penelope's feet.

From the look in her eyes, Morgan knew that Lily's throat was burning and tight. She loved that cup. He knew it. The children knew it. He had learned that she cherished very few things. But this cup had meant the world to her.

Penelope stood very still as if afraid to move, looking terrified. It was unsettling to see this in the child who elbowed her way through the world, rarely showing any emotion. Her widened eyes were awash with tears, though she tried to hide them.

Morgan's heart went out to her, much as it went out to Lily. But he also knew that the cup had been broken. Penelope deserved Lily's wrath.

Penelope stared at Lily, the muscles in her throat working. Then without a word, Penelope dropped to her knees in front of the cup and began to pick up the pieces, tears streaming down her cheeks.

"Careful, Penelope," Morgan said. "You could cut yourself."

"I told her to leave the cup alone," Cassie blurted, her chin trembling.

Even though her head was down, Morgan could see Penelope briefly squeeze her eyes shut.

And still Lily didn't move.

Cassie ran to Lily's side, wrapping her arms around Lily's hips. "Oh, Lily, I told her, really I did. Please don't hate us." Her voice cracked. "Please don't go away."

Morgan understood in that instant. Cassie was scared. And Penelope was scared but didn't know how to show it. The little girl desperately wished to turn back time. A time before the cup had been broken, a time before her father had died, leaving them alone in this uncertain world.

Still staring at the cup, Lily absently placed her hand on Cassie's head.

The eerie scene filled Morgan with the need to take control, to do something. But what could he do? How could he make Lily understand the girls' fears?

Gingerly, Penelope picked up one piece, then another. And just when Morgan had had enough, it was Lily who spoke.

"It's just a silly old cup, Penelope."

Penelope looked up. And Lily shrugged.

Morgan realized she understood.

"Really," Lily continued, the furrows on her forehead beginning to ease. "Everyone for miles knows that I break things every time I turn around. I can just *look* at a cup and it will break." She walked over to Penelope and dropped down in front of her, cupping the girl's chin. "Truly, it was just a silly old cup," she said softly.

Penelope crouched, looking horrified, unwilling to believe Lily's words.

And then Lily did something Morgan would never forget. She reached over and took a small china figure that graced a small table. Before he realized what she was about, she dropped the figure on the floor.

"Ooops," was all she said.

Penelope and Cassie looked on, stunned, their mouths hanging open.

Then in a motion that nearly toppled Lily to the floor, Penelope launched herself into her aunt's arms.

"I'm sorry," Penelope cried, her tears finally flowing over.

Lily stiffened, uncertainty and perhaps fear etching her porcelain features.

"I'm so, so sorry," Penelope added, holding Lily very tight.

Lily's hands fluttered uncertainly at her sides, making it clear she had no idea what to do. But then she seemed to ease, her features softening with an aching joy, and she awkwardly wrapped her arms around her niece.

"I'm sorry for making fun of you," Penelope continued through broken sobs.

"I know, I know," Lily murmured, stroking Penelope's hair.

"I'm sorry for being so mean. I'm sure you must hate me."

With that, Lily brought her hands to Penelope's cheeks, all uncertainty gone. Gently Lily turned Penelope's face up to hers. "I don't hate you. I could never hate you."

"Are you sure?"

Lily's smile was genuine, lighting up the room until even Morgan felt its force.

"Of course I'm sure. We're family. And families stick together. Now up with you," Lily said. "Rumor has it that there's some lemonade in the kitchen."

Penelope and Cassie exchanged hasty glances.

Lily laughed out loud. "It's good, I promise. I bought it from a vendor."

The girls left the room, their footsteps receding down the carpeted hall. Lily remained before the shattered pieces of china, her head slightly bowed so that Morgan couldn't see her face.

"That was very generous of you," he said.

Her shoulders straightened suddenly as if she had forgotten for a moment that he was there. "It's only a cup."

Very carefully, she began to pick up the pieces, cradling the fragments in her palm.

"But it's a cup that I know meant a great deal to you. A true mother couldn't have been kinder."

Lily stood then, and set the pieces into a trash pail before she looked him in the eye. "As I said, it's only a cup.

Broken, not broken, I don't care. Now if you'll excuse me, I have work to do.''

She turned to go, but Morgan blocked her way. It was more than a cup to her and everyone in the house knew it, including Lily. He wanted to ask her why she denied it . . . he wanted to ask why she had ignored him for the last week.

"Let it go, Morgan." She hesitated, her gaze dropping to his hand on her arm.

He felt his blood begin to surge. It had been so long since he had touched her. Unable to help himself, he pulled her close until their bodies nearly touched.

"Let me go, Morgan. Nothing good can come of this."

Then she was gone.

It was late that night when Morgan dropped into bed exhausted. But he couldn't sleep. He lay on the mattress tossing and turning until he pulled on his clothes and walked out into the night.

It had become a habit of sorts, walking through the grounds late, checking on the darkened house. But this night a light in the kitchen burned low. When he drew closer, he could see that Lily sat at the kitchen table. Alone. Intent on something before her.

Then her weight shifted and he saw that the shattered pieces of the china cup lay before her. With unskilled fingers, she was trying to put the cup back together again. His heart tightened in his chest at her inexperienced attempts at repair.

Finally she banged her fist against the table before she gathered the pieces, wrapped them in brown paper, then hid them in the back of a cabinet. Pulling her robe tight, she wiped her eyes and went to the gas sconce to turn the light low, leaving Morgan alone in the darkened night.

He told himself to do as she had already asked so many times—to leave her alone. He told himself that she wanted nothing to do with him, that as she had said, nothing good

could come out of their being together. And he knew that
she was right. But when he told himself to mind his own
business, to once and for all put Lily out of his mind, he
went into the kitchen instead.

Seventeen

The next morning Lily remembered Penelope and the cup. Her china cup. Lily suppressed the silly tears that started to burn in her eyes. Truly it was only a cup. Not as important as Penelope.

How would her niece act toward her this morning? Lily wondered. Would she be back to the same old angry retorts? Or had they achieved some measure of peace? Lily held a glimmer of hope about Penelope, but Robert was another matter entirely.

She shook her head. There was little doubt in her mind that Robert would ever love her. His anger and hatred ran deep, as if mimicking his dead father.

Lily pressed her eyes closed against the thought.

The kitchen was empty when she entered. Empty and quiet. Peaceful. She had loved this kitchen as a child. It was one of the few places where she could go and find people. Warm and lively. The servants had always been more of a family to Lily than her parents. Though Claude had disdained their company, Lily had found their warm exuberance welcoming.

Her throat tightened with emotion.

"Lily Blakemore," she chided herself in a whisper, "don't you dare get all teary eyed again."

But whatever control she might have gained was lost at the sight that met her eyes.

Her cup. In the very center of the kitchen table, the broken pieces magically sealed back together. Though the cracks were still visible, the cup was whole.

Lily pressed her eyes closed and fought to hold on. Emotion welled up inside her like a tidal wave, threatening to sweep her under. After the scandal, she had thrown herself into a new life, trying to forget the old. If she hadn't forgotten, at least she had achieved some measure of strength against it. After the recent article she had held on, barely, but she had managed. After making love to Morgan, she found she had to step carefully for fear of breaking down at every turn. But she hadn't. Somehow she had managed to hold on. But at the sight of her cup, the fragile pieces forming the best possible cup it could ever be again, Lily felt as if ten years of struggle had finally overwhelmed her.

Her resolve to be strong was gone. She reached out and clutched the table edge for support as she fought back her tears. Foolish tears, she chided herself. She couldn't let herself feel, she couldn't afford to break down now. Not after so many years of holding herself together.

But most of all, tears burned in her eyes because of what Morgan had done for her. She knew without having to be told that it was Morgan who had found her hidden burden, Morgan who had sat at this very table and pieced her cup back together again.

As if he could piece back together her life.

But he couldn't. He might want to, perhaps because he wanted her back in his bed. For a while. But she had seen the look in his eye. He might desire Lily Blakemore, but he hated Crimson Lily.

"What do you think?"

Lily whirled around at the sound. And found Morgan.

Of course he would be there. Hadn't she suspected as much when she saw the cup?

He stood at the back door, his hair still damp. How was it possible for any one man to be so beautiful? His full lips were spread in a boyish smile, revealing a glimpse of straight white teeth. So handsome, so perfect. Next to her ravaged soul.

She wanted to cross the distance that separated them, let him wrap her in his arms. Let him be the strong one—just for a little while.

Her chin came up resolutely against his devastating smile—and her weakness.

"What do you think?" he asked again, walking to the table. "Granted, you'll never drink out of it, but I thought it looked pretty good."

She wanted to cry out. Her hands fisted at her side as if holding on to a lifeline, keeping herself from being swept away. He looked like a young schoolboy, presenting his prize.

She took a deep breath. "You are a man who wants to fix everything. Painted letters on a wall, houses long neglected, pieces of a broken cup that should have been thrown away. But truly, not everything in this world can be fixed, Morgan. Some things we have to accept will remain broken forever."

With that Lily turned away. She didn't wait for his response, didn't want one, she hurried out of the kitchen, the door swinging to a halt behind her.

Morgan started after her. This time he wouldn't let her go. This time he would follow her and once and for all demand answers.

Lily had just started up the stairs to the second floor when Morgan came up from the kitchen. But Lily's flight and Morgan's pursuit were halted when someone knocked firmly on the front door.

They both stared at the door before Morgan pulled it

open and she caught a glimpse of a blue uniform. A patrolman. With Robert at his side.

"Mr. Blakemore?"

"No, Officer," Morgan stated, glancing from the patrolman to Robert.

Lily hurried back to the door. "I'm Robert's aunt."

The officer looked from Lily to Morgan, his hard glare censorious.

Morgan raised a brow, his voice growing dangerous. "Is there a problem, Officer?"

Morgan's demeanor instantly set the officer back in his place. "I'm bringing your nephew home," the man said to Lily. "Felt this was better than hauling him off to jail."

"Jail?" she gasped.

Morgan steadied Lily. "What happened?" he demanded.

"Your young man here got himself in a spot of trouble. A fight. Isn't that right, son?"

Robert stared at his boots.

"Is this true?" Lily asked, barely getting the words out. It didn't matter that she realized now that the officer was only trying to scare Robert in hopes that the boy would never want to fight again.

Morgan took hold of Robert's shoulder, gently but firmly. Robert looked up and for the first time Lily saw his rapidly swelling blackened eye.

"Good God," Lily cried. "Who did that to you?"

"You might ask what the other boy looks like," the officer stated with a nod of his head. "But I guess boys will be boys. I'm bringing young Robert home this time." He turned to the boy. "But if I catch you at it again, you won't be so lucky."

The officer left the three of them in the doorway. Lily could only stand and stare, a sickening dread beginning to fill her.

She was supposed to save them, not get them sent away. How would she ever manage?

"Why, Robert?" she whispered. "Why did you get into a fight?"

The boy dropped his gaze, then shoved his fists in his pants pockets.

"Robert?" Morgan demanded. "Tell us what happened."

"I can't," he said, his voice small.

"You can and you will."

The boy glanced at Morgan, then Lily. He looked directly at her as if seeing her for the first time. Then he flushed with embarrassment.

An unexpected rush of dread and understanding made Lily's knees weak. She had the sudden, desperate need to run and flee, to cover her ears. "Go on, Robert," she said instead, "tell us."

"I told you, I can't!"

"Of course you can, dear. You have to."

Robert shifted his weight from foot to foot. "Herbie Nylander said some terrible things," he mumbled.

Morgan's face turned grim.

"About who?" Lily asked, her voice like ice.

Robert looked away.

"Tell me," she insisted.

"About you, okay! He said things about you!"

She felt the sudden tension in Morgan. He was surprised, she knew it.

"We should talk about this later," he said.

"No, Morgan. We will talk about it now." She focused on Robert. "What did the boy say about me?"

"He called you Crimson Lily." His voice grew even smaller. "He said you were a . . . bad woman."

"Damn it," Morgan cursed without regard for who could hear.

Unlike Morgan, Lily had expected Robert's words, though it hadn't lessened the blow.

"I'm sorry, Robert."

"Why are you sorry?" the boy demanded, his voice

exploding, his face reddening with anger. "If that patrolman hadn't come along, I would have pounded Herbie even worse."

Her throat constricted.

Robert's bravado deserted him as quickly as it had appeared, and he shuffled his feet. "You may be silly sometimes, but you're not bad, not really."

She couldn't force words out of her throat, couldn't speak, could barely breathe. Robert had defended her—didn't think she was so terribly bad.

Tears burning her eyes, Lily stepped forward and pulled Robert into a fierce embrace. "I'm sorry," she finally managed. "So terribly, terribly sorry."

She held him tightly and was amazed when she felt his arms wrap around her. When she opened her eyes, she found Morgan looking at them, his eyes filled with a mixture of anger and pride. She started to extend her hand to him, but footfalls on the front steps outside drew her attention. Immediately Lily, Robert, and Morgan turned to the door. Lily was certain they all thought the officer had changed his mind and returned.

But it was someone else who arrived, a small man in stiff attire, looking ill at ease in his black suit. Everyone stared, no one spoke. The man held a satchel in one hand, and an official-looking document in the other.

"Miss Lily Blakemore?" he asked.

Lily barely nodded her head.

"Sign here, please."

"What is it?" Morgan demanded.

"A court notification."

Morgan reached out to take the papers, but the official moved them out of his grasp.

"They are for Miss Blakemore, sir."

With trembling hands, Lily took the papers before the man hurried off. Lily could feel Morgan's and Robert's questioning gazes as she stared down at the thick sheaf without reading

"Let me read it," Morgan said.

"No," she said quickly. "No."

Taking a deep breath, she broke the seal and began to read once, then twice.

She lowered her hands to her sides, the papers held loosely. Morgan reached down and took the document, and this time she didn't resist.

She stared out the door, down the now-empty path.

"No," Morgan bit out. "They can't do this."

Robert tried to get a look at the papers. "What does it say?"

Lily turned back, her tortured gaze meeting Morgan's. Then she turned to Robert—Robert who had defended her, Robert who didn't hate her as she had assumed. Anguish wrapped around her like a strangling vise. She had already possessed Cassie's love. Somehow she had managed finally to gain both Penelope's and Robert's. She nearly groaned with bitter laughter.

And now the courts wanted to take the children away.

Eighteen

Mere minutes after Lily learned that she was loved by the children, she was given notice that another relative had come forward and was contesting the will.

Who were these people? Where had they come from? How had they learned of Claude's death?

"Lily?" Robert said, his voice rising.

She turned her attention to her nephew, wanting to touch his silky hair, but didn't. She felt awkward and unsure of the situation. "It seems you have more relatives than we realized," she said, her smile forced.

"What are you talking about?" Robert demanded.

She glanced at Morgan, then back to her nephew. "It seems that a cousin of your mother's has filed for custody of you and your sisters."

"No!"

No, so emphatically. Lily was sure that as long as she lived she would remember Robert's simple exclamation.

"They can't have us!" he stated firmly. "You have to tell them no."

"I'm afraid it's not that easy."

"Of course it is. My father put you in charge. It's in the will. I've seen it."

Lily could just imagine Robert demanding a copy of the will right after it had been read, and poring over the document line by line in disbelief that she had been left in charge. But somehow his disbelief had given way to love and he wanted her to stay. She would have smiled her joy if she hadn't been so devastated.

She took a deep breath. "Yes, he did, but anyone can contest a will. And in two weeks the judge is coming here to see you and your sisters, to see where you live, how you live." Her voice caught. "In short, to see if I am a good mother."

Without waiting for his response, Lily hurried up the stairs, afraid that at any moment she would embarrass herself with tears.

Morgan watched her go, a sick feeling of dread spreading through his body. He had recognized the look in Lily's eyes when Robert had said that they couldn't let the others win. He had recognized her fear, her doubt. But then the look had disappeared, evaporated so quickly that Morgan could easily believe that it had never been there, just as he had done all along—disregarded her depth of emotions.

The fear and doubt had been there, had been there all along, he realized with a burning certainty. Only he hadn't let himself look deeply enough to see it, he hadn't let himself believe in the emotions, or her.

"Morgan?"

"Yes, Robert?"

"She'll fight for us, won't she?"

The boy's face was lined with worry. Morgan reached out and affectionately cuffed his shoulder. "Of course she will."

"But she might not want to." He glanced at his shoes. "I haven't given her much reason to want to stay."

"Hey, Lily loves you."

Robert shoved his hands in his pockets, then shuffled

his feet. "I don't care if she loves *me* . . . it's just for Penelope and Cassie."

"Sure," Morgan said. "But no need to worry for Penelope and Cassie. Your aunt will fight for all of you."

"How do you know?"

How did he know? he wondered. He didn't. He remembered talking to Beauford Tisdale at the Union League Club so long ago. Morgan had felt so confident, so sure that he understood Lily. Beauford had been right, and Morgan had turned out to be wrong. Lily never did what he expected.

Morgan was the first to admit that Lily didn't know the first thing about children. But now that he had allowed himself to see the truth about her, a kaleidoscope of images flashed through his mind. Lily pulling back her shoulders with bravado. Lily hiding her true feelings like a master.

Lily might have made a mistake in her past, but she regretted it every day of her life.

Lily loved her brother's children, and she might want to keep them. But though he had told Robert that he was convinced she would fight, in reality he wasn't so sure. And if she fought, could she win?

"She will, you'll see, Robert."

Morgan left Robert in the foyer and set off in search of Lily. He didn't bother with her suite of rooms. He kept going until he came to the narrow stairway that led to the room in the attic.

The bright sunshine that spilled into the room was a mockery of the desolate turn this day had taken. The sounds of the street didn't reach this height, not today. The room was quiet.

Lily stood, as she so frequently did, at one of the tall windows, leaning against the frame, her forehead pressed against the glass.

"You've been avoiding me long enough," he said, his voice shattering the quiet. "It's time we talked."

"I think you should leave. There is nothing to talk about."

"There is plenty to talk about, Lily."

"Not with you."

"Unfortunately you don't have a lot of choices in who you can talk with right now." He waited for her to deny his words. She could have said something about John Crandall. But she didn't speak, didn't offer up the name of the man who had all but rejected her since the article on Crimson Lily appeared in the paper.

Anger sizzled down his spine. But he recognized now that it wasn't irrational. He was angry at Crandall for not helping Lily. Morgan forcefully put aside his thoughts that he had done nothing to help Lily either, in fact, quite the opposite. Because he could help her now, and he would.

"I'm all you've got right now, and I can help."

"You?" She scoffed into the room. But her words held no animosity, just resignation. "You can't help me, Morgan. No one can help me."

"Stop it, Lily. Quit being foolish."

"Not foolish, just realistic. When I was forced to leave New York, I thought at least I could leave it all behind me, thinking to start over. I traveled far and wide. But no matter where I went, my reputation preceded me. Then I stopped going places. And of course, the talk stopped. Or so I believed. I was lulled into believing that people would forget. But they didn't forget. I can't leave Crimson Lily behind me. She follows me everywhere I go." Her head fell forward. "I can't hold on any longer. I'm tired of being strong."

"I used to think that it was the people who called you Crimson Lily that you were fighting. Now I'm not so sure. I think you're fighting yourself."

She shot him a sharp look, but he continued. "I think that you're giving up without fighting the real fight. You play the part that society assigned you instead of proving that you are more than your past."

"I'm not more than my past. I'm defined by those two words."

"Only because you've let it be that way. Fight, Lily. Prove to the world that you are more. You love the children and they love you. Fight for them!"

She turned away sharply. "I can't."

"Of course you can."

He closed the distance that separated them and pulled her around to face him. His thoughts faltered at the cornered look that ravaged her features. The bravado was gone. Naked fear etched her porcelain skin.

"Lily," he breathed, crushing her to his chest.

This time instead of pushing him away, he felt her fingers fist in his shirt. She clutched him tightly. But her features grew more ragged, her fear mixing with anguish. With her hands still clutching his shirt, she began pushing at his chest.

Unable to let go—or give in?

"Lily, why won't you hold me?"

"Because I am afraid if I do I'll never be able to let go." She pushed back until she met his gaze, her eyes wide.

As always, her beauty hit him hard. He realized then, as she looked at him with painfully tormented blue eyes, that he loved her. Loved her despite what she had done. He was in love with Lily—just as Trudy Spencer had surmised weeks before.

He had been unwilling to admit it before—to the art teacher or to himself. He had been willing to admit he desired her, and had even come to admit that they shared some kind of understanding. But he could no longer deny the truth. He loved Lily with an intensity more powerful than anything he had ever experienced. This strange woman-child had woven her way into his life until he felt that if she were to disappear he might unravel at the seams.

And that, he realized, was the reason why he hadn't been able to leave.

But his love came at a cost. And that cost was John Crandall. Could he afford the price?

His groan rumbled deep in his chest as he pulled her to him. "Lily," he murmured into her hair. "I love you."

With his words, Morgan expected her to hold him tightly. A sweet surrender. He was unprepared for the biting "No!" that resounded against the walls.

She pushed at him, surprise gaining her release.

"No!" she repeated, her eyes wild as she stood back from him. "You can't possibly love me."

"But I do. I love you, Lily Blakemore. I've loved you for months but have been too caught up in my own concerns to see it."

He watched the emotions work on her face. He knew she wanted to believe him, he could see it.

"How can you love me with all that you have heard?"

"I see beyond Crimson Lily. I told you before that everyone has made mistakes."

"Mistakes?" She pressed her eyes closed, then jerked farther away when he touched her arm.

"Lily, I'm trying to tell you that I don't care about your past. I believe in the Lily you have become." He forced her to face him. "And I believe that you can fight for the children and win."

She turned her head away. With one strong finger he turned her back. "I also believe you will be the best mother anyone could hope to have."

She stared at him for an eternity, and just when he thought she would demand that he unhand her, she spoke. "Then you must believe in magic after all."

He smiled, remembering their conversation from so long ago. "Not magic. It's all here, in you. And it's been there all along. So hold on to me, Lily. Hold on tight. You don't have to let go."

She sighed and shook her head. "Don't you see, Morgan. Everyone has to let go, because eventually everyone leaves. In the end everyone betrays—even if they don't mean to.''

''Lily, that's not true.''

She placed her fingertips on his lips. ''I will try to win the children. I will try to do what I need to do.'' She hesitated. ''But I can't do it with you here.''

Morgan couldn't have spoken if he wanted to. He stood there trying to comprehend.

''I can't afford to let you into my life, Morgan.''

''Of course you can.''

''You said that you loved me because you have seen beyond Crimson Lily.''

''And I meant it.''

''That's the problem. What you have failed to see is that I am not Crimson Lily.''

''You said yourself that you posed.''

''But just because I posed, does that make me a ruined woman? I am not what you think. Never have been . . . or at least I wasn't until the night when I came to you in your cottage.''

''Don't say that.''

''Hear me out!'' She drew a deep breath. ''The only thing that has saved me all these years was knowing,'' she laid her fisted hand on her heart, ''knowing that they were wrong. But after what I did, after asking you to love me, I no longer know in my heart that I don't deserve the name.''

''Damn it, Lily, this is crazy!''

''No! You asked who I was fighting. Always Crimson Lily. When I said earlier that I wanted you to leave I meant it. Not the room, but this house. I have no place for you in my life, Morgan. I insist that you leave.''

Emotions churned through his mind like a violent winter storm. His dark eyes grew dangerous. ''No!'' he stated. ''No, Lily. I won't leave.''

Her eyes widened, but he couldn't stop. ''I love you, as I have never loved anyone before.''

She turned away, but he grabbed her and turned her back. "You hired me to do a job and I'm going to finish it. This house is going to be finished. And beyond that I am going to help you win the kids."

She opened her mouth to speak, but he cut her off. "Every time I see you, every time I think of you I want you so badly it hurts. Regardless of that, I give you my word that I won't touch you. But I love you, Lily, and I'm not going to desert you like everyone else in your life. Not everyone leaves, Lily."

He let go of her abruptly, then started to go. But he stopped at the door. "I love you, Lily Blakemore. And now I'm going to prove it."

Then he slammed out the door, the entire house shaking from the force.

Nineteen

I love you, Lily Blakemore.

Morgan's words. Stated so adamantly. Did he really mean it? Lily wondered, her palms tingling. Was it possible?

It was the following morning, and Lily pressed her eyes closed with wonder. Morgan loving her, refusing to give up. She could hardly fathom the joy that surged through her. But on the heels of her joy, mind-numbing anxiety quickly followed.

Fight for the children—and win?

Lily scoffed. She couldn't imagine who she thought she might fool. Certainly not some judge.

After dressing with great care, thirty minutes later Lily stopped just outside the kitchen door.

Would Morgan really still be there? she wondered, her past making it difficult to believe that he would truly have stayed. Had he really meant it when he said he would show her the way? Or would his senses have returned after a long night's sleep, having realized the impossibility of his task?

A crooked smile pulled at her lips. No doubt with Morgan Elliott it was the impossibility of the task that would challenge him. She had never met anyone so unwilling to take no for an answer.

Her heart burgeoned with hope at the thought, and with her smile growing luminous, she pushed through the kitchen door.

No sooner did the door swing shut behind her than her eyes widened at the sight of not just Morgan, but Robert, Penelope, and Cassie as well, huddled around the kitchen table, conferring with great seriousness. Not until she cleared her throat a second time did they finally notice her.

As they turned to her they were smiling, but their smiles froze on their faces as they took in her attire.

"What?" she demanded, suddenly self-conscious.

She looked down at her clothes. "What's wrong with what I have on now?"

Morgan shook his head and groaned, Robert and Penelope grimaced, while Cassie stood up from her chair. "I think you look beautiful—perfectly perfect!"

"Perfect for a masquerade, maybe," Morgan stated. "I could deal with the feather boa, but those god-awful backless shoes?"

Red stained Lily's cheeks. "I thought old clothes would be appropriate. We are going to be cleaning, after all."

Morgan hung his head, then got up from his chair and came around the table with a sound rumbling in his chest that sounded suspiciously like a growl. Lily's eyes widened, then she sucked in her breath when he took her hand and pulled her out of the kitchen.

"Where are we going?" she demanded, trying to sound enraged, though all the while almost solely thinking about the feel of his fingers wrapped around her wrist.

"To change."

"To change what?"

"Your clothes."

Her heart slammed against her chest. He was going to

change her clothes, her mind shrieked. Lily dug her heels in, though it did no good. That was the problem with mules, she conceded. They weren't very good for maneuvering.

"Morgan, really," she said, trying to break free.

But he only drew her along easily.

When he pulled her to a halt in the middle of her bedroom, Lily blushed again. Though this time the flash of color had little to do with being aware of Morgan's body.

"This place is a disaster!" he blurted out.

Lily cringed. She hadn't straightened up before she had gone downstairs—and whether he realized it or not, she had spent a good bit of time trying to figure out what to wear, searching through every drawer.

"I wrote up a little something to put in the classified advertisements," she said, hoping to distract him. She picked up a slip of paper. " 'Needed: Butler, cook, and housemaid.' " She added the address, then lowered her hand to her side. "I still wonder why Marky and Jojo left without a word."

Morgan growled. Her distraction maneuver had failed to work. Lily stepped back.

"You need more than one maid, just to clean up this room."

He turned away and headed straight for the armoire that held many of her clothes. One by one he sifted through her wardrobe, discarding every gown he encountered. "Where in the world do you get your clothes? The Traveling Minstrels Secondhand Store?"

"I'll have you know that I've collected my gowns from around the world." She lifted her chin defiantly. "And if you've changed your mind and don't want to help me, fine."

"I wouldn't be here if I didn't want to help you," he groused.

"Then why are you so angry? This was your idea, not mine."

Morgan closed his eyes. Lily was certain he was praying for patience before he turned back to her.

"I'm not angry, Lily." He took a step closer, then stopped.

"You're acting angry. In fact you've acted angry with me since I walked into the kitchen."

The look in his eyes shifted. She saw it then. The heat. The desire. He wanted her. Badly. But he was keeping his promise. He was a man of his word. He wouldn't touch her, but it was costing him dearly.

Lily didn't know if she was elated or concerned.

Not wanting to press her luck, she hurried past him to a bureau. She pulled out clothes with abandon, adding to the mess, until she found what she needed.

"How about this?"

Morgan's dark-eyed gaze took in the riding pants and man's shirt that had been made to fit her.

"Don't you have any old gowns?"

She waved a hand over the finery she already wore. "This is it."

Lily returned to the kitchen a few minutes later, the riding pants smooth over her slender hips, the shirt billowing gently over her full breasts. She found Morgan at the table. She expected him to nod his approval. Instead, if possible, his dark eyes darkened even more as he scanned her form.

"Robert sent your advertisement to *The Evening Sun* and *The Times*," Penelope stated.

"I thought it was very good," Cassie said importantly. "We should have ever so many inquiries for the positions."

"But the work can't wait until someone is found," Robert interjected.

Cassie held out a sheet of paper. "We made a list. This is everything that needs to get done."

Even from a distance Lily could see that the list was

long. She took the paper with trepidation. "All this has to be done in two weeks?" she squeaked.

"Two weeks," Robert confirmed.

Lily groaned. It would take an army of servants to get this much work done in such a short period of time, and she hadn't even managed to keep the two servants she had. Where in the world would she find any more on such short notice?

"How in the world will I ever get it done?" she said out loud, bewildered, a sinking feeling washing over her.

"We're going to help!" the children announced in unison.

Lily's head shot up, her gaze taking in each of the children. "You're going to help?"

"Of course. Each of us will have a job," Penelope stated proudly.

"We'll get it done together," Cassie added.

"Because we're family." Robert said the words with gruff affection.

Lily took in each precious face, a happiness she could hardly describe lodging in her throat. And then suddenly Lily was engulfed by their young arms wrapping around her. Over her charges' heads, her eyes met Morgan's. He smiled at her and nodded his head as if to say, See, you're going to win.

"Come on, everyone," he stated, setting his coffee cup aside. "The clock is ticking. We don't have a second to lose."

They started with cleaning. Penelope produced a bucket and an assortment of rags and brushes. Cassie handed around aprons. Lily managed a bright smile, convinced that surely they wouldn't have to do this for long before servants were found to do the work.

They began to clean just as the clock tolled the hour. Nine o'clock. At nine-fifteen, Lily was convinced that the floors in the house had not been cleaned in a good many years. And by nine-thirty, she decided they weren't worth cleaning at all. But Morgan and the children were there every step of the way, or inch of the floorboards, she conceded wryly, and weren't going to let her give in. From floors they moved on to cleaning the peeling wallpaper and grimy windows, ash-filled fireplaces and mildewed tiles.

By the end of the day, Lily couldn't quite recall what it was about Morgan Elliott that had made her heart flutter. The man had been bossy since she met him, but now he had turned into an overbearing tyrant, she grumbled to herself as she emptied a bucket of dirty water out back, her hand on her aching lower back.

Lily wasn't certain she would ever be the same again. All she wanted to do was toss the scrub brush into the trash pail and find a nice tall glass of lemonade. And she was on the verge of doing just that when Morgan found her heading for the cool box.

"Where are you going?" he asked, his exacting voice making her feel like a guilty schoolgirl.

"I'm done for the day."

"No, you're not."

Lily whirled around to face him. "Who are you to tell me what I will or will not be doing?"

"Obviously the only person out here who has a lick of sense."

"Oh, that's right," she said, her aching body making her words slither out sarcastically. "You know everything. You, the demented taskmaster run amok. We can't do all of this. We have to find some servants. Do you hear me?"

"Yes, as does the rest of Manhattan. And you can scream all you like. But as Robert said earlier, you can't wait until you find people to do the work for you, Lily. You have to start now. And you will, because I'm not going to let you fail."

"Fail!" she shrieked. "I've worked all bloody day long."

Morgan's eyes narrowed angrily. "And you'll work all bloody night long if that's what it's going to take to get this place in shape. And from now on when I say Jump, you say How high!''

"How high?'' Every ounce of frustration and anger evaporated into the room. "How high!'' she gasped, before she doubled over laughing.

Morgan glowered, his eyes glittering ominously. "That wasn't supposed to be funny.''

"I know,'' she managed through another bout of laughter. "That's what *is* so funny! How high,'' she cried as she burst out laughing again.

But when she opened her eyes, tears of laughter streaming down her checks, she sobered quickly enough. The glitter in Morgan's eye had shifted and changed, and he moved toward her like a predator stalking its prey.

"What are you doing, Morgan?'' she asked, suddenly breathless, taking an instinctive step backward.

"What does it look like, Lily?'' he responded as he came closer.

Lily took another step back, but found herself blocked by the hard edge of the counter. She could barely concentrate. Morgan's gaze was locked on her mouth. Without realizing it, she ran her tongue nervously over her lips. "It looks like you are getting ready to break your promise.''

Morgan's eyes narrowed, his heated gaze rising to meet hers.

Lily held out her hands as if to ward him off. "You promised, Morgan. You promised you wouldn't touch me.''

His body coiled with tension, she could feel it. She nearly groaned out loud when he stepped away.

"Hell,'' he ground out, raking his fingers through his hair. "You're lucky I made that promise.''

Lucky? She thought not, her traitorous mind whispered before she could stop it. But before she could chastise herself appropriately, he reached out and very gently tilted her chin until she was forced to look in his eyes.

"Enough work for today. But we start again at first light." His gaze bore into her. "And don't be late."

Lily wasn't laughing the next morning when she woke up. She could do little more than groan at the unaccustomed feelings that pulsated through her body—none of them good. She ached in places she didn't know existed before Morgan Elliott had thrust a scrub brush into her hand.

Grimacing, Lily rolled over and burrowed deeper into her pillow. Morgan had said they would begin again at first light. She snorted into the downy softness. First light. Where did he think they were? On the frontier?

In the sophisticated urban confines of New York, first light did not signify a time in which something should occur, unless it was to go back to sleep. And she intended to. Though for just a little longer, she promised herself, exhausted at the thought of all that still had to be done.

Her eyes drifted closed, and she relished the feel of sleep-softened sheets beneath her. But her tranquil state was shattered when a harsh pounding sounded on her door.

Lily groaned into her pillow. "Go away!"

The door fell back on its hinges, the pictures rattling on the walls. "I told you not to be late. The children are up and ready."

"Get out!"

But Lily was granted no such luck. She had barely registered his pounding stride across the room before she felt the sheet and light coverlet pulled off the bed in one fell swoop. Lily shot up like a lightning bolt, leaping up to stand on the mattress, her tiny feet sinking into the downy folds.

"How dare you!" she raged.

"You're late."

"Late? Late! You are a deranged, unbearable beast, and I will not take orders from you a second longer. I'm in charge here. In case you have forgotten, you work for me!"

She reached out and grabbed at the covers, only to have him whisk them beyond her reach and toss them aside.

"Call me what you like, but employer or not, you're a pain in the hindquarters."

Lily's eyes narrowed. "It must be tough being a saint."

Lily saw the look in his eyes and the stillness in his body. Just as before, he became the predator. The desire. The heat. The need. He had controlled it yesterday, though barely.

This morning she had pushed him to some limit. She had survived yesterday. But today?

For one breathless moment she was certain he was going to damn his promise and pull her close in sharp demand. Her eyes fluttered closed at the thought. His lips on hers. The taste of him. The feel.

And that couldn't happen. Her eyes snapped open. *She* had promised. Had promised herself. She was not Crimson Lily.

"Just get out," she demanded.

He started to protest, but she cut him off, recognizing defeat when it was staring her in the face. "I'm up. Just let me get dressed in peace."

She knew he was studying her, trying to determine her degree of sincerity. "I promise," she said with exaggerated impatience.

"Five minutes. Not a second longer. And if I have to come in here again I will dress you myself."

His gaze darkened and he took a step forward. Lily leaped backward. "Morgan," she warned, her eyes wide. "You better get out of here before you do something you'll regret."

His eyes narrowed. "The only thing I regret is telling you I'd wait until you'd learned how to run this household before I touched you again."

"Again?" she squeaked. "I thought—"

"You thought wrong. We will make love, Lily. Again.

Make no mistake about it. But not until you have finished with this house. Now get dressed.''

With that he turned on his heel and slammed out the door. Lily stood on the mattress, her feet sinking into the bedding. *"Again."* He had said "again." And though she should have been outraged and insulted, she only felt a piercing sense of relief that she wouldn't have to live the rest of her life without the feel of his touch.

As one day turned into two, and two into three, the "house project," as Lily had come to call it, continued—never ending, until Lily felt she was cooking and cleaning in her sleep, and not a single servant had been found to do the work.

Not that people hadn't arrived to apply for the position. They had. But a more disreputable bunch of people Lily had never seen. Out of everyone who had applied for the positions of butler, cook, and maid, not a single person had known what they were doing. On top of which references looked suspicious, eyes were bloodshot, breath smelled as if they had stopped off at the nearest tavern on the way to the interview. Marky and Jojo had looked like prime specimens compared to what had arrived at the door of Blakemore House.

As a result, Morgan, Lily, and the children continued doing the work. Lily's every muscle ached from the sheer quantity of work, though for all the good her efforts did her she might as well not have bothered. Her laundered sheets were stiff as egg whites beaten to peaks, though her beaten egg whites were as soupy as bad bouillon despite the fact that she was certain she had beaten them within an inch of their lives. Her shirts gave witness to the fact that she couldn't quite get the iron just the right temperature. Every shirt she had worked on bore some sort of iron marking.

Sitting at the kitchen table on the fourth morning, Lily dropped her head onto her arms and groaned. How in the world were they ever going to get the house in order in time? As Morgan had pointed out, the clock was ticking.

Given that, as soon as Morgan directed everyone to gather the needed supplies and each of them had headed off, Lily headed out the front door. She hailed a hack in front of Central Park and within the half hour she was downtown at John Crandall's office. She only hoped that he had returned.

She knew that when Morgan found out that she had left the house instead of performing her assigned tasks she would have hell to pay. But her time would be well spent. If John could get her servants before, surely he could get some again.

Just as Lily entered the reception area of John's office, she overheard voices raised in anger.

"Blasted woman, we ain't been paid!"

"But I don't have your money."

"He should have left the money for us. We did what we could."

Lily was certain the voice belonged to Marky.

"But you didn't find anything," a woman's voice said.

"He wasn't payin' us based on finding or not finding. He was payin' us to look!"

"Really, sir. I can't help you."

Confused, Lily stepped inside. "Marky? Jojo?"

Marky and Jojo whirled around. "Miz' Blakemore," Marky gasped. "What are you doing here?"

"I've come to find some replacements for the two of you." She frowned. "Does Mr. Crandall know that you just walked out on us? And what was it that you were looking for?"

Marky shifted his weight while Jojo shuffled his feet.

"We had to leave your place, because . . . Mr. Crandall got us another job," Marky said.

"Yeah, that's right," Jojo interjected nodding his head. "We got another job. Mr. Crandall said we had to get on it right away. Otherwise we would have said something. But there wasn't any time."

Lily looked at the men askance. What did they take her for? A fool?

"May I help you, miss?" the secretary asked.

"I'd like to speak to Mr. Crandall, please."

"As I was just telling these men, Mr. Crandall hasn't returned to town yet."

"Hasn't returned?" Lily looked at Marky. "How could you have been called away from my house to something else if he wasn't in town?"

Jojo looked to Marky.

"He sent a messenger," Marky provided, nodding his head.

"Yeah," Jojo chimed in, "a messenger."

Lily knew that there was more to the story than met the eye. But just then she needed a butler and a cook. "Apparently you need money, and I need a butler and a cook. Why don't you come back to Blakemore House with me?"

Marky and Jojo exchanged quick glances. "Sorry, Miz' Blakemore," Marky said. "We can't help you."

"How is that possible? The children and I need help to get the place in order." She didn't want to beg, but what were her choices? "I have to prove to the courts that I'm capable of taking care of the children."

Marky sighed and Jojo groaned.

"Like I said, Miz' Blakemore," Marky finally said. "We can't." He hesitated. "You're better off without us anyway."

Then Marky and Jojo nearly ran each other down in their haste to be gone.

Lily stared at their receding backs. What had he meant, she was better off without them?

"I'm sorry, ma'am. However Mr. Crandall should be back next week. Would you like to leave him a message?"

Distracted, Lily glanced back at the receptionist. "No,

that's all right,'' was all she said before she turned and walked out the door.

"Where did you go?"

Lily stopped, her hand still holding the front door knob, to find Morgan standing in the foyer, impatience lining his face.

"I had an errand to run."

She didn't bother to tell him that she had run into Marky and Jojo. He would only make some snide remark about not being able to keep help. Instead, she hurried upstairs and changed into clothes that she could work in. For the first time she realized that they truly might not find people to do the work in time for the judge to arrive. Her blood ran cold at the thought. And if Lily thought things had started out badly that day, they only got worse minutes later.

"Someone's at the door!"

Lily was just returning downstairs. Robert pulled open the door just as Lily stepped into the entryway. Lily's steps faltered and Robert stood in the doorway staring. Neither of them spoke.

"Is this the Blakemore residence?" a middle-aged man asked.

Robert and Lily still only stared.

The man was nicely dressed and stood next to a woman about the same age, her hands decorously covered in net gloves, her hair hidden beneath the demure brim of a straw hat.

"Atticus, dear," the woman said softly, "we must have the wrong address."

"No, no," Lily interjected, taking the last few steps to the door. "This is Blakemore House."

"Well, then, fine. I'm Atticus Wesford."

Lily's palms grew moist.

"And this is my wife, Adeline."

Adeline smiled. Lily felt light-headed.

Atticus turned to Robert. "And you must be young Robert."

Robert nodded his head suspiciously.

"Who's here?"

Penelope raced down the stairs with Cassie just behind her.

"Well, well, well," the man said. "You two pretty young ladies must be Penelope and Cassie. I am Atticus Wesford, your dear mother's cousin."

Lily was certain she was going to be sick. The relatives who wanted custody were here.

They went into the parlor. Atticus did most of the talking, telling the children about their life in Pennsylvania, their prosperous farm, their friends, until finally they announced it was time they should leave.

It had been little more than twenty minutes. But to Lily, they were the longest minutes of her life. Once the door had shut behind them and the children had trudged back upstairs, their stunned faces matching Lily's own, Lily returned to the kitchen, barely aware that she had taken the steps.

Heaven have mercy, what was she going to do?

The couple who were fighting for custody of the children couldn't have been nicer. They were kind and caring, well-to-do, and desperate for children of their own. Anyone with a lick of sense could see they would make the perfect parents.

Standing in the kitchen, a scorched shirt and basket of stiff laundry before her, Lily knew that she should let the children go. Who was she trying to fool that she could ever make a perfect parent—or even a marginal parent for that matter? And the fact remained, the children deserved better than what she could provide.

But regardless of that truth, the thought that kept circling in her mind like a whirling dervish was that marginal at tasks or not, she loved the children. And they loved her.

They belonged with her. Not on some farm in Pennsylvania.

But if she wanted to keep them, Lily knew she had to prove that she was as good a parent or better than the Wesfords.

Fight, Lily. For once in your life fight. Morgan's words.

Defeat tried to seep into her mind. She *had* been fighting, and look where it had gotten her.

But then a streak of determination that she had thought was long gone emerged. She had to fight harder, and longer. She loved the children. She wanted the children. And she knew they wanted her, too.

With that, Lily set about her tasks with renewed determination. Whether she found servants in time or not, she would learn to do the laundry, she would learn to cook, and she would learn to do all the things most women could do in their sleep.

She was going to fight. And this time she was going to win.

Twenty

"How high?"

Morgan's head shot up and he nearly sliced his hand in two when the saw he was using slipped. "Damn it, Lily. Don't ever sneak up on someone with a saw."

But Lily only smiled, her face beaming proudly. "I said, 'How high?'"

Morgan sighed, his countenance grim as he set the saw aside, then looked at Lily. "What are you talking about?"

"From now on when you say Jump, I'll say How high? I promise."

His countenance grew suspicious. "What have you done now, Lily?" he asked, starting for the door, intent of finding what part of the house she had managed to destroy today.

"That is unfair! I haven't done anything!" She had to stop herself from adding "yet." "I just came in here to tell you that I am ready to do whatever you tell me to do. You won't hear another complaint out of me. I'm going to learn how to run this place if it kills me."

Morgan had the fleeting thought that it might just do

that, either that or kill him. He could hardly concentrate
anymore because his mind was constantly filled with
thoughts of this maddening woman. And that was dangerous considering how often he was working with tools that
could as easily mar something as fix it. And Lily Blakemore wasn't much better. He shook his head. He had never
seen any one human being so ill equipped to perform simple chores.

"I know what you're thinking, Morgan Elliott. But I
can do it. I really can."

Morgan studied her, his expression growing tender.
"I'm sorry about the relatives showing up here."

"How did you know?"

"Robert told me."

"Is he upset?"

Morgan's smile grew lopsided. "I think he will be relieved that you are going to apply renewed effort to the
tasks at hand."

"And I am. I promise."

"All right, then. You can start with that basket of laundry I saw on the kitchen table. Wash it again."

"Again! You want me to do it all over again?"

"This is how you say How high?"

Lily grumbled, then suddenly laughed. "You're right.
You're right. I'm on my way."

And within minutes she was.

She went to the laundry room where she lit the gas burn-
ers beneath the huge tub of water. She didn't bother with
more soap. She simply rinsed, then rinsed again, until
sweat dripped down her back.

She worked as she had never worked at anything in her
life. Morgan and the children stood back and watched, or
marveled really.

"It looks like all we have been telling her has finally
sunk in," Robert stated when Lily pulled soft, dried laundry down from the line at the end of the day.

Within a week no one, Lily included, could believe the progress she had made.

"I've done it," she announced, holding a perfectly pressed shirt out for everyone to see. "Not a burn mark in sight."

Penelope and Cassie cheered. Robert clapped. Lily bowed her head and curtsied.

Morgan looked on with a countenance so fierce that Lily knew he was proud. Elation filled her. She had done it— with not a minute to spare. Only one thing remained. The judge arrived tomorrow. And Lily had to convince him that she was a good mother.

With exhilaration and trepidation churning through her body, Lily walked out onto the back porch, the structure now sturdy and white. She stood at the railing, looking out, pulling a long deep breath of joy. The children were all abed. The moon was high in the heavens. She had bathed and pulled on the shimmeringly thin Indian ensemble she was so fond of. Loose top trailing over a skirt of the same material. Shamelessly she had left her stays and corset in her dressing room, and when she bent just so, she could feel the night air against her skin.

"I'm proud of you."

Morgan's voice didn't startle her, it was as if she had known he would be there. Waiting for her. His words drifting through the night, wrapping around her.

Lily smiled, tilting her head. "I have to admit, I'm proud of me, too."

The night was cool but sparkling clear. They had been close to one another for days, a circumspect dance of near touches and accidental brushings that left her breathless.

"Thank you for all your help," she said into the quiet night, staring out into the sky, her back to him.

"You did all the work."

"That's not true and you know it."

He didn't respond from where he stood behind her, leaning back against the wall. She could tell that he was smoking a cigar. And she could feel his dark eyes boring into her.

"I really should go inside," she said, afraid at any second that she would turn around and close the distance that separated them.

Morgan didn't answer, at least with words. Her heart leaped when she heard him push away from the wall, stamp out his cigar, then felt his footfalls as he crossed the wooden porch. He came so near that she could feel his heat, his chest almost brushing her back. If she leaned ever so slightly she would touch him.

With effort she cleared her throat. "Heavens, I ache all over," she managed to get through her throat, trying for innocuous conversation. "I've never done so much work in all my life."

A shock of sensation raced through her body when he touched her. His strong hands began to massage the muscles in her shoulders. Slow circles. Deep, penetrating. Then down her arms, down over the thin gossamer material until his hands rested on her hips.

Her breath caught when his hands began to move again, slowly, upward, though this time they slid beneath the material. His hands came up to her waist, his palms against her skin, then higher until he cupped her breasts and he gently pulled her back against him.

"Lily," he murmured in her ear.

Her head fell back onto his shoulder as he kneaded her breasts with reverence. Then he lowered one hand until it rested just above her womanhood and he pressed her back against the hard length of his desire.

His breath grew ragged at the contact. "God, you make me lose control."

And with those words, what little control he had maintained dissipated. He turned her around, and looked in her eyes.

"It's late, and tomorrow's a big day. I really should get

to bed,'' she stammered before she slipped beneath his arm and headed for the door.

Without realizing he had moved, Lily was startled when Morgan's hand flattened on the door, holding it shut.

"You promised,'' she breathed, her body tense.

He leaned down and kissed her ear, sending shivers through her body.

"Morgan.'' She forced the reprimand from her mouth.

"The house is done. Everything's complete. I'm going to make love you, Lily. Tonight.''

Sensation jolted through her body. "Everything isn't done,'' she barely managed. "I still have to meet the judge.'' Suddenly she whirled around. "Oh, Morgan, I can't do it.''

He pulled back and looked at her for an eternity. "Yes, you can, Lily. You can do anything you want. Only fear can defeat you now.''

But that was what she was afraid of. Fear and failing.

"Shhh,'' he murmured against her hair, gentling her. "You'll be fine.''

He turned her head until their eyes met. "You'll be fine,'' he whispered again, his eyes intense as his hand curled around her arm.

Lily's heart leaped in her chest as his other hand came down and touched her lower back. She opened her mouth to speak, but he wasn't interested in words as he pulled her to him and closed his mouth over hers.

He pulled her closer, fiercely, a primitive call that made her body tremble. He demanded that she open to him, and she felt his groan when their tongues intertwined.

Wrapping his arms around her, he molded her body to his, her hands caught between their bodies. Carefully, he took her hands away, his fingers grazing the peaks of her breasts.

"Hold me,'' he urged, his voice gruff and deep. "Touch me, Lily.''

And she did. She ran her hands up his back, relishing

the feel of him, his hard strength, his barely contained passion. He wanted her. Had wanted her. She knew it, and rejoiced in that wanting.

He had been waiting. And would wait no longer.

He ran his tongue along the contour of her lips, until he took her mouth once again. His kiss was both sweet and brutal, claiming her.

He kissed her deeply, and when she felt his hands glide down her spine and cup her hips, she melted against him.

"Yes, Lily," he said, his voice rough. "I've waited as long as I'm going to wait. I love you. And despite everything, we were meant to be together." He looked into her eyes. "We are meant to be together, Lily."

He took her hand, and led her down the steps. Her heart pounded as he guided her along the flagstone path, through the hedge toward his cottage. When they reached the porch, he turned back and looked into her eyes. Then without a word, he swept her up and carried her inside.

She tried to tell herself to leave, that she couldn't afford to act like Crimson Lily. But the thought no longer held weight. He loved her.

As she loved him.

And she did, she knew without a doubt. She loved him with her heart and soul. When she was with him she was complete. She had existed in an uncertain limbo for the last ten years—all her life, if she was truthful with herself. She had never felt she belonged, not with her parents, not with Claude.

Morgan might shake his head or curse his frustration over something she did, but he wanted her anyway—he loved her anyway, just as he had said. She wanted to cry out with joy.

The moonlight drifted in, washing the room with silver light. Morgan released his grip from underneath her knees, but he didn't release her upper body. He lowered her legs until her body ran the length of his. He leaned back against a writing desk and widened his stance, her small form settling between his thighs.

"Do you feel that, Lily?" he asked, his voice rough and sensual. "Do you feel how much I want you?"

Heat flooded her cheeks. She could feel the hard ridge of his manhood pressing against her.

"God, you are such an innocent," he murmured, and as soon as he said the words he was struck by the ring of truth. Innocent beyond the virginity he took from her mere weeks ago. An innocence of soul that he had questioned from the start. Had seen but denied.

The images of Crimson Lily and Lily Blakemore chafed more than ever. But why? he demanded silently, his analytical mind clicking into gear. But then Lily moved, unaware of what she did to him, and all thought vanished like snow on a summer day.

Morgan groaned, then stood, walking over to light the kerosene lamp. When he turned back, Lily still stood at the desk. She had found his watch.

"My father gave that to me."

"I know. I saw it the night . . . I came to apologize."

A smile broke across his lips. "I know."

Lily whirled around. "How did you know?"

"I could tell someone had gone through my belongings."

"I barely touched your things."

That was true. Morgan had been able to tell that as well. But he had been wary for too many years. Checking his room and belongings was like breathing. He did them without thinking.

"I know," he murmured against her. "But enough. I felt as if you had touched me."

The words sent a shot of awareness down Lily's spine, pooling in the core of her being. And when he very slowly turned her back around to face the desk, her limbs trembled.

"Morgan?"

He didn't answer, simply bent her over slightly until she supported herself against the desk.

"I want to touch you."

And he did. Touch her. His hands gliding over the shimmery material of her Indian gown, burning her with his heat. But unlike when they had stood on the porch, the fabric remained a barrier, a barrier he seemed unwilling to breach.

He whispered in her ear, and though his hands didn't touch her skin, he told her all the things he wanted to do to her. The words made her blush, but made her want him as well, until she thought she would go mad. She was on the verge of whirling around when his hand came up under her shirt, flattening against her ribs. He brought his other hand up to cup her breast, much as he had done earlier, pulling her back, molding her body to his.

"I've wanted you day and night," he said, his voice deep and guttural.

With one proficient movement, he relieved her of her skirt. In another, her blouse followed. But he wouldn't let her turn around.

"I've wanted to touch you," he whispered as his hand slid down her ribs to her abdomen, then lower. "I wanted to feel you wanting me."

She sucked in her breath when his hand came between her thighs, gently but possessively. She did want him, and standing so exposed she couldn't hide the fact. Morgan groaned his satisfaction as he slid his finger deep inside her slick wetness.

Her body began to writhe, matching the movement of his stroking finger. Only then did he let her turn around, his face lined with satisfaction at the passion in her eyes.

Fire darkened his features when Lily reached up and made to unfasten his shirt. Her fingers fumbled in their haste.

Morgan chuckled. "Here," he said. In seconds his shirt lay with hers.

He pulled her close and the feel of bare skin to skin took Lily's breath away. Startlingly intimate. And when he stepped out of his trousers, she wasn't shy, she only yearned to feel the hard planes of his body melded to hers.

But when she reached out to feel the chiseled contours of his chest, he took her hands and set her away.

For one interminable second, embarrassment swept through her like wildfire.

"No," he stated, his voice a command. "Never be embarrassed in front of me." His tone softened, filled with reverence. "I want to look at you."

Her embarrassment remained, but was fast mixing with a growing sense of awareness. At the look in his eyes, she began to revel in the amazing power she realized she had to awe him. His desire was apparent. And that desire no longer had the power to make her feel ashamed.

"Your beauty stuns me." His eyes took in every inch of her, his hand following where his eyes had traveled. Then a smile broke out on his lips.

"What?" she demanded, glancing down at her body.

"This," he said, his voice rough. He lowered himself to one knee. He held her firmly, his hands on her hips, as he leaned forward. He kissed her on her belly, to the side.

"Don't, Morgan." She tried to brush him away. She had always hated the angry red birthmark. Her mother had always told her as an adult she would have to learn to cover it up. But years had passed and she had forgotten. Until now.

"Morgan," she said plaintively.

"You are so beautiful," he whispered, kissing the mark again. "So perfectly beautiful."

"Ha!"

This time he held her hands away. "Don't you know that marks like these are made to drive a man to distraction?"

She looked at him as if he had lost his mind.

Morgan laughed out loud, but sobered quickly enough

when his gaze returned to Lily's curves. "Just as you have driven me to distraction with wanting you these past two weeks."

He kissed a trail up her body, shivers of yearning searing her. Beauty mark or no beauty mark, in that instant she didn't care. All she wanted was the feel of Morgan beneath her hands, the feel of his hard body joined with hers.

The boldness of the thought shocked her. But then he took one nipple deep in his mouth and she cried out, her fingers tangling in his hair, drawing him even tighter to her soul.

"Yes, Lily. Let me love you as you deserve to be loved."

The man, the sensation, the words all wrapped together and brought an overwhelming joy to her heart. *Deserved to be loved.*

And then he swept her up into his arms and carried her to his bed. He came down on top of her, the weight of him balanced on his forearms that outlined her face and shoulders.

"The house is finished," she whispered raggedly, meaning something very different from what the simple words implied.

And Morgan understood her meaning. Passion, fierce and wild, darkened his eyes. A primitive growl rumbled in his chest. "I love you. And always know . . ."

His words trailed off and he looked at her so deeply and so movingly that for a second Lily panicked. "Morgan, what is it?"

He stared at her for seconds longer. "Just know that no matter what, I love you. As I have never loved anyone in my life."

When she opened her mouth to question him, he covered her lips with his own, silencing her words.

He loved her then, as she had asked. He filled her body, slowly, lovingly, his dark eyes watching her as he brought her to her peak. Only then did he let go of his control.

Crying out her name, he buried his face in her neck, grabbing her hips and thrusting into her again and again until his body shuddered its release.

Morgan didn't know if they lay there for hours or minutes as their hearts slowed. He held Lily close, uncertain what tomorrow would bring. Would she win? Would she lose? In truth, Morgan didn't know. He only knew as he lay beside her that he could never let her go.

But first he had to tell her who he was.

$\mathscr{T}$wenty-one

The day arrived. At seven o'clock that evening, the Honorable Hayward Hartwell was to arrive at Blakemore House. Less than an hour remained until the appointed time.

Lily's heart pounded as she stared at her reflection in the mirror, all too aware of the importance of this meeting. Not even her newly made, perfectly proper silk gown made her feel any better.

She had gone to the dressmaker with Penelope and Cassie at her side. The girls, along with the seamstress, had planned the demure frock. Lily's only request had been the delicately woven ruffle of lace and beading that graced her shoulders and was fastened in the front by a beautiful brooch that had been her mother's. As Lily looked at herself now, however, she couldn't muster even the mildest of enthusiasm for how well the ruffle had turned out.

Closing her eyes, Lily clasped her hands to her cheeks, wondering how in the world she was going to survive this ordeal. And whose absurd idea was it anyway, she wondered in dismay, to have the judge to dinner—show him all the skills she had learned? It had been her idea, of course. And at the time it had seemed inspired. Today, however, dread pounded through her veins.

How had she been so foolish to think she could show this judge that she was an ideal mother who could guide the children through the vagaries of life, when it was the children who had been doing all the guiding? The children, that is, and Morgan.

Dear, dear Morgan.

A gentle burst of laughter escaped Lily's lips. Whoever would have dreamed that a day would come when she would call Morgan anything besides ornery, self-righteous, and more trouble than he was worth? Her laughter trailed off to a soft smile and a wave of emotion flooded her mind. He was all those things, she conceded, but he was so much more.

Sensation shivered through her body as she remembered their shared intimacy. With his touch he brought her body to life in a way she had never dreamed possible. She had never felt so cherished. His touch was filled with reverence, speaking if not with words, then with something equally as eloquent, expressing his emotions with every stroke and caress.

How had she ever thought she could put him from her life? He might simply be a hired hand . . . no, she amended, never simple . . . but that fact didn't matter to her. The strata of society she had been born to had shunned her. Morgan Elliott had helped her when no one else would.

And now she had to prove that all his help wasn't for naught.

Lily started to groan as thoughts of courts and judges resurfaced. But then she stopped the sound before it could leave her throat. With determination, she got up from her seat. She would not let the court get the better of her.

She would not let the court take her children away.

Sweeping down the stairs in her elegant gown, Lily

could hardly fathom the sense of pride and accomplishment she felt as her hand ran the length of the banister. Polished and gleaming. Though she had seen many a polished and gleaming banister in her life, never had she seen one that *she* had polished. She laughed at herself when she thought that this banister, the one that *she* had polished, looked more beautiful than any she had seen in her life.

The whole house made her feel that way. The new furnishings, the freshly painted rooms. Wallpapered walls that no longer had frayed spots and curled edges. Lily never would have dreamed that the finest of French perfumes couldn't compare to the fresh smell of lemon-scented polish on furniture. She also never would have believed so much could have been achieved in two short weeks. But they had accomplished everything. Together. As a family.

As she looked around her, Lily wondered how the judge could possibly find fault with this home. Her stomach clenched. Surely she would succeed. She had to.

The instant Lily entered the kitchen, she saw Morgan. Her heart filled with delight at the sight of him, and at the sight of his reciprocal smile.

"You look beautiful," he said, his voice sincere.

She smiled shyly, unaccustomed to the emotions he stirred within her, then searched out her list. "I think we're on schedule so far."

Morgan came up behind her, pulling her back to his chest. She knew as long as she lived she would never grow tired of the feel of him, of his strength.

"Everything is going to be fine, Lily." The words were a whisper against her ear.

"I want to believe you. But I'm so nervous."

"You are going to be fine," he said, turning her around. "The meal is ready. The finest French chef couldn't have done better."

"Let's not overdo here."

Morgan chuckled. "The meal is going to be perfect. And just as we planned, I'll have everything on the table at exactly seven-thirty. All you have to do is lead the judge into the dining room.''

''You know he's going to notice that I don't have any servants.''

''Tell him you've been doing it all yourself. He'll be impressed.''

''Are you sure?''

''Yes, I'm sure.''

''What if something goes wrong?''

''Nothing will go wrong. And I won't be far away if you need me.''

''You won't be far away if I need you?'' she cried.

It hadn't occurred to her that Morgan wouldn't be there, sitting at the table, helping her along. Panic rose through her body like mercury on a hot summer day. ''Please Morgan, you have to be there.''

He took hold of her shoulders, his grip firm. ''You know I can't be there, Lily. How are you going to explain the presence of a repairman at the dining room table?'' A smile pulled at his lips. Then he leaned over and pressed a kiss to her forehead. ''You will bowl him over, princess. You are going to be wonderful. I believe in you.''

If only she could believe.

At the exact second the hall clock struck seven, the Honorable Hayward Hartwell arrived, his expression closed, lips pursed, nostrils permanently flared. If looks were any indication, the signs did not bode well for the night.

But if Lily had worried about the children knowing how to behave around a guest she need not have bothered.

''Good evening, sir,'' Robert said politely, extending his hand like the young gentleman society would expect him to be.

Even Penelope and Cassie were pictures of perfection, each executing exemplary curtsies for the stiff man. Lily beamed with pride, then sobered at the thought that she might not do as well.

They sat in the parlor, the children exchanging niceties, regaling the judge with how wonderful their aunt Lily was. It was nearly seven-thirty when the judge cut them off and focused his narrow-eyed gaze at Lily. "I have a whole throng of people breathing down my neck about this case. Powerful people. People who got me appointed. I have never found myself in such a predicament. You are not a very popular woman, Miss Blakemore."

Lily's heart stilled in her chest. Her mind churned. She realized in that second that she wasn't fighting the courts, not really. She was fighting society—New York's elite. When the document arrived, how had she not realized it then?

The clock tolled the half hour, but Lily hardly heard.

"Aunt Lily," Robert said pointedly. "It's time for dinner."

Lily glanced at the boy, her mind trying to settle. She needed to talk to the judge, tell the judge all the things she felt. But the man didn't wait for her to sort through her thoughts, he stood and allowed the children to lead the way.

Lily was all but numb when she entered the dining room.

"Aunt Lily thought a less formal meal would be best, Your Honor," Robert explained, "so you could sit back and talk to us."

"Fine," the man responded curtly.

Lily's heart sank even further at his tone. But it rose just a bit when she noticed the table. It was grand, the meal waiting as promised. Glasses and silver, serving dishes lined up like soldiers down the center.

She sent up a silent prayer that they could turn the evening around—if nothing else, she had to at least convince the judge of her abilities. For tonight, she could do nothing more. She would deal with the rest of her detractors if they got through the evening—*when* they got through the evening, she corrected herself forcefully.

They started with soup served from a delicately wrought tureen standing high on a pedestal of porcelain flowers. Without waiting for Lily to begin, Judge Hartwell took up a spoon, then began to question each of the children with pointed seriousness, clearly no longer interested in niceties.

"How well do you know your aunt, Robert?" the man asked.

Lily's hand stilled.

"I know her very well, sir. And I can speak for my sisters as well as myself when I tell you that we love Aunt Lily a great deal."

A lump formed in Lily's throat, and it was all she could do to maintain her seat and not fly around the table and pull her nephew into a bone-crushing embrace.

The judge harrumphed, cleared his throat, then took another spoonful of soup. After a moment, he asked, "I can't imagine that lively young children such as you would want to be cooped up around here. I can see you on a nice big farm."

"We have Central Park within walking distance," Penelope supplied. "We have wide open spaces, but we have culture, too."

Judge Hartwell peered at Penelope closely. Anyone else would have squirmed. Penelope held his gaze until he returned his attention to his soup.

The questions continued much in the same vein. But at every negative the man offered, the children turned it into a positive. Lily had to believe the judge was impressed.

A bud of excitement began to grow in Lily's chest as she served plates of perfectly roasted beef around the table. Things were starting turn in their favor. Lily could feel it, and she knew the children felt it, too.

With a growing hope that things just might work out after all, Lily leaned forward to take up the gravy tureen, forgetting to use the thick linen supplied for the hot metal handle.

"Aggghhh!" she cried out, instinctively letting go, spilling hot gravy in her lap.

Not realizing that the lace and beading at the front of her gown had snagged in the tablecloth, Lily leaped up from her seat, pulling the finely crocheted heirloom with her as she jumped back.

It all happened so quickly that no one had time to react. The children sat very still, their eyes wide, their mouths agape as glassware and dishes began to tumble. And then it happened.

"Watch out!"

But Robert's call and frantic reach were for naught when the still nearly full soup tureen tilted over onto its side like a ship rolling over in a turbulent sea, its creamy contents finding a new berth—in the Honorable Hayward Hartwell's lap.

"Oh, dear Lord," Lily gasped, the tablecloth hanging from the front of her gown like an outlandishly sized napkin on a cowboy intent on eating barbecue ribs.

After a moment of stunned silence, Lily batted at the tablecloth, extricating herself from her predicament, then snatched up her napkin and reached for the judge.

At the sight of Lily coming toward him, the man's narrowed eyes widened to the size of silver dollars. He pushed back in his chair just as his hostess took the napkin to his person. She had gotten no more than "I'm sor—" out of her mouth before the man's chair teetered on its hind legs, Judge Hartwell still in it, then fell to the floor with a resounding crash.

Robert dropped his head to the table, Penelope groaned, and Cassie began to cry. Bending at the waist, Lily peered over at the felled judge, who was still sitting in the downed chair.

"Does this count against me?" she ventured tentatively.

Judge Hartwell burst into a flurry of activity, sputtering and scrambling about in a frenzied effort to pick himself up. Once he managed to stand, he snapped up his napkin

from the floor, wiped at his hopelessly ruined clothes, before turning a heated glare on Lily. "I will notify you
when I have reached my decision. Then I will see you in
court, Miss Blakemore. Good evening."

Then he was gone, showing himself out of the house on
Fifty-ninth Street while the occupants within stood
stunned.

Just then Morgan burst into the dining room, his mouth
gaping open when he took in the mayhem. "What happened?" he demanded.

"I suspect," Lily began, her voice knotted, "that when
you said I would 'bowl him over,' you had something a
little different in mind."

And then she began to shake, her heart seeming to stop
in her chest. *Dear God, what have I done?*

To make matters worse, she saw the devastated looks
on each of the children's faces and she felt a crushing
blow.

"Now they're going to send us away," Cassie choked
out, tears streaming down her cheeks.

Lily didn't know what to say.

Penelope took hold of the tabletop as if for support.
"They'll give us to some horrible monsters," she added,
her eyes overly bright. "They'll give us to that Artemis
and Audry."

"Atticus and Adeline," Robert corrected distractedly,
his fingers curling around Cassie's hand. "But it's all right.
I'll take care of you."

Lily felt as if a dagger had been plunged into her heart.
"We aren't defeated yet, dear hearts," she said over the
devastation that lodged in her throat. "How could anyone
take you away from me because I spilled some soup?"

But Lily knew it wasn't about soup. It was about New
York society once again turning her out. She was a fallen
woman. Not fit to be a mother. The judge was simply a
messenger of her fate.

The children murmured something inaudible, then

turned together and walked out of the room, leaving Morgan and Lily alone.

Lily felt the heat of Morgan's gaze, his questions, his concern. Unable to bear his scrutiny, she very carefully reached down, dipped her finger into the gravy that covered her new gown, then tasted.

"Delicious," she said, barely able to get the word past her lips. "Would you like a taste?"

"Lily, talk to me."

"No!" she blurted out, all pretense of calm deserting her. "There is nothing to talk about!"

Then she ran, up the stairs, around and around, hating the feel of defeat that wrapped itself around her heart. Trying to outrun the pain, she banged into the room in the attic.

Silver moonlight spilled in through the windows. She didn't stop until she came to the armoire, where she fell against the single piece of furniture as if it could offer the support and comfort that she so desperately needed.

The tears began to flow, gasping sobs racking her body as she beat against the door, beating against the unfairness of life, of the world. It was hard enough that she had been hurt, but now that the children would suffer because of her, she couldn't stand it.

She didn't hear Morgan approach until he stood behind her.

"Lily."

The word was a caress, filled with all the emotion she knew that he felt. But Morgan couldn't make things better. Morgan couldn't help her now. He had taught her what he could and that hadn't been enough.

"I failed," she cried, banging the armoire with her fist. "I failed."

But her words and tears were cut off by a sudden crack followed by a resounding bang that startled her away from the towering cabinet.

"What was that?" Lily gasped, wiping her tear-filled eyes.

Morgan stepped around the armoire, moving toward the wall. Lily peered around to see what had caused the noise. When she looked she could see that the back of the armoire had fallen off. But on closer inspection, Lily realized that what had fallen off wasn't the back, but something else altogether.

She stared, her mind failing to comprehend what she saw. Vibrant color, an image, but only a corner, as the rest was still behind the armoire.

"What is this?" Morgan muttered, taking hold of the corner and pulling it free.

Lily's brain refused to work, refused to assimilate the nearly life-size canvas of color, refused to acknowledge the painted blue eyes staring back at her.

"Dear God," Morgan whispered, when he stood back.

Lily wasn't certain what she heard in his voice. Disgust and outrage? Or perhaps awe?

She closed her eyes, hoping against hope that when she opened them again she would wake up and it all would be a bad dream. But when she opened her eyes she wasn't downstairs in bed, the sun climbing on the horizon, she was still in the attic room, Raine Hawthorne's betrayal of her staring her in the face.

The painting.

It was here, more bold than even she remembered, making it impossible to deny its existence any longer—making it impossible to deny that her brother had bought the painting as Morgan had said.

Her throat tightened, her heart hammering in her chest. Her shame was laid out for Morgan to see. She had been devastated before, but now, after all she had shared with this wonderful man, she hated that he would see it. Of course he already knew about the painting, but to know and to see were two very different matters. Now he had proof. He would see this image and see a woman of no virtue.

A woman he couldn't possibly love.

Lily wanted to race from the room, the house, and never look back. She had failed the children, and now her greatest shame was exposed before this man whose respect she desperately wanted.

"It's beautiful."

Lily turned sharply to look at Morgan. His eyes were intent on the painting, taking in each curve and line like a connoisseur of fine art. Her knees felt weak as his eyes traveled the length of the painted form.

Many had thought the work beautiful, but while they might admire a great painter's abilities, they did not admire the woman who would allow herself to be captured on canvas.

"But it's not you."

Lily's mind reeled. If this strong man had broken down and wept he could not have stunned her more. She tried to comprehend what he had said.

Morgan grabbed her arms and turned her to him, gentleness forgotten. His eyes were fierce, pained. "It's not you," he breathed.

Slowly, his words began to sink in, the meaning emerging, undeniable. He knew. He understood.

Her mouth opened as she tried to breathe.

"Dear God in heaven," he cried, the words torn from his chest, "he painted your face, but that is not your body."

"How do you know?" she demanded, barely able to breathe, desperately wanting Morgan to prove to her that he truly understood.

"Here," he directed, pointing at the canvas. "And here. This," he raged, "is not your body, these are not your hips, not your breasts. Not the swell of your abdomen. Where is your birthmark? I have known you intimately, I have made love to every inch of your body. I know you.

Even if this was painted ten years ago, this couldn't be you.''

He turned back to her. "Sweet Jesus, he didn't paint you. But you had no proof. You had no way to tell the world that you hadn't posed! So they believed the worst.''

His body grew taut with a palpable anguish. "Just as I believed the worst.''

The room seemed to swirl, light weaving in and out of her jumbled thoughts. Morgan knew. He saw her greatest shame and knew upon sight that it wasn't her. In that second, it didn't matter that he had believed the worst of her. How could he not? But even thinking the worst, he had come to love her anyway, for her.

"Lily,'' he said, taking her hands, "why didn't you tell me?''

A sad smile pulled at her lips. "Would you have believed me?''

He closed his eyes for a second. "Perhaps not.''

"Probably not. But that doesn't matter.'' She squeezed his hands as she realized that it *didn't* matter. "What fills me with joy is that there is someone in the world who knows that I didn't pose. New York doesn't know. Claude didn't know. But now there is someone who has seen the painting and knows that I'm not Crimson Lily.''

"You've got to tell the judge about this so you won't lose the children. You have to tell all of New York that you aren't Crimson Lily.''

"But I can't tell the judge, or anyone else. They won't believe me.''

"Then I'll tell them.''

Lily scoffed to cover her embarrassment. "And what are you going to say. That you know it isn't me because you've seen me in a particular state of undress and you know that the naked woman in the painting can't possibly be the naked woman you saw in your bed.''

Mortification stung her. "Your proving to the court that

I didn't pose will only damn me more thoroughly than I already am.''

Morgan turned away, ravaged. But then his body stiffened. She followed his gaze and she noticed a thin package that must have fallen off the back when the painting fell free. Bending down, Morgan retrieved an artist's portfolio. Very carefully, he unwound the binding ribbon. Quickly he leafed through whatever was inside, before he turned back to her, his face a stony mask.

At length, he extended the folder. "Here is your proof."

Confusion racked her mind as she took the portfolio. In some deep recesses she must have known what she would find, and that part of her didn't want to know. With fingers shaking, she emptied the portfolio, page by page. Sketches. Many sketches. Her in a day dress, her in an evening dress. From different angles, different expressions. But all undeniably fully clothed. Then others. Of another woman, posing in different ways. But all without clothing.

After a moment of study, Lily could even tell which sketches Raine Hawthorne had combined. A sketch he had done of her in this very room as she had stared out the window.

She remembered the day well. Remembered the storm. Remembered her brother's fury that she had allowed Raine Hawthorne to return to their home.

"You know that I hate him," Claude had raged once Raine had departed. *"You are doing this just to hurt me!"*

Had she? Lily wondered. She had wondered many times if she had intentionally tried to hurt her brother, berating herself at the possibility, refusing to think about the fact that he had hurt her. But all these years later, staring at the sheaf of sketches, Lily could no longer deny her brother's part in her demise. Claude *had* known that she hadn't posed. And still he sent her away.

"He hated me," she said, her voice barely carrying through the room.

She heard Morgan's sigh before he said, "Lily."

Just that, but what else was there to say.

"After I left Manhattan," she continued, "I wrote Claude every day. For months I wrote him, asked that he believe me that I didn't pose. I hated my new life. I wanted to come home. In my letters I reasoned, I cajoled, I begged, but I received no response. It was winter when a packet arrived. In it I found all of my letters, all unopened, with a simple note. 'Please stop writing. It is easier this way.' "

Lily drew a deep breath. "Easier? Easier! For who? For me? Was it easier for me to fend for myself as a woman alone? Or was it easier for Claude? Sending me away. Cutting all ties. Washing his hands of his ruined sister. All until he needed my help."

She turned into the moonlight. "I believed, had to believe, that he sent me away because of the shame, and that he couldn't accept my letters any longer because he was hurt too badly. It was the only way I could hold on to the last glimmer of the love that I had always believed we shared. But now that is gone. He'd had the means to extricate me from a nightmare, but hadn't."

Lily felt grief well up inside her, overwhelming her lithe frame, enveloping her in a cocoon so oppressive that she thought she might faint. "I had hoped that he loved me, but he didn't."

"Perhaps he loved you too much."

"Too much? Can someone love too much?" she asked, her voice weary.

"Perhaps he loved you . . . as he shouldn't," Morgan amended quietly.

Her heart hammered hard, once, echoing madly in the cocoon that surrounded her. How many times growing up had she explained away a look or action of her brother's? How many times once her body had begun to grow into a woman's had her cheeks stung with embarrassment over some look of Claude's when she would walk into a room? She had explained them away as Claude lost in thought, not really seeing her at all. But deep in her heart she had felt uneasy, sick. Could that have been what had led her to so flagrantly defy Claude's wishes regarding the beaux who had come calling? Had she realized subconsciously that if she didn't break away then, she never would have been able to break away at all?

The questions circled through her mind, unanswerable. Claude was dead. The answers were buried the day her brother was put into the ground.

She didn't hear Morgan come up behind her. She only felt the heat of him when his hands curled around her arms. She wanted to close her eyes and lean back into him. But she couldn't move. She was afraid that at any second the cracks in her soul would snake through her body and leave her in millions of tiny pieces. Broken. Shattered. Like her china cup.

"Lily," he said, pulling her back to him. "I'm sorry. I wish you didn't have to see the hard truth about your brother. But don't you see, by finding these sketches you are saved."

She jerked around in his arms until she faced him. "What are you talking about?"

"The sketches. All you have to do is take them to court. Let the judge and your detractors see them. Prove that you aren't a fallen woman. That you were wrongly accused. Then the judge will have no reason to take the children away from you."

For one glorious moment, she realized the truth of his words. But in the next, glory giving way to a crystalline clarity, she realized that she couldn't tell anyone what they had found.

"Lily," he breathed into her hair. "After all this you are going to win."

"No."

The simple word resounded through the room. She knew that Morgan didn't comprehend at first, but then he stilled. After a moment he set her at arm's length and looked at her gravely. "What are you talking about? Of course you will tell the court. And you will tell the people who are pressuring the judge to rule against you.''

"I will not tell anyone about these sketches, nor will you.''

"But you have to!''

"No, Morgan! I will not do that to the children.''

"Lily, you aren't making any sense. You have to do it *for* the children.''

"Oh, Morgan. Don't you see? The children loved their father, thought the world of him. What do you think it would do to them if they learn their father allowed me to be ruined wrongly? How would they feel if they learned he owned an indecent painting of his sister, as well as the sketches that would have proven her innocence? What kind of a man would do that to anyone, much less to his sister?''

"The kind of man who doesn't deserve the love of his children.''

"Maybe. But that's not for you and me, or even a judge to decide. And even if Claude doesn't deserve their love, could you possibly think that means the children don't deserve to believe in him? A child needs to believe that his parent is a person who is kind and good. A decent human being. How do you think it would make you feel to grow up knowing your father was a sordid man?''

"Sooner or later every child learns that their parents are fallible.''

"And it hurts. But eventually the child grows up and comes to know and understand their parents, and loves them in a different way. But Claude is gone. If I destroy the image they have now, they'll never have the opportunity to form a new one. They will live with the shame of their father forever. I will not do that to the children.''

"Damn it, Lily—''

"No, Morgan. My decision is final. Besides, not all is lost yet. I will go to court when I'm called. I will make my case. I will tell all of New York of my love and devotion to Robert, Penelope, and Cassie. Then I will remind them that regardless of what they think of me, Claude wanted me to have his children.'' She took Morgan's hand. ''You told me before to fight. And I thought I had by learning to cook and by repairing the house. But now I realize I haven't fought at all. It's time I fought the real battle, fight the people who sent me away, the same people who want to send me away again. My abilities as a mother are only an excuse. I have to stand up to them, Morgan, once and for all. Really stand up to them, show them that I'm not weak, that I will not let them send me away again. And I will not lose.''

A heavy silence sliced through the room.

''But what if you do?'' he asked.

Lily flinched inwardly at the possibility, but what could she say? ''Then I lose. I will not use the sketches. The fact remains that Atticus and Adeline Wesford are kind people who would provide Robert, Penelope, and Cassie with a wonderful home.''

When Morgan started to argue, she cut him off. ''Which do you think would be worse for the children, Morgan, living with me, but knowing that their father was a despicable person, or living with their mother's cousin and still having the belief that their father was a decent man?''

They stood in the middle of the room for long minutes as the moon drifted through the sky.

''I have admired very few people in my life, Lily Blakemore. But you have risen to the top of my list.''

Twenty-two

Morgan left the house early the next morning with a pervasive feeling of dread. He was on his way to see Walter. When he had gone to bed last night, his mind had churned with Lily's past and Lily's fall. She hadn't posed, but no one had believed her. Including him.

He had played judge and jury, trying and convicting her without giving her the chance to defend herself. He had arrived at Blakemore House, his biases already firmly in place, his evidence lined up like ducks in a row.

When had he forgotten that no story was a straight line? When had he forgotten that life was riddled with twists and turns, events occurring that would be hard to believe unless witnessed. If anyone knew, *he* knew that life was not always what it seemed.

But somehow with Lily Blakemore he had forgotten.

He remembered the times Lily had asked him if a person controlled their own fate, had the power to control what happened in their lives. Morgan had adamantly told her it was true. But he realized now that there was no black-and-white answer to her question. Only shades of gray.

While a person could affect the path his life took, there were some things a person could not control. Lily hadn't done something that ruined her. Others had. Lily had been nothing more than a puppet on someone else's string.

After they had seen the painting last night, when Morgan had asked why Raine Hawthorne would have done such a thing, Lily had taken him to her room and shown him a note the man had written just before his death.

March 1886

My dearest Lily,
  I hate to see the life drained out of you by a society that doesn't appreciate the type of woman you are. So I am leaving you my wealth so you can remain free . . . and I am leaving a gift, to ensure that you do.
Hawthorne

Morgan remembered closing his eyes in heartache at the tragedy of one man's good intent. Morgan realized that Hawthorne had left Lily his money and his gift to set her free, when in truth he had only made her a prisoner of the world more thoroughly than she had ever been before.

In some strange way, Morgan realized, the artist hadn't tried to hurt Lily. He had tried to help her—others had tried to hurt her, *had* hurt her. Morgan groaned. As he had hurt her.

The truth of Lily's innocence had stared him in the face since he met her. Even if he hadn't had the sketches in his hand all along, he had seen the truth in her eyes. And had disregarded it.

Shame twisted in Morgan's gut. He had condemned her, only to admit later that he loved her. Had he acted as he had because he was afraid of that love? Angry at himself for loving her? Taking his anger out on her?

For the life of him, Morgan didn't understand what had happened to him in the few months he had been living on the Blakemore estate. He only knew that he loved Lily

Blakemore with a fierceness that far outweighed anything he had felt before in his life.

But after all he had done, the devastating fact remained. He didn't deserve her love in return.

Morgan hailed a hansom cab, falling back into the leather seat, dragging his hand across his face. There was only one thing he could do. Once and for all. He had to tell her why he was there. And he knew he had to tell her that he wasn't who she thought him to be.

The thought seared him like a white-hot brand on flesh. But what else could he do? he wondered. Nothing. There was no choice. He would tell her who he was. He couldn't imagine that she would ever forgive him. For if there was one thing that he had learned about her, it was that she told the truth at every turn. Lily Blakemore was scrupulously honest, though he had believed she was an unscrupulous liar.

Morgan slammed his fist into the side of the carriage, welcoming the pain that shot up his arm into his shoulder. He would talk to Walter as soon as he got downtown, tell him that the deal was off. They would have to find another way to bring Crandall down. Then he would return to Blakemore House, tell Lily the truth, tell her every glaring detail because she deserved no less. If she passed the information along to Crandall and his henchmen, so be it. He deserved no less.

Morgan entered the downtown building thirty minutes later. He wanted to catch Walter before the day got too hectic.

The familiar smell of coffee wrapped around him as he entered. Walter sat behind his desk, his lips pursed as he read a report.

"Walter," Morgan said from the doorway.

Walter's head snapped up, surprise on his face. After a moment, the man settled back in his chair and studied Morgan. "Good morning, stranger."

"I guess I have been something of a stranger recently. But I've been busy."

"Busy spiffin' up that house over there is what I hear."

"Have you been spying on me, Walter?"

"Spying, no. I just wanted to make sure my best man hadn't run afoul of his prey and ended up on the wrong side of a knife or conveniently swallowed up by the East River. Didn't expect to find you on the wrong side of a broom, that I can say."

Morgan chuckled, though the sound was hollow. "Didn't expect to be doing housework myself." His smile drifted away. "But I was trying to help."

"You love her, don't you?"

Morgan sighed. Had it been so obvious to everyone but him? First Trudy Spencer, now Walter. Morgan shuddered. Had he truly been so blind?

"That's all right. Don't say. The answer is as good as written on your face."

"It doesn't matter what I feel. I'm going to tell Lily who I am. Then I'm leaving."

"Leaving what?"

"Blakemore House." Morgan glanced away, suddenly knowing what he would do. "And I'm leaving New York. I'm going home, Walter. I don't think I could stand seeing her around town by accident."

Walter slammed his fist down, startling Morgan. "What the hell are you talking about, man? You love her but you have to leave her? What kind of fool reasoning is that?"

"She thinks I'm a repairman."

"Well, you aren't. You have more money than she has."

"It's not about money, Walter. If there is any one person alive who cares little for money it's Lily Blakemore."

"Then what is it?"

"I deceived her."

"You didn't deceive her. You were working. The repairman was your disguise. It's your job."

"And how do you propose I explain that to her? 'By the way, I'm not really Morgan Elliott the repairman.' That should go over well. I'm sure she'll be clamoring after me to stay. I can hear her now. 'You may be a liar but that's all right, you have lots of money.' "

Walter cursed and shook his head. "Blast it, Morgan. If you love the woman fight for her. Okay, so tell her the truth, but when you're mentioning who you are, also tell her why you do what you do."

"Walter—"

"Damn it, hear me out. You're an admirable man, one of the finest I have ever met. You have devoted your life to righting wrongs. You can't start second-guessing now. Go to her. Tell her, Morgan. And no matter what she says, don't leave." He hesitated, his face becoming grim. "She's going to need you just about now."

"What are you talking about?"

"This," Walter said, holding out the report he had been reading when Morgan walked in.

Morgan took the single sheet of paper. Morgan read once, then twice, then slowly looked up at Walter.

"Yes," Walter said, "the judge is ruling against your Miss Blakemore."

"How do you know?"

"You know I can't tell you how I found out, but have I ever fed you erroneous information?"

Morgan tried to assimilate what he read. The court was going to rule against Lily. After Hartwell had left the house, deep down Morgan had known it would come to this. But still that didn't make it any easier to take. Dear God, he wished he had been wrong.

Morgan felt an impotent rage. How to fight back? How to help Lily?

His mind churned.

Perhaps he could put together a group of people who would be willing to testify on Lily's behalf. But where to start? Every single person he had met that knew Lily could only talk of her wild ways or passion for life—things that a judge would not think redeeming for the position of a mother.

"She doesn't deserve this," Morgan said out loud. "If only she could really convince the court and her detractors of her love for the children—convince them that she really is a good mother." Morgan shook his head and started to smile. "Lily truly has learned to take care of that house."

Walter cleared his throat. "We both know that her cooking and cleaning abilities aren't what's in question here."

"What do you mean?"

"According to my source, it's the Crimson Lily article that did it—that got everyone all worked up."

Morgan looked at Walter, confused. "What are you talking about?"

"That article," he prompted, " 'Crimson Lily Paints Town Red.' People were outraged by that. No appointed judge in his right mind would give custody to the woman portrayed in that article."

Morgan cursed.

"Yeah, apparently the judge doesn't appreciate a woman who wants to be a mother showing up on the front page of the newspaper—in less than stellar light."

"Hell." Morgan turned away. If that was the case, how could he help her?

"If there's anything I can do . . ."

Walter's words trailed off. Both men knew that there was nothing he could do, nothing most people could do to save Lily.

"Thanks," Morgan said before he shoved his hands deep in his pockets and quit the room.

His mind spun as he left the building. He was hardly aware of the carriages and horsecars that skittered by him. *What could he do?*

The thought circled around in his head as he made his way north to Fifty-ninth. He no longer cared if anyone saw him coming and going. He walked up the front path know-

ing that he had to tell Lily who he was, and then he had
to tell her of what the judge planned to do. Then he would
come up with a plan to save her. He had to.

He pushed the door open to chaos. The children huddled
together, tears on their cheeks.

"What's happened?" Morgan demanded.

"A messenger came. The judge has made his decision
and called Lily down to the courthouse."

Robert held his head in his hands. "She wouldn't let us
go with her. I just know it's going to be bad. I just know
it. Why else wouldn't she let us go with her?"

Morgan stood frozen in the foyer. Time had run out. No
time to make plans, implement strategy. The judge had
seen to that.

For one interminable second, Morgan thought of the
sketches that they had found. Without thinking, he raced
upstairs and found them—proof that Lily was not the kind
of woman that everyone believed her to be. But Lily had
been adamant. How could he go against her wishes?

Especially, he realized, when there was another way.

Seconds later, he returned downstairs without the
sketches. "Come on, kids. Let's go."

They made it to the courthouse in record time. Morgan's
chiseled face was grim as he took the steps two at a time,
the children hurrying along in his wake. Once Morgan had
made his decision, he knew he was doing the right thing.
The only thing. It didn't matter that by implementing his
plan he put himself in danger.

All that mattered was Lily.

He stepped into the courtroom. Everyone there was intent on the judge and they didn't notice his entrance. The
judge sat high on his bench, spectacles perched on his nose
as he spoke. Lily stood at a table below the court's high
bench. Silent. Tense.

Morgan halted at the back of the room and listened.
". . . Despite the will, and despite your declarations of love

for your nieces and nephew, Miss Blakemore," the judge intoned, "the court finds the best interests of the children are served by denying you custody."

The court erupted, onlookers nodding their heads in satisfaction. Morgan watched, enraged, as Lily's shoulders sagged. Defeat. Pain twisted in his chest. With that, the moment had come.

"You're wrong."

Shocked silence stilled the crowd for one startling moment before gasps reverberated through the high-ceilinged room and everyone turned sharply toward the back of the courtroom. Morgan recognized Edith Mayhew. He also recognized Winifred Headly, and swore. No doubt the women were behind this whole charade.

Morgan withstood the crowd's fiery gazes, and stepped forward.

"What did you say?" the judge demanded, his dark eyes narrowed in anger.

"I said you are wrong about Lily Blakemore—you've judged her unfairly."

A chorus of gasps shimmered through the room, but Morgan continued. "This entire court proceeding has been brought on because of an article—an article that wasn't true."

"How do you know that?" the judge demanded, outraged.

Morgan turned his gaze away from the judge and met Lily's eyes. He hated to speak, hated to deliver the crushing blow. He wanted to erase the past, start over. But Morgan had never run away from responsibility before. He wouldn't do it now. "Because I wrote it."

As long as he lived, Morgan knew he would never forget Lily's reaction. The look that said she must have misunderstood, then the dawning, as if all the inconsistencies finally fell into place like pieces to a puzzle. Followed by pain. Intense pain. A slow dying in her eyes.

Morgan remembered suddenly that she had said that

eventually everyone betrays. He had denied her words, only to painfully prove her right.

She reached out and grabbed a chair back, but she remained standing. Tall, stalwart. Determined. He knew that she stood before the world, telling herself that she would not be weak. She couldn't afford to be weak. She had lived a life unable to depend on anyone but herself.

Morgan wanted to close the distance that separated them and pull her into his arms, beg for her forgiveness. But he knew forgiveness was something he couldn't have—wouldn't even ask for.

He didn't deserve it.

"I'm speaking to you, sir."

Morgan forced his attention back to the judge.

"I want to know what the devil you're talking about."

"I am an investigative reporter for *The New York Times*. I took the job of repairman in Miss Blakemore's residence some months ago to . . . learn the truth about some people she calls friends."

"*The New York Times,* did you say?" the judge demanded.

"Yes, sir."

"Are you the man who brought down Bowtie Scotty?"

Surprise streaked across Morgan's face. "Yes, sir."

"Then you're a damned fine reporter, son."

"Thank you, but—"

"No buts. You are known for your truth and honesty. For getting the story right. Are you going to stand there and tell me you were wrong?" he demanded angrily.

"Yes, sir. I am. I was very wrong. I went to Blakemore House with my convictions set. I disregarded everything I learned that didn't support what I already believed."

"Good God, man. This is the craziest thing I have ever heard. Why would you do such a thing?"

"Because I love her. I loved her from the first moment I saw her. But I was too proud to admit it. I'd heard all the rumors everyone else had heard. How could I," he said with disdain, "a seeker of truth and justice, fall in love with a woman of lesser virtue?" Morgan shook his head in despair. "I once thought that Lily Blakemore rode through life flagrantly, carelessly, barely holding on to the reins." He closed his eyes, anguish shimmering across the chiseled planes of his face. "I realize now that I was wrong. She wasn't holding on because she couldn't, she was tangled up in the reins and didn't know how to extricate herself." He looked over at the crowd. "The Edith Mayhews and the Winifred Headlys of the world have passed judgment on Lily Blakemore without taking the time to learn who she really is."

Edith and Winifred gasped in outrage, their faces blazing with color when everyone in the courtroom turned to look at them.

But all eyes returned to Morgan when he continued. "I admit that I was blind to the truth. Just as society has been blind to the truth. But by seeing Lily Blakemore every day and watching her with the children, I was finally forced to face the truth about her. To accept that she is good and kind. Honest and caring." He looked straight at the judge. "Society has painted Lily Blakemore in crimson, when in truth she belongs in lily white lace."

In that second, Robert leaped forward. "Mr. Elliott is correct, sir. Our aunt Lily is not a bad woman. She is proper and respectable. Better than anyone around her."

"She loves us," Penelope added. "And we love her."

"We don't want another mama," Cassie stated shyly, but with a tiny stamp of her foot. "We want Aunt Lily."

The judge seemed as astounded as everyone else in the courtroom. After a moment, however, a stunned Atticus Wesford jumped up from his seat, his face mottled red.

"This is preposterous. You can't possibly take into consideration the words of this . . . this . . . yellow journalist," he said with a sneer, "or the words of mere children. How could they possibly know what is best for them?"

The judge focused his ominous glare on Atticus. "I

would think, Mr. Wesford, that children are a good deal more aware of what is best for them than you seem to realize. And a father should know that.''

The judge banged the gavel down. ''This court is in recess while I have time to review these new facts. And Mr. Elliott, I want to see you in chambers.''

''All rise,'' came the call as the judge stood from his bench and strode from the courtroom.

Morgan didn't want to follow, at least not yet. He wanted to go to Lily, talk to her. But Lily hadn't moved, she looked down at her hand that clutched the chair. Staring at her, Morgan felt as if his heart had been torn from his chest. He started toward her.

''Mr. Elliott.''

Morgan turned and found the court clerk at his side.

''Follow me, please.''

Morgan hesitated, but something caught his attention from the corner of his eye. He turned just as a man in a black hat pulled low on his head slipped out the back door. For a second, he thought the man looked familiar.

''Mr. Elliott,'' the clerk repeated. ''The judge is waiting.''

Morgan spoke to the judge for more than an hour before he emerged to the now-empty courtroom. Lily would maintain custody of the children.

Relief swept through Morgan, but it was followed quickly by despair.

He left the courtroom, and for the second time in one day he made his way north to Fifty-ninth Street. He came up the front drive, but he didn't go into the house. Instead he walked around back and went straight to the cottage. There was no need to go inside. He had told Lily the truth, owned up to his grievous wrong. And he had seen the look in her eyes. Devastation.

There was nothing left to do but pack.

Another day he would have been alert to the subtle nuances of the setting. But it wasn't another day. This day his mind was lost to thoughts of Lily. So when Morgan pushed inside, he was unprepared for the blow to his head that felled him on the spot.

Twenty-three

"Lily! Lily! Come quick!"

Lily stood in her room, barely aware of the frantic shouts.

"Lily!"

Slowly she turned to the sound, her mind no longer able to hold the shouts at bay. Robert stood in the doorway, out of breath, his normally perfect hair in disarray, clearly frantic. But still, Lily felt nothing. Didn't allow herself to for fear that if she did she would once and for all break apart into jagged little pieces.

She was numb. It was easier that way. She knew that—had learned that. How had she forgotten?

"Lily! They have Morgan!"

She felt a jolt of feeling at the name, and she started to move. But the moment was fleeting before memory returned and she quelled whatever concern that tried to surface.

"Lily," Robert raged. "Listen to me! When I walked into Morgan's cottage there were some men there. Beating him!"

"Beating him?" she gasped before she could stop herself.

"Yes," Robert said in a rush. "Big burly men. Now they've taken him away. You've got to do something. Morgan is bleeding, Lily. He's hurt."

She forced her eyes closed, trying not to see the image of Morgan in pain. It didn't help. Despite what he had done, she wanted to run to him. But she wouldn't. She couldn't.

Crimson Lily Paints Town Red.

And Morgan had written it.

So he was in pain, she thought, unexpectedly callous. He was hurt, just as she was.

Perhaps even broken beyond repair.

She knew who was punishing Morgan, or at least she could figure it out easily enough. She had seen one of John's men in the courtroom during the proceedings, had said hello to him when she first arrived—back when she had still thought the world was a just place where she would win the children because she loved them and they loved her.

What a fool she had been.

The world wasn't a just place. She didn't win the children, or at least wouldn't have if it hadn't been for Morgan.

With his announcement that it was he who had written the horrible article that had seared her to the core, he had caused the judge to rethink his position and award her the children. The judge's written notification had arrived only minutes ago.

Perhaps Morgan had come to her aid, but he was the one who had put her in a position of having to defend herself in the first place. She felt no obligation to the man, or so she told herself. Let John do what he would. Morgan Elliott was no longer a part of her life.

She fought down the wave of grief that tried to wash over her.

"Lily, don't you care?" Robert demanded, stunned. "Don't you care that they could kill Morgan?"

With a calm she had mastered over the years slipping into place, Lily met her nephew's disbelieving gaze. "Morgan Elliott can take care of himself."

Robert's gaze turned hard, censorious. "Everybody needs help sometimes," he stated harshly, an unexpected sheen of tears burning in his eyes.

When still she didn't move, Robert turned and raced out of the room. She heard the tread of his shoes on the stairs. He would try to find someone else to help Morgan Elliott—to help Morgan as she wouldn't.

Her body shuddered, both at the thought of Morgan, but also at the look she had seen in Robert's eyes. Disappointment. In her. For being less of a person than he had come to believe.

She didn't want to care. But she did. She had disappointed him. She knew that he was stunned and hurt by her callousness. Confused. His life had drifted so far from what he knew. First his father, then her arrival, and now this.

She understood that feeling. The brutal lessons that life wasn't what he had been led to believe. Happiness and love. Taken away. Leaving him alone in the world, unprepared for its harshness.

She had gone so long without his affection, and had enjoyed it for such a short period of time. Could she possibly ever win it back if she didn't help Morgan Elliott now?

Oh, Morgan. Why? she wondered. *How could you have written that traitorous article?*

She moved toward the window, wanting to see the sunshine, but saw her china cup instead. Cracked and scarred, but somehow holding together.

Why did you try to fix everything only to ruin it all with your words?

But then she realized in a startling rush that he had

wielded his pen *before* he had set out to fix everything.

Was that what had prompted his efforts on her behalf? Was that why he had prodded her to succeed?

Because he loved her?

Or because of his guilt?

She didn't know, no longer trusted her feelings about him or anything else.

But in her mind's eye, she could not wipe clean the look of Robert's searing disappointment.

And that more than anything, more than the concern she couldn't quite extinguish, sent her down the stairs and out the door.

The warehouse looked deserted when the hack pulled up to the back door. John had spoken to Lily about the warehouse, told her how difficult it was to keep the precious goods he imported from around the world safe inside.

Looking around her, Lily couldn't imagine that anything was safe inside or out. Never had she seen such abysmal wretchedness. Grime and trash. Scurrying rodents. A staggering poverty that was hard to imagine existing within such easy reach of the ostentatious wealth only blocks away.

"Please wait for me," Lily said, her heart pounding, uncertain what she would find in the warehouse.

Lily heaved open the heavy planked door and stepped inside. The space was nearly pitch black. She picked her way through the dimly lit passageway, through a series of storage alcoves that led deeper into the building.

She knew John well, and she knew he would be angry at Morgan for having hurt her. She had little doubt that John would have hurt Morgan in return. Roughed up. Cuts and bruises. Taught a lesson. But Lily was certain the minute she stepped in, John would let Morgan go. John was her friend, had helped her in so many ways. He would not hurt her now by doing something to Morgan that she would forever feel guilty about if she didn't have it stopped. Then she would see that Morgan got to the safety of his home, but beyond that she would do nothing more.

She tamped down the hollowness that snaked through her, and tamped it down easily when suddenly it occurred to her that she had no idea where Morgan really lived. In a tenement on the Lower East Side? A boardinghouse in Brooklyn?

Then she remember he had mentioned the South.

Would he return to his home there? Her head swam, but then she chided herself when she also remembered the watch. Fine silver watch. Etched and beautiful. Expensive.

Morgan was not a poor man, she realized with certainty.

Where did the lies end?

She turned a corner on that thought, but the sight that met her eyes stilled her heart. With a gasp, she fell back against the wall, and would have cried out had words been possible.

She had been wrong.

John hadn't merely roughed Morgan up, he had beat him until he was nearly unrecognizable.

Jerking away from the wall, Lily started forward, but the words that rang through the warehouse stopped her.

"Leave the gun," John said with an eerie laugh to three burly men with hobnailed boots whom Lily had never seen before. They weren't John's usual associates. The men with John looked dangerous, ominous.

John gestured toward a gun that lay on a crate. "Leave it here," he instructed. "I'm going to need it before the night is done. But first," he added, walking over to Morgan, who lay like a broken toy on the ground, "I want to have a word with Mr. Elliott."

"I have nothing to say to you, Crandall," Morgan managed to say, each word clearly a struggle. "I don't talk to scum."

Lily gasped, but the sound was washed away by John's hissing breath. John turned to his men, and Lily could see his eyes were wild. "Wait outside," he roared.

Lily fell back into the shadows, her heart lodged in her throat as the giant men passed by her so closely that had she reached out she could have touched them.

By the time the men left, Lily could see that John had regained his control. Once again he was the smooth, charming man she had trusted for so many years. But then the charm melted away and a cruel smile twisted his lips.

"Tsk-tsk-tsk," John said. "You should be nicer to me. In fact you should be respectful. I'm important, you know."

"You're a crook, Crandall."

"So you would like the world to believe. But have you found one shred of evidence to prove that? No," he answered himself with a satisfied laugh. "And you never will."

"That's where you're wrong. I will find what I need. Even if I have to dog you the rest of my sorry life."

"Morgan, Morgan, Morgan. I'm afraid that doesn't give you too much time."

"What are you going to do? Are you going to kill me? Just like you killed Jenny?"

John's face twisted with rage. "I didn't kill Jenny!"

"Face it, you're a liar, Trey."

Trey.

Lily's mind spun in confusion. Trey. Morgan's friend. How could John be Trey?

But then it came to her, from some foggy recesses of her mind. John Crandall III. The third. Trey, as Lily had once heard people say in the South. The Trey that Morgan had once told her about.

"You killed her," Morgan said, his voice tight and furious.

"*You* killed her," John screamed. "You were there with her. Not me."

Morgan pressed his eyes closed and flinched, his bloody features stricken.

John studied Morgan, cocking his head before he smiled,

his face sly and distorted. "I understand now. You have been chasing me all this time because *you* feel guilty." His haunted laughter echoed off the walls. "Of course. I should have known." His laughter broke off and he sneered. "Morgan the saint, Morgan the one everyone thought could do no wrong. What did you say to Jenny that day to make her jump?"

"I said nothing! I sat there and listened while she told me she was pregnant."

Satisfaction sliced across John's face. "And did she tell you how good I was? Did you think about the fact that *I*, poor boy John Crandall, sank my flesh into sweet little Jenny Moore. Not *you*! Not the great Morgan Elliott! You never had to worry about anything, damn you." John's face contorted with rage. "You had it so easy. Money. Looks. Everyone loved you. And they would have loved *me* if my father hadn't lost everything. Your father should have lost everything, too. But no. Only mine. *Only mine!* Leaving me to eke out a living to support my mother. And all the while you and Jenny pranced around like the chosen ones. But I took Jenny away." John sneered. "How did it feel, Morgan? How did it feel to have something you wanted taken away from you?"

Morgan lay stunned. "We were friends, Trey. You and me and Jenny. I didn't think less of you because you were poor."

"You did, damn you! I saw it in everything you did, everything you said. And I wasn't going to be poor any longer. Once Mama died I was free to leave. I was going to make my fortune. And I certainly couldn't do it with Jenny strapped to me just like my mother had been. I was free, I tell you. Damn it, I wasn't going to be poor any longer."

Tears of rage glistened in Crandall's eyes as he dragged a fine suit sleeve across his nose. "Look at me now! I'm somebody. I'm rich! I'm powerful, do you hear me!" He began to pace. "And I'm going to be governor. I am," he stated as if trying to convince himself. "I would be well on my way right now if it hadn't been for that damned Claude Blakemore. Everything was going so well. Perfect. Until he decided to bring Lily home."

Lily sucked in her breath at the words. Then a slow, sickening dread began to fill her.

"The ungrateful bastard," John hissed. "I'd been supporting him for years! If it hadn't been for me he wouldn't have had two nickels to rub together." John chuckled madly. "He would have asked Lily to come home long ago if I hadn't been smart enough to keep him angry at her. Lord, it was easy though. Just had to fill him with stories about her wild ways." He grew serious once again. "I couldn't afford for Lily to return. She might have started asking questions about her money."

"So that's how you started," Morgan said, his voice hoarse. "You used Lily's money. I always wondered."

John smiled slyly. "Smart, don't you think? I met Lily right after Claude sent her away. She needed a friend." John chuckled. "A friend who would take care of all the money that artist left her."

"You managed Lily's money?"

"Yes. Silly girl. She never asked a single question. Neither did her foolish brother, he never realized I used Lily's money to keep him afloat. For years everything went so well. At least it did until Claude became determined to bring Lily home."

"So you got rid of him."

John shrugged his shoulders. "It was so easy. Failure of the heart. It was rich, I tell you. No one suspected." But then his faced darkened. "If I had only known about his will. Everything would have been perfect except for that damned will." He shook his head. "Then to make matters worse you showed up like a bad penny. A repairman?" John scoffed.

"You knew?" Morgan asked as he tried to push up, groaning at the simple movement.

"Of course I knew. Why do you think I returned? I received a note from my man Marcus. If I had only gotten here a day sooner, I would have found you before you fouled up all my hard work by telling everyone in the court about the article. I would have gotten rid of you, the kids would have been sent off with those blasted relatives I spent a fortune finding, and Lily would have returned to Tarrytown, a defeated woman—right back in the palm of my hand."

Lily felt as if she had been struck hard and low. Pain and betrayal seared through her. How had she not known? She started to step out, to confront John for his grievous wrongs, but his next words stopped her.

"You fell in love with her, didn't you?"

Though she shouldn't care, Lily was desperate to hear Morgan's answer. But the answer didn't come. Only silence until John spoke again.

"Hard not to, I admit. But she's mine, old man. Just like Jenny was mine." He laughed. "I made it so you couldn't have Jenny. And now you can't have Lily either. Just like Claude, I'm going to take care of you, too. Once and for all."

"No, John. It's over."

Lily stepped out of the shadows.

John wheeled around. "Lily! What are you doing here?"

"I came for Morgan," she said simply, walking forward as calmly as she could, willing her trembling body to be still. "Let him go."

Lily's steps faltered as John's eyes widened, his face contorting. "*You want Morgan?*" he screamed. "You can't have him! You can't have him, Lily. Because you're mine. Do you understand me? Only mine! I'm the one who has taken care of you these last ten years, not him, not anyone."

"You didn't take care of me, John. You betrayed and used me."

"You ungrateful bitch!"

In that moment Lily realized that John was not only dangerous but perhaps insane, making him all the more unpredictable and threatening. "No, John. I'm not yours."

"A little late for that. You're here. I'm here. And nobody else is around to save you. Least of all Morgan Elliott." John sneered. "He won't save you, just as he didn't save Jenny."

And with those words, a shot that rang out. Once. Only once. But it was enough.

Lily stood frozen until John collapsed to the floor. She stared at the man she had called friend for so many years. The one person she had thought she could trust.

Slowly she shifted her gaze. Morgan leaned back against the crate where John's men had left the gun earlier, the gun in his hand. Morgan's eyes were closed and he didn't move. He looked dead.

Without thinking about the past, she raced to Morgan, falling to her knees at his side.

"Morgan." She pulled him into her arms, cradling him against her breast. "Morgan, please."

His eyes fluttered open and his body tensed. "Is he dead?"

Relief swept through her. "Yes."

His body sagged against her, his face pained. "He was my friend. I've known him since I was a child. But I never knew how much he hated me." He looked into her eyes. "Because of that hatred and because of my pursuit, innocent people have been hurt. Oh, Lily, I've wasted so much time, I've hurt people I love, all in a maddening . . . and futile attempt to cross an insurmountable distance to grasp a hand that reached out to me." He drew a deep breath. "I'm sorry, Lily," he whispered. "I'm so terribly sorry."

"For what? For saving me?"

"You know that's not what I mean."

"Maybe not. But I know now why you did what you

did.'' Lily smiled, tears glistening in her eyes. ''You may have dragged me through the mud with your article, but in the end you saved me. You may not have been able to grasp Jenny's hand,'' she touched his cheek, ''but you found mine. You pushed me to fight, and through the battle I truly learned who I was. I'm a fighter. I never would have known that if you hadn't come into my life.''

Just then the warehouse door burst in, the sound of several people running sounding in an echoing din. Morgan's eyes went wild and he pushed away from her, forcing her behind him despite his beaten state. And just as he raised the gun and leveled it at the entrance way, Marky and Jojo careened into sight, a pack of leather-helmeted policemen behind them.

At the sight of the gun, but more importantly at the sight of Lily and Morgan still alive, the former servants gasped in audible relief.

''We made it!'' Jojo called out.

''We got here in time!'' Marky added.

A policemen went over and crouched before John's body. ''He's dead.''

Several other patrolmen held John's burly men in custody. Lily looked at Marky who came forward.

''We'se sorry we came into your house and spied on you,'' he said. ''We were just doing our job. But when we'd been there long enough, we saw that you weren't like everybody said. So we left. But then we heard what happened at the courthouse, and that Crandall had Morgan, and we knew we had ta help.''

Lily's throat was tight. How her life had changed. ''Thank you, Marky. And thank you, Jojo,'' she said simply, not knowing what else to say.

The policemen came over to Morgan, looking over his wounds. ''You look worse than you are. Bloody and sore, and won't walk real easy for a while. But you'll be okay. Let us get you to a doctor.''

Morgan looked as if he would go with him, but Lily stayed them. "I'll take care of him, sir."

Morgan looked at her, his eyes deep and penetrating as if trying to see to that truth he had been looking for since she met him. "Yes, Morgan. I'm taking you back to Blakemore House, to the children . . . until you recover."

His dark eyes grew stormy but resigned.

When Lily realized that he thought she would send him away after he had healed, she smiled, carefully touching his bloodied cheek. "You'll not get rid of me that easily, Morgan Elliott," she teased softly.

His eyes filled with question.

"I'd like to travel," she said, her teasing smile gone. "I hear the South is beautiful in the spring. No doubt the children would love it." She hesitated. "And I wondered if you might show us this place where you were born."

She watched as his throat worked and his eyes burned. She waited with breath held for his answer. He still could say no—he might not want to take her to the place where he had loved Jenny.

At length he took her hand in his, his thumb brushing over her knuckles. Then he raised his head and looked at her. "I don't deserve you. But as long as you are willing to overlook that tiny little detail"—his lips broke into a smile, after which he grimaced at a flash of pain—"I will take you to the South—and build you and the children a home. I love you, Lily Blakemore, as I have loved no one else in my life. Will you marry me? Will you share your life with me, will you share my dreams?"

And that's when she felt it, and she knew he felt it, too. The shock of recognition that their world had finally slipped into place. They would not remain travelers in a foreign land. She would become this man's wife—the only man she had ever loved. She would leave Manhattan for good, and he would go home. They would build a new life together. Mistakes overcome if not forgotten. The children at their sides.

Their love to sustain them.

"Yes," she whispered. "Yes, I'll marry you."

Epilogue

"Uncle Morgan! It's beautiful!"

Morgan glanced down at Cassie and smiled. "I'm glad you like it, sweetheart."

"Well, I like it, too," Penelope stated obstinately, marching down the steps of the coach.

Morgan's smile tilted with fond amusement. "I'm glad about that as well."

"Are we really going to live here?" Cassie asked, her eyes wide.

Morgan's gaze shifted to the white-pillared home that stood before them, emotion tightening in his chest. "Yes, Cassie, we are."

Just then Robert jumped down from the carriage and stretched, a book held firmly in his hand, his finger marking his place. "Did you know that the state capital of Virginia is Richmond?" he asked importantly.

Penelope groaned. Cassie made a face.

Robert had read about each state they had passed through on their journey south, regaling his captive audience with every minute detail he thought worthy of being passed along.

"Another fact I found interesting," he began, but stopped abruptly when he turned and saw the house. "It's huge!"

Morgan chuckled. The house was huge—sprawling and elegant, but most of all, filled with memories. Morgan breathed deeply. Good memories, the bad exorcised from his mind.

All because of Lily.

As if sensing his thoughts, Lily stepped through the doorway of the carriage. She stopped on the top step to look down the long drive that led to the colonial mansion with tall white pillars and long wooden verandas.

"I'll race you to the house," Penelope said to Robert.

Robert looked as if he would refuse, but when Penelope shot him a superior smile, then twirled and sped away, he took off after her.

"Wait for me!" Cassie cried out.

Lily watched them go, her heart burgeoning with a simple joy.

When she didn't speak, Morgan couldn't help himself. "What are you thinking?" he asked, his deep voice carrying on the crisp spring air.

Lily met Morgan's gaze, her eyes filled with all the love that she felt for this man. "I'm thinking about how much I love you."

A low rumble sounded in Morgan's chest. "But what do you think about the house?"

Lily laughed out loud. "Your home is beautiful."

His dark gaze grew fierce. "Our home, Mrs. Elliott."

Lily breathed in deeply. *Mrs. Elliott.* Even eight months later it still amazed her that she was now Morgan's wife, that the children were theirs, and that he loved her and cherished her. But every day and every night he showed her his love in a million different ways. And she knew as long as she lived she would never grow tired of waking up every morning with Morgan at her side.

Looking at him now a sense of rightness filled her, intertwining with her joy. And whether the looming white mansion stood there or not Lily knew that indeed she had come home—to Morgan.

"Yes," she whispered, "our home."

Morgan closed the distance that separated them, and when he took her into his arms to help her down, she held on tightly, securely. Then she lifted her face to him and pressed her lips to his, never a thought about the boldness, because through the pain and anguish, through the trials they had been through together, she had finally come to believe, truly and completely, that she was not Crimson Lily.

"I love you, Lily," he whispered against her skin.

And she knew that he did.

Linda Francis Lee

__BLUE WALTZ
0-515-11791-9/$5.99

They say the Widow Braxton wears the gowns of a century past...she invites servants to parties...they say she is mad. Stephen St. James has heard rumors about his new neighbor. However, she is no wizened old woman—but an exquisite young beauty. But before he can make her his own, he must free the secret that binds her heart...

__EMERALD RAIN
0-515-11979-2/$5.99

"Written with rare power and compassion...a deeply compelling story of love, pain, and forgiveness."—Mary Jo Putney

Ellie and Nicholas were on opposite sides of the battle that threatened to rob Ellie of her home. However, all that mattered was the powerful attraction that drew them together. But selling the property would unearth a family scandal of twenty years past...and threatens to tear the young lovers apart.

__CRIMSON LACE
0-515-12187-8/$5.99

High society in New York, 1896 —the story of a disgraced woman returning home and discovering a renewed hope for love...